From o

Name

He's Done EVER SO WELL for Himself

Much love

x

Biography

JUSTIN DAVID is a writer and photographer. A child of Wolver-hampton, he has lived and worked in East London for most of his adult life. He graduated from the MA Creative and Life Writing at Goldsmiths, University of London, has read at Paul Burston's literary salon, *Polari* at Royal Festival Hall, and is a founder member of *Leather Lane Writers*. His writing has appeared in many print and online anthologies and his debut novella was published by *Salt* as part of their Modern Dreams series.

His photography collection of nocturnal performers, *Night Work*, has been exhibited in London at venues including Jackson's Lane. His photographic works have appeared on the pages of numerous magazines including: *Beige, Gaze, Time Out, Out There, Gay Times, Attitude, Polari Magazine, QX, GlitterWolf, Fluid, Pink Paper, Muso* and *Classical Music Magazine*.

Justin is one half of *Inkandescent*—a new publishing venture with his partner, Nathan Evans. Their first offering, *Threads*, featuring Nathan's poetry and Justin's photography, was long-listed for the Polari First Book Prize. It was supported using public funding by Arts Council England and is available in paperback and ebook.

Praise for Justin David and
He's Done Ever So Well for Himself

'A well-observed, charming account of small-town, working-class life and the move to the big, bad, brilliant city. This should strike a chord not just with gay readers but with anyone who's lived, loved and fought to become the person they're meant to be.'
MATT CAIN

'There's not much rarer than a working class voice in fiction, except maybe a gay working class voice.
We need writers like Justin David.'
PAUL McVEIGH, author of *The Good Son*

'An entertaining, highly detailed story form the perspective of a queer outsider. Insightful and inspiring. You'll love this book!'
RHYANNON STYLES, author of
The New Girl: A Trans Girl Tells It Like It Is

Praise for Justin David and
Tales of the Suburbs

'Justin David's *Tales of the Suburbs* reveals a true writer's gift for comic and poignant storytelling, in which pithy dialogue and sharp characterisation make for compelling reading.'
PATRICIA ROUTLEDGE

'Justin David's tale of working-class gay life is a bitter-sweet, beautiful thing. The audience at Polari loved it —
as well they should.'
PAUL BURSTON, *Polari Literary Salon*

Justin David

Inkandescent

Published by Inkandescent 2018

Text Copyright © 2018 Justin David
Images Copyright © 2018 Justin David
Use of photograph of *David Cabaret as*
'The Blue Lady' by Tretchikoff by kind permission of Perou.
Use of author photograph of *Justin David*
by kind permission of Holly Revell.

This work incorporates some real events as a backdrop for
fictional characters and their fictional dramas. Occasionally, real people
make cameo appearances and are treated as actors in an otherwise
fictional world. Beyond this, except in the case of historical fact, any
resemblance to actual persons, living or dead, is purely coincidental.

Publisher's note: a version of Chapter 8 *The Pharamacist* was published as
a novella by Salt Publishing in 2014

A CIP catalogue record for this book
is available from the British Library

Printed in the UK by Clays Ltd, St Ives plc

ISBN 978-0-9955346-2-9 (paperback)
ISBN 978-0-9955346-4-3 (kindle)
ISBN 978-0-9955346-3-6 (enhanced ibook)

1 3 5 7 9 10 8 6 4 2

www.inkandescent.co.uk

For Andrew Wilkinson

whose generosity and encouragement made
life worth living again

Contents

Tales of the Suburbs

Urban Nightmares

Fairy Tale Metropolis

Tales of the Suburbs

'And children who need to be able to count and multiply are learning anti-racist mathematics—whatever that may be. Children who need to be able to express themselves in clear English are being taught political slogans. Children who need to be taught to respect traditional moral values are being taught that they have an inalienable right to be gay. And children who need encouragement—and children do so much need encouragement—so many children—they are being taught that our society offers them no future. All of those children are being cheated of a sound start in life—yes, cheated.

Of course—in the country as a whole—there are plenty of excellent teachers and successful schools. And in every good school, and every good teacher, is a reminder of what too many young people are denied.'

Speech to Tory Party Conference, 1987
MARGARET THATCHER 1925 — 2013

Unicorn

Flamboyant. There's a word. Jamie's thinking about pop stars when he notices the bright red wool starting to unravel. 'I've dropped a stitch,' he tells Nan.

'Don't pull it, love. Give it here,' she says. She fixes it with her usual confidence. Just like that. Jamie loves being with Nan. She runs her papery fingers over the length of knitting beginning to form under the last row of stitches. 'Clever boy, ain't ya, our Jamie.' He can hear her voice but his eyes are fixed on the scrapbook in his lap, bulging with cuttings—photographs of pop stars he's collected. Jamie takes Nan's ballpoint pen from the arm of the chair and writes the word *flamboyant* at the bottom of a list he's started. 'Tension's a bit wobbly,' she points out. 'Nice and neat though—try to keep the wool taut when you bring it round the needle.' She finishes the row for him. 'There. That row was knit. Next row, purl.' She looks out of the window and nudges him. 'Look how dark it is a'ready. Not even five o'clock yet.'

Gazing into the tangerine twilight beyond the net curtains, Jamie's eyes become unfocused. His head fills with boys in turbans, quiffs and sequins, singers with eye-patches, feather boas and hairspray. This world of dry ice and neon and starburst light is only usually glimpsed in between the news and *Tomorrow's World* on Thursday nights and he wonders what happens to it when Grandad switches channels. While he likes to float off into his dream world, Nan has her own special way of keeping him in this one. 'That cabbage'll be done soon.'

It's quiet bar the bubbling pot in the kitchen and the ticking of the clock on the mantelpiece. Jamie puts the knitting down and sips the orange cordial mixed with a bit of whiskey that she allows him every Saturday evening—just him and Nan having special time. *Special time* means everything else stops. Television and radio off, Nan and Jamie do something together—sometimes bake a cake, sometimes crochet.

He lets his eyes pass over everything he loves in the room—Nan's Tretchikoff: a girl with red lips and a blue face hanging against embossed wallpaper, the cabinet of collected snow-globes, three carved wooden African figurines—until his eyes reach Grandad slouched in his armchair. His face is mottled with dark patches of skin and his eyes are red and wet, making him look both sad and angry at the same time. He used to be different. He used to be distinguished and sort of proud. Always had time to teach Jamie new things. They made a bird-scarer for the allotment and spent ages doing giant jigsaws. They loved spending time together. But all that has stopped. Poor Grandad.

Next to him is a pile of unread large-print library books covered with sticky backed plastic. There's also a scattering of rags, which he uses to wipe his runny nose, *festered*, Jamie's mum would say, from too much booze. He's joining parts of a model Spitfire together with a little tube of glue, which he's been doing since he lost his job as an electrician at the washing machine factory. Now he mumbles things under his breath: 'Boys of his age should be out chasing wenches, not messing around with wool. When I was his age... I used to have 'em flocking.'

'Oh, yes Alf,' Nan will nod. 'Heard it all before. Proper bloody Casanova.' This has been happening a lot recently; she'll say something cruel just to shut him up. The other day he'd been moaning about his waterworks playing up and she told him that if he didn't stop dribbling on the bathroom carpet, she would 'cut it off' while he was asleep.

Jamie's mum says it's difficult for Grandad to find a new job, him being too old to retrain and younger men prepared to work for less money. These men know about computers and stuff, which Grandad does not. His mum says Grandad is depressed. Jamie hasn't a clue what that means.

Grandad puts his glue down and looks at Jamie. Then he looks at the knitting, with an unhappy, disapproving sneer, shakes his head and turns back to his model without saying a word. Why is he being like this? Jamie tries not to dwell on it. The clock shows five o'clock and his head is filling with pop stars again, like the ones in his scrapbook: frilly shirts, lipstick, boys wearing eyeliner, dandy highwaymen, crazy female singers in white lacy dresses.

A car pulls up outside. There's the rev of an engine, doors slamming and then laughter. Nan jumps up out of her seat, runs to the window and lifts the net. 'It's them.' She lets the net drop and points to Grandad's Spitfire. 'Put that up now, Alf. They're here. Come on. There ain't room in here to swing a cat.'

Grandad huffs and puffs and grumbles. He leaves the Spitfire where it is. 'Why does everything have to change when that lot arrive? Bloody nuisance. We do *live* here, you know!' He used to leap up to answer the door when someone knocked, but not these days.

Nan dashes about the room clearing things away, collecting anything enjoyable. She moves the pipe that Grandad has loaded with tobacco but not bothered to smoke and the glass of whiskey he's poured but not bothered to drink and slams them away in his cabinet. She picks up a Curly Wurly from the mantelpiece and stuffs it into her pinnie. Arms full, she points at Grandad's bag of pork scratchings until he stuffs them, reluctantly, into his pocket. 'Freddie eats whatever he sees,' she says, heading for the back room clutching the fruit bowl. 'Jamie. Quick!' She points at his knitting. 'Put that up.'

Jamie doesn't need to be told. He's already wrapping the wool around the needles, stuffing them into the tapestry-covered bag that she'd given him to keep all his things inside. As Nan darts back in from the kitchen and over to the window, the smell of cabbage wafts in after her. *Must be boiled to nothing now*, Jamie thinks. Then he's startled by the thump of a knuckle against the window and a face pressed against the glass.

'Oh, look at ya!' Nan moans at Auntie Sandra's face through the curtain. 'Get yer nose off the glass, varmint! I've only just cleaned them windows.' Nan goes into the hallway and cheers as Auntie Sandra appears. Behind her is a deeper, louder voice: 'Hello Phyllis. Where's Nancy Boy?' Uncle Freddie sticks his head in sideways round the doorframe and grins—resting his black moustache on the edge of the door. Then his whole body appears, pushed in by Nan.

'Get in there—pest!' she says. That's her way of saying she loves Freddie—*pest, varmint,* and a good whack around the ears. They all like him. But Jamie doesn't get to see him very often as he's always on the beat. Nan's glasses are still steamed up. She wipes them on her pinnie. 'He's here again, ain't he, upsetting the applecart. Just don't bloody eat anything. You hear? Or I'll have your guts f'garters.'

Freddie looks past her at Jamie. '*There* you are, Nancy Boy,' he says. It makes Jamie cringe, that name. Uncle Freddie says it's a term of endearment, but deep down, Jamie knows Freddie is being mean. He throws himself on the floor with his scrapbook.

On TV is some quiz show that Nan and Grandad like to watch, with a toy bin as a booby prize. Jamie turns the pages of pop stars: Steve Strange, Midge Ure, Toyah Wilcox, Kate Bush. Behind him, he can hear a right commotion, Nan and Auntie Sandra laughing together. 'Alright Pops?' Uncle Freddie says, enthusiastically trying to fetch some life out of Grandad and failing miserably.

''Allo Dad,' Auntie Sandra says.

Grandad just mumbles, eyes super-glued to the television screen.

Jamie turns onto his back and rests on his elbows just in time to see Auntie Sandra staring at Nan, as if there is something she wants to say about Grandad. Nan is sneering at him. Looking back at Sandra, she shakes her head. There's a look of concern and confusion on Auntie Sandra's face, but it disappears when she notices Jamie looking at her.

'Alright our Jamie?' She smiles one of her big sunbeams that make him feel like the most important person in the world. He doesn't get to see her very often either because she's training to become a school-teacher. 'You been keeping Nan and Grandad company?'

'Been making a pencil case.' Jamie points at the knitting basket, with his things stuffed inside.

'Oh have you? You can knit me a mohair cardi next.' Her voice is full of belief. She always says Jamie can do anything if he puts his mind to it.

'Made anything else?' Uncle Freddie asks, prodding him on the shoulder.

Nan tugs the collar of Freddie's denim jacket. 'Ain't you come to stay?' she asks and goes into the kitchen. 'I'll put the kettle on,' she calls.

Uncle Freddie throws his jacket off, revealing a white t-shirt with the words 'FRANKIE SAYS RELAX' printed in bold, black letters across the chest. Everyone's wearing them. He thinks he's really cool. He perches himself on the arm of the settee, folds his arms and sits looking at Jamie, as if he knows a secret. Auntie Sandra gets down on her knees next to Jamie. Her golden frizz of curls dangles in his face. It's lovely when they are all together. There's always a lot of talk and laughter, but recently less from Grandad. Now he just grumbles about things like *privatisation* and *trade unions* and other things Jamie doesn't understand.

'Oi. Nance,' Uncle Freddie calls to him. 'Have you done it?'

'Done what?' Sandra asks, not appreciating being kept out of the secret.

'*He* knows!' Uncle Freddie nods.

Auntie Sandra slaps Freddie's leg. 'Leave him alone *you*!' She turns back to him. She smells of hairspray. 'Aintcha gonna give me a kiss?'

Jamie kisses her. Then she reaches into the pocket of her stone-washed denim jacket and pulls out a piece of paper. 'I found this stuffed in between the pages of my diary. It's an old one but I thought you'd like it for your scrapbook.'

Jamie knows what it is without even looking. She always saves them for him—clippings from her *Look-In* magazines - lots of them. Pictures of famous pop stars photographed in nightclubs or stills from pop videos. He takes the clipping in his hands and slowly unfolds it, taking care not to tear it, as if it's a special Christmas present.

'Wow.' It's Boy George and his friend Marilyn. George has a Geisha white face, heavily shaded eyes, glitter on the lips, and his famous braids. Marilyn is doing her trademark look: bright red lips against a powder white face and sharp cheekbones. She's smiling brightly. All teeth. *Glamour*.

When Nan comes back into the room, Uncle Freddie is eating a Curly Wurly he's found in Grandad's cookie jar, so she cracks him over the head with the back of her hand. 'Bloody gannet!'

'Ow! What was that for?' he says, eyes tearing up.

'I've told you before. Stop eating my bleedin' chocolate!'

'That hurt.'

'It'll hurt even more if I do it again,' she says, arm half-cocked ready to give him another one.

'You caught me with your wedding ring. Gonna have a right lump now.'

Nan cracks him again, even harder this time.

'What was that for?' Uncle Freddie rubs his head.

'That's for next time,' Nan says, looking very satisfied with herself.

Jamie and Sandra giggle and turn back to the photo of Boy George and Marilyn. 'Look at it, Jamie.'

'Amazing, ain't it,' he says.

Sandra spreads the photo flat under her fingers and smoothes out the creases. 'Imagine doing your shopping and seeing that.' She strokes the image of Boy George with a painted fingertip. 'So much... what's the word? *Mystique*.'

'D'you think you'd ever see Boy George on the street? I mean in London. Would you see him out?'

'Course,' she says. 'Pop stars *must* leave their homes—just like everyone else.'

Jamie shakes his head. 'He'd have servants,' he says. '*And* a driver. *And* someone to do his make-up.' They have this conversation a lot, Sandra and Jamie. They know that you'd be very lucky to see a pop star with your own eyes, but they both agree even pop stars have to go shopping, so if you tried really hard, you might find one being chased by a crowd of photographers.

Sandra tilts her head and says, 'I think I'd wet myself if I saw him and Marilyn knocking about the town, shopping for clothes.'

Jamie looks at the image of Marilyn—such a beautiful girl. Somehow, he knows she is much more than that. More beautiful than any girl he's seen before. *Dazzling*. Beyond human. 'Sandra, is Marilyn his girlfriend?'

'No, Jamie. I don't think she's his *girlfriend*. I think they're mates.' She winks at him and then taps the picture again. 'If you saw that in the street, it'd be like seeing a mythological creature.'

Mythological? Now there's a word. They'd done myths and legends at school. 'You mean like something from a fairy tale?'

'Yeah.'

Was Boy George a boy? Or was he a girl with a boy's name? Jamie wonders if anyone in his family really knows what he is. No one has ever seen anything like him. Nevertheless, they all love Boy George's music when it comes on the wireless.

Jamie grabs the sellotape from the mantelpiece and tapes the picture into his scrapbook. At the bottom of his list of words he writes *mythological*. Under the image of Boy George, he writes another word—*Unicorn*—and shows it to Sandra. She smiles. Perhaps he can use that word in a story he'll write later.

Uncle Freddie pipes up. 'So, Nancy Boy, have you done it?'

Jamie decides that if Freddie calls him that name once more he'll kick him really hard in the shins. He hates being teased by him and he isn't going to take it anymore.

When he turns over onto his back, Freddie is flexing his biceps.

'I've done it, alright.' Jamie blows out a loud sigh.

Nan is warming the backs of her legs near the fire. 'Oh, Freddie, just wait till you see it. He's made such a good job of it. Come on Jamie. Time for the unveiling.' She claps.

'Unveiling of what?' Sandra asks.

'Go and get it then,' Uncle Freddie says, impatiently.

'Who's Auntie Sandra going as?'

'Is this about the fancy dress party?' Sandra makes an excited squeal.

'Kate Bush,' Uncle Freddie replies.

'Uncle Freddie, are you going to wear the makeup as well?'

Nan tuts. 'He's not your real uncle yet. They're not married.' She shoots Grandad a stare.

'Course I'm going to wear make-up,' Uncle Freddie continues. 'Only for this though.'

Jamie sits upright. 'Sandra, d'you think Boy George looks like that *all* the time?'

Sandra giggles. 'I read that he doesn't leave the house without a full face of slap.'

Jamie tries to imagine the world that he comes from—a strange place where people don't have to be boys *or* girls. They can be a mix. And nobody cares. But the boys who don't behave enough like boys at school either get beaten up or ignored. That's how it is. Except in the pages of his scrapbook—not one of them looks like any of the boys and girls he knows from school.

'Funny looking thing, ain't he?' Nan says, tilting her head to look at Boy George. Nan can't really get a grip on him. To her, pop stars look like Buddy Holly. Or Cliff Richard, perhaps?

'Not right, if you ask me,' Grandad says, tapping a finger on the side of his head.

Nan plants her hands on her hips. 'Nobody asked *you*,' she says.

'Bloody whoopsies,' Grandad says. 'I blame Thatcher.'

'Oh yes... Thatcher's to blame for everything, isn't she?' Nan says. 'She'll be to blame for why I'm still waiting for a new fridge freezer, or why the windows are never cleaned, or why I always have to change a plug around this place, or why you can't afford your own daughter's wedding dr —' Her tear filled eyes snap onto Sandra who by now has completely lost her smile.

Oh no. They're not going to start all this again. Jamie's never seen her quite like this. She raises a trembling finger. 'Sandra! I swear if something doesn't change soon, I'll get the carving knife to him. I will.'

Jamie knows he shouldn't interrupt but he can't help himself. 'Nan, what's a *whoopsie*?'

'Oh dear God!' Nan rolls her eyes. 'Live and let live. That's my motto.' She looks at his scrapbook. 'There's enough heartache in the world. A man in make-up ain't hurting no one.'

Now seems like the perfect moment to go upstairs and get the creation he's made for Uncle Freddie.

Nan's bedroom is goldfish orange. The walls are orange, the bedspread is orange, even the carpet is orange. He likes Nan's bedroom. It's cosy and happy and full of pretty things that she's collected, like giant spiky seashells and seahorses she's trapped in little blocks of resin and made into paperweights and fancy fabric lampshades with furry tassels. Nan's very fond of cacti and has five different types lined up on the windowsill, which Jamie often dares himself to stroke. One day one of the spikes got stuck in his finger and he screamed blue murder until Nan picked it out between her false teeth.

The orange curtains are open but it's dark outside so he goes over to draw them. It's so dark he can see a trillion pinpoints of streetlight in pebbles of rainwater that have formed on the glass like the skin of a tangerine. He can just make out the row of houses opposite with their borders of privet and cars parked outside. Over the rooftops he can see the streetlights getting smaller as they stretch away into the distance until the last thing he can see is the floodlight of the factory where Grandad works. *Used* to work. He's been 'laid off'.

When Jamie was really little, his friend Stephen told him those lights were at the end of the world and Jamie was daft enough to believe him. Now, of course, he knows that it isn't true because Boy

George is from London. You can't see London because it's hundreds of miles away, but the lights of Grandad's factory, well they are only in the next town.

Jamie closes the curtains and turns to Nan's dressing table where his favourite photograph of young Nan and young Grandad stands in a gilt frame. You can tell it's really old because it's in black and white. Jamie used to think that everything in the world was grey in the olden days, just like in the pictures. In the photograph Nan's hair is black and done all nice in curls like an actress. Grandad looks young and macho like a real man from a Hollywood movie. This is how he likes to think of them. Some artist has gone over the picture with a pencil to make their eyes darker and Grandad's quiff stand out a bit more. They both look happy. He turns away from the photo. That's when he sees what he has come for—the cardboard box for Uncle Freddie, resting on Nan's bed. He picks it up carefully and creeps downstairs.

With his hand resting on the door handle to the living room, he listens to them all talking on the other side. There's still no laughter and it all sounds a bit serious, but at least Nan isn't shouting. He pushes the door open and they all stop talking, mid-conversation. He can't tell if they're annoyed that he's there or if they're feeling sorry for him, until finally, Auntie Sandra says, 'Alright, our Jamie,' and he starts to feel okay again.

There is a soft 'Oooooooooh,' from everyone, except Grandad. He puts the box down in the middle of the floor and lifts it out—his creation—a Boy George hairpiece of braided wool stitched into a black bowler hat. Each braid has been carefully woven with red, blue, and yellow ribbons, just like the one George had worn in the pop-video.

Auntie Sandra sits forward on her knees and touches the hat, fingering the braids. 'Oh look Freddie. Ain't he made a nice job of it? You're gonna look the biz. Look at all them ribbons. Must have taken him hours.' She looks at Jamie. 'Did you plait each one yourself?'

'Nan helped me get a few of them going. But mainly I did it myself.'

Nan is still wiping away inky tears and smudges of green eye shadow. She sighs, 'I ain't been able to go for a piddle all afternoon.' She points at the living room door where Jamie had been working. 'He's had them plaits tied around the door handle and I daren't disturb the artist at work.'

Uncle Freddie smiles. 'I knew he'd make a good job of it. He's got the right sort of hands.' He carefully lifts up the hairpiece and tries it on. Everyone laughs. Jamie thinks it's a bit of an insult. He doesn't look a bit like Boy George. Not with that big, dark moustache. More like Freddie Mercury in a wig.

'Watch him, our Sandra! He might be on the turn.' Nan roars with laughter.

'What's *the turn?*' Jamie asks, and they all laugh again.

Then Uncle Freddie makes his voice feminine and high-pitched and says, 'I'd prefer a nice cup of tea.'

Auntie Sandra joins Nan in laughter—shrieking, in fact, but it sounds a bit forced, perhaps to make Uncle Freddie feel better about a joke that clearly no-one understands.

'He's a clever lad, our Jamie,' Auntie Sandra says, hugging him tightly.

Then there's another thump of a knuckle at the window and they all turn to look; even Grandad this time. 'That'll be y'mother,' Nan says. 'Jamie. Get y'coat.' She goes into the passageway to open the front door. 'Alright Gloria? Oh my God, you're wringin'.' She comes back into the room with Gloria behind her.

'Alright everyone?' Gloria says, standing in the doorway, in a two-tone blue batwing jumper. She always makes a dramatic entrance. 'It's coming down in sheets out there. I'm not stopping. Just come to pick the bab up.'

'Alright Glo?' they chorus.

She takes one look at Uncle Freddie and says, 'What in the world have you got on your head? Y'silly bugger.' She squeezes in and steps over Uncle Freddie's legs. 'Alright bab? You had a nice day?'

Jamie flings his arms around her. They hug. Then she pulls her nose up and glares at Nan. 'Mother! You been giving him whiskey again?'

Nan shrugs. 'Only a dribble. Help him sleep better.'

'Mother!' Gloria snaps again. Jamie has his head pressed into her neck but he knows she's making mean faces at Nan.

'Don't make a fuss, Glo,' Nan says, settling herself into her seat, plumping the cushions behind her.

Gloria lets go of him and ruffles his hair. The room is so small she's standing in between Uncle Freddie's outstretched legs to check herself in the wall mirror. 'My hair's gonna go all frizzy now. I've only just had this perm.' She teases wet curls with the tips of her fingers. 'Come on Jamie. Get your stuff together. I've got to get back to get y'dads tea on. Give everyone a kiss.'

Jamie already has his coat on and is moving to begin kissing everyone goodbye. 'Love you, Nan.'

Nan leans forward and raises a cheek. 'See you soon, cock,' she says. 'And don't take any notice of him.' She points at Freddie. 'He's nothing but a bloody varmint. I'll put one on him if he upsets you.' At the same time she hands the afro-comb from the mantelpiece to Gloria.

'Bye Auntie Sandra,' Jamie says, leaning to kiss her.

'Mmmmmmmwaa! See you soon, Bab.' Auntie Sandra squeezes him firmly. She tickles his ribs. He struggles to escape. 'You're hurting me!' He squeals. She lets go of Jamie and he falls to the floor, squealing.

'I'll save you some more of them pictures,' Auntie Sandra says.

'Bye Uncle Freddie.' Jamie moves to kiss his stubbly cheek and Freddie squeezes him in his big muscly arms. 'See ya, Nancy Boy.'

The back of Gloria's hand comes down, crack! across the back of Freddie's head.

Freddie's hand shoots to the back of his skull.

'I've told you not to call him that,' Gloria says.

'Christ Glo, you didn't have to hit me *that* hard.'

She flashes her teeth at him. 'You'll be speaking on the other side of your face if you say it again.'

'What's wrong with it? He's one of a kind, ain't he?'

Gloria fixes him with her eyes. 'Just carry on. I'm warning you.'

Jamie moves to Grandad. There's a cruel look in his eye. He raises the palm of his hand to Jamie. 'What is it with all this kissing?' he says.

Jamie is stunned. Grandad can barely look at him. Jamie doesn't know what to say. At the same time, he feels something tug on his leg. He turns and looks behind. The red wool from the knitting has snagged on his shoe and he's dragged lengths of it out of the bag and across the floor.

'Oh Dad, he always kisses you,' Gloria says. 'He's your *grandson*. Give him a kiss, for heaven's sake.'

Something has changed. He always kisses Grandad when he's leaving. Jamie suddenly feels as if he's saying goodbye to them all for a very long time. It doesn't feel right. He's so very far away and so incredibly alone. Grandad should say something. He *is* his grandad after all. But he doesn't. His face turns to the wall. Deep lines curl away from his nostrils and his top lip disappears inside his bottom one. He seems to have lost interest in the Spitfire altogether and his sad, watery eyes are staring at the clock.

Jamie winds the wool back into the bag. 'Mum. What's wrong with—'

Gloria grabs him by the arm, as if there's something to be feared. 'Grandad's got a few things on his mind.' As she speaks, Jamie pulls out the partially knitted pencil case. 'Come on. I'm doing liver'n'onion tonight,' Gloria says.

He looks at the ruined work, red wool unravelling, stitches—loose from the needles. He can't for the life of him work out why Grandad has become so unfriendly, but he's sure it has something to do with the knitting.

Yarn

Gloria's about to lock up the wool shop for lunch. She places Mrs Hickingbottom's Sirdar order on the counter, ready for her to pick up, darts to the back of the shop to set the burglar alarm and then she's out the door, flipping the 'closed' sign as she goes. Keys in hand, she peers through the glass, checking the shop she's managed part-time for years. She turns the key, locking inside happy memories. It was the first job she'd had since having little Jamie and sometimes, during holidays, he used to sit with her on the bottom of a stepladder—a knitting mascot for the old ladies. The lights are off. The soft, comforting balls of wool sit in rows of many colours inside wooden pigeonholes.

She makes a move into cheerful sunlight—across town, through the cemetery where they would all sit—Gloria, Jamie, Nan and Grandad—on the perimeter wall, eating potato fritters in batter, followed by a jam doughnut. She has to walk all the way home in these damned heels—bloody idiot, should have worn flats. There are the dogs to walk, the meat to take out of the freezer for Roy's tea and her lunch to eat. She's cutting it fine if she's to make it back early enough for the afternoon rush. It's always busy when the shelf-stackers from Kwik Save clock off after lunch and they all rush in to get their needles, patterns, yarn, or just stand gas-bagging with each other. And today she's on her own. Margaret's under the doctor—peptic ulcer or some such trouble.

At home, she wolfs down her sandwich—cheese and Branston—adds Jamie's school uniform to a pile of freshly ironed laundry and carries it up to his bedroom.

On the threshold she stands, scanning the room—bloody untidy bugger. 'Lord only knows what he gets up to in here,' she voices to the empty room. His desk is cluttered with paints and brushes. There's a wooden box with seashells glued to it and inside it's stuffed with letters and photographs. Next to the desk, an easel carries a piece of board he's painted a picture on—a spaceship flying across the cosmos.

This is what he's into—science fiction and imagination. The walls are covered with pictures of now less-colourful pop stars—Boy George, washed-out, sadly lost in drugs, Holly Johnson lost behind the censors, and Freddie Mercury reportedly diagnosed with HIV, God love him. And there's Jamie's scrapbook—never grown out of it—big and red and bulging with cuttings.

She drops the basket of fresh washing on the floor, tidies the bed and arranges his teddy bears on the pillows. Then she hangs his clean laundry in the wardrobe, sniffing a school shirt—fragranced with fabric conditioner—and smiling inwardly. Fourteen and he's still her little boy.

The phone rings in the adjacent bedroom. 'Who's that now?' She dashes onto the landing, tripping over Roy's slippers, and into her own bedroom where she grabs the receiver. 'Hello?' From where she's standing, next to the window, she can see Mrs Tonks, waving up at her from the street, walking that daft miniature poodle—same route she does every day, wearing the same maroon cloche bucket hat.

'Oh, hello there. Is that Mrs Johnson?' comes a voice.

'Speaking.' If she's told Mrs Tonks once not to let that mutt urinate on the front lawn, she's told her umpteen times—piss burns ruining the grass.

'It's Annie—from the library.'

'Oh dear God,' Gloria says. 'Have we got overdue books? I thought I'd returned them?'

'No, no. It's nothing like that,' Annie says. 'It's about some books that Jamie's ordered through the inter-library loan service.'

'Go on.'

'Well, I've four books here. Art books. Paintings and such. They're ready for him to collect. Only I thought you'd better see them first.'

'Oh?' Gloria, turns away from the window now, one hand fiddling with her gold hooped earrings.

'Well, if it were my son, I wouldn't have a—I mean, it's not like he's—'

'Annie, what's our Jamie gone and done now?'

'I don't know how to put this. It's just that they're a bit, well, you know—*erotic*.'

Gloria pauses for a moment, absorbing what Annie's just said.

'Bloody Nora! You mean he's been ordering pornography?'

'It's nothing like that. I promise you.'

Gloria feels herself blushing. 'Dear God. What time are you open till?'

'Eight o'clock on a Thursday. It's my late night.'

'Right. I'll be in after work to vet them.'

'Alright Mrs Johnson.'

'Call me Gloria. Mrs Johnson makes me sound like an old woman.'

§

At the library Annie spreads the books out on the counter in front of Gloria. 'Do you see what I mean?'

Gloria flicks through the glossy pages of illustrations. Fantasy art they call it—Amazonian women wearing very little, voluptuous bodies, muscle-bound barbarians slaying dragons and sexy women riding winged beasts. She tries to keep her voice low. 'Some of this is quite tasteful, actually.'

Annie laughs. 'Mind you, you wouldn't want it on your bedroom wall, would you?'

'God no.' Gloria points at one female with an abundant cleavage. 'Enough to give you a complex.'

Both women titter, which draws a loud 'Shush', from behind one of the bookcases.

Gloria pulls a face and presses her lips together. 'I expect he's researching something. Our Jamie writes stories. Won a competition only last month. And he does a lot of drawing. Art's his favourite subject at school. Maybe he wants to copy some of these mythical creatures.' She exchanges a look with the librarian. There's an image of a muscular man seemingly being anally penetrated by a tree in the shape of a man, very artfully done, but —

Gloria bites her lip. She closes the book and looks at Annie. 'I'll make sure he doesn't take them to school.'

'I just wanted to be sure, Mrs... sorry... Gloria. Better safe than sorry,' Annie says. 'I'll just check these out to Jamie's account and you can take them with you, okay?'

§

In the dark, she's sitting on the edge of his bed, playing with his knitting bag, when he comes in from his after-school art class. She watches him through the bedroom door, coming up the stairs, alongside the slatted banisters, pulling off his school tie, and unbuttoning his shirt.

'Alright, Mum,' Jamie says. His voice is deep and slightly husky, in a way she'd never noticed before. When he reaches the top of the stairs he looks taller than she thought he was. Taller than his dad now. 'You checking my tension?' he says, leaning on the doorframe, the landing light behind him casting his face into silhouette.

'You still into this?' Gloria asks, thinking that she preferred it when he was.

'Not really. Grown out of it.' He gestures to his tube of paintbrushes, which replaced his knitting needles a few years ago. He walks in without switching on the light and places them on the desk.

She stands up. 'The librarian called today. I went to pick these books up for you.' She hands him a carrier bag with the books in. '*Art* they call it.'

'Oh, brilliant.' He reaches into the bag, excitedly. 'I've been waiting for ages for these.'

Gloria looks at her son—a furry shadow on his chin, Adam's apple, greasy hair, pimples—not so *little* anymore. 'I know you only want to look at the tits!'

'Mum!'

'Your Dad says you'll go blind.'

'Mum!'

'I'm only saying.' She punches him on the shoulder and leaves him alone in the darkness of his room. 'If I catch you playing with yourself, I'll ban you from that library. Do you hear?'

Mirror Ball

Ray's Volvo smells of warm plastic and lemon air freshener. It's all mock-luxury: leopard print seat covers and faux mahogany panelling. Jamie, Paul and Debs are in the back. Angie, Paul's mum, is in the front passenger seat doing her hair. They're waiting for Ray, Paul's dad, to drive them all to the baths. They call it 'The Baths', but for as long as Jamie can remember the pool has been covered with a semi-permanent wooden dance floor. It's used for ballroom dancing now, and prom nights.

It's New Year's Eve and they're all going to party, just like they do every year. No school for another week. They're all dressed up. Paul and Jamie are in grey chinos, black slip-on shoes and cotton shirts. Jamie's is pink. Paul's is lemon. Debs is wearing a sequined dress with a lace over-skirt and mesh fingerless gloves.

As per usual, Ray is the last one to get ready. He sticks his head through the driver's side window. 'Angie, have you seen my gold bracelet? I can't find a stick of jewellery anywhere.'

'It's on the dressing table next to your cufflinks. And hurry up— we're gonna be late.'

He disappears again. Angie carefully divides her hair into sections with a comb and applies portable curling tongs that she's connected to the cigarette lighter. She looks over her shoulder. 'Looking forward to it, kids?'

'Highlight of my year, Mum.' Paul laughs and elbows Jamie playfully.

Finally, Ray gets in, suitably bejewelled, patting his hair, quiff at the front, duck's arse at the back. His shirt is open to the fourth button down, revealing the flash of a gold chain and a mat of chest hair. He reeks of eau de toilette, but Jamie knows he must have rushed in the shower because there's still the undercurrent of armpit odour beneath cheap deodorant.

He throws his leather jacket at Jamie and says, ''Ere Cock, put that on the back shelf, will ya.' He pulls the plug of the heated tongs out, chucks it into Angie's lap, pushes the cigarette lighter back in and says, 'Have you got the tickets?'

'Ray! I was using that.'

'You look fine. Don't make a fuss,' he says, picking a cassette off the dashboard and inserting it into the player. He turns the rear-view mirror to face himself, licks a finger and smoothes down his eyebrows. Then, he adjusts his seat and belts up like a fighter pilot in an F-14 Tomcat.

As he turns the ignition, Angie says, 'Did you lock the back door?' and the car lurches forward to the sound of *Take my Breath Away*, nearly causing her to doodle lipstick over her cheek. She punches him hard on the shoulder. 'You left it wide open when you went out last Wednesday. That's why the place stinks of cat's piss. I come home to a kitchen full of stray moggies.'

Jamie's still trying to find room for Ray's jacket behind him. The whole back seat shelf is cluttered with Debs' dancing trophies.

Angie hands two ten-pound notes over her shoulder. 'That's for your drinks, lads. Don't spend it all at once.' She didn't do that last year.

'Where's mine?' Debs says.

'Your Dad'll buy *your* drinks. You're not old enough.'

'Neither are these two. They're only sixteen.'

The lighter pops out again and Ray says, 'Angie, light me one of them cigars, will you luv.'

'You're a girl,' she says, ignoring Ray. 'I don't want you going near that bar. Understand?'

'It's not fair. You never let me do anything because I'm a girl.'

Jamie takes the tenner and puts it in his pocket. 'Thanks Angie.'

Angie turns around in her seat and looks directly at him. 'Jamie sweetheart, keep your eye on her, will you?'

'Alright Ange,' Jamie says. When Angie sits back, he nudges Debs. She looks at him and he puts a finger to his lips, tapping his trouser pocket at the same time. She smiles and touches her top lip with her tongue. Jamie and Paul have been doing extra paper rounds for beer money.

Angie turns round in her seat again. 'Here, Jamie, it might be your lucky night,' she says, perhaps a little too enthusiastically.

'How do you mean?' Jamie asks, feeling himself blush.

'You might meet your future wife,' she says.

Paul rolls his eyes and inspects his biceps.

Debs shakes her head. 'Are you kidding? At the *baths*?'

'It's where me and y'dad met,' Angie says.

'A marriage made in heaven,' Paul says.

'Pure Barbara Cartland,' Debs says, and looks out of the window.

At the baths, they pull onto the muddy car park where Alan, Janice and Darren are waiting at the bottom of the steps. They all get out of the Volvo. Debs runs to Darren and snogs him. Ray walks over to Alan, his drinking partner. They shake hands and slap each other on the shoulder.

'All right, mate?' Ray says and then turns to Paul and throws his car keys at him. 'Park it round the back, Son. And don't scratch it.'

Paul's eyes widen. 'Thanks Dad,' he says, watching them all walk up the steps to the dancehall. Angie and Jamie struggle behind them all with plastic bags of picnic food, soft drinks and undelivered Christmas presents. Her shoes are sinking into puddles.

Angie shouts to Ray, 'Do you really think you should be letting him park that car?'

'Why?' Ray asks.

'I only washed it yesterday. He's gonna drive it through all that mud.'

'Oh, stop going on, woman!'

From one of her carrier bags, Angie pulls a fire extinguisher sized canister of hairspray and mists her head as they go through the double doors. She passes it forward to Janice who does the same, walking down the corridor.

'Fuck's sake Janice!' Alan says. 'I can fucking taste the stuff. Leave it out.'

§

It's ten o'clock. The bar at the side of the dance floor is packed. Jamie's drinking cider, because it's all he can stomach. He hasn't yet acquired a taste for ale, like the other men. He's been buying double shots of Vodka in pint glasses of lemonade for Debs, so her Mum won't find out. Even Darren doesn't know. He's like the fucking thought-police, eager to score brownie points with Angie.

Paul's off sharking. Darren is talking to some older boys from school and Jamie is soaking up the smoky atmosphere. It's the kind of place that time left behind: beer stained carpets and toilets that stink of sick.

The mirror ball sends a dotted trail of light along the wall. Jamie follows its path around the room until it crosses the faces of Ray and Angie, finishing their first dance of the evening. They're perfectly matched, height-wise. Short. Ray's in Cuban heels and Angie is wearing very gold, very high heels, and *now*, very shiny, since she's wiped off the mud with a tissue. They go well with the gold sequined frock she's wearing and her golden, shimmering, not-quite-finished hair-do.

The track comes to an end. 'Shit,' Debs says, getting all jittery. 'Mum's coming over.'

'It's alright. Remember, it's only *lemonade*.'

'Alright, me luvs,' Angie says, smoothing down her lamé skirt.

'Yeah,' Jamie says. 'Did you enjoy your dance?'

'Probably the last one I'll get. He's gone off to talk to Alan now, about a motor. You know what they're like. Ain't you found a nice girl yet?'

Angie is showing a lot of cleavage. She's wearing a pendant on a long gold chain, directing the eye deep into the folds of her sparkly dress.

'No,' Jamie says, lazily, and looks at Debs, who is rolling her eyes.

'Y'mum and dad didn't want to come, Jamie?' Angie asks.

He can just imagine his mother's face at the thought of it. When he left the house she was wearing a black and cream peplum jacket over a pencil skirt and pair of two-tone patent leather court shoes. And that's just what she throws on to run the vacuum cleaner round or walk the Alsatians.

'They're at home watching television. Dad's been working long hours lately.'

'They don't know what they're missing,' she says. 'Is he still roofing?'

He nods. 'I think he's doing all right. Can I buy you a drink, Angie?'

'You save your money, luv.' She lowers her voice and nods over to our table in the corner. 'Me and Janice have got a bottle of Vodka stashed.' Then she slaps Jamie on the shoulder and points a sharpened fingernail at him. 'You looking after *her*?' she asks, nodding at Debs, leaning sheepishly, behind him.

'Yeah, course.'

'More than I can say for that boyfriend of hers.' Angie folds her arms and looks around the room. 'Where is he?'

'He's talking to some of his mates,' he says.

She looks at Debs. 'I thought I told you not to come near this bar?'

Debs pinches her face into a fake smile and holds up her glass. 'Lemonade,' she says.

'Even so. Why don't you go and have a dance with Jamie? You'd like that, wouldn't you, Jamie?'

Before he can decline, Debs says, 'Why don't you worry about Paul as much as you worry about me?' Jamie leans back against the bar, out of the firing line.

'Your brother can look after himself.'

'Really?' Debs says.

Angie turns again and looks over her shoulder. 'Where is he anyway?'

'Probably in the toilet selling something.'

§

Paul is unzipping his fly next to Jamie. Jamie looks at him out of the corner of his eye, as Paul liberates his undercarriage in strong, muscular hands. He lets out a loud groan of relief as a steaming flow of liquid hits porcelain. Paul rocks his head back, relishing this moment. Then he says, 'Alright, cock?' which Jamie remembers is what he'd said to him the first time they ever met. He'd been racing his radio control model car in a spot of wasteland called 'The Burn', a quarry, half-filled with rainwater, a couple of miles from where he lived.

A group of older boys from another school ambushed him and tried to steal the car. One boy, the tallest, had a mean look in his eye and blonde highlighted spikes in his hair. He'd started mouthing off at Jamie. 'That's ours now. Hand it over.'

The boy wrenched the car from Jamie's hands, pushed him to the floor and kicked him hard in the ribs. The boy was just about to make off with it when Paul appeared brandishing the butt of the snooker cue he always carried around. 'Go and play in the traffic,' he said. He put the control to his own car on the floor. The gang laughed at Paul, but when he went for them, showing no fear, swinging the cue hard enough to fracture a skull, they scarpered. He laughed and turned toward Jamie. Jamie had seen him at The Burn before, with his model car. They went to the same school but this was the first time he'd spoken to Jamie.

'Alright, cock?' he'd said, holding out his hand to help Jamie up off the ground.

Jamie can't piss. He looks down. Nothing. He bears down on his bladder harder, squeezing his abdomen. He closes his eyes in embarrassment.

'False alarm?' Paul asks.

'Something like that,' Jamie says, and feels his cheeks burning red.

'It's no wonder,' he says. 'Have you seen the birds in here? That one behind the bar—Linda Lusardi look-a-like—she's had me like a compass near north all night. I thought I was gonna have to piss standing on my hands.' Then he whistles. 'Fantastic tits,' he says. He exaggerates the consonants in 'tits', as if he really enjoys the sound of the word in his mouth. Jamie hears the guy on the other side of him grunt in agreement.

A stream of piss from between Paul's legs hoses down the porcelain. He moves away from the trough. Jamie hears the tap go on behind him and the sound of running water in the sink, and suddenly he can go. He lets his eyes roll back in his head for a moment as the pressure of liquid, seemingly backed up somewhere inside his ribcage, releases like a lukewarm hot-water bottle being emptied down a drain.

Paul's hand is on his back. Jamie senses him playfully sniffing his neck. 'Mmm. Nice aftershave. Who are you trying to impress?'

Jamie laughs. 'Wouldn't you like to know?'

'Lock up your daughters,' Paul calls out to the toilet and giggles. 'Do you want another pint?' he asks, stepping away. Jamie glances over his shoulder at him, preening his curly dark brown hair in the mirror, muscles in his forearm flexing as he runs his fingers through his hair. It's unlikely he plays with that radio-controlled car anymore.

Jamie nods acceptance of a fresh cider and then Paul leaves the toilet.

The guy next to Jamie at the toilet trough is pissing some kind of radioactive yellow fluid that makes Jamie think he might need a new set of kidneys. It trickles along the trough and merges with Jamie's relatively clear urine and collects in the drain cover, inches away from his toes, foaming up like Coca-Cola. Jamie turns his head for a second and snatches a look at him: old fella with a stoop, red face, broken veins on a purple nose.

Jamie shakes, zips himself up and takes a deep breath. The air is noxious. His head swims. He leans, almost touches the wall, but notices the decaying water pipe—sweating rust pushing through caked gloss paint. The look of it makes him shudder. Jamie steps backwards from the trough and moves to wash his hands in a grimy ceramic basin. He stares at himself in the mirror, ruffles his hair, loosens his tie and undoes a button. His skin is smooth, uniform in colour. He has a few spots, but nothing to worry about. He frowns at the soft down around his chin. He's not yet developed stubble, like Paul but he is changing. He's slimmer, faster—like a whippet. Paul can beat him in an arm wrestle, but he doesn't read books. He's not interested in the world, or at least not Jamie's world. Jamie's eyes are brighter, more vital.

In the mirror he sees guys walking in and out of the toilet. Their eyes are different, dull beads of glass, set deep in their skulls, like something has been stolen from them. Jamie is determined not to become like them.

He walks out of the toilet and onto the dance floor. He sways to the music on his own. An old lady gives him a dance lesson. It's Ada, one of Ray's mum's friends. She teaches him the quick step, and he picks it up pretty quickly. Then he hears Ray's voice behind him. 'Who's he think he is? Lionel Blair?' It smarts a bit, because Jamie can't tell if he means it as a joke or not.

§

It's now eleven o'clock and Debs is on the stage doing a solo number. It's like this every year. She's won so many of those dance competitions for the district, she always gets asked to perform, just before they do the raffle - some modern dance routine to Whitney Houston: 'I want one moment in time... When I'm more than I thought I could be... When all of my dreams are a heartbeat away...' *The irony*, Jamie thinks. He's still here where time has stood still, where the highlight of the week is Sharon Moody's mid-week power-ballad night at The Winking Frog and if he's lucky, a joyride around the estate in the back of one of his older friends' cars. Same as last year and the year before.

He watches Ray making a fuss over Debs, telling everyone around him that it's his daughter on stage. It's laughable really, because Ray thinks she's made it. But Jamie knows better. She's just cutting her teeth. If Ray has his way, he'll have her in the back of a van, driving her around the country, singing and dancing in working men's clubs. That's not what she wants. She's a brilliant dancer, but it's history she's always liked at school.

From across the room, Jamie can see Angie and Janice standing together, arms folded, dots of reflected light from the mirror ball gliding across their faces. Janice is top to toe in silver. Together they look like a couple of second-rate game show hostesses. Angie is looking over at Ray, shaking her head. He looks annoyed. He beckons her to go nearer the stage, next to him, but she sticks out her tongue at him.

The room is hushed and all eyes are on Debs while she's dancing and there are a variety of ooooohs and aaaahs from the audience as Whitney reaches the key change and Debs segues into her final sequence. Ray is jubilant. It's like Torvill and Dean's Bolero all over again. Old ladies dab tears away from their eyes as they watch Debs. She pirouettes, cartwheels and spins across the stage, all the while twizzling a bit of pink ribbon on the end of a stick. Suddenly, it gets caught on her foot and she trips. Jamie looks over at Ray who now looks crestfallen. Unbeknown to him, the vodka and lemonade are getting the better of his daughter and she nearly topples off stage. She makes a professional, tits and teeth recovery just in time for Whitney's money-note and a rapturous applause. 'Stunning!' says one of the old ladies, as if it were all part of the routine. 'Bloody breathtaking,' says another.

Next, a stocky woman in a grey trouser suit and a gent's haircut steps up to the tombola. With fingers like sausages strangulated inside gold sovereign rings, she pulls numbers from it and calls them out.

Each time she does, the amp shrieks with feedback and she tuts with great annoyance, her big moment being spoilt. Anyone would have thought it was the Oscars instead of a silly raffle. Still, the audience are very excited about the prizes. Jamie's already checked them out— nothing anyone would really want to win: a bottle of bubble bath, a magnum of sparkling Perry, edible knickers, cuddly toy and a compact disc of *Love Songs from the Movies on the Pan Pipes*. Compact discs are all the rage but he doesn't have a player yet. Shame. His dad is a big fan of the pan-pipes.

One of Jamie's numbers is called and he collects his prize. The butch woman with the mic, hands over a bottle of Opium by Yves Saint Laurent. Ray falls about pissing himself. 'Are you gonna give it y'mum or wear it yourself?' he says.

After the raffle, the DJ puts on some slower music, so finally, Jamie dances with Debs. They're the same height. Tall. They rest their heads on each other's shoulders. Jamie nuzzles the gold curls of her hair with his nose. They smell of hairspray and perfume. Nice. They fall around in the music, bathing in it, as if it were tropical water. The floor is dappled with tiny shards of mirror-light. She leans back to look at Jamie. For a second, she's not a girl, but a woman.

'I'm fucking drunk,' she says and bites her lip.

'I know,' Jamie says and they giggle. 'I thought you were gonna come off that stage on a stretcher.'

She pulls him close again. Over her shoulder, Darren is frowning at them. For a moment Jamie thinks he's going to walk over and get in between them, but as Darren steps forward Angie grabs his arm. Jamie can lip-read her saying 'Oi, no y'don't!' and then 'dance with me, face-ache.' She's all flirty-mumsy. But as he tries to step away again, she points a finger and shakes her head. And then, miraculously, they're dancing. The top of Angie's head comes just to where Darren's nipples would be.

'Do you love him?' Jamie asks Debs.

'Who?'

'Darren.'

'Are you mad?' she asks..

'Why d'you go out with him then?' Jamie asks.

'Dunno. What else is there to do in this hole?'

He remembers the time they first listened to Whitney together. He'd gone round to call for Paul but it was Debs who answered the door. 'He's gone out with one of his girlfriends tonight,' she'd said. 'But you can come in and talk to me, if you like.' They ended up getting burnt on her portable sun-bed, singing *Didn't We Almost Have It All* at the tops of their voices. And that's when he told her. Well, maybe he didn't tell her *anything*. She just knew.

He feels Debs' hands moving, down his back, over his bum.

'You've got a nice arse,' she says. He feels her fingers gently squeeze flesh through the seat of his trousers and he wonders, for a second, if her brother might have a firmer grip.

'Thanks,' he says.

'My mother would say, 'It's a waste. Good looking guy like you.''

'I know,' he says and he feels her kiss his neck.

'Where's me Dad?' she asks.

'He's over there, dancing with the woman from Woolworth's again.'

'He's not?'

'He is.'

§

It's five to twelve. Angie and Jamie are sat at their big table eating crisps. The remnants of smuggled party food, cold fatty sausage rolls, pork pies and potato puffs, lie scattered on a beer-swilled tablecloth.

Paul comes up behind Jamie and puts his arms around him. 'It's nearly time mate.' He's drunk. 'How many girls have you snogged?'

'How many have *you* snogged?' Jamie says.

'Four,' he says.

'Five,' Jamie lies.

'Nah! You're a dark horse, ain'tcha. What you got, that I ain't got?'

'Must be my aftershave,' Jamie says.

Paul smells good. Manly. Jamie breathes him in deeply. Paul moves away. 'You coming then?'

'Where?' Jamie asks. He looks round. He's got his arm around some bird now. Christ, what toilet did you scrape her out of? It's mean of him but all the same, Paul doesn't have great taste.

'For a dance,' he says, pulling the girl onto the dance floor.

'Oh, yeah,' Jamie says. 'In a minute.'

What's all the fuss about? It's just another fucking year. Nothing changes. The world will still be the same tomorrow morning. If he has to dance with Paul's mum another year, at twelve o'clock, he's going to kill himself. No, really, he will. He'll kill himself. He looks across the crowded dance floor at Ray. He's not going to leave that woman alone.

Angie gets up and heads over towards them. She stubs her toe on the empty Vodka bottle that she and Janice have discarded. 'Fuck!' She pushes her way through the crowd and nearly goes over on her heel. Jamie can see her talking to Ray. There are raised voices for a moment, and then she's walking back. 'Lousy bastard!' he hears her say. 'Looks like it's me and you again, Cock. Come on, get your dancing shoes on.'

The music, it's the Nolans. Why couldn't it have been *It's Raining Men*? He forces a smile. He swallows, heaves his unfortunate carcass off the seat and takes her hand. She lifts their hands up high and they cross the floor like *Come Dancing* partners in the Blackpool Tower ballroom.

The room seems like a drunken merry-go-round, Jamie in the centre, barely moving, all the dots of mirror-light shooting around the perimeter. He lets his eyes follow one, a glass butterfly in a hurricane, hitting people in the face. Ray is drunk, slumped over the shoulder of the woman from Woolworth's. Alan and Janice are two-stepping together. Darren is dancing with Debs, if you can call it dancing—he's got two left feet. Her eyes are glazed over. She looks like she's thinking, *get me the fuck out of here*, which is not far from what Jamie's thinking. Angie puts her head on his chest and they go round to the music. He fakes a smile, closes his eyes and dreams he might find something new and unexpected in the darkness.

Then, he feels something touch his crotch—just a brush at first, and then something grabbing hold. His eyes snap open. Angie's hands are on his shoulders. He wonders if he could've imagined it, but there's a furtive look in her eyes and she lets out a wicked cackle, fluid rattling in her throat. Why do middle-aged women think they can do this? No luck with their husbands, so they turn to the boys.

Jamie's head is swimming. He's looking at Paul snogging the toilet bird, strong, well-developed forearms wrapped around her. His hand is on her tit. Jamie wishes his hand were—

And suddenly, everyone is counting down... ten, nine, eight... the music stops... everyone has let go of their partners... Angie is smiling... they're all smiling gleefully... three, two, one, zero... and there's a flash of light, a loud explosion and thousands of bits of glitter falling on them from above and... HAPPY NEW YEAR... and there's that expectation of resolution and turning over a new leaf and everyone kissing each other. Beery men hold each other in headlocks and the room spins and everyone is still smiling and then suddenly Toilet Bird is in front of him—her breath, a mixture of fags and Pernod.

'Happy New Year,' she says and her open mouth and tongue come straight at him. His hands come up in front of him and he goes rigid. She's shocked and bristles at the rejection. 'Bender!' she says and walks away. And then it's Auld Lang Syne and they're all standing in a circle. Except he's mouthing some shit because he doesn't know the fucking words... and then it's just the light that engages him... fractured light, shooting in every direction. For a moment, in his eyes, everything is frozen. Only the mirror ball turns, Seurat-speckling faces. Alan and Janice are arm in arm. Ray and Angie are snarling at each other. Paul, the reason for him being there, is absent. No surprises. Debs and Darren are in a static clinch. He's kissing her full on the mouth, tongue down her throat, big brutish hands inside her blouse, except her eyes are looking directly at Jamie. And he knows, in that one moment, they're both thinking the same thing.

The room starts turning again. This time, something has changed. It's not the same this year. Next year he won't be here.

Mandarins in Jelly

'Secrets. One day, you'll know all mine, Soft Lad,' Billy says.

Jamie listens to Billy prattling behind him while he thumbs through an interiors magazine. Raising his head to face the mirror, he reconnects with Billy's reflection smiling back—both of them enclosed inside the surround of full-length glass. Billy covers the shoulders of Jamie's 1950s cream polka-dot shirt with tea towels. Jamie muses upon Billy's rats' tails and his own low sideburns: Jamie favours Britpop, while Billy is still holding on to Grunge.

Jamie lingers on their reflection; Billy takes a brush from Jamie's free hand and butters magenta dye into his bleached blonde side parting and deep fringe. 'This stuff stinks,' he says, and moves to open the window.

'There's only one person who knows everything about me,' Jamie says. 'Paul Fullbrook.' The magazine drops to the floor as Billy dispenses a bowl of pink gunk into one of Jamie's hands and a comb into the other. The two of them work in sync.

'Your mate studying in America?'

Jamie looks around Billy's childhood bedroom. It's covered with images of black and white movie stars: Gloria Swanson, Bette Davis, Greta Garbo.

'Keep still,' Billy says and taps him with the dye brush. Billy steps around paperbacks and magazines strewn across the floor of his bedroom. 'What did you tell him?'

'It's possible he's so disgusted by what I wrote that he's decided never to speak to me again,' Jamie says.

Jamie feels Billy staring at him from the mirror, head tilted a little, as if Billy were soothing a troubled boy. 'Christ! We're not that different,' Billy says. 'We'll be just like your parents when we're older. We can get a mortgage and a couple of puppies—semi-detached in Leamington Spa and an obsession with interior design.'

'I don't think Paul would be offended by a bit of interior design.

It's the other stuff I wrote.'

'Oh, I see. The *other* stuff,' Billy says, smearing more pink paint onto Jamie's head. 'It's not only gay men who like a bit of anal, you know. I'd put money on it—your mother's had it up the arse more times than I've had hot dinners. And if Paul is *that* prissy...' Billy wipes pink dye from Jamie's forehead with a pad of cotton wool.

Jamie glances over at the open door, through to the landing at the top of Billy's mum's stairs. 'Keep it down a bit will you.'

'Stop being such an apologist. This *is* nineteen ninety-five not nineteen forty-five,' Billy laughs. 'They can't lock us away anymore. I'd be more worried about what Gloria's going to say about your hair. You're going to look like a giant fuchsia.'

'My mother loves fuchsias. Patio's covered,' Jamie says.

Billy scoops up Jamie's fringe and combs it back. 'If she didn't know you were gay before, she certainly will now. What are you going to do? Spend the rest of your life pretending to be something you're not?'

Jamie lifts a hand to his eyebrow. 'Careful, you're going to get it in my eyes.'

'There,' Billy says. 'We have to wait for twenty minutes.'

Billy clears away his hairdressing tools and wipes down the little table cluttered with brushes, foils and bottles of peroxide and ammonia. 'So anyway, what did you write in this letter that was so scandalous?'

'Everything.'

'Everything?'

'Everything!'

Billy rolls his eyes. 'What possessed you?'

'I was lonely. I kept a lot in,' Jamie says. 'Things got better when I met you in London.' He looks at Billy's reflection—his head is angled to one side now. 'But when I started writing, well—'

'It just poured out.'

'I expect Paul's told everyone by now.'

From downstairs, Jamie hears the sound of the living room door opening. He flinches.

'It's only Mum,' Billy says, as her footsteps reach halfway up the stairs.

'You can stop your funny business.' She appears at the bedroom door, holding two mugs of tea. She sets them down on top of the bookcase. Everything about her is relaxed from her functional boyish haircut and her sloppy grey sweater. She leans against the doorframe and looks at Jamie's hair. 'Jesus Christ! What fucking colour is that? Anyone would think you two batted for the other side or something.' She grins.

'Or *something*,' Billy says, ushering her back out of the room.

'Don't do anything I wouldn't do,' she calls back to Jamie.

'Leaves us plenty of scope,' Billy says and presses the door shut on her.

Jamie smiles, stands inelegantly, rearranges the tea towels on his shoulders and flicks on the radio in the middle of *Smells Like Teen Spirit* by Nirvana. 'Paul Fullbrook. Jesus! Paul loved this.' He sits again in the chair they'd borrowed from the kitchen. 'We watched films together. Nothing else to do in Welston, so we used to walk the best part of two miles to the cinema together and get drunk on White Lightning on the way home. When I started at art school in London, I hadn't heard from Paul for ages. Then his letter came out of the blue. I was really surprised when I heard he'd decided to go to university. Always thought he'd join the family building firm. He'd finished his term early and was working in a summer camp in the US.'

'And?' Billy sighs impatiently.

'The letter: details of the many shags he'd had, list of clubs he knew, parties he'd been to, the substances he'd used... everything you're supposed to do on your first flight away from home. And questions... *Fallen off the face of the Earth, Jamie? Forgotten how to use a pen? I know there's something you're not telling me.*'

Jamie feels Billy's hand on his shoulder. 'So you took this as an invitation to spill the beans?

'This stuff has been fermenting for years.'

'Meaning?'

'I'm twenty and only now experiencing the kind of starry-eyed relationship that people like Paul Fullbrook form in their early teens. He was a girl-magnet. Probably lost his virginity at twelve.' Jamie smiles into the mirror. 'Before I met you, it felt like part of me hadn't been born.'

There's a knock at the door. Jamie stiffens. 'I'm going to the fish'n'chip shop,' Billy's mum calls. 'Do you two want your usual? I thought we'd have a treat before you go back to London.'

'Yes please,' Billy says.

'Are you two coming out?' Billy's mum shouts. 'Or are you going to stay in there and play with each other all night?'

'Fuck off,' Billy shouts back.

'You don't fancy a battered sausage then?' she says before her footsteps can be heard on the stairs again.

Billy shakes his head and turns to Jamie. 'I suppose writing to your mate felt cathartic.'

Jamie nods. 'We'd been close at school. There was no one else to tell. And the States seemed so far away. At least I didn't have to look him in the eye and say it.'

'It.'

'Yes. *It*,' Jamie says.

'Are we really worth so little, it has to be whispered?'

Jamie laughs. 'I didn't whisper. I evacuated my bowels onto the page. Everything came out. I wrote about the tantalizing, twilight excursions I'd had to parks and toilets and canals of London.' Jamie remembers every word vividly. *Imagine a derelict tram-shed littered with intravenous needles, crack pipes and foils, left by junkies, and bottles of amyl-nitrate discarded by seekers of furtive nocturnal pleasure. We had sex in the dark. The only sounds were our grunts and the skitter of broken glass beneath our feet. Hardly glamorous but it was exciting to do something that has a sense of the forbidden—outdoors, public, under the moonlight.* 'I wrote about the porn, the dates, the drugs, the many, many men... I wrote about you.'

'Jesus! You told him all that?' Billy turns to face him in the chair. 'Not as green as I thought you were.'

'I don't expect Paul had ever read anything like it. I wrote about 'The Black Cap' in Camden Town and the drag queen, Regina Fong.' *The last of the Romanoffs. A Russian princess who fled to Britain after the revolution. Some of the other students and I go every week to see her lip-synching to scenes from Coronation Street and Are You Being Served? She's wicked. One night I got right next to the stage, close enough to pull her skirt and get her attention. She said, 'You touch these silks again and I'll put my stiletto heel straight through your fucking skull.*"

Jamie fingers an itchy patch on his head where the dye has started to burn. 'I wrote about this initiation into a new world. It wasn't poetry. It had all the warmth of an autopsy report. But my god it felt good to get it out. Line and verse splurged onto that thin blue airmail paper—the first and last time I ever used it. I kept accidentally making holes in it with the nib of my pen. Ironic, isn't it—the burden of so many years carried by that frail, weightless paper.'

Billy pulls Jamie out of the chair. For a moment their faces are so close together, their lips almost touch. Jamie lifts a hand and it lands on Billy's dewy abdomen, the way it had when they first met. After just a year in London, during an excursion to a nightclub, he had discovered Billy, a lad who, studying just one year behind him at St Martins, had by coincidence shared one vital peculiarity; they both hailed from neighbouring nowhere towns in the Midlands.

Cliques of clones in leather S&M harnesses held glasses of G&T as if they were standing around at an afternoon barbecue. Dancing cadavers mingled with muscle men transformed by steroids, many of whom were disguising the disfiguring effects of AIDS and antiretroviral drugs. Gym-fit, hairless and tanned had become the prevalent fashion.

Jamie was the only guy still wearing a shirt, rocking his head to the trance music he couldn't abide. He felt insignificant next to their swollen bodies, chests and arms pumped like inflatables, nipples like rivets. He wished he occupied more space in the universe. He couldn't wait to get out of there.

Through a mosaic of airbrushed centrefolds, a young man moved towards him. He was toned and striking but not plasticized like the others. It couldn't be, thought Jamie. His naked chest was partially scribbled with unfinished tattoo. Peeping from underneath a blue and white denim baseball cap, his dark brown hair was dappled with an unbecoming orange. But Jamie knew. It was *him*. The one. Why there? Why then, in that place? And why that *orange* hair?

Jamie bundled deliberately and drunkenly into his path, and they clashed.

'Watch it,' the man said, steadying Jamie with both hands, preventing him from tumbling.

'Sorry,' Jamie replied, straightening his back and lengthening his vowels. 'Dancing. I wasn't looking where I was going.' He looked into the man's sparkling eyes.

'Mind on other things?' the man said, releasing him from his grip.

'I was just leaving.' Jamie smiled, perhaps a little too flirtatiously. 'Maybe you could help me.'

The man looked beyond him, over his shoulder. 'Actually, I'm looking for someone right now.'

'This place is so big. I need to get my coat,' Jamie said.

'What do you want me to do about it?' the man said.

'Cloakroom. Do you know where it is?' Jamie asked.

'Over there.' The man pointed. 'Up the stairs. Next to the bar.'

Jamie was still gazing into his eyes. 'Over there. Up the stairs. Next to the bar.'

'Yeah.'

Jamie recognized those flattened vowels anywhere. 'You're from the West Midlands? I'm from Welston.'

The man winced. 'You noticed, even in this din. I ran away as soon as I could.' He wasn't going to be drawn in. He arched his neck to see above the bobbing heads.

'I'm Jamie.' Jamie beamed and extended his hand, trying to make himself more noticeable.

'Billy,' the man said and they shook hands. He smiled and gently moved Jamie out of the way. For a moment their faces were so close together, their lips almost touched. Jamie lifted a hand and it landed on Billy's abdomen. Billy gave him a condescending little smile, as if he were an adolescent trying to prove he fitted in.

'Wait!' Jamie said. 'When am I going to see you again?'

Now passing him and slipping back into the crowd, Billy looked over his shoulder. 'You're not.'

'Love the shirt,' Jamie called after him.

Billy looked down at his naked torso. 'Thanks.' He smiled and vanished.

Right now, he'd still be tortured by his eternal dissatisfaction if Billy hadn't eventually been wrenched into the sewery depths of Soho, where they found solace amongst vintage-clad sexy boys. Week after week, they danced dreamily to Placebo and Pulp and Morrissey and

Blondie at *Poptarz*. They cruised, they hooked up, they found possibility on the dance floor, but it wasn't long at all before they found themselves falling in love with each other and Jamie had taken Billy home, where they made the beast with two backs, over and over.

Jamie stares into Billy's eyes. Billy wrinkles his nose. 'So you sent it?' He kisses Jamie gently, careful not to touch the strands of dyed hair.

'You know what I'm like. I almost didn't. I stood at the post-box for ages before watching the little chevrons of the airmail envelope fall into its cavernous red belly.' He throws his eyes up and slides his palms together, as if brushing away cobwebs.

'He's not written back?'

Jamie shakes his head. 'And Mum hasn't mentioned any mail for me at their place.' He walks to the mirror.

'You have your mail sent back home?'

'Post at the YMCA is hardly reliable. In between terms, post often got lost.' Jamie inspects his eyebrows, wondering if they should be pink too.

'You'll see your mum before we go back to London. You can ask her.'

'That mate of yours, Les—does he still want to take us to that gay bar?' Jamie asks, deliberately changing the subject. 'I didn't know gay bars existed in Welston.'

Billy wiggles pink stained, latex covered fingers at Jamie. 'The provinces never cease to amaze me.'

Jamie inspects his eyebrows again. He was right. They should be pink. 'I expect he is living it up in some New York nightclub.'

'Who?'

'Paul Fullbrook. Probably surrounded by girls. Fuck, he had bad taste—Pamela Anderson types with fake *everything*. What Paul thought of as *feminine,* I always thought of as drag.'

Jamie leans forward, peers at his reflection. 'I think this has been on long enough now. Shall we go and wash it off?'

Billy wrinkles his nose and picks up two bottles—one shampoo, the other conditioner. 'Yes. Come on, I want you to fuck me with pink hair.'

'Animal!'

§

Under luminous clouds passing in front of a halogen moon, men shuffle between ramshackle buildings of corrugated iron and zigzag-roofed factories. This is the canvas into which Jamie steps—a jigsaw area, shattered by economic decline, of shadowy gullies and industrial streets. Outside a blacked-out doorway, more men loiter, waiting to be allowed in.

Les and his boyfriend, Mark, are bickering over what colour floor tiles they should have in the new conservatory. Billy is taking photographs with a new camera. Jamie presses a buzzer painted with gelatinous black gloss. A little hatch opens in the door. Jamie turns and throws a surprised look at Billy. The gay bars and clubs of London are not secret or underground. Their names are scribbled in shouty bold colours and bright neon—*Heaven, Freedom, Compton's*. Yet here they are, Jamie and Billy, displaced and dispossessed, at The Pink Flamingo, too fearful to kiss or hold hands, standing outside a bar with no windows, waiting for the voice of a bodiless mouth to invite them in.

'Been here before?' the voice asks, sharp and waspish. It waits for Jamie's affirmative reply. 'You know what kind of bar this is, yeah?' Again, he nods. And finally, 'This is a bar for gay people and their friends. Any trouble and you're out! Understand?' Jamie nods once more. The door swings open and they're in. Immediately, a contrasting world of colour and exultant popular music is found inside. The revealed figure behind the door is, to his surprise, a boy who Jamie knew from school, who was bullied and ostracized from the others. He says, 'Alright Bab,' and Jamie nods, unable to say much else, wondering if the lad recognises him or not. The lad points to Billy's camera. 'No pictures. Sorry, Bab.'

'Oh?' Billy says. 'We were only going to take pictures of us lot.'

'Management policy, I'm afraid. You'll have to leave it here and pick it up later.'

They pass on through the entrance hall into a room decorated in nicotine-stained flock wallpaper, a mock-Flemish chandelier and a standard lamp with a tasselled shade. There's a video jukebox belting out camp classics and Eurovision hits. The clientele, whom Jamie senses all know each other, snap their heads round to look in their direction. *Know each other?* They've probably all *fucked* each other. Not much on the menu and so it seems Jamie and Billy are the new dishes on offer.

'I'll get the drinks,' Billy says, walking away, leaving Jamie standing with Les and Mark. All around him—a surreal scene for this area of Welston: young lads sitting with each other, holding hands, some of them kissing. Lesbians play a game of pool. A woman smokes a cigar and two muscly, tattooed guys lean over a fruit machine. Jamie never expected to find this on the edge of the council estate, where he grew up.

'We've just bought a place together,' Les says, sliding onto a banquet behind a table. 'One of those new starter homes, up in Bushbury. We couldn't afford much until the divorce comes through…'

Mark is nodding his head, urging Jamie to sanction this plan. 'Obviously, he's still paying maintenance for the kids. So the decorating has been put on hold for now.'

'Having said that,' Les says, 'We've just booked a cruise. Mark's always wanted to go to the Seychelles. I said, Babe, if you want to go. Let's go.'

Part of Jamie feels envious. To be like his mother and father, to fall in love and when the relationship tires, to work at it—is that the right thing to do? Though he also knows one of the benefits of being of his disposition is that you don't have to choose that model. A lifestyle can be invented—one that doesn't involve children or the Monday to Friday grind.

Jamie looks at Mark. 'You do know, I think, in the Seychelles, you can go to prison for being gay.'

'Oh, it'll be fine,' Les says, slipping out of his glittery Buck Rogers jacket. 'We're very discreet.'

On the other side of the smoke-filled bar, Billy is pulling notes from his wallet and handing them to a bald, fat man whose fingers glint with gold sovereign rings—a man who Jamie instantly recognizes. It's the fella who lives in the council house next door to his grandmother. He'd lived all his life with his mother, now dying of lung cancer. Jamie remembers him in the back yard, seen across the picket fence, hanging out washing with wooden clothes pegs in his teeth. The phlegmy rasp of his decrepit mother would call, 'Fetch us a cabbage from the yard, our Brian,' and he would point his eyes skyward, pick up a trowel and retrieve the vegetable. Now, with those same fat bejewelled fingers, he hands Billy his change with the grace of a gull swooping from the sky to catch a fish. Brian's eyes follow Billy, carrying drinks back to the table, until he and Jamie lock eyes; Brian winks with warm-hearted recognition.

Les draws hard on his cigarette and stubs it out in an ashtray. 'I'm dying for a piss.' Les stands. His hands clasp Mark's hips.

'Alright. Les!' Mark says, swatting away his groping hands. 'Go to the toilet then.'

Les looks a little hurt as he enters the gents'.

'Jesus Christ! He's suffocating me,' Mark says, as Billy falls into the seat next to Jamie. 'I can't fucking breathe.'

Billy lifts his beer and holds it up to Jamie. 'Come on, let's get pissed.'

'Cheers.' Jamie winks at Billy and they clink glasses.

A crowd of gay boys and lesbians are arriving, some from home, after hours of getting ready, some still in their work clothes from the office, the factory, the hospital.

Jamie watches the meaty tattooed couple snogging against the fruit machine.

'Fucking hot,' Mark says, rubbing the fabric of his crotch where an erection stirs and looks at Billy. Billy punches Jamie, affectionately, on the shoulder. 'So, what have I missed?'

'Les was telling me how content he and Mark are together now that they have fully assimilated. Cruise holidays and all. Proper little marriage made in heaven.' Jamie kisses Billy on the cheek. 'That could be us, one day.'

Mark looks away. 'I don't know what the hell I've let myself in for.' He lifts his beer and slugs.

Billy smiles. 'You're not going to elope and adopt Romanian orphans?'

'Told him a thousand times. I want to do something with my life before I settle down.'

Jamie frowns. 'Isn't it a bit late to be saying that?'

'Les bought the house, not me. He goes on and on until I find myself going along with him. I never wanted to move in. It was just meant to be a bit of fun.'

The room is filling up now and Brian, the barman, flounces across the room and opens up the second room, from which spills an effluence of loud pop music and dry ice. The crowd begins to peel off through the doorway towards the shimmering mirror-ball light.

'Have you thought of leaving him?' Billy says, warily. Jamie jabs him hard in the ribs.

'You like it here?' Mark asks, abruptly as Les exits the toilet.

Jamie nods. 'I never imagined this could be right on Mum's doorstep. Even if I'd known about it when I was growing up, I'd have been too young to explore it.'

Les is back at the table. 'Not bad eh, Jamie? I don't suppose it rivals your fancy London clubs.'

'It's this or the Bricklayer's Arms,' Mark says.

'Oh, the *Layers*,' Jamie says. He remembers being dragged there with Paul Fullerton and glimpsing the married men taking advantage of a dimly lit car park, skirts hitched up around their mistress' waists, knickers around their ankles. 'Isn't the Glasshouse Sauna more your thing?'

'The *Gentlemen's Health Spa*? Prowling around in nothing but a towel?' Les looks at Mark. 'No. We're strictly monogamous. Aren't we, Mark?'

Jamie looks at Billy and catches him rolling his eyes. He knows the sauna from an advert he'd seen in a magazine. He's never bucked up the courage to try but now he's with Billy—who knows?

Over Les's shoulders, the tattooed boys are still snogging. What might they do for a living? This is not Soho. This is not The Black Cap in Camden Town. Typical occupations taken up by gayers—make-up artists, magazine editors, art directors are few and far between here in the Midlands. These men are more likely to be shift workers at a local factory. Jamie fetishizes the idea in his head—the smell of engine oil, the dirt and the grease that his father used to scrub down with astringent Swafega.

Jamie exchanges a look with Billy, then glances at Mark and realizes they are all captivated by the same image of constructed masculinity.

Les jumps out of his seat, postures—hands clasped behind his head, in an exaggerated pretend yawn—a display so distracting it draws them from the floorshow and Les sits again.

Mark throws his eyes up, knocks back his beer and stands up. 'Who's coming for a dance?' He looks at Billy.

Les sits again. 'My feet are killing me. We've been walking around IKEA all day.'

Mark snatches Les' silver Buck Rogers jacket and flings it at him. 'And who's fault is that?'

The dance floor, populated by a group of guys who look like they might go home to their wives at the end of the night, is a small square of dirty plastic releasing an acrid fragrance left over from a dirty mop. Jamie finds himself dancing next to Les, to some ridiculous genre of high-energy pop.

'So, you're up from London to see your folks?' Les shouts over the din.

Jamie nods. 'Couple of nights at Billy's mum's... then I'm having a night at my parents'—'

§

The following morning, Jamie steps into his mother's kitchen after a quick trip to see Phyllis. He pulls off his shoes and calls out, 'I'm home!'

On the kitchen work surface is a glass dessert bowl full of partially-set orange jelly with pieces of fruit floating in it, like suburbanites in suspended animation.

'I made your favourite pudding.' It sounds like an accusation.

'So I see.' He turns to see his mother in the living room, runs one hand through his newly-dyed hair and holds out a bouquet in the other. Gloria is staring at him as if she has just caught a stranger stealing money from underneath his grandmother's mattress. 'You and I need to talk,' she says coldly and heads upstairs.

'Alright, Son.' Roy, in his usual inert manner, dips the newspaper resting on his paunch and peers over the rims of his reading glasses. 'Nice hair.'

Jamie frowns. 'What's got into her?'

Roy shrugs and returns to his paper, as Jamie follows Gloria upstairs. They sit on the bed that used to be his. All his posters are gone now. She changed the wallpaper after his first three months at university. Now, everything is pink and floral. Her hands smooth down the bedclothes.

From behind her, like a magician pulling a white rabbit from a hat, she produces a letter, pale blue in colour with holes in it made by the nib of a pen, held between trembling fingers. In her other hand—an envelope. Red and blue chevrons around the edge. Jamie's mind frantically retraces imaginary steps across the Atlantic. Jamie's letter to Paul sent months ago—opened by a complete stranger, noted *not for me* by the recipient and readdressed to the address at the top of the page. She begins to read, '*It was the danger of it that was most thrilling. I could smell what he wanted. We only stood at the urinals, staring at each other for a few moments, before he was leading me by the hand, into a toilet cubicle where we clumsily, eagerly wrenched belt buckles, tore at shirt buttons, unzipped flies to hold each others'*—'

'Stop!' Jamie cries. 'Stop!'

'Is it true?' she snaps, throwing the letter down onto the bed and staring now at his plumage of pink hair.

This isn't coming out. This is falling out. This is worse than being George Michael caught in a public toilet by a policeman.

No one ever wants their mother to read *this*—the forensic pathology report of her son's other life now drawn to a dramatic end. But this is what she's got. He can see it all on her face. *Are you being safe? Are you going to die of AIDS? I'll never have grandchildren.* And, 'Don't tell your Dad.'

'Why?' Jamie asks, bluntly.

Silent for a moment, she jerks her chin back into her neck, as if the question is a confrontation he ought not to be making. Regardless, he holds his gaze. 'Well,' she says, 'We don't know how he'll react, do we?'

Jamie doesn't see any point in keeping it a secret from others. 'What do you think he'll do?'

'I don't think he'll break open the champagne, if that's what you're thinking.'

§

From Billy's clapped out Vauxhall Nova, Jamie looks back at the house where he's spent the night—a modest suburban semi with its square front lawn and its conifers, rosebushes all neat and tidy, just like his parents. The silence of the neighbourhood is deafening—no dogs barking, no police sirens, no sound of noisy public transport.

Billy laughs. 'Don't tell me. She's not a fan of fuchsia?'

On the verge of tears, Jamie stares into the mirror mounted inside the passenger side sunshield—eyes as pink as his hair.

'Come on, let's get out of here,' he says, and suddenly sobs into his hands.

'Hey, what's wrong? What's happened?'

'I can't tell you here,' Jamie cries. 'I just want us to get away.'

Billy drives, passing rows and rows of houses, neatly delineated by regimented flowerbeds and neatly mown lawns—each of the houses an imitation of the other with their tidy TV aerials, their garage doors, and their floral displays in a bay window. After half a mile, Billy parks up on the side of the road. 'We can't drive all the way back to London like this. You have to tell me what's happened?'

Jamie takes a deep breath. Billy undoes his seatbelt, turns and touches Jamie on the cheek. 'It's all right, Soft Lad. This is *me*. Just tell me.'

He covers his eyes with a hand. 'I *knew* there was something wrong.'

'Oh god!' Billy says. 'She's not ill, is she?'

Jamie thrusts the letter into Billy's hands—pale blue in colour with holes made in it made by the nib of a pen.

'Jesus! This is—'

'Yes.' Jamie hangs his head.

'Bugger me!'

Jamie sobs. 'I think it's buggering that's got me into all this trouble.'

Billy laughs. 'So you've come out?'

'Not entirely.'

'What do you mean?'

'She said, 'Don't tell your Dad.''

'But you *did* tell him?'

'No.'

'Why not?'

'She said, 'If you tell your father, he'll throw a fit. You know what he's like. I'll end up coming down on your side and then we'll have to get a divorce."

Billy lets out an angry gasp. He slams his hands on the steering wheel.

'She said she'd made my favourite pudding. As if that would make it all better. Can you imagine? I haven't wanted mandarins in jelly since I was ten.'

'Fuckers!' Billy is suddenly red in the face. 'Fuck them! This kind of thing makes my blood boil. You go through school being beaten black and blue, picked on, called names, spat on. If you can get through that you've done well. But then you finally build the courage to tell your folks—the people who are supposed to love you, protect you, nurture you—about this essential part of yourself, that is by now malformed and unnourished, only to find it's a truth so unpalatable to them, so beyond their comprehension that they ask you to keep it a secret to save their sham of a marriage.'

'Billy, calm down. This isn't helping.'

'I'm sorry. This has hit a nerve. You're basically told repeatedly that you're a reject, that it's something that must be whispered in corners. It's no surprise guys think so little of themselves that they throw themselves into alcohol, drugs, meaningless and dangerous sex. Ha. And they wonder why there's a fucking AIDS epidemic. Well fuck them!' Billy belts up and slams the car into reverse.

§

'I'm sorry boys, we don't really have time for this. We're off to the *Scan'n'Pack*.' Gloria's heavily plucked brows arch so high that her usual startled appearance is almost a touch *Divine*.

'Go on then,' Billy says. 'Tell him!'

Jamie stands at the edge of the room shifting his weight from one leg to the other on Gloria's burgundy Axminster.

'Tell him what?' Gloria asks, the tips of her curls twitching maniacally.

'Gloria?' Roy appeals, shaking his car keys.

'I won't be forced into this,' she says. 'You can't just come in here shouting the odds.'

Jamie clutches Billy's elbow. Roy has noticed this action and peers at his son, tilting his head a little.

Jamie looks at Billy's hard face staring at Gloria. 'This is not your story, Mrs Johnson.' Her eyes are wet now and she's trembling.

Jamie breathes deeply, an electric chill running down his neck, hair follicles all over his body standing on end.

'Roy—Jamie wanted to tell you something. Something honest and truthful and good. And *she* wants him to keep it a secret from you.'

'Jamie?' Roy says.

'Dad,' Jamie says. Jamie's hand tightens on Billy's elbow.

Billy's face softens. 'It'll be alright.'

Finally, she breaks. 'You'd better sit down, Roy.'

Roy flops onto the leather sofa. 'I hope this isn't going to take long. She's given me a list of jobs to get through.'

Gloria sits next to him, resting her hand on his knee. 'Now Love, this might come as a bit of a shock to you. I don't want you getting upset.'

Roy folds his arms defensively. 'Whatever it is, I'm ready.'

'It's just that, well… you know… Billy and Jamie… you know how you thought they were best friends… Well—'

'We're not best friends, Dad,' Jamie says. His fingers curl around Billy's hand. Billy squeezes them tightly. 'We're—'

'Is that it?' Roy looks at them all, as if they've all gone completely mad. 'God I thought someone had died.' Roy gets up walks into the kitchen. Jamie can't look at the other two. He finds himself staring at Gloria's faux Grecian plaster fireplace. There's the sound of the fridge door opening and closing and he comes back with a pack of four beers. He hands one each to Jamie and Billy, snaps off the ring-pull on his own and raises the can up. They, all three, touch beers together, making a dull springy noise. He shakes his head at Gloria and chucks the last beer into her lap. 'So do you still want to go shopping then?'

§

'It's over now.' Billy's hand falls onto Jamie's leg as he changes into fourth gear.

'I felt invisible,' Jamie says. 'How can something that's about me, suddenly become *her* drama?'

'It's done now.' Billy accelerates towards the brow of the hill in Welston, just before the motorway.

Jamie lays a hand over the top of Billy's fingers. 'I love you.'

The sky above the trees and houses is layered with globular masses of clouds suspended in sunset, under which Jamie and Billy turn towards the motorway slip-road, London bound.

Trifle

Phyllis works a good look: a whale-blubber slick of pearlescent pink bleeding into wrinkles, antique brooch with headscarf, emerald green eye shadow. She scrubs up well, especially at Christmas. Today, the pearls and clip-on earrings have come out. Everyone thinks she's frail, with her angina and her watery eyes, but she's got anti-corrosive in her blood and radiator sealant in her bladder—nothing wrong with *her* waterworks. Gloria always says, *She'll outlive us all.*

'Merry Christmas, Nan,' Jamie says.

'Give us a cuddle.' She walks in, arms wide, like a Mafioso boss, pulls him to her tightly and whacks him on the back as if winding a baby. 'Hardly get to see you these days. Bloody defector. Where's your mother?'

'She's doing the dinner,' Jamie says.

Phyllis lets go of him, smacking her lips together. 'Something smells nice.' Then she looks at the music-centre. Doris Day sings *White Christmas.* 'I love a bit of Doris Day at Christmas. It's traditional, ain't it.' Her eyes sparkle a little. Jamie joins in while she sings along. 'Her and Rock Hudson—they used to call 'em *Hollywood's Golden Couple.* A fairy tale made in heaven.' Jamie smiles. 'I used to do my hair like her, but it was always too dark.' Phyllis turns, sprightly, arms spread, ready again to guide and usher. 'I've brought the invalid with me. We've had back-to-back Max Bygraves all morning at our place. *You're a Pink Toothbrush, I'm a Blue Toothbrush,*' she says. 'Come on, get him in.' She points at Alf in the doorway where she's left him and then at the armchair, as if instructing removal men with a piece of furniture.

Alf shuffles in, leaning on his walking stick, struggling with two plastic carrier bags full of Christmas presents. 'Alright, Grandad,' Jamie says over Phyllis's shoulder. He moves around her to take Alf's arm and help him lower himself into the armchair by the window. He's more cheerful than usual. The walking stick and the bags of

presents crash to the floor, like rubble from a crane grabber, as the
bulk of him finally makes contact with the seat.

'Alright, our Jamie,' Alf says, squinting at Jamie through lenses the
thickness of a glass ashtray. 'How're things down in the Big Smoke?'

'Oh, fine, y'know,' he nods, hoping for no further inquisition. They
don't talk about what happens in *The Big Smoke*. In fact, Jamie and
Alf haven't made proper conversation for years. Alf would usually be
in one room with the men watching the football. Jamie would be in
another with the women watching *Emmerdale Farm* on the portable.

'Making a go of it down London with that mate of yours. Ah,
doin' well for himself, ain't he, Phyllis?' Alf says. Phyllis's attention
is elsewhere.

'I'm coming to the end of my degree. I'll be looking for a job. So
hopefully, we'll have enough money to get a flat,' Jamie says, trying
his best to sound as if 'best friends' set up house together all the time.

'How long are you here for?' Alf asks, rearranging himself in the
armchair.

'I go back the day after boxing day,' Jamie says.

Roy comes in from the kitchen, pulling up the sleeves of his Aran—
the one Gloria knitted for him. 'What can I get you two to drink?' he
asks, despite the fact that they are both still in their coats. He goes to
Alf and struggles to get him out of his sheepskin while he is still in the
armchair. 'Lift up Alf, and I'll get it off you.'

Phyllis has been looking over Jamie's shoulder at the display of
Christmas cards on the mantelpiece. Gloria's trying to transform this
two-bed semi into a national treasure. She likes *traditional* - false oak
beams and fake leaded windows. She likes white weddings and meat
and two veg. She likes fish and chips on a Friday and wash-day is
always Monday. She likes brown sugar in her coffee. She likes Cath-
erine Cookson novels and floral curtains.

'*To a Special Couple?*' Phyllis remarks and makes a bee-line for the
card that Gloria and Roy gave him. Jamie had meant to slip it into
his suitcase last night. Phyllis is making the face of someone who's
just had a baby's dirty nappy thrust under her nose. On the front of
the card is a picture of two cuddly teddy bears, both grey with blue
noses, holding a Merry Christmas love heart between them. At least
Gloria hadn't chosen a card with one blue bear and one pink bear.

Now, Phyllis opens it up to read aloud the message inside. "*To Jamie and Billy. Hope you have a wonderful Christmas, love Mum and Dad.*" She turns to look at Jamie with bewilderment. He can see the idea congealing in her mind. She looks at Roy with raised eyebrows and a faint knowing smile. 'Funny sort of card to send two fellas.'

'Let me take your coat, Nan,' Jamie says, gently easing the card from her hands and setting it back on the mantelpiece. He thinks of something else to say. 'We should listen to the radio later. I want to see if the Spice Girls are at number one.'

'It's a bit early to start drinking, isn't it, Roy?' Phyllis says, surrendering to the question he asked moments ago, but keeping her eyes on Jamie, weighing him up. He can feel the pressure of an inquisition coming. She'll put him on the spot in front of everyone and watch him squirm. He knows it. But at this point, she just says, 'I'll have a whisky. With a drop of boiling water and half a spoon of sugar stirred in.' Then she throws her coat and scarf at Jamie. 'Here, pest. Take that.'

'On its way, Phyllis. Alf?' Roy says.

'Lager please, Roy.'

Roy gives Alf's coat to Jamie and disappears into the kitchen from where Jamie can hear the clattering of kitchen utensils and the ferocious slamming of doors and drawers.

'I hope you haven't squashed them presents,' Phyllis says.

Alf shakes his head and says, 'I can't hear what you're saying, Phyllis.' He adjusts his hearing-aid and turns sulkily to face the window.

Phyllis turns to Jamie. 'It's been one of those mornings. I've had a right game with him. One thing after another. He won't do as he's told. I told him to put his glasses in his jacket pocket and he didn't, so we had to go back for 'em. And just as we were leaving the house, he decides he needs the toilet. Well, that's an issue all in itself, isn't it? I had to get him back inside and upstairs and onto the khazi. And y'know how long it takes him, with his bleeding haemorrhoids and his bleeding moaning! 'I think I've strained meself,' he says. Oh and Jamie, the most graphic descriptions. He has to tell the precise colour and consistency and I say…'

'Don't go on, Phyllis,' Alf pleads, mysteriously regaining his hearing.

'…and his hands! That's another story. *Do you know* he insists on

washing his hands before *and* after using the toilet. He makes himself
red raw. What's the doctor call it? Obsessive compulsive. That's it!
Washes his back passage too. It's no wonder it's all dry and cracked.
I've told him he's washing the natural oils out of his skin, but he
knows best, doesn't he.' She prods Alf. 'If you want to end up with
flesh like the arse end of a wind-burnt rhino, keep on. Just don't come
crying to me for a jar of E45 when you're too sore to sit down... And
of course, he marked his underwear, so now I'll have to do another
boil wash.'

Alf turns and looks at Jamie. 'It's bloody Purgatory, I tell ya. She
won't let up.'

Phyllis waves him away and calls to Roy in the kitchen. 'I can't wait
to get my lips around that turkey.'

Taking that as his cue, Jamie dashes upstairs with the coats and
looks at the bed—the bed where he was made. He begged and begged
Gloria for a brother, but there was no chance. *You were too bloody
painful.* Days after he'd been released into the world, Roy was up the
clinic to have his tubes tied. And that was that.

He pulls his new phone from his pocket and types a message.
HOW R U?

A response comes almost immediately. *HAVING LOVELY TIME.
HOW R U?*

Jamie struggles to type a response with his thumb. *LIKE A FISH
OUT OF WATER. MISSING U,* he replies, clicks send and puts the
phone in back in his pocket.

The bedroom is all chintz, lacy frills and plaster coving. There are
doilies on top of doilies and collections of *stuff*, ornaments and photographs in frames, working-class proof that the Johnson's were here.

Jamie throws the coats on the bed. Then he has second thoughts.
Phyllis will curse him if her gabardine gets creases in it. She likes it
to be hung up. So he opens Gloria's wardrobe to look for a hanger.
It's crammed full of clothes. He has to push hard against the clump
of dresses and blouses to retrieve a hanger and something heavy falls
out and hits him on the foot. He bends down to pick it up and feels
the supple article in his hand—a heavy cylindrical handle with black
leather bound all around it, ending in long strips of leather—a *cat-o-
nine-tails* type of object, the likes of which he's only ever seen used to

flog people in old oceanic costume dramas on the television. Oh god! Scenarios, involving his parents, flicker through his mind—he sees one end of the leather instrument in his mother's hand and with the quick movement of her arm, the leather straps of it lash his father's milky white bottom producing a cartoon yelp. Heart pounding, he thrusts the hanger and the leather object back in the wardrobe. He slams the door, throws Phyllis's coat on the bed and rubs his hands on his trousers.

He can hear raised voices as he runs back downstairs. Phyllis, holding a whisky, is looking daggers at Roy. Gloria is striding in from the kitchen, hair stuck to her face, now that she's grown it long, glasses steamed, pink Marigolds dripping. 'What do you mean, Roy? *We're not having turkey?'*

Gloria pushes her glasses back up her nose with her upper arm, avoiding suds from the rubber gloves that might spoil her lenses. 'Don't start Mother! You do this every year.'

'Look, don't upset yourself.' Roy tries to appease Phyllis.

'Be quiet a minute, Roy,' Gloria says. 'Why don't you choose another record or something?'

Phyllis's eyes burn into Gloria. She purses her pearlescent pink lips together in exaggerated indignation. 'Do *what* every year?'

'Complain. I could have put Beluga caviar and white truffles on the bloody table and you wouldn't be satisfied.'

'We always have turkey! It's *traditional.*' Phyllis's voice is barbed.

'Well, I decided to do pork this year. Something *different* for a change.' Gloria's eyes flick over at Jamie. 'If you don't like it, Roy can drive you back.'

Phyllis looks aghast. She throws back her whisky and scratches the back of her liver spotted hand.

'Doesn't seem much like Christmas without turkey, Gloria,' Alf says. 'Everyone has turkey at Christmas.'

Now she blasts her parents, the air a blur of her pink gloved fists and extended fingers. 'Well who ever said we all have to be like everyone else? I don't suppose Doris Day is sitting down to a turkey dinner right now.'

Jamie holds his breath as he waits for Gloria to trounce some long-held opinion about Doris Day and Rock Hudson.

'Oh, go on,' Phyllis rasps. 'Break my heart. Tell me why.' Her head is wobbling so that the neatly teased grey curls on her head quiver like the hair on a ferocious Bichon Frise.

'Because she's a bloody vegetarian,' Gloria says. 'Allegedly.'

Jamie battles with the image of his mother holding a whip in her hand, which is now contaminating his view of the situation. He pictures her wearing painfully high black stilettos and black high-necked all-in-one PVC body suit, the type he's only ever seen worn at clubs called *Thrash, Skin Tight, Rubber Masque, Torture Garden.*

He cuts in, 'Hey, Nan, your glass is empty,' and throws himself in between them, trying to break the tension.

'I'll have an Advocaat this time,' Phyllis says, quickly.

Then Jamie turns to Gloria, nodding enthusiastically. 'It's after twelve you know, Mum, *you* could probably do with a drink as well.'

'You're bloody lucky that you get a Christmas at all,' Gloria continues rasping, even as he ushers her back into the kitchen. The sequins of her harlequin patterned Capri pants sparkling, despite the darkened atmosphere. 'You know, I do Christmas lunch *every* year and what thanks do I get?'

'Don't get yourself upset, Gloria,' Alf calls after them. 'Come on, why don't we open our presents?' Jamie can hear him rustling his carrier bags in the living room.

Gloria shouts, 'No. We'll do presents later, Dad. Your dinner's nearly ready.'

After Jamie returns with Phyllis's drink, they all sit smelling the food wafting in from the kitchen. Jamie is thrown a list of topics by Phyllis: *the cost of living in London, work, friends* and, despite the fact that she saw the card on the mantelpiece, *is he courting?* Every time Billy's name or their life in London are mentioned Jamie jumps out of his seat and refills the glasses until Gloria finally calls them all in to the dining room.

Gloria is dishing up an enormous feast of delicious Christmas grub minus the turkey. She's removed her apron and glasses and is now the picture of glamour. Roy carves the joint and Gloria serves vegetables. Alf is hunched over his plate, salivating. Phyllis is tight-lipped, eyeing the joint of pork as if she wants to wrestle it to the ground.

'Roasters, Dad?' Gloria asks, holding a dish next to his plate.

'Yes,' Alf replies, smacking his lips together like a hungry dog. 'Your roasters are the best I've ever tasted, all fluffed up at the edges.'

Jamie wonders at Alf's appetite; even with his grumbling appendix and his piles, his plate is piled high with vegetables.

'There's plenty left, Dad. You can come back for more later.'

'Go on, save yourself the journey, Glo. Put a few more on there. I'm famished.' Being of the Protect and Survive generation, he places his arms on either side of his plate as if worried someone might swipe his roast potatoes. He would always put four boxes of teabags into the shopping trolley, four bags of rice, four tins of beans, four of everything. Hoarding, just in case nuclear war broke out.

Phyllis is surrounded by drink, unable, as ever, to turn it away. She has a cup of coffee, into which she's poured the remaining Advocaat, joined by yet another whisky, a large glass of bubbly and a red wine. Jamie is surprised to see she hasn't brought her usual bottle of Lambrusco.

His mobile phone buzzes in his pocket. Another text. *I LOVE U*, Billy says. Jamie thinks about Billy having Christmas lunch with his own family.

HOW MUCH? he replies.

'What's that, our Jamie?' Phyllis asks, pointing to the phone.

Before he can reply, Gloria calls over, 'They've all got them these days. Mobile phones are the new craze.'

Billy's response comes back. *4 BAGS OF SUGAR, 2 PINTS OF MILK & A PKT OF CHEESE & ONION CRISPS.* Jamie smiles.

'Put it away now,' Gloria says. 'Not at the dinner table.'

Alf is tucking into his dinner already. 'Wait 'til Mum is sitting,' Jamie says. 'She's the one who cooked it.'

'You won't change him, Jamie,' Phyllis says, picking one glass up and putting another empty one down. 'He's got the manners of a pig.' Then she looks at Alf. 'Couldn't you get any more on the plate?'

'You enjoy your dinner, Dad,' Gloria says lovingly. 'Don't you worry about me.' Jamie frowns at her but she shakes her head. 'At least he's not causing trouble while he's got his head in the nose bag.'

Jamie watches the gravy dangling from Alf's four-day old facial hair. He can't help but smile. 'Couldn't afford a razor today, Grandad?' He hands him a napkin and points to his top lip.

'Thanks,' Alf grumbles and wipes his mouth. Gloria and Roy join them to eat. Gloria makes them all put party hats on. 'It's traditional,' she says, pulling one over Grandad's sweaty forehead. 'Right, I want everyone to have a nice time. Tuck in.'

'Raise your glasses. Raise your glasses,' Phyllis says. She rearranges the selection of drinks in front of her and finally goes for the red wine. They all cheer, 'Merry Christmas' and clink their glasses together.

Then there is a hush—just the sound of them chewing loudly and Alf scraping his cutlery on the side of his plate. Phyllis is enthusiastically biting down on a piece of crackling.

Then Alf nudges her: 'Pull a cracker with me, Phyllis.' They pull the cracker with a grand commotion, both cheering like school children. Glasses and cutlery shake as Alf unwraps a pirate's eye patch and puts it on. Then he puckers his drooling lips at Phyllis. 'Give us a kiss,' he says, and they start canoodling.

'Don't be disgusting,' Jamie laughs. 'We're eating!'

'Jamie, lighten up,' Gloria says. 'Nice to see they're still in love at their age.'

Phyllis pulls away. 'Stop it, Alf. You're upsetting, Jamie.' She takes another slug of wine.

'I just don't like all this fruitiness at the table.' Jamie says.

Everyone joins in the laughter. 'I'm sorry, old *fruit*', Phyllis says and winks. Jamie enjoys her casual use of the word *fruit* and wonders if she knows it derives from ancient gay slang. 'Billy at his Mum's today?' she asks. He can feel that she is working up to a question—some uncomfortable query, to put him on the spot.

Alf says. 'It's only because I love her.' He looks at Roy. 'Can't keep me bloody hands off her.'

'Oh, aye?' Roy says, nodding at him, encouragingly.

Alf turns to Phyllis who is not smiling and trying to ignore the whole carry on. She pushes a roast potato around her plate with the end of her fork. She has begun to look a little pale.

'Is that right, Phyllis?' Roy asks. 'Does he give you hot loving?'

Gloria bursts out laughing hysterically. 'Roy, stop it. That's my mother you're talking to. She doesn't need any encouragement.'

'If I could have my time again,' Alf says. 'I'd show her.'

Jamie can see Phyllis rising to the occasion, doubling in size like an angry wildcat, hair standing on end. She places down her knife and fork, cleanly on the tablecloth, and takes a quick swig of red wine, leaving greasy lipstick on the glass. Her lips are pursed, creating vertical wrinkles under her nose. '*He* don't give me hot love anymore! You must be bloody joking. He can't. That *thing* went cold years ago.' She wiggles her little finger in the air. That should be enough but, no, she goes on. 'It's bloody useless. Shrivelled up and no bigger than the end of my finger. I don't know what he thinks he can do with it. He can't even piss through it properly. Do you know, our toilet-bowl has got to be at least fifteen inches or more in diameter and he can't hit the middle of it. The bleeding bathroom carpet stinks of stale piss.'

'Mother, that's enough!' Gloria growls, showing her teeth.

Jamie's cheeks are hot. Roy is hiding behind his wine glass. Jamie looks at Alf fiddling uncomfortably with his hearing-aid again and looks down into his dinner. He looks destroyed. His watery lower eyelids are more wet and bloodshot than usual.

'Hot love? You must be joking.'

'Mother!' Gloria shouts this time. Her hand comes down hard on the table making everyone's cutlery rattles against the plates. Alf spills his wine.

'Now, look what you've gone and done, ya bloody silly oaf,' Phyllis says.

'Enough!' Gloria snaps. 'I swear to God, Mother, if you spoil another Christmas... Just eat your bloody dinner and shut up.'

They eat in silence while Gloria mops up the wine. After they have finished, without a word, she clears all the plates away. They sit obediently as she collects the cutlery and replaces the spit-sodden serviettes with crisp clean ones. She moves methodically around the table, removing the gravy boat, the remaining meat from the joint and the vegetable dishes.

Jamie rises to help her load the dishwasher. Gloria, rigid with anger, quickly brings her hand up to her mouth to stifle a sob. Then she's crying on his shoulder. Phyllis rushes past. 'Oh God! I think I'm going to be sick.' They all look at her dashing out of the room, clasping a napkin to her mouth.

Gloria is shaking her head, wiping tears away with a tissue. Her lips are stretched across clenched teeth. 'Roy, how much has she had to drink?'

Roy closes his eyes at the sound of Phyllis retching into the toilet bowl. 'Jesus,' he says, 'I've only just decorated that bathroom.' They've had it done modern. Plush white, no fuss. Roy moves to get up out of his place. 'Gloria, let me help you?'

'No. Just let me do it.' She shows him the palm of her hand. In Jamie's mind, she's in black PVC again, holding a leather paddle—only this time the PVC suit has morphed into an image Gloria and Jamie had once seen of the renowned performance artist, Leigh Bowery, in the arts supplements of one of the Sunday newspapers. And he wonders, after all, if they really are as different as he'd first thought. Gloria blows out, as if breathing through fury. 'I'm fine. Just leave me. I'm fine.'

Roy settles back into his seat. Gloria takes the remaining dinner things and places dessert-spoons, bowls and a jug of single cream on the table. She goes to the fridge. Alf watches attentively. She's returning with dessert as Phyllis shuffles back into the room, wiping her face with toilet tissue, her mouth a gash of smudged lipstick.

'That really was a lovely bit of pork, our Gloria,' she says, though she's looking directly at Jamie.

Oh no. She's got that look on her face. Maybe it's his turn to visit the toilet.

'So, our Jamie…' she begins.

Jamie can feel his neck getting warm and redness in his cheeks.

'…what colour are you and Billy going to paint the bedroom?'

'Fuscia!' he jests, and everyone laughs, including Alf, despite his selective hearing.

The phone buzzes in his pocket again. He looks at it. *U WILL B SWIMMING IN THE SEA AGAIN SOON. FOUND ANY COMMON GROUND?* Billy asks.

MORE THAN I'D LIKE TO ADMIT, Jamie types back, clicks send and then wonders to himself if it might be nice to stay a little longer than he'd planned.

'Right,' Gloria says sharply, taking a deep breath. Alf, Roy and Phyllis all stop to look at her. In her hands she's holding a glass vessel layered with broad stripes of white, pink, yellow and deep red at the bottom. 'Who's for trifle?' she says, jubilantly.

Phyllis's mouth drops open. 'But what about the Christmas pudding?'

OR ENTRY AND
BERSHIP CARDS
ARE NOT
NSFERABLE
Y MUST ONLY

USED BY THE
SON NAMED
THEREON

Two Little Ducks

'Six and nine, sixty-nine... Two fat ladies, eighty-eight.' The bingo caller, brushed with glamour—rhinestone jacket, black quiff, solarium tan, stares over his booth—a moist grin, white teeth, something obscene in his eyes.

Mid-game, Billy weaves through grey air saturated with fag smoke, down the gangway of old ladies. Phyllis sits at a table with her entourage, stabbing their sheets of bingo numbers with inky dabbers. 'Here he is,' she says in between numbers and indicates the space she's kept for him. 'Put y'bum down there.' Billy places drinks down for Phyllis and her friends and slides into the seat, where her newspaper is open at the classifieds. 'Pass me that dabber, Ivy. This one's dead.' Phyllis presses a finger to her lips, ensuring silence, until somebody shrieks an orgasmic—

'Here y'are!' and the caller confirms the winner's numbers.

'Can I speak now?'

'That's it,' Phyllis says, taking the last drag on a cigarette so carefully smoked, at least an inch of unbroken ash remains attached. 'I won't be going to the Bahamas this week.' She leans over and kisses Billy. 'No Jamie?'

'Nah, not tonight... he's working on an assignment,' he says, pushing a whiskey and soda towards Ivy Warner, Phyllis's bingo partner. 'So he's sent me instead.' The bingo caller steps down from his podium as music begins to play—*A Design for Life* by the *Manic Street Preachers*.

'You didn't have to come out alone on my account.'

'A night out with my Phyllis? Wouldn't miss it for the world.' His eyes track rhinestone jacket and black quiff from the caller's booth, past the tables until he reaches the bar.

'You know, Jamie's been coming to the bingo with me since he was knee-high,' Phyllis says.

'Shouldn't you be here *together*?' Ivy says, from across the table.

'Last night before you head back to London?'

'Where's *Mr* Warner?' Phyllis spits, then looks back at Billy. 'Remember last time? You and Jamie won all that money—enough for a weekend in Amsterdam.'

'It won't last,' Ivy says, scratching the back of her liver spotted hand.

'You can't say that, Ivy,' Billy says. 'We're a proper couple. Just like you and Mr Warner.' Billy breathes out and lets his eyes fall onto the newspaper classifieds. *An Oasis of Pleasure in a Hectic World. Glasshouse Health Spa. Looking for escape? Open 365 days a year.*

'I expect we're not enough for Jamie.' Ivy's lighting up now. The fringe of her long platinum-grey hair is browned from nicotine. 'Ideas above his station, that one—now that he's living the high-life in London.'

Billy half-laughs. 'Hardly, Ivy. He lives in a box room in student digs.'

Ivy tears up her bingo tickets and throws them into the centre of the table. 'Yes, and when he does hit the big time, he won't remember us.'

Phyllis throws her dabber at Ivy. 'That's my grandson you're talking about.'

'He won't forget you, Ivy,' Billy says, gently. 'He just wants different things out of life, and round here, you know—'

'Round here, what?' Ivy asks.

Scanning the room of drinkers, glass collectors, men playing a game of darts in the corner—Billy's eyes pause on a poster near the bar. *Welston Constitutional Club. Mon—Quiz Night (Chicken in a Basket), Tues—Bingo, Wed—Karaoke, Thurs—The Gone Wrong Sisters Drag Show, Fri—Disco, Sat—Country and Western Night, Sun—Shanice.*

'Mr Warner can't control himself anymore,' Phyllis says. 'He's having a bag fitted.'

Billy sighs. 'Where you are born and who you are shouldn't exclude you from anything, whatsoever.'

'Don't get deep, Billy,' Phyllis says. 'You'll lose her completely.'

'What you talking about my husband for?' Ivy says in disgust and then turns back to Billy. 'Jamie's not excluded. If he'd learnt a trade like his father, he'd have a bloody good business in roofing.'

'Yes, I expect that would be true, Ivy, if he'd wanted to do that. He'd have a very strong network. But the thing is—'

'We're all looking for something to carry us away from the mundane,' Phyllis says, 'while we're crawling our way across the globe… even you, Ivy. Don't deny it.' Phyllis lights up another cigarette. 'She doesn't like to brag about it but our Ivy used to work in Soho. A rather well-kept secret, Billy—our Ivy here used to answer the telephone in a—'

'A madam?' Billy says.

'It wasn't like that,' Ivy says.

Phyllis mimes a telephone with her left hand and mimics madam Ivy. 'Hello. House of Sin. How may I help you? Oh, yes I'm sure that can be arranged. It's sixty for a half hour or a hundred for the full service. All tastes catered for.'

Ivy looks a bit wounded. 'It was a change of scenery.'

'Exactly!' Phyllis says. 'Nothing so edgy round here, is there? You should be with your own kind, Billy. Not sitting here with the old women.'

§

Billy steps from his car and walks with nervous excitement towards the innocuous doorway, pausing as he waits to be buzzed in. He'd never do this with Jamie. He'd never understand. Too vanilla. The door opens and he's in. He hands over his money at the reception desk to a bald man, attractive—perhaps once handsome. He collects a towel and walks through into the busy locker room—smelling of men and chlorine. It's almost the same as going to the swimming baths.

Undressed, naked—wearing just a towel, vulnerable, Billy pads round—a sauna, steam room, cinema, swimming pool with Grecian ornaments (reminding him of Gloria's living room and prompting a wave of guilt) and then a darkened sex maze only dimly lit with red light.

He decides to visit the bar for a drink before setting out on adventure. A beer. The man on the stool next to him drinks whiskey and soda. The barman flounces up and down in flip-flops. Scanning the many men perched on barstools, wearing just towels—Billy's eyes pause on a poster on the wall. *The Glasshouse Gentlemen's Health Spa. Mon—Sports Day, Tues—Bears, Wed—Underwear, Thurs—Leather, Fri—Disco, Sat—Cruise, Sun—Cruise.*

'First time, honey?' the barman asks.

'Does it show?' Billy says.

'You're safe, darling. We're all friends here. Go on. Go get 'em, tiger.'

He finishes his drink and goes on the prowl. All he can hear are the fetid whispers of strangers in the dark, the sounds of heavy breathing and of bare feet on the sticky floor.

'Fancy a threesome?' a disembodied voice asks in the darkness. It unnerves him. Billy weaves through air saturated with amyl-nitrate, down the maze of corridors. Only a few narrow shafts of red light filter through the gaps between the door and the doorframes of the cubicles where men collect for sex. The floor is peppered with sachets of lube and empty condom wrappers. Along the corridor twenty or more figures can be seen. Silence, but for the grunts, snorts and spit of men shuffling around in the dark and the groan of an occasional orgasm.

Billy stops. He has his eye on a man who has come to stand just next to him—rugged, tanned, short neatly trimmed stubble, black hair sculpted into a shiny quiff. In the half-light he gives the impression of being shy but Billy can see he knows exactly what he's doing. There are a couple of men opposite, passing a small bottle back and forth, and holding it to their nostrils.

Sweaty palms.

Tingly neck.

The tanned guy rubs his chest and fingers his left nipple. He leans closer to Billy then steps backwards into one of the empty cubicles, his silhouette now defined by the red glow from inside. Billy edges forward. He's trembling, adrenaline coursing through his veins. His hands go up in front of him, tentatively feeling his way through the darkness. On the threshold, he knows. This is him. This is part of who he is.

Inside, there's a padded leather bench, just long enough to lie down on. The glow of red is brighter in here and it's possible to see the man's smile. They lock the door behind them.

'What's your name?' the man whispers. He finds the man's voice a little disturbing. Billy hasn't come here to make conversation.

'Billy,' he says, not encouraging anything further.

'I'm Russell.' He feels the man's hand stroke his nipple and ruffle his chest hair. 'Been here long?'

They kiss for a moment. 'Long enough to have a scout around.'

'I just arrived from work,' the man whispers.

'What do you do?' Billy asks, instantly wishing he hadn't.

The man's hands go to Billy's now flaccid penis and says, 'I'm a bingo caller.'

Urban Nightmares

'We've got a job to do—all of us. You, me, everyone. Together we can do it. Together we can change Britain, change Britain for the majority of its people and together we can win. We've all got a part to play, no matter how small. Every contribution is an important one. We've a great team in place and you—each and every one of you are part of that team. Between us we can build a better Britain for everyone.'

The Road to the Manifesto, 1996
JOHN PRESCOTT 1938—

Kissing the Lizard

Old Compton Street is simmering. Jamie registers the summer joy outside the coffee shop and rests his chin on a hand with listless resignation. Everyone has gone wild at the first sign of moderate sunlight. T-shirts are wrenched from milky torsos, men kiss in the street, shirtless bikers ride roughshod through Soho. Everyone's leaving work early to grab what they can of the rays. Businessmen drink beer in the street, abandoning ties, collars undone at the neck. Jamie can't join in. He's cut off. Three years an art student, in the capital, and no closer to being part of it.

The broken air conditioning in The Crêperie has resulted in a thick haze of steam and smoke.

'Do you think we'll ever see America?' Billy asks, looking up from a book. He draws deeply on a Marlboro—a duty-free gift from when Jamie's mum and dad spent a package holiday in Magaluf. He exhales into the already choked room.

'I don't know,' Jamie says, waving away smoke. 'I'm not convinced I'll ever get back to London, let alone reach the States.'

'Well you're here now, aren't you?'

'For one more night but then I have to go back to that wretched place.' Jamie says, rolling up the sleeves of his paisley shirt and unbuttoning his waistcoat.

Billy places the fag in his mouth and leafs through the other books Jamie has piled up on the table. A volume about alien abductions by Whitley Strieber provokes a curl from Billy's lip. Another one—*Feel the Fear and Do It Anyway,* incites a cartoon scowl. He holds up a third book and frowns. '*The Prophetic Insights*' he says. 'Really?'

'I'm searching.'

'What for? The knit-your-own-aura-brigade?'

Jamie returns to the accommodation pages of *Time Out*. 'Nothing under seventy-five pounds a week.'

'Well if you hadn't run back to Mummy and Daddy so quickly...'

'I didn't have any money, Billy.'

Billy stares at Jamie's hair. 'You could save ten pounds a month if you stopped bleaching that mop.'

A clique of art students Jamie recognises from St. Martin's cackle over cappuccinos near the window. Plates clatter. A radio crackles, losing and regaining its signal—issuing a broken chorus of *Tubthumping* by Chumbawumba. The coffee shop is full of French and Germans and Turks and Americans. Everyone else seems to be having a great time.

'If you'd taken that job with the magazine you'd be on an all expenses paid trip to India by now.'

Jamie throws the *Time Out* across the table. Billy, still within the cosy confines of his final year, hasn't yet felt freedom slipping away.

'Free holidays don't pay the rent,' Jamie says. 'If I could afford to work for nothing, I'd have a huge portfolio and a contract at *The Guardian*—not living back with my parents in the arse end of nowhere.'

A tanned rent-boy brushes past the table—an outline of an unfinished William Morris design peaking out of a loosely buttoned shirt. Jamie watches Billy's eyes trail his studded leather belt and bubble-butt. The youth takes his window seat, from where he has solicited every weekend during Jamie's time at art school.

'Some folks know how to make money,' Billy says.

'You're meant to be with me, not eyeing up the local trade.'

Billy leans across the table and takes Jamie's hand. Jamie pulls back but Billy holds on tight. 'This is Soho. Not the West Midlands. You think anyone gives a shit if I hold your hand?' Billy squeezes even tighter. He is looking into Jamie, his gentle opalescent eyes lined with kohl. Jamie feels himself yield. 'Maybe you should take more notice of those books you read—meditate or something.'

Hard to stay positive, Jamie thinks. 'You know, that talentless bitch, Saffron Delany—'

'Still gnawing away at that bone?'

'She left St Martin's last year and did three months at Vogue without pay. She's done pop videos, photo shoots and now she's famous for doing fuck all. Can't open a newspaper without seeing her smug face. This time next year, her father will probably *buy* her Channel Four for her birthday and she'll be married to Lance Lewes.'

Billy laughs. 'It won't last. Everyone knows he's got a touch of lavender. You'll get your chance.'

'Will I?' Jamie asks.

'*Anything* is possible,' Billy continues. 'I might win one of those photographic competitions I entered. Who knows? I could get a big contract.'

'You're deluded, Billy. It doesn't happen to people like us.'

'Oh, here comes Tess of the D'Urbervilles again.'

'When I finished my degree, I thought I'd be on my way—list of contacts, a little place to live in London. Look at me now—working a supermarket checkout. Mother's driving me mad.'

Billy nods at the books on the table. 'She'll wipe the floor with you if she catches you reading that rubbish.'

Billy's right. Gloria has a temperament neatly suited to British border control. Jamie touches the cover of *The Prophetic Insights* protectively. 'It's the key.'

Billy picks up the book and reads the blurb. '*From six-hundred hours of channelling extra-terrestrials, Prunella Small brings to us a new wisdom for the New Age. For anyone questioning an ever more confusing cosmos, The Prophetic Insights offer the reassurance and knowledge required to go beyond fear and trust the universe.*' He drops the book on the table as if having discovered a turd in his hand. 'We've got to get you out of this situation. Up there, you're not surrounded by people who can nurture you. We've got to get you back to London.'

'I'm twenty-two. There are things I should have done by now. List of clubs I should know. I want to publish a novel before I'm thirty.'

'Come on, what are you having?' Billy urges. 'We've sent the waitress away twice.'

Jamie fingers the space in his wallet where he might keep a few notes. Empty. 'I'm not hungry.'

'I'll treat you.' Billy turns the menu to Jamie—an entirely vegetarian selection, couscous, pancakes stuffed with spinach—the sort of fare that bores him rigid.

Jamie sighs. 'I—'

'Don't be proud. You can pay me back later.'

Over Billy's shoulder, a very tall man is walking in, carrying a satchel and a carrier bag of baguettes. His overall look is disco back-packer—citrus neon green t-shirt underneath a sleeveless maroon pullover, shorts, walking-boots with neon coloured rolled over socks. A long, thin face on a bulbous head, accentuated by a closely shaven hairstyle—skin taut and shiny. The man cranes over Billy who's smil-ing unconvincingly. As the man's satchel swings forward, Jamie no-tices a fabric *I heart USA* badge sewn onto one of the front pockets.

'I *thought* it was you,' the man blurts, gay as a daffodil. 'I saw you as I was walking past.' He ruffles the fronds of Billy's dyed black spikes. 'How the devil are you?'

Billy angles his face to the man, who towers over him like a giant stick insect. He obviously can't remember this guy's name and Jamie enjoys letting this run on, briefly, until he weakens. 'I could wait for-ever for an introduction. Hi. I'm Jamie.'

'He's so rude, isn't he?' the tall man laughs. 'Matthew. Pleased to make your acquaintance.' He extends a long limp-wristed arm, hands littered with silver, slightly loose on bony fingers.

Jamie winks at Billy. 'Lovely to meet you, *Matthew*,' he says, watching Billy relax.

He shakes Matthew's hand and as their gazes meet, his eyes seem to move, vibrate almost, from side to side. Jamie is first to look away.

'Well, what a surprise to see you, Billy, in a vegetarian bistro, of all places. I thought you were a meat eater.'

There's an affected air about this man, behind an attempt at re-ceived pronunciation, Jamie detects an un-disguisable top-note of guttural North, which brings to mind the telephone voice his mother uses to ingratiate herself with the more genteel classes, or else trying to get her own way when returning an item of silk lingerie to Marks and Spencer's.

'Room for one more?' Before Billy can reply, Matthew slides into the banquette. The waitress walks over and hands him a menu. 'I was only stopping for tea.' In the early evening sunlight, his complexion has an unnatural greenish tinge, somewhere between vomit and chlo-rophyll. Fresh scratches criss-cross his sinuous arm. Could he be ill? Twenty-eight? Thirty? It's not beyond comprehension. Jamie knows three men, at least, who died of AIDS in the last half year.

'Gardening,' Matthew lifts his arms. 'Bloody rose bushes.'

Jamie reproaches himself. His morbid conclusions are ignorant. Though there's something about Matthew—his clothes, his manner— unlike anyone else he's encountered.

'I finished my shift at the bakery. Just popped into the Chinese supermarket and was on my way home to cook a soup. Now I've seen you two, I might stay for a sandwich,' Matthew says. He drops his satchel and the baguettes on the floor.

'The more the merrier,' Jamie says, though Matthew strikes him as pushy. Back at the table the waitress presses a pen against a pad, waiting for them to order—sandwiches, carrot cake, coffee.

'Are we drinking?' Matthew asks. Before Jamie can mutter something about not being very flush, he produces a grating—'I'll have a dry white wine.' Jamie deduces, from Matthew sickly sweet breath, he's already been drinking. Matthew sucks in his cheeks and purses his lips with exaggerated feminine enthusiasm. 'Billy, do you know, I was pruning the rhododendrons the other day and it just came to me—I could see your face in my mind and I just knew we were going to bump into each other.' He pauses, draws breath and articulates his impossibly long neck. 'So Jamie, what do you do?'

Jamie searches his head for something to say, not wanting to look like a complete loser. 'I finished my fine art degree last year but now I'm focusing on my writing.'

'I'm a writer too,' Matthew says.

'Really?'

'Anything published?' Matthew asks.

'I'm working on it.'

'You're very young to be a writer. Perhaps you'll experience a bit of life first.'

'He's an apprentice,' Billy says, supportively.

'Don't mock,' Matthew says.

'I'm not.'

'Is that how your support yourself?' Jamie asks, breaking the tension.

'Well, I do a few shifts at the bakery. I don't think one needs a lot of money.'

Jamie wonders what he means by that. 'So how do you two know each other?'

Matthew looks away at Billy, tearing the corner of a paper napkin with his eyes shut. 'Long story, best left for another time,' he says.

Billy opens his eyes to Jamie. 'A while ago, before I met you.'

The smile drops from Matthew's face. 'Well, maybe it wasn't *you* I was supposed to meet that time,' he says with witchlike illumination. 'Perhaps I've been brought here for another reason. Serendipity. The universe is constantly rearranging itself.' He taps the table in front of Jamie with his forefinger. 'Do you know what I see when I look at you?'

Jamie recoils slightly at the direct challenge.

'I see a person who's afraid of life,' Matthew says, 'Afraid of letting go of the edge. But there's a great big world out there.' Matthew turns to Billy. 'Am I right?' He touches fingers to his temples and then rubs his thumbs and fingers together, as if absorbing oil into his fingertips. 'That's what I'm picking up here. You're just not living your life the way it's meant to be lived.'

'He needs a good kick up the arse,' Billy says.

'Grasp the nettle, Jamie.'

The waitress returns with food. 'You'll have to move that,' she says, sniffing at Matthew's satchel. 'It's a fire hazard.'

Matthew kicks the bag under the banquette like a rebellious school-boy. 'What's her problem?' He raises his hands, as if, resisting an invisible force field and eases them down, until they reach the table. 'I won't get annoyed. I'm just going to let this slip off me.' He turns to Jamie once more. There it is again, his eyes—vibrating from side to side. Jamie didn't imagine it this time.

'Happens to me all the time and I say to myself, 'Matthew, don't get yourself involved.' Because, you know, while there's all this chaos going on in the world, I'm the one who has control.'

Jamie senses Billy inwardly recoil from their new friend's hippy-dippy claptrap.

'You're an old soul. Just getting used to your new skin, aren't you?' Matthew says, regaining his genteel tone. Jamie is gripped with magnetic curiosity.

'What makes you say that?' Billy's voice has a challenging note in it.

'Vibrating on a higher frequency—more evolved,' Matthew says.

'I can feel it.' He nods at the books in front of them. 'Searching for something though. Why else would you be reading *The Prophetic Insights?*'

'Everyone's reading it,' Billy says. 'It's on special offer round the corner.'

'Isn't that fortunate?' Matthew says. 'The message is spreading far and wide.'

Billy makes yawning shapes with his mouth. 'We're trying to find Jamie somewhere to live in London.'

'Oh?' Matthew leans forward with interest.

Jamie lifts up the accommodation page in *Time Out.* 'Everything in here is way too expensive. I viewed two flea-pits in Zone 4 this morning.'

'The universe provides us with everything. Just ask.' Matthew clutches empty space and makes a clenched fist in the air. 'Think of what you want. Bring it into being. Manifest!'

Jamie giggles nervously. He thinks of the poor emperor being swindled by the weavers promising to make clothes from invisible fabric and, not really knowing what to say, he takes a huge bite from his sandwich.

'Go on,' Matthew insists. 'Close your eyes and ask it.'

Jamie stares at the shape his mouth left in his sandwich, contemplating Matthew's last words. He closes his eyes and pictures himself living in London, a room of his own, traveling on the tube, making new friends. Then he opens his eyes.

'When are you thinking of coming? Matthew asks.

'As soon as possible,' Jamie says.

'If you can wait until the end of the month, I'll have a room for rent in my house. I've a flatmate moving out.'

Jamie feels his mouth open a little wider than before.

'Willesden Green—forty pounds a week. Nicely decorated. Zone 2.' Matthew makes a magician's flourish with his hands, silver rings sparkling in sunlight. 'Well, something for you to think about. You don't have to decide right now. Give me a call when you are ready?' He gets a pen from his backpack and scribbles his phone number on a serviette.

'How many flatmates do you have?' Billy asks. Jamie feels like someone had performed a card trick in front of him and he's still trying to work out the illusion.

'Well, Adrian has just gone and Mark's moving out, so there will just be me. I promised myself a bit more time on my own, but...'

They finish their sandwiches. Matthew regales them with stories of his travels across Europe before slugging back wine and announcing, 'Listen, I must go.' He drops some coins in the middle of the table. 'That should cover my order. See you both soon. Lovely to meet you, Jamie.' Matthew leans to kiss him on the cheek. *A kiss*. His large almond shaped eyes penetrate Jamie, for a moment. 'Billy. Until next time.'

'Yes.' Billy stands to kiss him goodbye but Matthew's hand comes up evasively. 'There's absolutely no need for us to kiss.' He slips out of the banquette and pulls his satchel over his shoulder. He glances outside. 'Look at them, out there. They're running amok!' He laughs and walks out of the door.

'Did you see what he did there?' Jamie says.

'His crystal ball needs an MOT, if you ask me.'

Jamie asks the waitress for the bill, even though he can't afford to pay it. Then he turns back to Billy 'Well? *Did* you?'

'Did I what?'

'You *know*. With *him*?'

'God, of course not. He tried. I wasn't having any of it. He's bloody creepy.'

Billy counts the money Matthew left on the table and scowls.

'What's wrong?'

'He ordered *wine* and *carrot cake*. There's about enough money here to pay for half a sandwich. Self-seeking fucker.'

'That's not very spiritual,' Jamie says.

Billy holds up Matthew's telephone number. 'Still, looks like you've got your accommodation sorted out.'

Jamie pulls a face. 'Move in with someone I just met in a coffee shop? What would Mum think?'

§

'A complete stranger!' Gloria's voice cracks into falsetto as she parts the curls of her hair, pressing them against her head revealing the dark rootage, in the little mirror inside her sunshield—bloody hell, must get it done.

Roy nudges her knee, which, resting against his gear stick, is preventing him from changing down as they reach the end of the motorway in North-West London. 'We're almost there, Glo. It's a bit late to talk him out of it now, don't you think?'

In the back, Jamie sighs. 'You've decided you don't like him before you've even met him.'

Gloria rubs away smudged mascara with the tip of her index finger. 'Honestly Roy, he hasn't been this much trouble since he brought home that dried snake skin from Paul Fullbrook's house and left it in my side of the bed. Jamie, I don't like this. It's history repeating itself.'

'I'm not doing this to hurt you, Mother.'

That look again in the mirror. 'You're not in love with him, are you?' she asks, flipping his reflection against the upholstered ceiling of the car.

'You know, if you gave Matthew a chance, you might even get to like him. He's travelled—speaks different languages. I could learn from him. He's amazing.'

'Oh, well I can't wait to meet this *amazing* person—'

She turns to her son, suspiciously. He's wearing clothes she's never seen him in before—a black woollen cap and a second-hand sheepskin jacket. Looks like something from *Fiddler of the Roof.* 'Where did you get that coat?'

'Matthew gave it to me.'

'Dressing you now, is he?'

Roy wrenches open the glove compartment and pulls out an A-Z. 'I'm going to need you to navigate from here, Glo. I've put a bookmark in the right page for you.'

'People move in with strangers all the time,' Jamie says. 'They find them in newspapers, on postcards in shop windows…'

'I've never heard the like.' As they shuttle forward towards a slowing car in front of them, Gloria's right leg reaches for an imaginary brake pedal. 'Roy, you're going a bit quick, aren't you?' She covers her eyes, peeping through splayed fingers.

Jamie says, 'It's all about control with you, isn't it?'

The car radio crackles and the dour voice of a BBC newsreader makes yet another announcement of the death of Princess Diana. They've been occurring periodically since the car crash in the early hours of the morning. Gloria can't help thinking of the sons Diana has left behind.

'Roy, speak to him, please!'

'Don't bring me into it,' Roy says. 'He's old enough and ugly enough to make his own mistakes.'

Gloria changes tack. 'How will you support yourself?' she snaps.

'I've got a job. You know the supermarket gave me a transfer and—'

'A transfer? You talk about it like you have an executive job in the city. Is that why you studied for three years—so you could wear a little blue waistcoat and sit on a supermarket checkout?'

'*You* work in a shop!' Jamie retorts.

'I've got your dad.'

'Some people don't even have or need jobs.'

'Oh, here we go! What type of people, Jamie? *Alternative* people? Or are you referring to those lazy bloody slobs conning the arse out of the country. I bought you up to stand on your own two feet.'

'You know what your problem is, Mother?'

'Pray tell.'

'Your need for protection is so great that you build up a wall. You cling to what you know. You hate change. You hate difference. You're threatened by anything new, anything you don't understand and you won't allow it in. You look down your bloody nose at everyone. But instead of feeling more secure, you'll be alone.'

'I didn't raise you to speak to me like this.'

Roy over-revs the engine at Neasden Junction and weaves, aggressively, across four indistinct lanes of kamikaze traffic. 'Will you pair just give it a rest!'

This time Gloria presses both feet into the footwell. 'Bloody hell, Roy.' She flings the A-Z at Jamie and continues to work her way through the packet of stomach settlers she'd started at Milton Keynes whilst Jamie reads directions. But Roy manages mainly on his own, treasure that he is. He'd studied the map as if revising for an exam before the journey.

As they pull up outside Matthew's house, Gloria turns and asks,

'Did you remember to pack your toothbrush?'

'Yes, Mum.' Jamie scowls.

'And a flannel?'

Roy shakes his head at her, 'Muzzle it, would you?' he says. 'Come on, Sunshine. Let's get your things.'

Gloria looks up at the Edwardian house, rather looming and imperious for a modest suburban semi-detached. Something about its miniature turrets and grinning bay window, give it its own devious personality. A tall man is standing at the front door in shorts and a torn shirt. He's holding a small gardening fork. That must be him, watching her as she adjusts her blouse. Look at him! Gloria gets out of the car and rushes up to Jamie and speaks in his ear. 'Don't be walking around barefoot, our Jamie. Got to be careful. Hypodermic needles!'

'Gloria!' Roy barks. She's overstepped the mark. 'Behave yourself and grab hold of this.' Roy swings a suitcase at her and, as he lets go of the handle, the dead weight of it almost pulls her over.

Jamie, ahead of her, is first at the door. 'Hello, Matthew,' he says, quietly. Gloria watches their smiles of allegiance as Jamie passes into the hallway.

'Dump your cases there,' Matthew says, pointing to a spot at the foot of the stairs. 'I can help you unpack your things later. I'll make a pot of tea.'

'Oh, good. I'm parched.' Gloria reaches the front door. 'Gloria,' she says, straining with the large suitcase. She drops it at Matthew's feet. Useless bugger!

'You must be Jamie's mum,' Matthew says. 'I love what you're wearing.'

A little flattered, she laughs. 'Oh, how kind of you to say!'

'I love that colour. It's quite nutty. Would you say that's grey or beige.'

'It's taupe.' She steps in through the door and moves to stand next to Jamie.

'I'll get that, shall I?' Matthew says, lifting the case across the threshold and placing it at the foot of the stairs. He then holds up hands, fingernails caked with soil. 'Spot of gardening, Gloria. Won't shake your hand.'

She's relieved. 'My feet are throbbing. Just let me sit down.'

'Don't mind her,' Jamie says. 'She's a martyr to her swollen ankles.'

Gloria cracks him across the back of the head and he lets out a voiceless, embarrassed squeal. 'Been asking for that all morning, cheeky swine.'

She's alarmed by Matthew—so tall and gaunt. 'Jamie hasn't stopped talking about you,' she says, forcing a show of niceness. 'I've been waiting to see what all the fuss is about.'

'Only good things, I hope,' Matthew says, in a posh accent but Gloria can see through it. Got a lot of shit on him.

'This is my husband, Roy,' she says, proudly.

Roy sticks out his hand. Matthew raises soiled hands again. 'How was the journey?'

Roy pauses heavily.

'We made good time,' Gloria answers for him. 'The traffic got a bit busier as we came into London but the motorway was relatively clear.' She tilts her head at Roy, apologetically.

'Go on through,' Matthew lifts a third suitcase into the house. Roy hesitates, steps inside, closes the door firmly behind him and stands for a long moment in the hallway, motionless, eyes fixed on one of those brightly coloured Sacred Heart images that Gloria once spotted in a street market in Alicante. Now that the daylight has been blocked out it's possible to see candles flickering. Roy's face is lit up—his nose is wrinkled like the arse end of a cooked chicken, detecting what Gloria has already spotted—a burning stick of some scented rubbish.

Matthew points to a room off the hallway. 'Make yourselves at home.' He disappears into the kitchen.

Gloria doesn't move from her spot. What a dump! The hallway walls have been stripped bare, washed in some sort of transparent brown muck with a gloss surface. This has left them with a fake medieval appearance—the kind she's seen on TV in those ridiculous makeover programmes. A thick red bell rope accessorizes the banister, leading to a candlelit upstairs. Gothic candelabras and Moroccan tea lights illuminate the downstairs area. The only other decorations are a cluster of gaudy Jesus or Mary pictures spread throughout the hall and stairwell. One large Sacred Heart takes pride of place above the telephone table and a pile of directories. Her eyes come back to Matthew, sashaying from the kitchen with a tray. Look at the colour of him. Doesn't look well.

Matthew clears his throat, perhaps annoyed to find them all still standing in the hall. 'Tea,' he says vividly, and ushers them all past an empty room that Gloria has already guessed will be Jamie's, into the living room. 'Please, take a seat—'

'Forgot to pay the electric?' There's no shortage of candelabra, even though this seems to be the side of the house that catches the afternoon sun. Coloured stalactites and stalagmites of candle wax have collected on wrought ironwork and parquet flooring.

Gloria heads to a large patio window and peers out. Polythene bags of soil lie around on the flagstones. A compost heap at the rear of the garden harbours fresh scraps of carrot and orange peel.

Matthew is arranging cups and saucers on the dining table. Well at least he makes tea properly, with a teapot. She'll give him that.

'Milk and sugar?'

'Milk for me please. Neither for Roy. He's being careful,'

The Earl Grey tea he pours only succeeds in increasing Roy's stiffness. He can't stand that bloody scented muck. And Jamie sits fidgeting on the sofa, probably embarrassed that his parents are even here. He might be in his early twenties, but in reality, look at him, still a kid with a ridiculous bleached mop and a t-shirt she'd only ironed for him this morning. Matthew won't get his whites *that* white.

Gloria makes an effort to keep conversation going. 'Lovely garden. Roy loves gardening, don't you Roy?' Conversation isn't Roy's thing at the best of times, unless coaxed out of him with a bit of boiled ham.

'It's my pride and joy,' Matthew says.

'Roy's just installed a pond in ours. He deliberated for some time over whether to put in a preformed fibreglass pool or use a liner. In the end, he went for a liner. Such a perfectionist, my husband.'

Finally, she sits down next to Roy on the sofa. 'So this is *your* house?' she asks, locking eyes with Matthew.

'It's my *home*,' Matthew says.

'And what are you charging him?'

'Mother! That's my business.' Jamie looks aghast.

'Forty pounds a week,' Matthew says.

Jamie tuts.

'Well I suppose he'll just afford that on his wages from the *supermarket*, won't he?' she says, spite getting the better of her. 'But he won't be here for long. I expect he and Billy will want to get a place of their own.'

'There you go again,' Jamie says. 'Making decisions for me.'

'Thank you.' Gloria takes a teacup. She slurps on tea, hiding her displeasure at its funny taste. 'Dreadful shame about Diana, eh?' she hurries along. 'I suppose it will hit you Londoners hard.'

Matthew looks at her, quizzically, for a moment, as if he's misheard. 'Yes, I suppose it will. But I'm —'

'Not a real Londoner?'

'No,' Matthew says emphatically, as if stamping his foot. 'Not a fan of royalty.'

'Are you not? We've got a lovely commemorative wedding mug. Who would have thought it would end up like this?'

Matthew averts his eyes. He's got something to hide; Gloria knows it. She feels the skin on her face tightening—perhaps the beginning of a hot flush. They have been coming more frequently lately. She bit the postman's head off the other day just for walking on the lawn.

'So where are you from, originally?'

He deigns to lift his eyes again to look at her. 'Sheffield. But I haven't been back for years.'

'I'm sure it will be a kick in the teeth for some people,' she says.

'Sorry?'

'Diana. I mean the papers thrived off her.' She finishes her tea.

'Gosh, you can drink it *that* hot?' Matthew says.

'Asbestos mouth,' she says. 'Right then. We'll be off. If I can just use your loo.'

'Top of the stairs, first door on your right.'

She points a forefinger at Roy. 'Hurry up and finish your tea.' She leaves them in silence. When she reaches the top of the stairs, the floorboards creak on a hexagonal landing stinking of incense. The walls upstairs are covered with more of those kitsch pictures of Jesus. The landing has five open doors off it. Three bedrooms, a bathroom and a toilet hardly big enough to sit down in.

There's a high-level cistern with a flush handle on a rusty chain. A smell of damp reminds her of the cold outside khazi she'd used as a child, where she discovered her first period.

The interior of Matthew's loo has been entirely pasted over with cuttings of news photos from the Eastern Bloc. Shirtless Soviet boy soldiers, flaunting themselves in front of the camera, feature dominantly. The pictures have been varnished flat to the plaster. Who in their right mind does this to a perfectly good wall? Why would her son want to stay here, of all places, with this man—a cross between ET and Peter O'Toole?

She closes the door—no latch, flicks her clothes up out of the way, squats over the toilet seat without actually making contact—a practise she's rehearsed many times. Thighs trembling, she reaches forward with one hand to hold the door closed and pees. She checks the seat for dribble and flushes. The bottom of the toilet bowl, is covered in a thick layer of lime-scale, in dire need of a bottle of bleach. And a crack! A cracked seat harbours germs. She leaves the toilet and walks into the bathroom to wash her hands. *It's my home.* Home? What the hell does that mean? It's a bloody squat this is. A *squat*. No bloody wallpaper, no carpets anywhere, nails sticking out of floors. She looks at the bath, which has a tidemark running all the way around it and a plughole bunged up with the tiny bits of soap and hair. No towel. She wipes her hands on her jeans.

On the landing, one of the doors is ajar. Creeping about, trying to avoid squeaky floorboards, she sees clothes on the floor and the starry edge of an American flag on the wall. But that's all. She hasn't the nerve to pry, even though she wants to turn the place over and find evidence that Matthew is a total creep.

Trailing a finger along the banister, she descends, breathing sharply through clamped teeth. 'Dirt,' she whispers. Then her eyes come back to Matthew, waiting at the foot of the stairs. I know what *you* are, she thinks—eco warrior, *never-paid-national-insurance*, dog-on-a-rope sort. That's what you are.

'You ready, love?' Roy asks, man of so many words.

She looks directly ahead at the door in the hallway they'd missed earlier.

Matthew opens it. 'This will be Jamie's room,' he says, reassuringly.

She pokes her nose around the door. Clean and tidy, at least. *No curtains.* No furniture—just a bed and a clothes rail.

'You'll have to get some nets put up those windows.'

'I'll be alright Mum. I'll sort it.'

This doesn't feel right at all. Jamie wouldn't come back with them, even if she demanded. He'd dig his heels in. It's enough, for now, that Matthew knows she doesn't trust him. But she'll be there, when it all goes wrong. Because it will, won't it?

Turning at the door, she hugs Jamie. 'Call us as soon as you've got yourself settled in.'

'Yes. I will. I'll wave to you from the bedroom window,' he says and retreats inside.

Roy looks at Matthew smiling down on him. 'Well, nice to meet you, fella.'

'Good to meet you too,' Matthew says. Roy jangles his car keys and walks off down the driveway.

Gloria can feel herself lingering slightly—one leg on the driveway going after Roy, the other straddling the doorstep. She turns back into the doorway and Matthew fills her vision—too close—close enough that she can smell his offensive breath. And *Oh my God! What's wrong with his eyes?*

'It's time to let go now, Gloria. He's a big boy.'

She's intimidated, caught adrift from Jamie and Roy. He's one of those sexual ones—a predator. If he so much as lays a finger on her son she'll—

She eyeballs him, making sure he looks away first. She lets go of the doorframe and walks away.

From inside the car, Gloria fights back tears and waves to Jamie, standing at his bedroom window, as Roy accelerates away.

'Well, that was bloody awkward,' Roy says.

'It's not right. I'm always right about my instincts—as you well know.' She touches him on the leg, reminding herself of the familiarity they share. 'Get us home.'

§

Truth be told, Jamie's glad to see the back of them. For the first time since they'd set off this morning, there's a space in his head where Gloria's voice had been.

In his new bedroom, he hangs the last of his pitiful assortment of clothes on the rail, a jacket, and checking the pockets, finds a little piece of paper inside it.

I love you, Soft Lad.

He smiles. He hasn't worn this jacket since the last time he saw Billy. It's the fifth one he's found today—one inside his shoe. *I miss you.* One was inside the chest pocket of a shirt, one inside the zipper of his suitcase and another inside his jeans. This is Billy—little gestures of kindness.

'Are you hungry?' Matthew's voice echoes from the kitchen.

Jamie can hear his music—a minimalist classical arrangement with lots of bells and strings. Jamie loves it. The rest of his belongings are on the floor, along with his well-thumbed copy of *The Prophetic Insights*. Matthew's sorted out some nets *to put up the windows.* His mother was right; the window exposes the room to the whole street.

'Starving.'

'It's Thai. Trust me, this is going to be delicious.'

'I'll be right in.' He makes the bed, checks himself in front of a glass mirror, leaning against the lilac anaglypta. There are two versions of himself—the one in his mind's eye, the shy schoolboy always covering up, aping some idealistic notion of heterosexuality. Look where that had got him—fondled by lonely, desperate middle-aged women at parties. The other version, staring back at him from the mirror, is altogether different to Jamie Johnson of the West Midlands. This is the type of gent he hopes would stand out in the crowd. His parents accept the gay thing, in their own way. You're alright if you're like them—settle down, spend Sunday afternoons shopping for garden sheds in B & Q. But, Jamie wants to be *queer*—a word his mother thinks is rude and distasteful. He imagines Billy in his student lodgings, surrounded by photographs by Mapplethorpe and books about Jarman.

When he enters the living room, Matthew is absent. The table is set. Candles are lit, flames flickering with the gentle breeze from the open patio window. A large steaming saucepan of green broth sits alongside glasses and a bottle of fizzy wine. Jamie edges further into the room toward the wide sliding door. Just outside, a couple of planters with masses of flowers are made visible in the spill of light from inside. Beyond that it's dark. Jamie finds the switch for the garden lights.

He calls out into the night, 'Matthew?' He moves closer to the window, his feet touching the lip of the window frame, eyes becoming accustomed to the darkness. A ghostly outline is visible, arms outstretched, at the top of the garden, only metres away.

'What are you doing?' Jamie whispers. Matthew spins, like a child deliberately trying to make himself sick. Round and round—counting his revolutions, 'One hundred and six... One hundred and seven... one hundred and eight... one hundred and nine...'

Jamie watches with red-faced confusion—he might as well have caught him masturbating. Matthew stumbles giddily for a moment. Jamie scuttles back to the dining table and pretends to be arranging place settings.

When Matthew flounces back in. 'Do the honours!'

Jamie wonders what he means?

'The wine! Let's pop.' Matthew laughs.

'I love the music,' Jamie says.

'Philip Glass.'

Jamie smiles and marks a few notes in the air with his fingers.

'She's ever so uptight, isn't she?'

'Who?'

'Your mother.' Matthew sits down to stir the soup. 'She needs to loosen up,' he says, apparently finding great amusement in this idea. He sucks in his cheeks and flares the whites of his eyes in a pretentious, self-important gesture. Then Matthew softens. He must have noticed Jamie bristle. 'My parents are the same.' Jamie can't imagine Matthew's mother is anything like his own.

Jamie pops the cork and sprays them both with Cava, provoking a little squeal from Matthew who claps his hands together. He pours two glasses. 'She's not all that bad,' Jamie says.

'Don't get me wrong. Gloria's a beautiful human being. But Jamie, all mothers have to let go at some point, even yours.'

They drink and talk over dinner—Matthew's love of throbbing techno, favourite films and where Jamie can go out in this part of London. Jamie's never tasted Thai food before. The soup has an unusual flavour. Like everything around him now, he's not sure if he likes it or not, but it makes a refreshing change from Gloria's traditional English roasts.

Matthew's voice grows ever grander. 'It was Caribbean and Creole food when I was a child. Dad liked roast beef and Yorkshire pudding but that would only happen if he cooked it himself. Mother insisted on traditional cooking.' Matthew gazes into the middle distance for a moment.

'You never say much about your parents,' Jamie enquires.

'What's happened to the lovely Billy?'

'Didn't think you'd appreciate me inviting guests so soon.'

'I thought he'd be over to christen that bed in there.'

Jamie looks into his soup. He examines the ingredients before ladling another spoonful into his mouth. Chilli, ginger and green peas are about all he recognizes.

'All good stuff. Lemongrass, galangal, pak-choi... And some spirulina .'

'What's *spirulina*?' Jamie asks.

'Micro-algae from deep under the ocean. Boosts the immune system.'

Jamie remarks that he'd once read a book all about a woman who, riddled with cancer, had healed herself by altering her diet and remodelling her thought processes. When the doctors tested her, the cancer had not only gone into remission but had disappeared entirely.

'The mind is a very powerful thing,' Matthew says.

Jamie's eyes fall on a row of large photograph albums lined up on the floor, each spine labelled with marker pen—*Berlin, Bucharest, Thailand, Auschwitz, Moscow, Kosovo* and *Moldova*.

'I'm envious of your travelling,' Jamie says.

'You'll do it too.' Matthew gulps down wine. 'Just as soon as you start living your life instead of letting your mother live it for you.'

Jamie grasps the wine now and pours himself a large one.

§

'Stop the car, Roy.' Gloria's voice rises above a passing police siren.

'What now? We're nearly home.'

'Stop the fucking car!'

Roy swings into a roadside layby and skids to a standstill, tyres spitting up gravel. 'Jesus, Glo!'

'You're freaking me out, Roy. All this time I've been going along with it because you're the rational one. And now you say *you're* not comfortable.' She's unravelling, like rows and rows of stitches free of knitting needles. 'We've dropped off our son in a house worthy of Norman Bates and just left him there.'

'Gloria, I don't like it any more than you do.' Roy has always had a brand of non-stick robustness that made her feel secure, like *Teflon* or *Kevlar*. The world is always all fine because Roy is there—as sure as the tide comes in. But here, now, his voice has a note of uncertainty. 'If I thought we could change his mind, I'd turn around right now.'

'I'm living on my nerves, I am,' Gloria says. 'We've bought our Jamie up in a decent house, with decent things, to live a decent life. And now this! Oh, it doesn't bode well. Roy? Are you listening to me? This isn't like that time he decided to give up eating meat and start growing his own vegetables. This is something else. Something's going to happen. It's like he's under a spell! And now he's even wearing Matthew's clothes. The look that *thing* gave me when we were leaving —'

'Gloria, let's not turn this into something that it's not.' Roy squeezes her hand tightly.

'And if you'd heard the way he spoke to me. He's got breath the kind you'd back away from holding a crucifix.'

'What do you want me to do—put him in a straightjacket?'

She looks at her fingers—chipped polish. 'My nails won't take this, Roy.'

§

'Moldova?' Jamie ponders a topic of conversation that will a) not reveal himself to be a complete idiot and b) elevate him, in Matthew's eyes, to protégé status. He's thinking of the photo albums in the living room, where Matthew is stalking with an incense stick like a witch doctor exorcising evil spirits as Jamie squirts washing-up liquid into a sink filling with hot water—something chemical free and environmentally friendly. Submerging plates and cutlery into bubbles, he smiles at the decadent contrast between the elegant cut-glass in his hands and the uneven stone floor of the kitchen—appliances askew like listing boats in a harbour.

He closes his eyes and pushes his hands down into the comforting warm water. Ah. This house pulsates with exotic aromas. Colours and stylish embellishments clash everywhere he looks. There's still the trace of something in his mouth. What did Matthew call it? His mother's never heard of coriander, let alone introduced it into her cooking.

They'll be arguing over something by now... Should they have a water-feature in the fish pond? Or, whether to set the table for dinner or have it on a tray in front of the telly—those sorts of really important conversations.'

'Sorry, didn't catch that.'

Jamie opens his eyes. 'It's an unusual place to visit.' Geography was never his strong point.

Matthew discards the incense. 'Well, in those days, you could buy a train ticket that would get you thousands of miles across Europe. I was halfway across Romania when I met a young couple who'd been travelling the same way. We befriended each other. They were heading for a town near the border. I forget the name of it. Call me naïve, but it wasn't until the last minute I realized we were entering a conflict zone. I saw roadside graves and a roadblock.' Matthew pauses dramatically, as he puts the kettle on.

'I just knew if I did the wrong thing, or said the wrong thing they'd shoot me. I mean these guys weren't messing around. They took my luggage and smashed my camera. I'd been really foolish. I was going to have to be very clever if was going to get out of such a dangerous situation.' Matthew's voice grows low and dark—a master of storytelling. 'So I just spoke very calmly. I didn't want to piss them off. They kept me in a shed near the roadside for a couple of days. No proper buildings. Strip-searched me and took my clothes away. They just shouted at me in pidgin English. The soldiers kept touching me, pushing me around. At one point I thought they would rape me, but they didn't. I knew I couldn't descend into that. I knew I had to banish those thoughts.'

'You must have been terrified,' Jamie says.

'Naturally. They interrogated me for days.' Matthew continues tea making. 'I think it was all about massaging their egos, making them feel powerful. I was their toy, you see. Somehow, I just managed to talk myself out of the situation. Strength of mind,' Matthew says, his voice brightening. 'They let me go because of who I am.'

Jamie wipes the kitchen surfaces and lets his dripping hands fall to his sides. 'What do you mean, *because of who you are?*'

'I knew that if I could survive that experience, I could get through anything.' Matthew lifts teacups. Jamie follows him through the dining room towards the garden. 'It was very liberating.'

'Look at this,' Matthew says, lifting up a postcard he spotted on his way through the living room—an advertisement for a New-Age convention called *Anything is Possible.* 'I picked it up the other day, in the esoteric shop I like to visit. It spoke to me. Like, *I'm for Jamie.*'

Jamie smiles. 'Shall we go?'

'Anything is possible.'

The sky in Welston would be black and prickled with white dots. Here the stars are lost behind a viscosity of light pollution. The moon, though, is bright and large. In the dilute light, Matthew's face looks otherworldly, as he stares up at it. 'Ask the universe…'

Jamie says, 'Can I ask *you* something?'

'You can ask me anything.'

'Why do you collect those pictures of Jesus?'

§

'Look at all these,' There's a bread-crate outside the *Scan'n'Pack* full of discarded sandwiches. 'It's the universe at work.' Matthew picks it up. 'That's dinner sorted out.'

Jamie's phone rings. 'Oh, please come tonight,' Jamie starts immediately before Billy can get a word in edgeways. 'We've hardly seen each other this week.'

'If you will insist I come to that house.'

'It's where I live!'

'Will *he* be there?' Billy asks.

'Of course.'

'He's a freak.'

Jamie looks at Matthew, handing out sandwiches to a homeless guy sitting on the pavement. 'Not from where I'm standing.'

§

Jamie lurches after Matthew up the steps of Shoreditch Town Hall and into the Gilbert and George art opening, tipsy from the bottle of cava they'd guzzled on the journey. Jamie's excited to see that Matthew knows *everyone*. In a film-star entrance of mouthed helll-loooos, Matthew gestures to people on the other side of the hall, well-known members of the art world—the 'Bitterati' he calls them. Jamie recognizes faces he's only ever seen on the covers of magazines and on television—Andrew Logan, Phillip Salon, groups of freaks in flamboyant attire and fantasy make-up and his hero, Boy George, whose appearance leaves him speechless. It's almost as if Jamie has seen... a unicorn.

'I can't believe I'm here,' Jamie says.

At the edge of the crowd, Matthew turns. He presses his hands onto Jamie's shoulders. 'Do you mean to say you wanted to be *anywhere* else? Don't underestimate yourself, Jamie. Only *you* could have brought this into being.'

Jamie nods. 'The universe provides us with everything we need.'

Matthew smiles back at him—his unearthly almond-shaped eyes, unblinking hazel rimmed with blue. 'You're very special, Jamie.'

He leads Jamie by the hand across the room. 'So many people I want you to meet—David, Gracie... so many people.'

Within minutes Matthew is holding court. 'I thought I was going to die,' he says to a fixated crowd, mouths agape.

'Oh, that's terrible.'

'How did you get away?'

'You must have been terrified.'

Matthew appears to be devouring every second of it, perhaps making a meal of it for Jamie's benefit. 'Take it from me, if it hadn't been for my strength of character, I might not be alive now.' Jamie wonders if the god complex Matthew developed as a child had really gone for good: are those religious icons back at the house simply souvenirs from an angst ridden adolescence or does he believe he really *is* Jesus Christ reincarnated?

Beside Jamie, a handsome man in lederhosen seems to be enjoying the story. 'Hi, I'm Jamie,' Jamie says, suddenly conscious of his supermarket uniform. 'I'm a friend of Matthew.'

The man's smile drops. 'Oh, really?' He moves away.

Amongst the throng is a man who Matthew is keen for Jamie to meet. He's been dubbed as being all glamour and no shame—performance artist, costume designer and club host—Bond villain minus the pussy. He's staring. A bleached platinum quiff with a subtle lilac rinse is set off by a navy 1940s double-breasted suit, over a ruffled shirt. He sidles up, wiggling his fingers inside lilac silk gloves.

'David. David Cabaret,' he says. 'Wonderful to make your acquaintance.' He drags out the vowels in exaggerated feminine abandon as he takes Jamie's hand in his own and kisses it.

Matthew can be heard over the buzz of the room. 'We're all connected, everyone. Take it from me. We're all from the stars.'

David rolls his eyes and whispers into Jamie's ear, 'Take no notice. He talks a load of old shit.' He drains his glass through a straw and dumps it, as if needing both hands for a fight. Then he looks coquettishly at Jamie, from behind lilac contact lenses. 'Come on, *you*!' David tugs Jamie's sleeve. 'You can get me a drink.' Jamie steps back and presses his hands against empty pockets, feeling for coins.

'It's an art opening, daaarling! No-one pays for the drinks,' David says, grasping two glasses of bubbly from a passing waiter.

Relieved, Jamie sighs and accepts one from him. 'I love your outfit.'

'Oh, this old thing.' David holds out his sleeves, pretending to brush a bit of dust from them. 'Well, it'll do for these two—' he says, motioning to Gilbert and George who are holding court on the balcony. 'I usually make more of an effort.' David does a little twirl. 'Tell me you're not one of his conquests.'

Jamie touches his forehead, drawing a blank.

'Pinocchio, over there,' David nods in Matthew's direction.

'Oh, no. He's my housemate. I already have a boyfriend.' Jamie scans the room again. Boy George has vanished and there's no sign of Billy either.

David looks around. 'He's not here?'

'No. Not yet.'

David purses his lips. 'My lucky night then. Oh look, there's Princess Julia and...' He stands brazenly pointing and reels off a list of names, some of whom Jamie recognises as veterans of 80s club society, Blitz Kids and 'faces' of Leigh Bowery's infamous Soho nightclub, *Taboo*. 'There's Molly Parkin and Mr Pearl and there's—Oh! God! Isn't! He! Lovely! Michael Clarke the dancer, I-made-a-costume-for-him… and oh, look there's —' David shifts from side to side, annoyed by the crowd obstructing his line of vision to a young man in a white vest and jeans, revealing a chest inked with William Morris tattoos.

Hypnotised by the man's beauty, Jamie wobbles. 'Who is that?' he whispers.

'That's Simon Jones.' David licks his lips.

There's still no sign of Billy. The last time they'd seen each other there had been an unexplained distance, into which Jamie had read a need for Billy to untangle himself. Jamie also suspected he'd smelt someone else's aftershave on Billy's neck.

David licks a finger and rubs a stain on the cuff of his jacket.

'You made this?' Jamie asks.

'Of course. This jacket got me on the pages of all the scene magazines,' David says in a fit of unbridled flounce. 'I make all my own costumes. I'm just *fabulous*.'

A voice booms from behind them. 'All the fun-fur in the world won't make *you* fabulous, David Cabaret!' They spin. A helmet of bleached white hair with darker dyed layers beneath, pussyfoots towards them. She arcs her cigarillo, turning the art of smoking into a ballet. Her 60s feline eyes are the result of expertly applied shadow and liquid liner.

David gasps, 'Gracie Sharp! Speak of the devil and she shall—'

'Davey-baby. Long-time-no-see. Where have you been, you little recluse?' Gracie's voice is deep enough to be a touch masculine. Dusty Springfield—but with finer features and flawless skin. The rest is a black kaftan affair with black culottes.

'It's been all go,' David replies. 'London Fashion Week and all.'

'*You* need to get out more, David. People will forget who you are.'

'Me. Nooo,' he roars at her.

'You want to be a *has been*?'

Jamie plucks up the courage to tell Gracie, 'You look amazing.'

'It's all drag, baby,' she says, throwing a limp hand at him. She draws the last puff from her cigarillo and drops it into David's empty glass.

'Charming.' David tuts.

Gracie turns her attention to Jamie. 'Oh David, isn't he just sweetness personified? I could eat him.'

Jamie feels himself blush.

'Bring me a knife and fork,' David says.

Gracie squeezes her eyelids together. 'So how do you know David?'

'We only met tonight. I know Matthew.' Jamie indicates his ganglylegged friend. 'He's a friend of David.'

Her face is fixed, as if someone has pressed a pause button. '*Is* he a friend?'

'*I* didn't invite him,' David says, sauntering off. 'Only met him a handful of times. The man's a mystery.'

Jamie spots the man in lederhosen again. 'Who's that?' he asks.

Gracie grins. 'He's single, if that's what you're asking.'

'He was laughing at one of Matthew's stories.' Jamie says. 'But when I introduced myself as Matthew's friend, he just blanked me. It's happened a lot lately.'

Gracie lets out a loud giggle. 'Darling, I don't expect it's *you* they're snubbing.' She touches him affectionately on the cheek.

'You don't like Matthew?'

She plucks a glass of cheap fizz from a tray and leans in to Jamie. 'Don't take this the wrong way because I'm sure you know him better than anyone—it's simply that he's just *appeared*. No-one seems to know who the fuck he is.'

Gracie links arms with Jamie and strolls him, in a motherly fashion, around the room. There's a long story about her meeting David. 'He made all the costumes I wore while my band were touring South America. Never known anyone so talented. I've seen him take a piece of tin foil and turn it into a Russian space suit. Total magician.'

'Why South America?'

'Why not? Growing economies—seriously, *here* nobody knows who the fuck I am. *Peru*—I'm like Madonna.' She rubs him on the arm. 'So, you're a student?'

'I just finished my degree.'

'So you're looking for work?'

'I want to write.'

'So you're looking for work.' Gracie smiles.

'I am working.'

'As a writer?'

He lowers his head, shyly, avoiding Gracie's eyes now. No one seems to have noticed his uniform yet. Perhaps his attire stands out so much, they think he's selected it deliberately as a statement. 'I work at the *Scan 'n' Pack*.'

She squeezes his upper arm. 'Never mind darling—you can write about what goes on in the locker room.'

Then she's distracted by someone on the other side of the room. 'Nice tats.'

Jamie squints. It's that guy again. Simon.

'I'm looking for someone with a great ass. He'd be perfect.'

'What for?' Jamie asks.

'Darling, I direct porn.'

'Porn?' Jamie can't help sounding surprised.

'Keeping the wolves from the door.' She peers at him from beneath her fringe. 'Maybe I could give *you* some work. Twink like you—made for it.'

Jamie giggles shyly.

'Don't knock it 'til you've tried it.' Gracie tells him about the other members of her crowd—a mixed bag of creatives and strays—none of whom had ever held down what Jamie's mother would call a 'proper job' or paid any tax. 'Marcel over there —' She points. 'He's a club promoter. Richard designs film-posters. Jeremy is a rent-boy and...'

'And Matthew?'

'I don't know about him.' She drains her glass. 'I'm just going to have a word with tattoo-boy. Get yourself another drink and grab me in ten minutes. We'll talk about how you're going to break London.'

She snakes elegantly into the crowd. Jamie's attention is diverted by Matthew, standing close to a man sporting a beard and a baseball cap. Even from this distance, Jamie can hear his American drawl, agreeing enthusiastically with Matthew.

Matthew splits off. Jamie approaches him and asks, 'An old friend?'

Matthew falters. 'We only just met.'

'Oh. I thought I saw a connection there.'

'I've never even been to America,' Matthew says emphatically.

Then Billy is in front of Jamie, giving him a start. 'What did I tell you about turning up in your work clothes? For fuck's sake!' Billy smiles. He's wearing a loose denim jacket, and a vest Jamie bought him when he still had money—black cotton with a print of a bulldog across the chest. Jamie recognises a familiar feeling—knees like water, the rest of the room blurring. Billy leans towards him and kisses him on the lips. Jamie is just about to habitually scan the room for onlookers, but he checks himself and instead pulls Billy towards him.

'You forgot to get me on the guest list,' Billy says. 'I had to flutter my eyelashes at the doorman.'

'Shit. Sorry, I was supposed to ask Matthew.'

'You're so preoccupied these days.' And there it is, that distance again.

'He's been so encouraging...' Jamie tells him about the tarot reading that Matthew had given him, and their trip to the *Mind, Body and Spirit Centre*. Billy stiffens, the way Jamie's father had on the day of his arrival.

'How can I talk to you about him, if you're going to react every time?'

Billy sighs. 'Okay. Try me...'

They walk around the periphery of the crowd. 'Do you think he's ill?'

Billy looks up at the panelled ceiling. 'Are you asking me if I think he's got AIDS?'

'Yes.'

'How the fuck should I know? You can't tell just by looking.'

'*Billy*, he's greener than Kermit the Frog. And there's something wrong with his eyes. They flicker from side to side.'

'Drugs can make you go a bit cross-eyed.'

'He's totally anti-drugs!' Jamie says. 'He doesn't even use surface cleaner. He wipes the kitchen down with half a lemon. You know, I can't work him out. He works just four mornings a week and —'

'How's he surviving? Maybe you're right. Maybe he's on some sort of sickness benefit. It wouldn't surprise me.'

'What do you mean?' Jamie stares indignantly.

'He's a charlatan.'

Fear rises up in him. What if he's making a terrible mistake? And there it is again, the voice of his *mother*. 'You're wrong!' Jamie says. He throws back his glass of fizz, burps and thrusts it at Billy. 'Here, hold that. I'm going to the toilet.'

'The ladies toilets are over there,' Billy says, pointing to the corner of the room.

'Sexist!' Entering a vintage deco space of duck-egg-blue porcelain that he's sure is the gents', he's surprised to see Gracie Sharp standing in front of the mirror. She's concealing something on the side of the basin with her purse.

Damn Billy. 'I'm sorry, I must have the wrong —'

'No no,' she says. 'You've got the right loo. There's a queue in the women's and the boys here won't make a fuss.' She smiles, fluffs in the antique mirror and moves her purse gently. Underneath is a credit card and four lines of white crystalline powder. Jamie feels a rush of adrenaline.

She pulls a business card out and scribbles on it with eyeliner. 'This is home… and this is work,' Gracie hands it to him. 'Call me. Whenever you like.' She rolls up a note, puts it to her left nostril and snorts a line from the porcelain surface. Then she presses a finger against her other nostril and sniffs back, sharply. Tilting her head back, she leans into the mirror, checking for residue and wipes the back of her credit card against her tongue.

When Gracie looks back at him, Jamie feels himself blush. She offers him the note. 'It's cocaine. You want to try?'

'Isn't it very bad for you?'

'Extremely,' she says and touches her top lip with the point of her tongue.

'But doesn't it kill people?' he asks. *Shut up, Mother! SHUT UP!*

Bending to finish another line, Gracie's voice is lower, graver, 'Listen sweetheart, if you want to stay ahead of the plot—you've got to get to know the enemy.'

§

'What the fuck have you got on?' Billy flicks his fag butt into the driveway.

Jamie looks down at his turquoise tie-dyed kaftan. 'You don't like it?'

Billy throws his eyes up. 'Another one of Matthew's hand-me-downs?' He barges past Jamie, into the hallway. 'Is he home?'

'We're alone.' Jamie closes the door behind him. 'I got a job today.'

'Really? Where?'

'Gracie pulled a few strings at the Walter's Gallery. I went this morning. They told me straight away.'

'The woman from the party? You've learnt to schmooze then.' Billy hugs Jamie tightly. 'Well done, Soft Lad. When do you start?'

'Not for a few months yet. And I'm brassic...'

'Well, at least it'll fill Gloria's cakehole.' Billy sniffs the air. 'Mmmmm.'

'It's Thai.' Jamie closes the front door behind him.

'Thai?' Billy's eyes suddenly flare wide. 'Is this wise?'

'I thought I'd try.' Jamie's been at it all day, trying to get it right. 'I know you'd probably prefer a burger.'

'I'm happy to trying anything when it comes to your cooking but I'm talking about this shit.' Billy points at Matthew's collection of gaudy religious icons. 'You wonder why I don't want to come and visit you.'

'Open your mind, Billy.'

'Don't give me that clap-trap. This is *me* you're talking to now.'

Jamie sighs. 'You're beginning to sound like my mother.'

Billy pulls at the fabric of Jamie's kaftan. 'Listen, Soft Lad. I don't give a shit about the dust, or the décor. But your mother has got a point about the rest.' He lets the fabric fall again. 'And if you think I'm going to the theatre with you dressed like that, you've got another thing coming.'

§

Jamie cradles his programme in one arm as he springs down the street towards home. It's been a wonderful night with Billy. The tickets were expensive but so worth it. He can't wait to tell Matthew all about it. Oh London. Oh world! Isn't it beautiful to be so part of everything...

'Helloooo,' he calls as he enters the house. The hallway is imbued with the smells that Matthew always calls juniper and patchouli but

Jamie doesn't know which is which.

'I'm just in the bath,' Matthew calls. 'I'll be down forthwith.'

'Relax. Enjoy your bath,' Jamie says.

'How was the play?'

'Amazing.'

'And the boy?'

'Tucked up in bed now.'

Jamie walks into the living room. There's a pot of tea on the table next to a pile of papers. As Jamie pours tea into a china cup, he can't help noticing the letter on top:

RLP Solicitors
Dear Matthew Morris,

Our Client: Mr MJ Nkanti
Property: 86 Gillet Street, Willesden Green, NW10
Re: Outstanding Sum Due

We act on behalf of the landlord Mr Nkanti and enclose a notice terminating your tenancy of the premises on 31.01.98. We require payment of rent arrears in the sum of £30,750 failing which—

'You still haven't christened that bed then?'

Jamie turns to Matthew in the doorway—snake hips and slim torso rising above his towel draped waist. 'Who's Mr Nkanti?'

§

'What do you mean, it's not really *his* house?' Gloria throws her oven gloves across the kitchen work surface. 'Whose bleedin' house is it?' she asks.

Her fingers loop anxiously around the telephone cable. He'd better not spin her a tale. She'll see straight through him. Terrible liar. But if she pushes too much, she knows he'll withdraw and she'll get nowhere. She's already the *meddling mother*, slated by *that thing*.

Jamie's voice is distant on the other end of the line as he tells her how Matthew had lived in this house for over a decade even though he's not the landlord. Her fingers move to her neck, scratching skin, already sore with anger. Initially, a guy in Africa owned it and a property management company collected the rent. Then Mr Nkanti moved back to England and came once a month to collect his money. One summer, he just stopped visiting. Matthew later found out that he'd died. Didn't leave a will. The estate went to probate. There was no one else to pay the rent to. And that was that. Until the letters started arriving.

A likely bloody story. 'So it's a squat. I knew it.'

'I wish you'd—' Jamie's voice is trembling.

'And what's been happening to all the money?'

'He's been saving it to give to the landlord. Why do you always have to think the worst?'

'Because I'm the one who picks up the pieces. He's not being honest with you, Jamie. He's not at all who you think he is. He barely works. Just some tuppenny-ha'penny job in a bloody bakery. He's constantly travelling. And you're just—'

'What's your aversion to me spreading my wings? Have you never felt like just running away—to live in a different places, meet different people?'

She casts her mind back. People like her just didn't do that. At nineteen, she got a job as a telephonist, met Roy and got married. They worked to save for a deposit on a mortgage and before long she was expecting. 'Never had the opportunity, Jamie.' She sighs. 'Well, that's a lie. When your dad pisses me off, of course, I could run for the hills.'

'What about the swinging sixties, when everyone was taking drugs and ripping their clothes off? Did you never feel like joining in?'

'No, love. That never happened in Welston.'

'Mum, can't you just learn to trust the universe…'

'That bloody vampire must have seen you coming, you soft sod.' She knows she shouldn't be speaking to him like this—like a child. She wants to leave it at that but she can't. 'So what's going to happen now?'

§

'America?' Jamie blurts, quickening his pace to keep up with Matthew.

'I know, I know. It's unfair. Especially as we've only just become friends.' Matthew's flapping his hands with excitement, walking heroically towards the funfair—a whirling light of red and yellow mathematical roulette curves and strobe.

Jamie stammers. 'How long are you going for?'

'I'm not sure. Who knows? I might like it so much I—'

'But you've only just met him! At the Gilbert and George exhibition.' Jamie can feel the floor of his stomach dropping from beneath him.

'Oh Jamie, there's the voice of your mother again. I thought you were going to put a stop to that? This is an amazing opportunity for me. And just think… you could come visit.'

'What if the Nkantis come back?' he says, voice rising above the generators and the din of a power-ballad issuing from the waltzers.

'We've been through this,' Matthew says. 'The house will be repossessed at some point but I have certain rights as sitting tenant. Don't worry about it. You'll have the place to yourself.'

Jamie's throat constricts. 'What about the convention we were going to go to?' His words come out high pitched and strangulated. 'The New-Age thing?'

'I know. I'm sorry.' Matthew's voice a tone of robotic mercilessness. 'You can take Billy instead.'

'How can you just drop everything and jet off in three days time to *Boulder, Colorado* or wherever it is? You've only known the man a matter of weeks.'

'There's no need to get upset, Jamie.'

'I'm not.'

'Clearly you are. His name is Dale. I met him in the Crêperie actually, where I met you. I knew as soon as I saw him that he was beautiful and kind and loving.' There's an impatient edge to his voice that makes Jamie retreat inwardly. 'He's really into crystal therapy—something I want to learn about. Jamie, it just feels right. The universe has offered this to me. I have to go.'

'Well I'm not trying to stop you.' Jamie can't look at him.

Matthew stops, grabs him by the shoulders. 'Jamie, what's really bothering you? It's not like we're in a relationship or anything. You've got Billy.' They've reached the middle of the park now. Families walk past them towards the fair.

'I'm being selfish.' Jamie offers after a tense silence.

'I'm sure you're not.' Matthew makes tight fists.

'It's just that...' Jamie looks down at Matthew's neon green socks peeping above suede hiking boots, even though it's nearly October. Even in this light, Jamie can see his gangly, hairless legs are covered with scratches from his rose bushes. He wonders just who is going to tend the garden. 'It's just that I've always dreamed of going to America.'

Matthew's fists open. 'Oh, fuck. Give me a hug.'

Relieved by this release of tension, Jamie flings his arms around him.

'You're going to love it,' Matthew laughs.

'Love what?'

'The USA.'

Jamie pulls away. 'I thought you'd never been?'

Matthew is stunned. 'I haven't,' he says eventually.

'Then how do you know I would love it?'

'I just do.' Matthew pulls Jamie to him again and kisses him on the lips. 'Pull yourself together. I feel like a spin on the waltzers.'

In a carriage on his own, legs spread, locking himself into position, Matthew rides the waltzers three times in a row. He throws his head back and laughs wickedly. Jamie feels sick just to watch.

'You must spin,' Matthew says, stepping off the ride. 'Every day. It helps to make the chakras spin faster, allowing you to interpret and process information faster. Why don't you come on with me?'

'I can't.'

'Why?'

'I'm scared.'

'Trust the universe, Jamie.'

§

Jamie is listening to the music of Philip Glass. Every time he hears that music, it connects him to Matthew. Since he's been away the house has felt so empty. There's been no exotic food or smells. There are no magical conversations about the mysteries of the universe. Life is just a bit dull.

But—no uniform, no checkout—Jamie's booked a week off from work to do *nice* things. He can be like Matthew—hanging out in coffee shops with a notepad, going to the cinema during the *daytime* while it's quieter and cheaper. And ordering takeaway Thai meals.

When the doorbell rings, Jamie checks his appearance in the hall-way mirror and opens the door. He was expecting a delivery man on the doorstep, but instead a tall, smartly-suited and dark-skinned black man, carrying a London A-Z, stands sideways to him on the doorstep.

'Hello.' Jamie smiles widely, yet regrets opening the door—*bloody double-glazing salesmen.*

'I'm looking for Matthew Morris,' the man says.

'I'm sorry. He's not here right now. Can I help?' Jamie folds his arms across his pounding chest.

'I'm Mr Nkanti. I am the owner of this house.'

§

'The desert? You? Oh, Jamie you're not going to last two minutes out there. You're just so...'

'Green?' Jamie replies.

'I was going to say *homely*. A nester.'

'You think I'm not capable.'

'I don't think you should go.' Billy shakes his head. He's wearing the same baseball cap that he'd been wearing when they first met.

'Where else am I going to go? The job at the gallery doesn't start for another few months.'

'Well, you could—'

'I can't stand another *day* with mum and dad, and if I move in with you... Well, you've said it yourself, we'll be tripping over each other in this little room.'

'Jamie, just think about it.'

Jamie looks away. He'll show Billy. 'I have thought about it. You know how much I've always wanted to visit America. Here's my chance. I can go and stay with Matthew. He says it won't cost me a thing. This must be the universe speaking.'

Billy sighs deeply. 'The money is the least of your worries. One sign of a spider and—'

'Watch me. I'm going on this trip. I'll be a different man when I come home.'

§

Wispy threads of silver swirl across a cerulean sky streaked with rose and violet and bright, blinding tangerine. The setting sun reflects off the bonnet of Dale's jeep like a laser, as they pull onto the ridge of Sandia Crest. A halo in front of them is dramatic enough to inspire an almost religious experience in Jamie.

He clutches his copy of *The Prophetic Insights,* the one personal item he didn't leave at Billy's place after the eviction. A photograph of Billy, standing in for a bookmark, is sticking out of the pages. Jamie touches Billy's youthful face with a fingertip. Did they need this much space?

'This is only the beginning,' Matthew says, his mood, perhaps, warming after his strange behaviour at the airport.

'Incredible,' Jamie whispers, unsure if it's Matthew's conduct or the altitude that is unsettling him.

'I wanted you to see this,' Matthew says, now with childlike candour.

As they drive on in silence, above the twinkling lights of Albuquerque and beyond—the meandering snow-capped mountains, Jamie ruminates. They do things differently here. Only an hour ago he'd been on the connecting flight from Houston, Texas to Albuquerque, New Mexico. His first ever long-haul journey had been fucking turbulent. As soon as he'd set foot on American soil, he'd been greeted by stern airport staff, who had been military in their handling of passengers. He'd rushed from one side of the airport to the other to check-in his bags for the connecting flight.

Matthew and Dale met him at the airport in Albuquerque, as arranged. Something was different in Matthew. Perhaps the two of them, Dale and Matthew, had quarrelled prior to his arrival.

'One thing, Jamie,' Matthew said, quite sharply, before Jamie could even set his rucksack down on the tarmac. 'We've used a hell of a lot of diesel getting here and it costs such a lot. We wondered if you would fill the tank up.'

There was absolutely no question of Jamie not paying his way but he hadn't factored in the cost of diesel. On the phone, Matthew had been emphatic about the trip not costing him anything.

'October will be a fantastic time,' Matthew had said. 'It'll be just nearing the end of summer and the *light*—Jamie, the sky goes on forever. You must come for at least a month. It'll still be warm.'

'But you're in the middle of the desert —' Jamie had offered.

'Let the universe take care of everything.' Matthew had said.

Okay, there were a few hundred pounds in his account, saved from his extra shifts at the *Scan'n'Pack*, to get him through the next few months. There was also an overdraft, set up in case of emergencies. But... 'But I only have enough for the airfare. Catching a bus—'

'Dale has money. We'll collect you in the jeep.'

The implication was that they'd changed their minds and he was now just a great inconvenience to them. Realising the cost of filling up that jeep might be all he had in his wallet, Jamie shifted his weight, nervously, from one leg to the other.

He had observed, with some confusion, that Dale seemed a friendly enough person. The blackest of moustaches only served to embellish an already good-natured mouth, through which he'd cheered, 'Heard so much about you.' He carried Jamie's bags to the jeep and offered him water to drink. Matthew, on the other hand, had seemed to be enjoying Jamie's edginess.

'You should ride in the front. You'll get a better view. I don't want you to miss a thing,' Matthew said. 'It's a long drive to Taos, especially at night. So we thought we'd make a stop off, if that's alright— a couple of friends. Tomorrow we'll take the Turquoise Trail, as it's commonly known. We'll be in Taos by tomorrow evening. Take lots of photographs.'

'Yeah, whatever, that's fine,' Jamie said. 'I'm easy.'

'It's just that Dale had to drive all the way here, nearly a day and a half travelling, and it's really not fair for him to have to drive back right now.'

'Oh, I should have brought my driving licence,' Jamie said.

'Don't say 'should' Jamie,' Matthew said. 'It implies a sense of guilt. I 'could', but I didn't. You see, it's not the same thing at all.'

Matthew was so direct. Jamie wanted to believe he was teasing, but it felt like an accusation. He breathed out. 'No, all I meant was—'

'Well, maybe it would have been better for you to have caught a Greyhound,' Dale said.

Now, as they drive from the dark airport, the sky gradually turns lighter as they rise higher up into the mountains, racing towards a disappearing sun. Albuquerque glistens, an emerald city beneath them. On the dark road, the yellow markings curve underneath the jeep as they ascend a serpent of sheer hairpins into the distant Sandia Mountains.

'Pale and Gegger—they're not a couple,' Matthew asserts. 'They live in Gegger's Grandmother's old shack. You're going to really like them.'

Jamie fiddles with his seatbelt. It's all happening so fast. Jet-lag? Altitude sickness? Jamie can't read the situation at all. Maybe he just needs some sleep. 'Are you sure it's alright? I mean, turning up with a complete stranger.'

'Gegger said it would be fine, whenever we were passing.'

§

It's *Pumpkin Season* in New Mexico. With his weighty rucksack leaning against his ankles, Jamie views the front of a duck-egg-blue shack, glowing with pumpkin lanterns in preparation for Halloween. It's reminiscent of a gingerbread house in an illustrated version of Hänsel und Gretel. Rows of dried chilli-peppers hang from the eves of the shack, an ancient pueblo custom according to Matthew.

Night has closed in. Except for the brilliance of the pumpkin lanterns, it's difficult to see. Jamie wonders who could be bothered to light so many candles, out here in the middle of nowhere—such a time-consuming and whimsical thing to do, yet beautiful in effect.

The air is filled with the clicking and popping of insects. A willowy, squinting figure makes its way from the shack, through a hinged bug screen, carrying out trash. Jamie takes the figure for a female in this light: long blonde hair tied back, a lacy, blousy shirt, loose fitting trousers and flip-flops. As his eyes grow accustomed to the darkness, he can see the figure is actually male. The screen slaps shut behind him. He dumps the rubbish, and walks down the small steps towards the jeep.

'Pale,' Matthew calls in a slithery public-relations intonation that Jamie has become familiar with. 'Hi.'

'Hey.' This mono-syllable, in contrast, is not altogether friendly. 'Now what in tarnations do we have here?' Jamie watches Pale's face as they make their *hellos*. It's smooth and elegant and finely boned, as if carved from ivory. Lines like Russian filigree have been hand-tattooed around his lips. He wears eyeliner around deep-set eyes and his long witchlike fingers are tipped with black nail varnish.

'And you must be Jamie,' he starts, in a comparatively kinder manner. 'Look at this. Is this the 1940s?' he says, pointing to Jamie's clothes.

'Original.' Jamie grins, instantly warming to him. He's wearing a vintage Bretton sailor jumper and pair of bell-bottoms, a rather eccentric get up for Houston airport. The outfit had turned a few heads—not in a good way.

'You look fantastic,' he says. 'Let's get inside before the grizzlies come and get you. Gegger has just put the kettle on.'

'Bears?' Jamie says, shuddering.

'If *they* don't get you, the snakes and spiders will.'

'*Spiders?*'

'Tarantulas.'

Jamie lifts his arms into the air and looks around his feet.

'Don't worry.' The man laughs, registering his fear. 'All the spiders will be hibernating now. Too cold for them. Snakes too.' He steps forward and takes Jamie's rucksack. 'I'm Pale.'

Jamie's reticence falls away inside the shack. It resembles a grotto, adorned to excess. Every surface is covered with spooky paraphernalia—skulls, voodoo dolls, incense burners, dream-catchers, masks. Old Indian curios are collected on top of shelves and dressers. There are candles everywhere and the walls are lined with shelves of books about witchcraft and UFOs. A mannequin standing in the corner, is made up to look like Jane Mansfield.

'You like?' Pale asks.

'Oh yeah,' Jamie says. What strikes him most are the paintings that cover the wall surrounding a small fireplace.

'They're mine.' Pale says. Matthew and Dale, have been forgotten, still standing in the doorway. 'Come in, guys, and take a seat.'

They walk in and sit on couches covered in old Indian woven rugs.

'They're beautiful,' Jamie says, staring at the brutal images. Each one seems to be a portrait of a child with a mature adult face, painted with impossibly smooth brush strokes, wearing decorative smocks and suits, like Victorian cameos. Jamie instantly understands that they are therapy for Pale—a seepage of exquisite pain and oil on canvas. The paintings make him feel grounded again.

'I'm looking to have a show in LA. And maybe later in London,' Pale says.

Another man, enters from the kitchen. 'Hello, Jamie,' he says. His unkempt bespectacled face is reminiscent of a young Allen Ginsberg. 'I'm Gegger.' His voice is an aristocratic Vincent Price-like drawl.

After their introductions, Gegger hands Jamie a cup of steaming liquid. 'Green tea. It should help with the fatigue after the distance you've travelled.'

'A fantastic home you have,' Jamie says, admiring the shack.

Dale has made himself comfortable on one of two Arabian style divans, fiddling playfully with his facial hair. Pale seats himself on the opposite divan and pats the space next to him, rearranging cushions and a crocheted blanket to make room for Jamie.

Pale and Gegger amuse Jamie with stories of their past. Pale had been a go-go dancer in various nightclubs—first in San Francisco and later in Los Angeles. The sincerity about his personal life makes Jamie comfortable, even though the subject matter is intimate.

'I started doing porn during my mid-twenties. Easy money. But the filmmakers—they were pretty narrow-minded. They obviously had a certain role in mind, because of my build, and the way I look. I always ended up being the bottom.'

'That must have been pretty demanding.' Two days before, Jamie hadn't expected to find himself talking about the precise details of a sex worker's life but here they are.

'It's difficult to get fucked when you're not aroused. So I took drugs.'

'What kind of drugs?' Jamie imagines a scene in his head: Pale, ass in the air before a shaky camera, surrounded by a camera crew, while having to appear relaxed and desirable for the viewer.

'I got hooked on Tina—crystal meth.'

He'd heard of whole towns in the US that had been ripped apart by this substance. 'It keeps you up for days and you can fuck forever on it.'

Matthew is sucking the inside of his cheek between his teeth, his motif of disapproval. He gets up and walks to the bathroom.

Gegger makes more tea while Pale tells the rest of his story—of moving away from the city to rebuild his life. Gegger, also a recovering addict, from time to time falls off the wagon. 'Pale, darling, I think it might be time for my heroin.'

It was good judgement not to have taken Gracie up on her offer of a career in porn. He admires Pale for his frankness and strength of character—a man whose stories resonate with authenticity. Clearly, Pale's recovery from crystal meth abuse fuels his paintings. Jamie wonders how long it will be before this destructive white powder reaches the streets of Soho. Then he overhears Matthew and Gegger in the kitchen. 'Actually, Jamie hasn't eaten since he got off the plane. Would it be alright to cook something?'

Jamie registers a look of *He's got a nerve!* on Gegger's face.

'If you'd given me more notice,' Pale says. 'I would have prepared something earlier. When you called, I assumed you just—'

'I can do it,' Matthew says. 'I'm at home in anyone's kitchen. Do you have any vegetables? Garlic?'

Jamie leaps up, detecting an obvious animosity between them both. 'I hope you're not going to any trouble on my account.'

Pale touches him on the arm. 'It's fine, honey. You just relax.'

An hour later, they are surrounded by food. 'This is lovely,' Jamie says, looking at the table—cups of wine, bread, soup, green vegetables. 'It's so good of you to do this, Gegger.'

'Thank Matthew. *He* did all the cooking.'

'But I mean to put us up, like this, at short notice.' Jamie locks eyes with Gegger.

'It's fine, our pleasure.' Gegger smiles, reassuringly.

'So, New Mexico?' Jamie asks, shovelling food into his mouth.

'This is the home of Roswell. The infamous airbase where a UFO crash-landed in the 40s. The government allegedly quarantined beings from outer space here.'

'Do you believe all the stories?' Jamie asks.

'If I were to believe all those stories, I really would go mad,' Gegger says. 'New Mexico does have its fair share of crackpots.'

Pale nods. 'Weird tales are official currency in New Mexico.'

Matthew latches onto Jamie's enthusiasm. 'When I was much younger,' he says. 'I went to visit a friend in Cornwall. South of England, Gegger.'

'King Arthur territory.' Gegger sips wine.

'That's right. I was staying in a large house. I was in a room on one side of the building away from everyone else.' Matthew's eyes sparkle; he seemingly loves the attention. Jamie leans closer. 'On the third night, I woke up in bed, sensing something in the room. I'd been sleeping on my own, of course. I was startled. I tried to move to get up. I was fixed. Paralyzed.'

'Were you actually awake?' Pale asks.

'I felt a gentle pressure on the side of my legs, which moved to my thighs.'

'Did you scream?' Pale giggles.

Matthew continues in earnest. 'I couldn't move my lips. The more I tried to move, the more helpless I became. My eyes became accustomed to the light. A thin black figure was leaning over me, face hidden. I knew it wasn't human.'

Here we go again, Jamie thinks.

'I felt it move its hand to my crotch.'

'Oh, brother.' Pale stands and starts collecting plates.

'I was determined not to let this continue. I forced the sound out of my body and shouted a firm 'No!' And then it just faded away.'

'And you say New Mexico is bad.' Jamie looks in Gegger's direction.

Gegger exchanges a look with Pale who's moving behind Matthew with the plates.

After Jamie finishes the washing up, they all settle in the cosy living area. 'Jamie, you know, it's a real pleasure to have you here,' Pale says, in earnest. Jamie feels such joy for having met them both. Yet he senses Matthew isn't so smitten with the idea of them all getting on.

Gegger asks him about his writing and Jamie takes the opportunity to tell him about a collection of stories he's written.

'You didn't tell me you'd published a book,' Matthew says, blankly.

'I wrote three. They were rejected,' Jamie says.

Out of Matthew's deadpan face seeps spiteful satisfaction.

'Three books! It's those who keep going who make it in the end,' Pale says. 'Don't give up. Rise above the competition.'

'We'll get up early and drive along the *Turquoise Trail*.' Matthew says. 'Stopping off at Madrid, Cerrillos and Santa Fe. You'll be amazed by the sights, Jamie. Then we'll head to Taos and the desert where our dome is.'

'Gosh. You live all the way out there, do you?' Gegger asks.

'Taos is to the New-Age movement as Mecca is to Islam.' Pale says, emphatically. 'There are no children in the town. It's full of transients, nomads and orphans. No-one actually grows up there.'

'The day after tomorrow, we'll be getting ready for the party,' Matthew says.

'Party?' Jamie blushes nervously.

'In *your* honour. It's going to be just wonderful.'

'Swell,' Pale says, an odd look passing across his face.

'It'll be Jamie's initiation to things,' Matthew adds.

Initiation. The hairs on the back of Jamie's neck stand on end.

'You'll be coming, of course?' Dale asks.

Gegger looks at Pale.

'You must,' Matthew says, placing a bony hand on Jamie's shoulder.

A corner of Pale's mouth curls up. 'Yes. We'll come.'

'You don't have to come on my account,' Jamie says. 'It's so far!' Drive across the desert? To go to a party? It's inconceivable to him.

Gegger tilts his head at Jamie, a look signalling something between alliance and fatherly reassurance. 'We can't let this be the last time we see you, Jamie. And a party in Taos desert—who could stay away?'

§

Shaken from sleep, Jamie feels Matthew's fingers probing his ribs.

'We have to go *now*, if you're going to catch it,' Matthew whispers.

'Catch what?' Jamie moans and pulls sheets up over his shoulders.

'The sunrise from Sandia Crest.' Matthew looks at him in

astonishment, as if he'd committed an act of blasphemy.

Jamie's so tired his eyes roll back inside his head. 'What time is it?'

'Five-thirty.'

§

The rising golden disc behind translucent cotton wool clouds makes the sky look as if it is on fire. From an aesthetic point of view, no one can argue that it's not spectacular but Jamie has never really understood the symbolism that people attach to sunrises. They're a bit like New Year's Eve; expectation unreached. He casts his mind back to the last one he'd seen. He must have been about fourteen. He, Gloria and Roy had sat looking at the golden fire above the ocean from the coastland of the Gower Peninsula. A week before, at school, he'd been beaten, badly: the usual thugs. From the beginning of that holiday, he'd been afraid to take his shirt off on the beach, ashamed of the bruises, fearing that he would expose who, no, *what* he was. There are darknesses that no amount of sunlight can take away.

Sitting next to Matthew on a rock at Sandia Crest, the sun has started to spill onto the buildings out in front of him, vast swathes of golden light seeping out of the mothership.

'Just look at it. A new day,' Matthew says. And then he turns to Jamie. 'A new life.'

§

Miles of open road stretch out in front of them, punctuated now and then by old colonial church buildings, disused gas stations and telegraph poles. Desert plains turn incongruously into mountain ranges low on the horizon as the lone jeep cruises languidly along the tarmac. The sun, at its zenith, creates no shadows on an alien landscape that seems to beat and breathe as if it is alive.

They stop off, firstly at Madrid, a mining town, almost exclusively populated by lesbians, then spend a few hours in the state's artistic capital, Santa Fe, where they load up the back of the jeep with pumpkins. It seems Matthew wants so much for him to like all of this. Dale had been so kind in fetching him from the airport. It would be

ungrateful and ridiculous to whine about homesickness. He misses
the concrete reassurances of Billy. He'd do anything for one of his
hugs. And any talk of London lowers the temperature and triggers a
change of subject. Matthew points to the decorative dried chillies on
the eaves of the buildings and collections of pots. 'This is traditional
Indian pueblo work.'

In the afternoon they set off for Taos. The jeep roars down through
sagebrush desert. Jamie feels the wind tickle his hair. He's connected
to something primal as they move over one more ridge and toward
the Sangre de Christo Mountains ascending before them.

'It's so different here. Sometimes I feel I'm on another planet,' Matthew says. 'The people are extraordinary. Everyone has some sort of
quirk. Prunella Small—'

'Author of *The Prophetic Insights*?'

'Yes, I've been doing some housekeeping for her.'

Jamie twists to look behind at Matthew. 'You're kidding?'

'She has this healing machine, invented by a Russian scientist.'
Matthew's voice is flat, as if talking about something banal like having forgotten to empty the laundry basket. 'It works by analysing a
person's aura and presenting the results visually.'

Jamie reaches into this rucksack for a pad and pen. Glimpses of
character and dialogue like this will surely make it into a book he
writes one day.

'Aurographs are a bit old hat, Matthew, no?'

'It's not an aurograph. *This* is interactive. Let's say for instance, you
have bowel cancer—just hypothetically. The defective energy pattern
would show on the machine.'

Jamie nods.

'They use the machine to project energy into the affected area. Thus
making you well again. It's revolutionary.'

'Sounds rather Frankensteinian to me.'

'Listen, it could help people with all sorts of cancers. It could help
people with HIV and AIDS. And they have it here, right in the middle of New Mexico.'

'So how come they're not using this technology in England, on the
NHS.'

'Only just scratched the surface,' Matthew says.

Jamie looks at Matthew's sickly pallor and hasn't got the nerve to ask if this is why he came here. 'Suppose it got into the wrong hands. Too much energy in the wrong areas. You could really fuck someone up.'

'Exactly. She's had her fair share of detractors.'

The Taos desert fills his vision like the sound of an organ filling an empty church.

Matthew points to a tiny speck in front of them. 'See the groove? That's the Rio Grande. See the tiny dot in the desert about a mile above it?'

'Yes.'

'That's the dome.'

'Incredible, isn't it?' Dale says. 'Home.'

The setting sun bathes everything in a final warm glow, as they pull up outside the dome. It then falls behind the mountains, and an immense shadow flies towards them, covering the surface of the desert, as swift as a bed sheet being drawn across a mattress.

Speechless, Jamie steps from the vehicle and almost loses his footing, as he makes contact with Taos soil.

'We rented it from an architect,' Dale says.

The geodesic dome, constructed entirely of tessellated triangles, is set in the desert like a crash-landed spaceship. The living quarters, it would appear, are partially above and below ground. There's a freshwater tank to one side of the dome and large solar panel. The smell of shit, floating in a barrel of chemical is masked, only partially, by a small herb garden and fruit trees.

Matthew sets about lighting a fire inside a ring of stones. Inside the dome is decorated with bright colours and Mexican patterned textiles, which remind Jamie of retreats he's read about in books. 'It's like a hippy commune,' Jamie jokes.

Dale shows Jamie to the loft that will be his sleeping area, in the upper hemisphere of the dome. 'The walls are plastered adobe style to keep the room cool during the summer and warm in the winter.'

Jamie changes into jeans and a fleece before joining them beside Matthew's fire. It crackles and pops. Dry rocks, packed with air trapped inside them, explode spectacularly, sending Matthew wild with childlike joy. He turns around on the spot, beginning his spinning routine. The fire draws up dry leaves and dust, the way fire does, sending a blizzard of burning snowflakes falling upwards.

'Does it get cold like this every night?' Jamie says.

'Yes,' Dale says. 'I think it may snow, very soon.'

Matthew stops revolving.

'Snow?' Hadn't Matthew said the weather would be warm? Jamie's hardly prepared for winter. Matthew turns away. Jamie feels like he's been set up. He clenches his teeth together, thinking about two months here in the cold.

In the distance, there are a few caravans, a couple of earth-ships and a stockade surrounding a large motorhome. Further away, highlighted by the last strip of orange sunlight, Taos glistens like a spillage of caster sugar on a kitchen work surface. This is the only other sign of real civilization for miles and separating Jamie from it, the valley of the Rio Grande.

'How long does it take to get to Taos centre from here, Dale?'

'About forty-five minutes.'

'Walk?'

'No. Drive. You couldn't walk, really. There's only one bridge across the ravine and that's over there,' Dale says, pointing blindly into the expanse, which is now mostly in shadow. 'I suppose you could hitch-hike. But it's fine, you'll come with us, in the jeep.'

Jamie squints at the sprinkling of golden sugar. Dale points to the snow-capped Sangre de Christo Mountains. That's a ski-resort, at this time of year.'

'What's behind the mountains?' Jamie asks.

'Colorado,' Dale says.

'And beyond that?'

'Utah.'

Jamie processes a thought. He looks across the landscape at Taos, and the thought emerges.

Snow.

§

A chill nip wakes Jamie. Through a little window in the domed loft he can see a panorama, as if sprinkled with desiccated coconut, interrupted occasionally by the skeletal branches of sagebrush and a baleen of aspens bristling at the edge of the forest.

The many thousands of miles travelled have left an impression on Jamie's aching body. Matthew and Dale are already up, making breakfast, listening to the weather report. He struggles to lift himself off the bed. 'Morning all.'

They watch what can only be described as *limited news*—something about homeless pets in Albuquerque, a mystery shooting in Roswell, 120 Elk found dead near to a crop circle, while Matthew serves omelettes. There's nothing about Britain, London, the rest of the world.

'We're lucky if we hear anything about the rest of America, let alone the UK. It's how they control us,' Dale says, from the round sofa in the circular living area.

'They like to keep people impaired.' Matthew turns off the TV in protest.

All day they prepare for the party. Jamie collects firewood. Matthew spends hours cooking and Dale carves hideous faces in the pumpkins they transported from Santa Fe.

'It's going to be just wonderful,' Matthew says.

But who will come? Apart from the odd caravan plot and the four or five nearby earth-ships, there are no neighbouring desert inhabitants. Not enough guests for a knitting circle, let alone a *party*.

'They'll come,' Matthew says. 'Believe me.'

At eight o'clock, Jamie stands before the large picture window, as the sun creeps down an orange and purple sweet-wrapper sky. A faint sketch of road, crosses the Rio Grande, picked out by a fine trail of car head-lamps twinkling like fairy lights. 'Look at that,' Jamie says. He feels a sense of dread, as if about to go on stage in front of thousands to sing a song to which he does not know the words.

'The guests,' Matthew squeals.

'There must be forty or fifty vehicles in convoy,' Jamie says, pointing and counting. 'Who would cross a desert for someone they never met?'

'I told you it's going to be special.'

Twenty minutes later, the three of them are outside smelling the creosote bushes still wet from frost and the smoke from a beacon of fire lit earlier by Dale. A lady in a turquoise jogging-suit springs out of a rusty old car. The car cannot be hers, *surely*. He knows she's got money to burn, with that book selling out worldwide.

'Prunella!' Matthew shrieks, performing a sycophantic pantomime of bending and flapping. 'You made it!'

'Mercury might be in retrograde but of course I made it,' she says. 'What did you expect—that we'd miss the turning and plummet into the Rio Grande? I brought my faithful driver with me.' A portly man climbs out of the driver's side. He looks like he's going woodcutting rather than to a party. Matthew had sketched in the details earlier, local sheriff, always 'on duty'. Though what sort of heinous crime could occur here in the desert, Jamie couldn't guess.

'Steve!' Matthew cries, as if they are long lost relatives.

Prunella might be anything from fifty-five to seventy-five years old. It's impossible to place her age. Her face, framed by a helmet of curly white hair, is hidden behind large turquoise sunglasses. She's tiny next to Matthew, not at all like the image Jamie had in his head. Flinging her arms wide, a bottle in each hand, she greets Matthew with a hug. He has to stoop. *Inside,* he beckons, *come, come.*

As they move inside, Matthew introduces Jamie to Prunella. Tiny as she is, she's also a gushy and expansive *let's talk about me* sort of character. *Look at me—my aura is clean. I can turn lead into gold. You too can be like me. I even wrote a book about it. Positivity is the key. Banish negativity. Out! Out! Out! Open your heart to the universe. Behold the new era. Let the vibration of light penetrate you. See it. Create it. Grasp it. The Universe will support you in your work.*

Jamie is mute. He'd always imagined meeting her. He would be vivacious and entertaining and she would find him charming. But no—he cannot find the words. He'd thought she might be more, well, friendly.

'Jamie,' she purrs, standing in the middle of the dome. 'It's so wonderful to have you here in Taos, after so long. Matthew tells me you're writing a book,' she says, with an affirming smile.

'Well, I have a few ideas but—'

'You wanna write a book—*write a book*! Put the energy out there and it will come back to you, tenfold.'

'Thank you. I'll give it a go,' he says, politely.

'Trust me, honey.'

'It's good to meet you,' he says, awkwardly.

'We've been waiting for your *return*, Jamie.'

What does she mean? There's no sense in challenging her. A question would only open up another can of spaghetti symbols. It might be easier just to go along with it all.

By half-past eight the dome is crowded with people. How Matthew has got to know so many people in the short time he's been here, Jamie has no idea. There must be fifty or sixty people and more arriving all the time. Matthew hands Jamie a tray of food to take round, a task he exploits in order to meet everyone in the room. He can feel their Taos eyes upon him, working him out; even fingers pointing. That's *him. He's the one Matthew told us about.*

He bumps into a woman, swathed in purple crushed velvet. She's about fifty. *Dyed* hair. If she's prepared to use chemicals, then she can't be *that* New Age.

'I'm Bunni,' she says. 'Jamie, yes?'

Everyone in the room knows who he is but *he* doesn't know any of them.

'You're going to do great work here, with Matthew. I know it.'

'I'm sorry... *work?*'

'Well, I don't mean *work*, work. You'll take to it easily.'

'I don't follow.'

'You're working on *The Book*, aren't you?'

'You mean, my writing.'

'I mean *The Book*.' She nods and smiles.

He inhales deeply. 'I'm working on *a* book.'

'You know, the light coming from your aura is extraordinary.'

A few months ago, he might have fallen for this. He'd have even convinced himself that he could see his aura—beautiful colours surrounding him like a halo. Matthew had once said he could read them—stare into the invisible light and say how someone was feeling or what kind of person they were.

'Same colour as Matthew's,' Bunni says. 'Well, it would be, wouldn't it?'

'Why? Jamie fixes a smile and forms his eyes into a question.

'You being *brothers*.'

'Is that what he told you—that we're brothers?' He hears his voice slide high, as he looks over at the kitchen—Matthew slicing lemons, mixing some concoction with herbs in it.

Bunni's arm, strangled from wrist to elbow with bangles, reaches out and clutches him. Jamie looks at the hand squeezing his arm, aiming, possibly, to reassure, until it retreats again, fingers sparkling with clusters of opals. 'I know you're not siblings in your *human* form. Perhaps you've blocked it out.'

'I'm not blocking anything,' he assures her, stiffly folding his arms.

'This is the site, where you landed. From the Hermetes.'

'Hermetes?' Now he feels a violent urge to bite her.

'A star constellation, on the other side of our sun.'

'Look, I didn't. I'm from the UK.'

'Still holding onto personal information that you've learned to carry. Usually, folk have worked through this by now. Don't worry. We'll help you prepare.'

They've got him entirely wrong. He's partly incredulous, partly—

'Listen to me.' She leans into him. 'You and Matthew were separated and now you're reunited, at last, to do great work here in Taos.'

Jamie has brought himself to this place. So many unanswered questions about the universe—now he wishes he'd never asked. Obviously, extra-terrestrials exist but to suggest that *he* is one of them— no, that's going off the script. If only he'd listened to his mother. Sceptical and scared of taking risks she might be, but she is at least a good judge of character. It is all rather *Emperor's New Clothes*. What should he do now? Pretend that he can actually see the finest silk and blend in with the others, or—expose them for what they are?

Bunni is prattling on about them all being from the family of light and all this important work they have to do while they are in the physical plane.

'We are all emerging from denial,' she says. 'Even Prunella has found it hard. In fact, her own family have turned against her. She adored her grandson. They won't let her see him anymore. They think she's a bad influence. But she's committed to the project, so she accepts she has to let go.'

Jamie's chest tightens. Her mad glassy eyes drill into his as she burbles on and on about him needing to let go of the personal information that comforts him during his time on Earth. 'It anchors you to the physical realm and keeps you separate from the universal pool of wisdom—your family, your birthplace, your name. You must let it all go before you become non-physical again and return to the light.'

He hears no emotion or irony in her voice. 'After the initiation, a process to remove this information will commence.'

'Initiation?'

'I think it will make Matthew feel better when you return to the family. Must be a bit strange for you. Though I wouldn't say too much to the others about that. Resistance tends to cause negative vibrations.'

Across the room, Gegger and Pale have arrived. Pale's wearing a black cat-suit with a silver O-ring belt. His blonde hair, plaited and swirled up on his head, is more suited to a swanky art opening in New York City, than a glass dome in the sagebrush desert. Gegger looks gloomy in his beat blacks and his wayfarer half-framed glasses. Jamie grins in their direction, eager to catch their attention and escape Bunni. Matthew sweeps Pale and Gegger from him, across the room to the hexagonal couch near Prunella.

Bunni touches him on the elbow. He flinches and she withdraws, as if expecting him to hit her—her fat little fingers tipped with green nail varnish, remain hanging in the air.

'Matthew has been through a lot recently,' she says. 'He was almost abducted again, when the *others* came.'

'Abducted?'

Recovering now, she opens cigarette papers, preparing to roll. 'They're constantly fighting for occupancy of this land.'

'They should give it back to the Indians, if you ask me,' Jamie says, partially under his breath, trying to bring things back to reality.

Bunni looks across the room at a Native American Indian man. 'Shamboo, over there. He'll tell you about it. He was abducted too. It's not uncommon in these parts. And so was my son. And then we found out about you—'

'You've made a mistake. I've never been abduc—'

'It's the block again.' She puts the joint in her mouth and sparks up. 'The others—the dark ones are trying to deplete our resources. They want to see how we've evolved. That's why they perform the abductions.'

Jamie surveys the room. 'Bunni, I really must say hello to a few more people. Do you mind if I circle the room? We can continue later.'

She holds the joint up to him. 'Do you think they'll mind?'

He shakes his head. 'Matthew doesn't like smoke.'

'He's so pure, isn't he? Do you want some?'

He'd love to numb the evening away but he doesn't trust what might be inside the joint. 'No, thank you.'

He heads for Gegger and Pale. Matthew catches him by the elbow. 'Getting to know everyone?'

Jamie tries to look cheery. Pale and Gegger are chatting to Prunella Small, stunned looks on their faces.

'We're extremely lucky to be amongst such special people,' Matthew says. 'Come on, I want you to meet Steve. He's one of us.'

One of us? Fuck! They're all bonkers. Steve, ordinary as he looks, in his plaid shirt and Stetson, sounds eccentric to say the least. 'You're waking up from that trance state, Jamie,' Steve says. 'Try not to be sceptical. You are an artist. An artist's job is to tell the truth.' Jamie fiddles with his shirt cuffs, trying to avoid Steve's intensity. 'Think of the great artists and writers. Look at Orwell, Verne, Arthur C. Clarke. We are living in their future. Do people need any further convincing? All will become clear after the initiation.'

Steve rambles on, turning now to Prunella, using words that Jamie struggles to catch the meaning of. Prunella rattles off soundbites from the self-help universe—about enlightened beings, a new world order. When the subject turns to some conspiracy at government level, Jamie is able to peel off and finally makes his way across the dome to Gegger and Pale.

'Jesus, am I glad to see you two.'

Their forced smiles can't disguise their alarm. 'What on Earth are you doing here?'

Jamie stares, unsure of the answer.

'You don't fit with these people,' Pale says. He leans in close and lowers his voice. 'These people are not your friends, Jamie. I knew from the moment I met you at our shack. You've been unfortunate to get mixed up with them.'

A mixture of fear and loyalty rises up in Jamie's stomach. 'Hang on a minute—Matthew is my friend.' He glances over at Matthew, who is raising his voice to Bunni in the open plan kitchen area. 'What's the problem? It's just a doobie,' he can hear her saying over the din of the party. Then Matthew is pouring some green liquid infused with herbs from a bottle and laughs spitefully at something with Prunella.

'You should hear the stuff they've been telling us,' Gegger says.

Jamie turns back to them, now less defensively. 'Thank God I'm only staying for two months.'

'*Two months!*' Gegger leans forward to rest a hand on Jamie's shoulder, close enough for him to get a whiff of Gegger's peppery cologne. 'Look, we know we've only just met you, but we have no hesitation in telling you this. You are lovely person. We really like you. Matthew, no.'

'Like I said, he's my friend.'

'*Is* he though?' Pale asks.

On the face of it, Matthew knows far more about Jamie than Jamie knows about Matthew. For all those months, what does he have to show for it? A collection of half-believable stories.

Gegger sits back on the couch, his black velvet undertaker's suit crushed behind guardedly folded arms.

'He's different now,' Jamie concedes.

'You think he was ever interested in you?' Pale asks. 'I can't believe they dragged you out of bed yesterday morning to see the sun come up. You'd been on a plane for thirteen hours, for fucksake.'

'But he's your friend too.'

Gegger snorts. 'Oh brother! Is that what he told you?' He lowers his voice, forcing Jamie even closer. 'We met at an arts festival in Santa Fe. Pale only mentioned we had a shack in the mountains and that was it—couldn't get rid of him. This is only the fourth time we've met him.'

Pale sits forward now, in a persuasive gesture. 'It's so isolated here. Why don't you come back with us, to Sandia Park? At least you'll be closer to Albuquerque.'

'I came all this way to see Taos, to visit my friend. I think I have to give it a chance. After the conversations I've had tonight, I could run screaming into the desert. But I ought not to overreact.'

He remembers what he'd said to Billy. There's no way he's going to

go back on his word and have Billy harp on about him being a feath-
erweight. In any case, where the hell would he go? It's the American
trip or back to Welston with his tail between his legs. No. Just no.

He tells them about the things Bunni and Steve had said to him.
Pale and Gegger stare at him. 'Jamie, we've been talking to that lady,'
Pale says, finally. 'The one with the glasses. I think she's in control.
She told us about a crazy old machine that she has at her place.'

Gegger takes over, 'This whole story has been documented in *Esoteric Magazine*. They look human. But on their own planet, they
manifest as reptiles. Lizards. I think *these* people are *them*.'

Jamie laughs. 'Now you're starting to sound like them.' The feeling of being in danger disappears. 'That machine! How can anyone
take it seriously?'

Even Pale has turned to Gegger now with a look of incredulity.
'You don't really believe in all that, do you, Gegger?'

Gegger says, 'Doesn't matter if *I* do or don't. The point is, *they do*!
They say they're the oldest living civilized race on Earth. *They* were
here before we were.'

Pale shakes his head slowly and pulls an object from his bag,
wrapped in tissue. 'For you,' he says.

'From both of us,' Gegger says.

Jamie tears the paper away to reveal a candle in a glass jar. This
one has a brightly coloured image of the Virgin Mary emblazoned
across one side, not unlike the iconography that adorned the house
in London.

'It's the Mary of Guadalupe. We want you to keep this for a time
when you need some help,' Pale says.

Jamie frowns. He'd thought they were generally spiritual but not
religious. What should he do—risk fate with the lizards or allow himself to be saved by two guys who might also have an agenda?

Gegger shakes his head. 'Not any old trivial problem, like losing
your door key or forgetting your mother's birthday.'

Pale takes over. 'No, save this for when something is really getting
to you—when you meet with a difficult situation that you just can't
get through on your own. Whatever the problem is, write it here,' he
taps Mary on the chest. 'Then burn the candle down. Burn it every
night until it's gone.

'I know it seems like a strange gift to give to somebody, but if you really won't come with us, we'd like you to have it. Please. Just humour us.' Pale looks over at Matthew in the kitchen. 'At least until you are safely back home.'

Jamie nods. 'Thank you. That means a lot.'

He looks at their sombre faces fixed with horror. 'I'd like us to keep in touch,' he says. 'I'll write and give you a debrief, as soon as I'm home.'

'You'd better,' Pale says.

Would they bother writing back? 'Don't forget to let me have your address before you leave,' he says.

Later, Matthew draws everyone's attention by clinking a spoon on a wine glass. He makes everyone charge their glasses, points in Jamie's direction and makes a toast to him, the new member of their family. Pale and Gegger's glasses remain on the table.

Billy would taunt him over this. This was like one of those daft action-adventure comedies in which one character always ends up unwittingly lost in a desert, or kidnapped by smugglers, in need of rescue by the romantic hero. Well, he doesn't need rescuing. He'll show them all. Later, he'll hold court at dinner parties, quaffing good wine. He'll know about wine, of course. He'll share this moment with his friends. *Academics*. They'll all laugh at the absurdity of it all.

Through the large picture window at the front of the dome, Jamie stares into the blackness of the desert. The red brake lights of Gegger's car burn bright like two hot embers in dwindling fire. If he ran out there now, he wouldn't be too late to stop them. Then Gegger lets the brake off and pulls away so that now only the rear red lamps glow, getting smaller, as they move down the track away from the dome towards the road across the Rio Grande. He is overwhelmed with self-pity, homesickness and terror as they disappear.

§

As Dale drops them in the sleepy town that is Taos, Jamie rubs his temples, his hangover only now beginning to ease. There aren't many people around. Matthew remarks that it's a tourist trap, but to Jamie it appears an out-of-season holiday resort. Shutters cover most of the shop windows and only a few little galleries are open.

'You know, it might be an idea for you to spend more time on your own. You could hitch-hike into town.' Matthew strides ahead. 'You have all this to explore.'

Jamie scampers along the street, a few paces behind. 'What would I do? Everything is boarded up. Why would I come to town on my own? I came here to spend time with you.'

'Don't forget, I do need a bit of time for myself.'

This is cold water in his face but as they reach Cafe Christo, Matthew smiles so widely and in such a friendly manner, Jamie wonders if he'd misheard. 'Deep at my centre is an overflowing pool of love,' he says, repeating one of his affirmations. 'I am safe in the universe. I am at peace wherever I go. I trust life.' He winks and pushes open the door.

A bell above the door jangles. Inside, Shamboo and Prunella are reading the morning newspapers at opposite ends of a long bench with a table each to themselves. Steve serves himself coffee and carrot cake and leaves the cash on the counter. Does this man do any work in a town devoid of crime? Jamie wonders why he's not rushed off his feet with all the UFO landings and alien abductions.

'I'll have a piece of walnut cake and an Earl Grey tea,' Matthew says, taking a seat at Shamboo's table. Jamie seems to be paying for everything. Already he had parted with cash for diesel, alcohol and food for the party. When the waitress returns, Jamie buys drinks and cake, and shyly slips in next to Prunella, who is tapping the seat beside her.

'Lovely to see you again,' she says, shaking the newspaper out in front of her. 'The world is very ill. *Your* time has come.' She pats the paper down and stares into Jamie. 'We waited so long for Matthew. And now *you're* here.'

Steve wipes coffee from his mouth with a serviette. 'Prunella has been channelling the Hermetians for a long time,' he says. 'And then he came.'

Jamie contemplates the validity of her convictions. '*He* doesn't seem to know...'

'He has a little way to go,' Prunella whispers and marks the air in front of her with a pointed finger. 'Like yourself. He's still to let go of a great deal of personal information.' Glancing over at him, it occurs to Jamie that Matthew has already started letting go. He had never called his own mother, not in front of Jamie at any rate, and he never, ever mentioned his family. He'd become remote. Is this what they wanted? Rather than letting go, Jamie had always thought the point of being human was to become more connected, to evolve and share thoughts and ideas until a kind of hive mind could be achieved. Or maybe he'd just been watching too much *Star Trek*.

'Everything alright, dear?' Prunella asks.

Jamie tries to think of a way to ingratiate himself with her. 'You remind me of my grandmother,' he says, finally.

Prunella rubs him gently on the arm and whispers into his ear. 'Did you bring the book?'

Jamie lifts the book from his satchel and sets it on the table. Prunella raises a hand over the worn copy of *The Prophetic Insights,* hovering above the cover. 'You've been busy.'

'I've read it three times,' Jamie says.

'A scholar. But there are more important books to read than just mine. Dip into Betty Shine or Shirley MacLaine.' She opens the book and writes:

> *The divine truth will set you free, Jamie.*
> *Prunella Small*

Jamie thanks her and hides the book away. 'It's odd, don't you think, that you don't really get any 'world' news here?' he says.

'Don't we?' Prunella asks.

'In the UK, we get news reports from all over. Here, the news seems to be very localized.'

'It sounds to me that England is a completely awful place to be at present. There's talk of this 'foot 'n' hoof"

'Foot and *mouth*,' Jamie says. 'It's like flu.'

'And then there's 'Mad Cow's Disease'. I read only yesterday that there are actually crazy animals walking the streets of England.'

Jamie levels his eyes at this bestselling author. 'The animals are mostly contained in farms. You don't honestly believe—'

She touches him on the hand. 'I like you, Jamie. If there's one thing

I respect, it's emotional honesty.' Prunella tilts her head to one side, as if sympathising with a naïve child. Then she looks over at Matthew pontificating.

§

The spite in Matthew's voice has been ringing in Jamie's ears for days. And the days, filled with so much space and so little activity, are long. Jamie sits on Matthew's bed, confronting the mirror wondering how long it would be before they return. It's been five minutes already since they went off in the jeep to run errands. He leans toward his reflection and tugs at an eyelash, pulling it from the space where he has pulled six or seven others, leaving a little gap. He pinches the tiny hair between his thumb and forefinger, and then brings it to his mouth, feeling its end, as sharp as a cactus spine, on his tongue. He resists the urge to pull another and then another until a noticeable break appears in the row of eyelashes. Though as soon as he stops pulling and looks at the vast desert just outside the window, the thoughts rush in again. How did he end up here? What has he got himself into? Why is Matthew behaving so differently? He can't stop the thoughts. Round and round in his head they go. In just a few days, Jamie's heavy-duty reality has become unreliable and nebulous. Every time he allows his mind to dwell upon the situation, his world becomes askew and he feels like running to the toilet.

He presses fingernails into the flesh of his forearm and tries to focus on one real thing at a time. He's in New Mexico, yes. He's here of his own free will, yes. Matthew is his friend and everyone has been nice to him. Yes and yes. They believe in things from another planet. Yes. And Jamie doesn't because those things are lizards. *Lizards.*

Four crescents glow red from where his fingernails dug into the skin—an attempt to keep him in the here and now. He rubs his face, greasy with anxiety. He's twitchy and unable to rest. His mood isn't helped at all by sleep interrupted by a howling animal outside his window. Lizards from another planet. It can't be real.

He lies back on Matthew's bed, staring at the telephone—his only link to world he calls home. If only he'd never started reading those damn books.

He pulls Matthew's duvet up to his neck and clasps the phone to his ear. When he dials Billy's number the first time, there's just the unobtainable tone. He tries again and it rings and rings. Come on, Billy. Please pick up. He leaves it ringing but can't even connect to his answering machine.

After sitting numbly for a minute, he dials his mother's number. He swallows, straightens his back—she's always telling him not to slouch so—takes a breath, ready to deepen his voice—so as not to sound shrill or frantic. Ringing out. Same pattern, no answer, no beep. He *needs* to speak to someone in England, about the mundanity of life, weather, salacious gossip—anything other than crystals, lizards and *Mercury* being in *retrograde*—whatever that means.

Has he brought this upon himself? That's what they'd say. *Every thought we think manifests itself physically. We create our reality.*

He makes three more calls—Gracie, David and Auntie Sandra—the only numbers he can remember off the top of his head. He can't get through. It's like being in the Bermuda triangle. He wonders if he might have slipped through a gap in space and time.

Slamming the phone back on its cradle, he stares out of Matthew's window. It frames the emptiness stretching away into infinity. The flat grey of the sky meets the green-grey of the land, reminding him of an abstract painting made on a giant canvas with a roller. Loneliness consumes him. Across the room in the mirror he sees, dark circles around his eyes, sunken cheeks. He's wasting away. 'All is well where I am,' he whispers, really needing it to mean something. 'The universe supports me in all that I do. I am surrounded by love.'

'The universe loves you, Jamie.' The voice is unannounced from behind him. Jamie spins round, grasping a pillow to his chest. Matthew stands in the doorway. 'Isn't it beautiful?' he says.

Matthew stares out of the picture window. A fine sprinkling of snow is settling on the ground for as far as it's possible to see.

'Do you think it will get worse?' Jamie asks.

'I guess it could. Imagine, white over. It'll be like a dream—picture postcard.'

§

'Mable Dodge House was once home to artists and writers such as Georgia O'Keefe and D.H. Lawrence,' Matthew trumpeted, tourist guide fashion, when he dropped Jamie off. Now alone, Jamie trudges through the snowy ghost town, towards the most famous adobe building in New Mexico. It's nearest equivalent in England would be a stately home. Leaving Matthew behind for his tarot appointment with Dorothy at Cafe Christo, Jamie tries to focus on something else: his father. Roy had always enthused over the *National Trust Guidebook* when Jamie was a young boy. When he was a teenager they had targeted the castles, houses and ruins of the UK. Mable Dodge House is simply another historic building to add to his list. He remembers vividly the long walks, the hours of staring at exhibits—when, in fact, Jamie had always wanted to go to Butlins. But now the musty smell of the rooms, antiquated books, the linseed of the oil paintings makes him feel closer to Roy. With a close friend or a travelling partner he might enjoy the artwork, the scenery, the atmosphere. Alone, all he can think of is going home. He writes as much as he can in the little journal, knowing that, when this is over, when he finally gets back, he'll want to plunder these emotions, these episodes, for a novel perhaps.

Matthew insisted he would love the house. 'It's full of curiosities that you will find fascinating,' Matthew had said as he pressed a couple of books on to Jamie. Not his thing, at all. He'd once felt an obligation to like the things that Matthew liked but he's given up trying to be so agreeable. He doesn't like the spooky old house.

Alone amongst the relics—an opportunity to reconnect with himself—Jamie searches himself for a fragment, something buried deep within him—an abduction, an arrival, a half-brother. The memory must be there, if it actually *happened*. When Matthew talks about them all 'coming from the stars,' this is what he means. Jamie's seen programmes on television about people who have repressed memories of having been taken in flying saucers, intrusive scientific experiments performed on them. He's waiting for it now, a horrifying flashback of having been violated. He would know if that had happened to *him*. Wouldn't he?

Back outside in the chill air, vapour plumes from his nostrils, as he strides, to the Zen Garden, an art gallery supporting Taos painters.

The plan was to walk to Taos Plaza where he would meet Matthew and Dale. The anticipation of being with them again makes him feel a little sick. All three of them are to travel to the ancient Indian Pueblo—a museum, as it were, where Native American Indians live as they did before their land was taken. The very idea of it upsets Jamie.

Dragging his feet along the dirt road, Jamie comes across a phone booth. For a moment, less than a moment, his heart springs. Speak to Billy. Though there's the seven-hour time difference. He'll be getting ready for college. Perhaps his mother then? She'll be on her day off. He feels for coins in his pockets, paces up to the booth. Scanning his mind for the international dialling code, a lump forms in his stomach, as he lifts the receiver. A clump of silver now in his fist. It's ringing. A click and a beep and he's emptying coins into the slot.

'Hello.' There it is—his mother's voice.

'Mum!' He pictures Gloria immediately—hand on hip, self-assured, immaculate hair, even for the housework, silk-dressing gown, mules—lounge kitten.

'I was just thinking of you. Couldn't you have called a bit sooner?'

'I tried to call at the beginning of the week. I've had trouble getting through.'

Click-click-click. The phone gulps his money.

'I'm in a phone box.'

'Doesn't Matthew have a phone?'

'I've not got many coins. I just called to let you know I arrived safely.'

'Alright, love,' she says. Her voice is tender and homely. He wishes he could be transported to her right now. 'Save your money. Have a lovely trip.'

'I will.'

'Are you eating properly?'

'Matthew cooked a lovely soup with coriander and ginger.'

'Coriander?'

'They use it in Indian cooking.' Jamie pauses. Breathes deeply. 'Are you okay?'

'Yeah, I'm fine,' she says. 'Why wouldn't I be? Auntie Sandra's coming over for coffee. I think she and Freddie are arguing again. What's the weather like?'

'Oh it's, you know—' He runs out of coins. The line goes dead. Damn!

Why hadn't he listened to his mother? Why hadn't he gone to Albuquerque with Pale and Gegger?

He sets off for the plaza, assessing the situation. He'll go to the café for some change. He walks across town, snow crunching under his feet, until he sees Matthew outside a bookshop. Jamie walks over to join him. 'Hey. Don't suppose you've got any loose coins?'

Matthew's face contorts into a twist of anger. 'You've not listened to a word I've been saying, have you?' Jamie takes a step backwards. 'I thought I made it clear yesterday. I need time to myself.'

'Matthew—' the word comes out shrill and begging.

Matthew's eyes bulge. 'I can't look after you all the time,' he snarls.

'I don't expect you to,' Jamie says, bracing himself now. 'Matthew, this is ridiculous. I've been reading, writing. Do you really expect me to hitchhike into town? No one around. It's fucking snowing, for Christ's sake. I didn't come all this way because I enjoy travelling. I don't know what strange ideas you and your new friends have got, but this is not a quest. I came to see *you*.'

Matthew might combust. 'I don't think we should talk about this any more.' He turns, walks away from Jamie, down the street.

'Where are you going?'

'Away from you.'

Jamie feels in his pockets for money. He'll be stranded. His passport. All his things are at the dome. 'You can't just leave me here. I don't know what's got into you, but you've changed. You're not—'

'You know who you sound like?' Matthew hisses over his shoulder.

Jamie wants to fly at him. 'You don't know my mother. You don't know the first fucking thing about my mother.'

After travelling back to the dome in silence, Jamie feels hungry. Their meal portions have been so small he feels he needs more food. He doesn't mention it to Matthew. Not now. It crosses his mind that they might be conspiring to weaken him. He goes straight up to the loft, pushes his face into the pillows so they can't hear him sobbing.

Recovering, he sits up on the bed, wiping his eyes, rubbing his damp hands on the bedclothes. Just a half metre away from his fingertips—a dark clump, like a ball of wool. It moves like a brown hairy hand. Then he shoots across the room in sudden terror—a tarantula.

§

From a rock, some two hundred metres away, Jamie can see the dome's interior lights glowing, now that the dusk sun has fallen low on the horizon. The dome seems to pulse and hum ominously, jutting out of the earth like a broken UFO, perhaps surveying his every move, watching him, knowing him. One hundred and eighty degrees of sky, orange to purple, threatens to engulf him. The flat plain of desert, finely textured with loose rocks, stretches out in front of him. The depersonalised feeling of being a speck, a cell in a greater body, fills him with fear. He could disappear from the face of the earth and no one would know.

Jamie shifts uncomfortably inside the warm jacket that Dale lent him for the walk, its papery rustle oddly amplified, in the otherwise deafening silence. He pulls up the collar around his neck, imagining walking in a line from the geodesic dome. His feet and head ache from lack of sleep. As far as the eye can see is a human-less grey-white blanket of snow and frost, interrupted only occasionally by a deeps faults in the Earth.

There are signs of life dotted about. Matthew told Jamie about the mule deer, the prairie dogs, who roam the scrubland. But he's not in the mood to think of beauty.

He strides back to the dome and shunts open the door. He hangs up Dale's coat and walks around looking for a sign of life, eventually reaching Matthew's bedroom, where the benevolent host welcomes him to join him.

Even though he is free to go wherever he likes—there are no locks, no doors bolted—nowhere is there an available exit route. The dome is a veritable prison.

'I can see it in your eyes.' Matthew smiles kindly, as if the situation at the bookshop hadn't happened. Jamie fully expects him to grow a pair of fangs. They sit on Matthew's bed in front of the large picture window, the way they used to in the house in London on a Sunday morning—Matthew, brewing tea; friendly, warm, safe. 'It frightens you, doesn't it?'

'What?' Jamie says.

'You know, this place can swallow you up if you're not careful. It takes a certain type of person.'

Jamie says. 'Dale told me all the spiders would be hibernating at this time of year. How did it get there?' Jamie's eyes are fixed on the miles of snow-covered desert before them—inches thicker now. A drift has formed against the window. 'I've decided, I can't stay here much longer.' Jamie wraps his fingers around his wrists. 'It's not you. It's me. It's all very exciting, but it's wrong that I'm here. I've come in on the wrong vibration,' he says, throwing in a bit of ingratiating new-age babble.

Even without looking at Matthew, he can feel his incendiary anger. 'You've barely given it a chance.'

'Matthew, I know you think I'm unadventurous, but backpacking, hitch-hiking—it's just not my idea of fun. It's been great to see you. But now I want to go home.'

Matthew's head drops. Jamie turns to face him head on. He needs to look him in the eye for this. When Matthew starts to speak again, his words are slow and deliberate. 'I don't think that's going to be possible now.' He brings his head up and their eyes meet. 'What about the initiation?'

Jamie pauses. 'Matthew—I don't really want to join your thing— whatever it is—I think they're getting me mixed up with someone... something else.'

'How will you get home?'

Jamie shrugs. 'You said that Dale would take me to the airport.'

'Dale has already made arrangements to visit his brother in Colorado,' Matthew says—seeming to enjoy tormenting him.

'If he can take me to Taos, I can get a bus back to Albuquerque. It'll be fine.'

'In this snow? It's far too dangerous.'

'Life doesn't stop in Taos for a layer of snow. Dale drove into town only yesterday.'

'Dale won't be able to take you. You'll have to face the snow, alone.'

'Thirty minutes drive across the desert to Taos?' Jamie says, infuriated. 'Half a day to walk—in the snow—across the Rio Grande. And you said there were bears. I can't walk.'

'Then you'll have to hitch-hike.'

§

The days, like the unending forested sections of skyline, bleed into each other. After trying again, unsuccessfully, to make contact with his mum, Jamie feels beaten. He doesn't have the energy to stand up to Matthew. If Matthew wants to be left alone, then so be it.

Jamie knocks back a cup of brown-green herbal sludge that Matthew brewed for him. He wraps up warm in a thick sweater borrowed from Dale and wrenches on his walking boots. Camera and journal in hand, Jamie cheers goodbye, disguising sullen discomfort, and walks forthrightly up hill towards the woods. Perhaps he'll sit and attempt to write something.

Any life from their nearest neighbour in the trailer home is tucked away inside. Jamie glances over. Other people might be different. He could ask for a lift into town. There's a light on, but no sign of movement. No sound. On other days, he could hear dogs barking. He continues into the brush, towards the aspens, on the crest of the hill.

From up there, the view is something to behold: a desert floor of pastel shades partially covered with frosted shrubs, brittle like pieces of coral.

The dome is just an insignificant dot. He sneers at *them* with their silly stories. How can they know all the answers? When he thinks of the vastness of the universe, the ocean of time that has lapsed since what—say, the big bang, it seems foolish to believe their stories, so inconsequential when you consider the meagre time humans have walked the planet.

A superior race of reptilian overlords governing the universe since long before we were here? To Jamie's mind, any extra-terrestrial race must have evolved at the same time as everything else—from what? Atoms and molecules, algae and other microscopic what not. If only he could lie on his mother's sofa now and watch *Coronation Street*.

He kneels and presses his trembling hand against the icy sand—debris that has been around for thousands of years—pieces of seashell and water-washed stones, marooned miles above sea level. It feels difficult to differentiate between himself and the sand. Flashes of an idea—if everything in the universe is connected, possibly he's made of the same stuff that the sand is made of. The idea comes together in his head like particles of water joining to form a distinguishable vapour. Then he stands and shakes the notion away. In the city, he doesn't feel such things. There he feels like one of the cogs that make everything work. Here, he is nothing—and he is everything, all at the same time.

From the crest he snaps away with his camera, as he's done since he arrived here. There are plenty of pictures religious buildings, local artists, strange pieces of landscape. He's used rolls of film, recording the whole nightmare. The sound of his camera clicking away is the only thing that can be heard. The remoteness of the place only amplifies his feelings of fear.

Come on, Jamie! You're going to get back to Taos. Get a bus or a coach or something back to Albuquerque. People do this. People climb fucking great mountains in the freezing cold and they survive.

He walks back down the hill, through the sagebrush—startled by the sounds of the dogs now, over at the trailer. He quickens his pace, there being no sign of human supervision.. A mix of sand and pebbles slide under his feet. Down the incline, a little too quickly, he stumbles, falls on his knee, sharp pebbles jabbing into his flesh.

The barking grows louder. Dogs don't usually spook him; he's not prone to being harassed by them. One dog—a yappy-snappy little creature. The other looks like a wolf. He brushes himself off, breathes deeply and walks on, deliberately steady this time, so as not to entice them into a game of chase. They continue to bark, less than a hundred yards from him. He's mindful not to make eye-contact. Louder. He turns. Closer. The wolf is upon him, growling and baring its teeth—blue eyes, piercing. It pads the ground, and then leaps forward.

'Stop!' Jamie shouts. Then more softly, 'I'm not going to hurt you.' He bows his head trying to appear docile, hoping the owner will come and round them up. No one appears. The wolf dog runs at him, snarling and foaming at the mouth.

A spark of fear—suddenly he's detached from his body, hovering above himself, watching the dog. He pushes it off—swings his camera, on the end of its leather strap. It misses the dog.

He runs for the dome, too far away, slipping on pebbles, jumping over rocks—the dog just behind. Faster. Teeth sink into his leg. He screams, cries out for help. It bites—bites again, drawing blood, tearing his trousers. Pain. A jolt. A stone in his hand. Misses. Stumbles backwards, arms flailing frantically

The dog snarls—leaping—fangs just missing his face. Jamie pushes it away, fingers inside its mouth. 'Fuck off, fuck off.' Its teeth, needles through flesh. Saliva loose from its tongue hits Jamie's cheeks. He falls. Hits his head on hard rock. Hands search blindly for another stone. Seizing a jagged piece of rock, he stabs at the dog's side, inducing a painful yelp. It backs away.

A strange filmic sensation of being an observer, while at the same time, being observed—makes Jamie feel a presence other than the dog. Is he hallucinating? A twinge of remorse condenses in his mind before the dog snarls again.

On his feet now, exhaustion overcomes Jamie. The dog licks the bloody wound in its side. Jamie takes this chance. He gallops toward the dome. At the threshold, he glances back; the dog has vanished. He collapses emotionally, just for a moment and feels himself jerk, like a television regaining its signal, back into his body. Seeing through his own eyes, in his own skin, he sobs. The wounds beneath his trouser leg—blood, teeth-marks. He touches his head—battered.

He staggers into the wooden antechamber, locking doors behind him. The inner door into the living area is open. He looks into the kitchen, expecting to find Matthew cooking. Silence.

Slowly regaining perspective, he breathes, wanting to leave the drama outside. Maybe Matthew is napping. Jamie kicks off his wet shoes and suppresses his urge to cry.

In the living room, he pulls off clothes. He spots eight red flashing lights dotted around on the carpeted area of the dome and becomes slowly aware of a very low-pitched vibrating hum. The lights were not there before; not when he left. Just get out of these bloody clothes. He pulls Dale's sweater over his head and, steps further into the room. They are, Dale, Matthew, Prunella and Bunni, on opposite sides of the dome, cross-legged in what looks like a deep meditative trance—all of them, eyes closed.

Close to blacking out now, his thundering heartbeat slows dramatically. His vision greys. He gently moves the door towards its frame but at the last second decides to let it slam, making his presence known. They don't move. What the fuck are they doing—invoking spirits? They don't even appear to be breathing. The vibrating continues.

'Matthew?' he calls across the room. Even his freaky fucking eyelids are still. Jamie stares at his face; it appears to shift for a second. His features undulate—not bones or the muscles, it's the flesh of his face itself, moving independently of the structure beneath. Now more. Cheekbones swell; the chin becomes subtly elongated. The shiny flesh on his forehead ripples, the beginnings of horns pushing through angry red skin like hot boils. Jamie wants to scream but no sound emerges. He's still dizzy—drunk, even.

Matthew opens his eyes. Behind the lids, his eyes have rolled back so that only the whites show. They roll forward again and flicker from side to side.

Jamie is transfixed. He wants to look away but his eyes are hooked on Matthew's lips which part into a thin opening, through which slides a repulsive green tongue, long and forked. What the fuck is that vibrating hum? He feels a stomach cramp and wretches on the floor in front of him. Then—blackness.

No humming. When Jamie opens his eyes, his vision is filled by the image of Prunella Small kneeling over him—a mass of white curls. Her large blue glasses hang precariously on the end of her nose.

'Matthew said you'd popped out for a stroll. What happened?' she asks. 'You've been gone for hours.'

It takes a few moments before Jamie can orientate himself. Is he imagining this? 'I got bitten by a dog.'

Matthew sneers, towering over both of them. Lying on the floor of the dome, Jamie tugs up his trouser leg, showing them his wounds. Prunella rises, stands back and folds her arms.

'You've brought it all upon yourself,' Matthew says.

'Matthew!' Jamie says, pushing himself up, onto his elbows.

Prunella purses her lips. 'If it's sympathy you want, you've come to the wrong place.'

'Aren't you going to do something? I need some antiseptic.'

Prunella, Dale, Matthew and Bunni move in on him. Collectively, speaking in unison—'Every thought we think makes our universe.'

Their eyes roll back into their heads and they chant, reciting words and sounds that Jamie cannot decipher.

§

'Yes, I'm well aware that the departure date is over a month away, but now I need an earlier flight.' Jamie's stomach churns. 'Aren't there any flights to London at all this week?' Inside his mind: a black abyss. A sensation that often creeps up on him without him realising. It's the same sensation that overcame him at school, where he was relentlessly bullied. It was the dull leaden helplessness that came when he realised his mother might die of meningitis or when his parents were fighting, and he had to go and live with Phyllis and Alf for a week. It will pass. It usually passes, with sleep, with the conversation of a close friend. But this is heavier than usual. Tears fill his eyes and his throat, and he struggles to suppress the *what if*.

'I'm sorry, sir,' the voice of the reservations assistant says. 'Could you read the ticket number to me again?'

Jamie does so, twice more. He clutches the blankets on the edge of Matthew's bed.

'Sir, I'm sorry but there's no record of this number logged in our system. It might be a printing error. If you paid with a credit card, I should be able to trace the booking.'

'I have it here.' Jamie runs a finger across the embossed plastic numbers, reminding himself that he's here, now. He reads each one carefully, holding his breath between each number.

The enormity of the silence at the end of the phone line is held back by a tiny glimpse of light. He waits on the brink of good news; his stomach uncoils slightly.

'I'm really sorry, sir. I can't help you. There's no trace of your ticket number *or* your credit card booking on the computer system.'

Jamie's mind bungees back into the abyss. 'I have it here in my hand. Flight AB132 to Houston, flight LG495 to Gatwick.'

'I'd really like to help you, but there is no flight AB132. It doesn't exist.'

He's going to throw up. Just breathe. He rubs the sharp edge of the plastic card against the soft flesh on the inside of his forearm, leaving angry pink tramlines. When he returns home, he'll start a steady job, spend the rest of his life holidaying in the Med, eat boring food and numb out on crap television just like ordinary people do.

'I can sell you a new ticket, sir. I can make a booking for you now over the telephone.'

'You don't understand.' Jamie's voice cracks. He looks at the bedroom door, hoping he won't be interrupted. 'I don't have any more money. I assumed everything would be... I bought the tickets all together. I still have the boarding pass for my outbound journey.'

'Mister Johnson, I can only suggest that you bring the ticket, along with your credit card to the airport. Perhaps it *is* a printing error.'

'Can you guarantee that I'll get a seat on the plane?'

'Let me check availability for when you might be travelling.' Jamie listens to the sound of fingers running across plastic computer keys. 'Mister Johnson, all flights on Friday, Saturday and two flights on Sunday are fully booked.'

'And in the next three weeks?'

'There are often cancellations. I'm sorry I can't be more helpful.'

When he puts down the phone, Jamie wants to curl up and weep. His mind falls, this time without a safety line, back into that black hole. He sees one image in his mind far, far away. Almost an indistinct dot: his mother.

§

Gloria isn't home, so Jamie takes advantage of the line in Matthew's bedroom actually working to make another call.

'Jamie! You need to calm down,' Billy says.

'I'm terrified of finding more spiders!' Jamie nervously scans the bed sheets for arachnids, thinking better of mentioning what happened the other afternoon. He's still not sure if he has been dreaming, drugged, or else experiencing something quite out-of-this-world. All he can think of is getting away from these freaks.

'You were right, Billy,' he speaks quietly into the receiver. 'I should have listened to you. I should have listened to Mum.'

'Well, don't think about that now.' The line is so clear, Billy could be in the next room. 'You've enough to think about without beating yourself up.'

The dog bites are healing, slowly. He hooks his fingernail underneath the edge of a scab, until fresh blood seeps out and he feels a twinge of pain. This helps to focus his mind.

'Don't waste your holiday time. Go to New York, Jamie. Just get on a plane.'

Jamie hears footsteps. 'I'd better go, Billy. Someone's coming.'

'Wait.'

'It's not a good time.' Jamie can sense Matthew on the other side of the door.

Billy's voice gets louder. 'What's going on?'

'I'll call you soon,' Jamie says.

'Jamie. Wait!'

'What?'

'I love you—'

'I love you too, Billy.' The line is dead. 'Billy?'

§

Jamie waits for them to go out for their afternoon walk. Then he follows the telephone cable along the skirting-board into the darkened spare room. He's keen and alert. He breathes steadily. Pressure builds on him, while on his knees, tracing the cable. They won't be gone long. Why is this phone line so unpredictable? One minute it's working, the next it's dead.

It's hard to see in this dimness. Jamie stands and switches on the light. He sees a second telephone on a little table. He walks over and picks it up—listens. There's that perfectly clear *brrrrrrrr* ringtone. A different line? He places the receiver down and kneels. Next to the table is the end of the line to the phone he's been trying to use, the end of it completely free of the socket.

§

Initiation? Healing machines? There's no way they're getting him to go to that woman's house. If he's quick, he can be out of here before they come back. He doesn't know if he should pack the big rucksack or not. He doesn't want another confrontation with Matthew. No. The big rucksack will draw too much attention. He kicks it under his bed and packs his small holdall instead—just the essentials: reading material, waterproofs, camera, passport, plane tickets, money, the candle given to him by Pale and Gegger and his notebooks. There's nothing amongst the remaining things that he can't obtain again in London. He'll leave in the clothes he's standing up in and slip away unnoticed into the night. Are there really bears out there, or have they told him this in order to keep him prisoner?

Jamie arranges things in the holdall, hands shaking from a mixture of nerves and low blood sugar. Has he got everything? He looks round the room at his stuff scattered untidily around the room. Check. Check. No, he's forgotten something. He remembers his camera. Must take that. He finds it lying on a chest of drawers. Just as he's placing it carefully into the bag, he hears Matthew's voice. 'I've been meaning to have a word with you about that.' Jamie looks up and catches Matthew staring at him from the doorway. 'The camera. I expect Prunella would love some good pictures of the event.'

Jamie is speechless.

'Are you ready?' Matthew asks.

Jamie looks out of the window at the desert. The dirt road leading to Taos still visible even under light snow. In trembling hands, Jamie turns, lifts his camera to his eye and shoots Matthew.

§

In her basement, Prunella sits, large thick-lensed glasses balancing on the bridge of her nose, needles rhythmically clicking like the sound of woodland insects.

'Ah, you came,' she says, as Jamie steps down into the sparse room. 'You're knitting?'

Prunella holds up the mass of webby green wool. 'A shawl.'

'My grandmother taught me when I was a little boy.'

'And I taught my grandson,' she says, a sad lilt of remorse in her voice. 'I don't see him now, I...'

'She used to pick up my stitches when they unravelled.' He feels tears in his eyes. He wants to see her so much.

'I've had to let go. We *all* have to let go. But... you remind me of him.'

She puts down her knitting and turns his attention to her treasured possession. 'I thought you ought to see this.'

In the middle of a white room fitted with chrome units sits the *machine*—a computer—all screens, knobs and buttons, inside a curtain of translucent surgical-green plastic. Next to the machine is something like a dentist's chair upholstered in white PVC. It's surrounded by breathing apparatus, electrodes and a monitor screen.

'Isn't it wonderful? Your reading will be displayed here and we'll be able to see where all the imperfections are.'

The sight of it all chills Jamie's blood. Is this what they have in store for him? They're going to strap him on that thing. He imagines himself wrestling with them—Matthew, Dale, the others, holding him down.

Jamie forces a smile. He's knows he's leaking emotions from every corner of his face. He can't fool Prunella. 'And then what?' he asks.

'We will make you complete,' Prunella says. 'The way you were before you were incorporated on Earth without the flaws you have now.'

Jamie scans the room for another exit. It's a cellar: there is only the doorway he's standing in.

'It's perfectly safe, Jamie. Imagine, we're just returning you to your factory settings. You'll feel a little dizzy at first. The whole experience will accelerate the spinning of your own chakras.' Prunella strokes her hands across the shiny white surface of the chair. 'We've all been done. But you, Jamie, you will benefit the most.'

Jamie edges into the room to get a better look. He wonders what it would feel like to erase it all: the bullying at school, all his neuroses, all the shit that haunts him. What a relief it might be to let go of all that weight.

'You'll have to be naked of course. You have a problem with that?' Her head is cocked slightly to one side, a contradictory earnest look in her opal eyes.

Jamie feels his face fixed like marble. Prunella softens. 'It's not easy, honey. We all feel we need that personal connection,' she says. She looks at him as if she's saying goodbye for a very long time. It feels right, for some strange reason. Prunella leans forward and kisses him on the cheek. It feels like a kiss that has waited a long time to be planted.

'I think I better get back upstairs to help Matthew.'

§

Dale, Bunni and everyone else are in the kitchen, preparing for the party, assembling paper lanterns and unpacking glasses. On the surface of one of the preparation areas sits a bottle of brown-green herbal sludge, labelled *Yagé*. It has the same devious appearance of the tea Matthew had made him drink before being bitten by that damned dog. Through the window, Jamie can see Matthew is outside moving fence posts to make space for the extra guest vehicles that will arrive tomorrow evening. The road where Prunella's house stands has been gritted and cleared of snow.

A moment of clarity, blade-sharp, hits Jamie. Absolutely no good can come from any of this: the violation, the manipulation, his own puerile behaviour. He needs to be back home with Billy. It's the most awake, the most grown-up he's felt since he arrived here. He'll confront Matthew and tell him that they must take him to the bus station. They can't keep him here, a prisoner. He darts through Prunella's kitchen, and outside. As Jamie approaches, Matthew is trying to move a boulder from the gravel driveways.

Matthew turns his back, pulls up the collar on his jacket. Even in this weather, he's still wearing those daft shorts, exposing his yellow knees to the elements. 'I have nothing to say to you, Jamie.'

Jamie is expecting this. 'Well, *I* have something to say to *you*.'

Matthew is scraping earth from underneath the boulder with a kitchen knife, trying for more leverage. Don't they have a shovel? A trowel? As Jamie steps towards him, Matthew spins—the knife in his outstretched hand, whistling through the air. 'Get away from me,' he screams.

'Why are you so angry?' Jamie dodges.

Matthew's eyes are on fire. 'You've done nothing but *take* from us.'

'That's rich! *Me* taking from *you*?'

'From the moment you got off the plane you wanted to stir up trouble between Dale and myself.'

'Where the hell has this come from?' Jamie gasps. 'You're delusional.'

Matthew continues his blind rant, conjuring up stories about what he thinks has been going on during Jamie's stay. 'And that energy you ooze, it's so damaging.'

'Oh, you know,' Jamie begins quite frankly, 'the energy thing—it's gone far enough now.'

'Your negativity is putting the entire project at risk,' Matthew says.

'I had no idea I had such power.' Jamie laughs. It's the first time he's really laughed in weeks. 'You've brought me here under false pretences.'

The knife is just inches away from his face. '*You* wanted this,' Matthew says. 'I opened a door for you.'

'Yeah, you *opened* a door. I was in awe of you. You made me think it was *your* life that I wanted, sitting around in cafes all day long with a notebook. I thought you were going to teach me how to beat the system, not give me bullshit about extra-terrestrials before strapping me to a machine to have my DNA poked and prodded.'

'Ungrateful wretch!'

Jamie eyes him defiantly. 'Certainly pulled the wool over my eyes, didn't you? Making me think you knew all those people—David, Gracie and the rest of them.'

The knife moves even closer; Jamie doesn't flinch. 'I should never have chosen you,' Matthew hisses. *Chosen him?* Again, he sees an image of himself strapped into that hideous machine, flashing through his mind.

'I'm your friend. Stop being ridiculous. How you got yourself mixed up in this nonsense, I'll never know.'

Matthew lunges, the point of the knife quivering just a hair's breadth away from Jamie's face, causing him to lose his footing and fall.

Scrambling around on the muddy driveway, Jamie feels his arse cut by grit and salt. Looming over him, Matthew's face bends. Reality distorts like a funfair mirror. The knife becomes liquid. Matthew's eyes become sacks of blood. His face reddens, temples swelling and undulating just where horns might grow. Jamie's seen this before. He closes his eyes for just a moment, hoping that this is all a—

It's not going to go away. When he opens his eyes, the bones protrude where Matthew's temples are, the skin—leathery and shiny with beads of sweat.

He refuses to let his own mind turn on him. But his vision buckles. He might vomit. A lizard in the shape of a man—forked tongue, flickering eyes—lurches forwards, now thrusting the knife right at Jamie. Misses. Jamie screams, voice cracking, leaving just air hissing over vocal chords. Jamie scrambles to his feet. Pushes Matthew away. They tussle. Buttons tear from Matthew's coat. Runs back to the house. Where else to run?

'He's trying to kill me,' he shrieks, running right into the kitchen-diner, scattering place settings, glasses, vases of flowers.

Prunella spins round with her knitting in her hand. The green ball of wool falls and rolls across the floor. 'What in the name of—'

'You're all fucking crazy,' Jamie screams, knocking crockery out of Dale's hands. Plates and glasses clatter to the floor.

'What's wrong, dear?' Prunella stands there in her tracksuit bottoms, arms wide now, the knitting dangling. She looks at Dale as he reaches for broken plates on the floor. 'He was fine a few minutes ago. I don't know what's got into him.'

Jamie points at them all. 'I know what you're doing.' He gags. Barely able to breathe, heart—pounding. 'I should have listened to them.'

'Calm down!' Prunella calmly takes off her blue rimmed glasses and rubs them on her cardigan. 'Dale, get him a chair,' she says, replacing her glasses on the bridge of her nose.

Jamie recoils. 'Don't any of you come near me!'

'He's in shock.' Prunella says to Dale.

'I just want to go home!'

'Hush a minute,' Prunella says. 'I can't think with all your hollering.'

'I need to get out of here.' Jamie cries.

'You can't just leave us now,' Dale says. 'Don't you want to be welcomed into our family?'

'I have my own fucking family!' How can he connect with them? Nothing he says will make them hear him. 'I want to see mother, I want to see my grandmother, please...'

'No one is holding you prisoner,' Prunella says.

'But you are!' Jamie laughs hysterically. 'It's fucking snowing. They refused to take me to the bus stop.' He points at Dale. 'I can't *walk* across the desert.'

Matthew walks in now, face congenial, no sign of the knife.

'Is this true, Matthew?' Prunella says. 'Did he ask for your help?'

Matthew shrugs. 'You want us to let him go, before tomorrow's initiation?'

Prunella presses a hand to her head. 'This is a reality *you* have created, Jamie. This is what you must have wanted for yourself.'

It dawns on him. He *had* made this real. It was a sick fantasy nurtured by loneliness that began long ago. But from that fantasy he'd plagiarised more sick fantasies. Whatever he'd thought was going on is not what was going on at all. He wants to go back and rewrite the script. He should be at home now, working on a novel, looking for an agent—not wasting his time in the desert. 'I even called the airline but they have no record of my booking!'

'You're being selfish,' Prunella says. 'After all our hard work? The least you could do is stay for the party.'

Jamie shakes his head. 'I want to go home.' He can feel himself unravelling—yarn free of needles. But now there's no-one to pick up the stitches for him.

Prunella looks down at the length of knitting in her hands. Then up to Jamie again. 'That's settled.' She stoops for the ball of wool and starts to wind it back up. 'Tomorrow morning. Dale will drive you to the bus stop.' She looks at Dale, 'No buts,' and then at Jamie, 'What company are you flying with?'

'Continental.'

Prunella looks out of the kitchen window, as if consulting some higher source. Outside it's beginning to snow again. 'Okay... okay...' She looks back at Jamie. 'There'll be a seat on the Continental. An afternoon flight. I'd say around five o'clock. You'll need to rise early if you're to get a bus from outside the Taos Inn.'

Matthew scowls. 'We can't just let him...'

'He's of no use to us now,' Prunella says.

'We must press ahead with the initiation.'

Prunella laughs. He is trying to take the upper hand. She turns on him. 'He's of no use to us now. If there's one thing I can't cope with, it's negativity.'

Jamie feels his world coming to an end. Who can he trust now? Matthew makes a grab for Jamie, and Jamie sees it again—the tip of that forked tongue. With a brief flash of bravery, he dashes out into the blizzard.

§

A spectator in his own movie, Jamie is running as fast as his feet will carry him. He's lost track of time. Hard salt-like snow bites into his face. White biscuit crunches beneath his feet. He snatches a look behind him. Alone, thank *fuck*—he must be miles from the house by now. Before him the road leads through a thick wooded area and beyond, what he assumes is the Rio Grande. The sun is sinking behind the trees. The day is closing in.. His breath freezes into white spirits.

The dangers—the bears, the drop in temperature, the distance he might have to cover to reach the bus garage—running away was perhaps not the most sensible choice. But what choice does he have?

It might take him all night to find his way in the dark. Could they follow his tracks? This thought forces him off the road and he dives into the woods, where the floor has been protected from the snow by the brush and the aspen. His trail is no longer visible as he rushes on through the damp mulch. Only a trained hunting dog could come after him now.

The setting sun casts the vertical prison bars of the aspen into silhouette. He's determined to reach the other side before the light fades. Cold air burns the back of his throat. On the other side of the woods, he perceives the beam of headlights along the distant carriageway. What will he do at the road? He has none of his things with him. Why did he ever come here in the first place? Why didn't he listen to his mother?

Closer to the road, the air is filled with a revolting stench. Catching his foot on a log, he tumbles headfirst into snow, inches away from the dead thing. He is jolted into the present.

Now has never been so vivid. The world clarifies: a mangle of disfigured fur, snout, teeth, bloody broken ribs, crushed—flattened limbs, lies decomposing. A bear, road-kill crushed by the wide tyres of a truck, rotting at the edge of the carriageway.

Car headlights throw a beam onto the carcass, followed by the screech of tyres. The passenger door is flung open. Prunella looks over the rims of her glasses from the driving seat. 'You want to get eaten by one of those things?'

'I'm not going back there,' Jamie shouts. 'You can't make me.' He runs in the opposite direction, into the driving snow. Behind him, he hears the revving engine, and the vehicle slammed into gear. She drives alongside him again, the open door almost swinging off its hinges.

'Are you out of your fucking mind? You'll die in this weather. Get in.'

Jamie holds his hands up. 'I'm going home.'

'Time to put the stitches back on your needles,' she says.

'What?' Jamie feels an almost hypodermic rush of relief.

'Trust the universe, sweetie.' She indicates something in the back seat—the bag he'd left at her house. Then picks up something from the passenger seat and holds it up.

'My passport!'

'Jamie, when you're so close up to an idea, most of the time you can't see its true significance. Is it new? Is it old? Only when you get some distance from it do you fully comprehend it.'

Jamie shivers.

'I'm packing you off.'

'What about Matthew?'

'He and I will be having words.'

§

Across a brown-white canvas of desert, Jamie rides a small bus equipped with snow-chains. It climbs up steep roads through the night and once again into bright blue skies. He's lost a friend, a bad one. But it still feels as if he's leaving something behind. He remembers remains of the bear—drags a sharpened thumbnail down the inside length of his forearm, bringing up a welt of pink flesh, angry enough to trap him in the present.

Just as Prunella had predicted, there *is* a seat for him on the

Continental. A last minute cancellation frees up a single window seat, as if the universe had rearranged itself for his journey home. And they exchange his ticket with no hiccups.

The lady in the seat next to him tries to make polite conversation several times. Eventually, he pretends to be asleep. He needs to decompress. But images flash behind his eyelids—the desert, the snow, Matthew. His voice says, 'We're all from the stars.' Jamie opens his eyes. Through the window he can see a velvety blue blanket pricked with glittery dots whose essence may, in fact, be contained within him, but whose light is long gone.

§

Gloria's nearly done the housework—the vacuuming, the washing. She's only to put away the laundry, walk the dogs and do a spot of dusting, then she's done. Everything is in its place. She arranges two candlesticks on the fireplace with an eye on symmetry. She uses a feather duster and a hairdryer on her silk flower arrangement.

On top of the TV is a china Pierrot clown sculpture that Jamie bought her when he was little. Bless. Saved up all his pocket money. Lifting it gently in one hand, she dusts it and places it back. Just a centimetre to the left. She's been like this all her life—taking care of everything. She's had that clown for years and there's not a mark on it. She doesn't like anything to get ruined.

It reminds her of the time when she had to go to the eye infirmary, as a child, to have a squint corrected. The pain was excruciating and she cried for days. Phyllis bought her a set of china dolls to cheer her up. They had beautiful satin dresses, realistic hair and carefully painted faces. She kept them on a shelf in her room. Sometimes, she would sleep with one. One day she came home from school to find them all lined up on her bed, spectacles drawn on them with a ballpoint pen. Her favourite, the one with the red hair had a moustache and a pince-nez. Bleeding Sandra. She always lost interest in her own little trollops and had to deface Gloria's.

The sound of a parcel through the letterbox, falling with a heavy thwack, brings her back. It brings a smile to her face. She tears open the brown paper packaging to reveal the catalogue from the cruise ship holiday company that she'd ordered a couple of weeks ago. Time she and Roy broke out of the mould.

§

The fatty sludge of the in-flight meal reminds Jamie of the road-kill he'd seen. Its pieces will be carried away by the beetles, washed into the ground by the rain, perished by frost, blown away by the wind until nothing remains. But it must still exist. Each microscopic piece of it, every molecule, every atom, redistributed to the universe. He can imagine himself, disintegrating like the bear, returning to the nebula. We're all particles of carbon, hydrogen, whatever, and everything in the universe is made of the same stuff. We are all one and the same thing. He feels his mind expand like elastic, suddenly reassured by the permanence of life.

§

'I'm not having it, Roy,' Gloria says, three steps ahead of the shopping trolley. The sun, low in the sky, casts a long shadow on the car park. 'It's gone downhill ever since that new manager started.' Gloria glances over her shoulder at Roy, who is angling the trolley to compensate for the camber of the tarmac. Such an expert. 'Two luncheon vouchers for the Wacky Warehouse—do they really think that's recompense for what they've put me through?'

Roy sighs, as they reach the car. 'You've got your money back, haven't you?'

'It's the inconvenience, Roy. And I won't be made a fool of. Did you see the look that cashier gave me? Smug bitch.'

Roy opens the rear door so they can chuck the carrier bags in the back. 'Don't upset yourself, love. Come on, we'll pick up fish and chips on the way home.'

'You have fish if you want,' she says. 'I think I'll have one of them shish-kebabs. I feel like something exotic.' She's organizing the shopping in the back of the car, moving items from one bag to another. 'Roy, what have I told you about putting the washing machine powder next to the salad? You'll have us all poisoned.'

Roy holds up something that she's snuck into one of the salad bags.

'Oh, that. It's just coriander,' she says, as if it were something dull and everyday like a jar of Branston Pickle.

'Is it foreign?'

Why does he do this—raw meat next to a bottle of Domestos? 'You could say that. They use it in Indian and Thai cooking. Thought I'd give it a whirl.'

They drive in silence for a mile or so until Roy reaches the industrial estate near to where they usually pick up supper. The road runs adjacent to an old factory covered in graffiti and barbed wire. The *Glasshouse Gentleman's Health Spa* is set in what looks like an old public house. Gloria waves her hand irritably, indicating that Roy should slow down.

'If I go any slower I'll get done for kerb crawling.'

'Don't be ridiculous,' she says. 'Not with me in the passenger seat. Just stop, outside the gates. I want to get a better look.'

'A better look?'

'I'm just curious. Nothing wrong with that, is there?'

Roy pulls up in front of the building.

'I tell you something, Roy. They must be making a mint here. Pink pound they call it. Look at the cars on that car park. '

'I'm surprised there's much call for it round here, Glo.'

'Sandra says it's all married men what use it. Swingers.'

'I'll bet it's awash with disease,' Roy laughs.

'You keep away. D'you hear?' She giggles. 'I can do without crabs at my age.'

Roy tuts. 'As if.' He revs the engine.

She prods his legs with a fingernail. 'And don't mention it to our Jamie when he's back here. I don't want him getting ideas.'

Roy pulls away. 'Don't knock it, Gloria. After everything, he might be safer there than anywhere else.'

§

Jamie is disturbed by the muffled noises of Camden Town floating through the front door of Billy's bedsit, up the stairwell and under the duvet. He hears the door slam. Billy's footsteps. It feels like he's been asleep for days. The homely smell of Billy's cigarette brings him to a halfway state between sleep and wakefulness. Next thing he knows, Billy is above him with kisses and a mug of hot chocolate. 'How are you feeling?'

'I think I should go and stay with Mum and Dad.' Jamie feels maimed.

'Commute to the gallery? Don't be ridiculous. Why don't we get a little place together?'

Jamie sits up in bed. 'Buy? That's a big jump from sofa-surfing in student digs.'

'I've been looking at a few places. Dalston. It would be cheaper than renting and it would be ours. Our own little piece of London. I can't see you lasting long at your mother's.' Billy leans over and kisses him. 'There's a letter. Postmark *New Mexico*.' He sits down on the bed.

Jamie tears open the envelope. 'It's from Pale. I gave him *your* address. Don't want any mail going to my mother, eh?'

Dearest Jamie,

For sure you must be home by now. I know you won't be able to stand those creeps for long. I only hope your heart is in one piece. You're in the small percentage of people who see and feel with their hearts. Just keep hold of the thought—everything happens for a reason. Back home, you'll start making sense of everything. Matthew must have had something very unhappy and cruel happen to him to have got himself involved in this nonsense. A lot of times, people do not survive their past and are unable to heal. We are not lizards! Our tails do not grow back when they fall off. When it all gets too much for me, I go out in town to breathe and dance with the neighbourhood dogs.

I have to say, I was not very thrilled to meet you at first. I thought only a creep must hang out with them, but I was incredibly wrong. You are not at all a miserable or negative person. But clearly you had no idea what you were being led into. I was never comfortable around either of them. Matthew has monsters living in his head and Dale is just a bore.

You know, we had no idea that they wanted to stay the night. How

absurd, to turn up like that and take over our kitchen! Rest assured,
Gegger and I had it all worked out. We were both sure they were in
a cult. And the good thing is, you and I have a friendship created out
of darkness. Highly dramatic things seem to happen to people like us.
And dragons are attracted to angels.
    Write, as soon as you get home and tell me everything.
Love Pale x

§

Jamie looks at the bank clerk in disbelief.

'What do you mean, 'Could *I* have authorized these transactions?'
The money had been taken out of his account yesterday, in *dollars*.
'I've been back a week.' He can't afford to be further overdrawn.

'Can you verify the following transactions for me...' The clerk
turns the monitor screen to Jamie: *Human Light Research. BioGas-*
VisCorp. GDVsystemtech.co. The dates of the transactions and the
names of the businesses don't tally with any places he'd actually vis-
ited. His mind races. The card was never out of his sight. He knows
that much. He thinks of the spider in his bed, the disconnected telephone. He wouldn't put anything past them.

'Have you reported your card lost or stolen?'

'I didn't authorize these transactions. I need you to put that money
back in my account.'

'We can only assume that the card was cloned while you were in
America.'

'Cloned?'

'Criminals sometimes use devices that copy the information off the
magnetic strip. This enables them to make an exact replica of your
card.'

'But how would they know my pin number?'

'They don't need it to buy stuff from the internet. I need to speak
to the manager about this. We'll keep the account active in order to
investigate the problem.'

§

Billy is lying on the bed channel hopping. Something catches Jamie's eye. The scenery, then whiteness, a plastic curtain—the camera pans, a dentist's chair. Billy hops again.

'Put that back.' Jamie jabs a finger at the television screen.

'It's just some crap documentary.'

Jamie wrenches the remote from Billy's hands. 'Listen.'

The narrator describes a cult in New Mexico who believe themselves to be the children of a group of enlightened beings, from a star system on the other side of the universe. 'This is it, Billy. That's the place,' Jamie says, shaking Billy's leg.

The documentary reports members recruiting in the UK, convincing young people to initiate themselves in the desert near Taos, New Mexico. They believe originally they had an extra strand of DNA, which got lost when the *children* manifested on earth. A special machine perfects their humanized bodies. And the thing that strikes home to Jamie—the narrator reports the building of vast funds, conning new recruits out of thousands of pounds. The gay communities of London, Berlin, New York and San Francisco have become targets of the cult because it's believed that people of a homosexual orientation have less 'personal information' to hamper their induction: fewer family bonds and paternal links mean a smoother initiation to the *family*.

Jamie's mind shoots back to the morning he met Matthew for the first time. 'How could I have been such a fool?' he says. Now on the television a distorted home video sequence, intermittently interrupted by static. Roaming footage reveals the machine room Jamie had stood inside. Jamie and Billy watch a naked woman strapped into the dentist chair, electrodes all over her body. Figures in white protective suits spectate. She's writhing around in pain.

'This is going to give me fucking nightmares,' Billy says, grabbing the remote control. 'Turn it off.'

'No.'

The narrator explains that the group use dangerous sleep-inducing delta waves to slow the heartbeat of the victims they wish to incapacitate. Then they can reveal themselves in their purest form. These lizards feed off negative energy produced by humans.

'Makes sense. They made out that they couldn't stand my

pessimism but they deliberately pushed me into a situation in which I was terrified.'

'You don't really believe this shit, do you?' Billy says.

'Have you got a lighter?' Jamie is out of bed and rummaging in a drawer.

'You haven't started smoking?' Billy asks.

Jamie finds the candle tucked inside a pair of Superman underpants. 'What?'

'The Mary of Guadeloupe.'

§

'Jamie. They're here,' Gloria calls up the stairwell. She primps before the hallway mirror and then opens the front door. The puffiness under her eyes betrays disturbed sleep last night. 'Alright Sandra?'

'Alright Glo?' Sandra is wearing a strappy red, white and blue sequined top the pattern of a Union Jack. Taking fashion advice from Ginger Spice now?

'Bit daring, even for you.' Gloria looks at Sandra's newly dyed red hair.

'How is he?' Sandra asks, stepping into the living room.

Gloria folds her arms. 'To be quite honest, Sandra, there was a bit of a 'to-do'.

Freddie is in a grey round neck t-shirt under a black blazer. 'So how did he get on with the aliens?' he says, playfully and whistles the theme tune from the *X-Files*.

'How do *you* know about our Jamie and all that UFO nonsense?' Gloria presses the anger into her pelvis somewhere. This, she has learnt over the last year. Letting it out in public never gets her anywhere, except in the supermarket where the staff all run for cover. It'll probably give her a tumour one day.

'He's been reading it. That book everyone is talking about,' Sandra says, inching slightly closer to Freddie. 'What's it called—*The Prophetic Insights*?'

'I don't think he is.' Gloria laughs, anger now leaking out of the seams. 'Our Jamie grew out of that rubbish a while ago.'

'Nah. I expect that's why he went to Taos,' Freddie says. 'That author, Prunella Small—she lives there. Says it in her biog.'

Gloria feels red mist rising around her. 'That *book*?' She's unable to find other words. Sandra and Freddie are both looking at her now, as if she's mentally ill. 'Well it had better not be in *this* house,' she says, eventually and heads to the door. 'Jamie, get down these stairs *now*.' She spits the words, the way she had when he was ten years old and had failed to tidy up after himself.

Roy walks in from the garage, a puzzled look on his face. 'What's going on?'

'Just keep out of this, Roy.' The palm of her hand comes up. 'This is between me and him.' Jamie's face appears at the door. 'Where is it?' she says. 'Don't pretend! You know exactly what I'm talking about. That book.'

Sandra touches Freddie on the shoulder. 'Perhaps we ought to just go.'

Roy says, 'Is this entirely necessary, Glo?'

Jamie leans against the doorframe, just as he had when he had been a boy in his pyjamas, upset that he'd been told to go to bed early. 'I-put-it-on-the-bookcase,' he says.

'Oh—I—could—bloody—swing—for—you!' She flies up the stairs. Even from the spare bedroom she can hear them talking about her.

'She's off,' Roy says. 'I knew it was a mistake to reduce her medication.'

On her knees, she reaches the bottom shelf, and finds it. 'I knew it.' Flicking through the pages, she notes, it's been signed by the author. 'The divine truth will set you free,' she reads out loud, standing again, almost wrenching the door from its hinges and flying back into the living room.

Jamie is backed up against the bay window, nervously hugging a tasselled cushion cover. Roy asks again, 'What's going on?'

'*This* is what's going on,' Gloria confronts Jamie with a look of disgust. 'You know, I always granted you half a brain. But now I see that you don't even use that.' She raises the book at him like a weapon. 'Do you know how *worried* you've had us?'

Jamie holds out the palms of his hands in a gesture of apology. 'Mum, I didn't—'

'*He* got you reading this, didn't he?' she says. 'That Matthew. Oh, if I saw him now, I couldn't be held responsible—'

'I read it before I met him. Though he *had* read it. That's why we connected.'

Sandra reaches out for Gloria. 'Don't you think you should just calm down?'

'Connected?' The pitch of her voice is rising now, outside her own control. 'Like you had some sort of special bond over a fucking book.'

'Gloria!' Roy snaps, his face a little purple now.

'Well, *he's pushed* me to it. He'd make a saint swear,' she waves the book in the air. 'Everyone in the country has read it. But that doesn't mean it's any good.'

'How would *you* know?' Jamie says, flushed with embarrassment. She shouldn't be doing this in front of them all. It's humiliating for him but she can't keep it in.

'I *know*,' she says, feeling she has the upper hand now, 'because I've *read* it.'

Jamie gasps. 'You're lying! You'd never read a book like that.'

'You think you know everything,' Gloria says, spitefully. 'You're not the only one who reads. What did you think you'd find in there?' She starts tearing pages.

'No, Mum! Please!' Jamie rushes towards her, grasping for it.

Sandra shifts uncomfortably on the sofa. 'Maybe I should make the tea. Who'd like a nice cup of—'

Gloria pushes Jamie with a fist wrapped around a clump of torn paper. 'Get away from me,' she snarls, lips stretched across clenched teeth. 'Or I'll be sorry for what I do.'

'Mum, that's mine. Please—'

'Look what a bloody mess you got yourself into—moving in with that freak. I'm getting rid of this rubbish.' She tears more pages and throws them at Roy. 'This is because of you, this is.'

'Don't you start on me,' Roy says.

'*I* wanted to bring him back, that day. But it was you who said it was okay to leave him there, in that dump. That *squat*. With that cretin—the bloody Pied Piper of the self-help universe.'

'Good God!' Roy says, at last. 'I work all day and have to come home to *this*?'

Gloria looks at the ruined book in her hands. *Just breathe*, she thinks. She coolly passes the book to Roy, grasps a bit of dignity and wipes away angry tears.

'I only wanted some answers,' Jamie says.

Gloria looks at him now with incredulity. 'You know, some mothers take their kids to church, or mosque, or whatever. We didn't. We thought it'd be better you make up your own mind. I'd have saved up to send you on a Buddhist retreat rather than this. How could you let yourself get so taken in—to travel halfway across the world. Good God, I spent hundreds putting you through college. You're meant to be educated.'

'It wasn't meant to be like this,' Jamie says.

She looks around the room—the armchairs and sofa of her three-piece suite all pointing at the wide screen television that she and Roy sit in front of every weekend, hoping they might win the national lottery while the dust settled on her memories.

'Is this about the trip to America?' Roy says.

'Oh, the penny drops!' Gloria says.

'What was it? Was it some cult?' Roy asks.

'For want of a better word! He was in the middle of it! Our son, the *Pilgrim*. *You* saw that programme the other night. I told you at the time what he was getting mixed up with, but you wouldn't listen.'

Roy looks at the savaged book in his hands. 'What's the bloody book about?'

Gloria's hands go to her sides. 'Oh, it's just a load of old New-Age bullshit about how the universe is made up of energy and how we've come to evolve, you know, from energy to hydrogen atoms, from atoms and molecules and then into us.'

'Sounds pretty scientific,' Freddie says, smirking.

'When I want your opinion, Freddie, I'll ask for it.'

Sandra sits forward now. 'I don't think there's any need for—'

'The problem with it is,' Gloria continues, 'it suggests that we can harbour this energy in some way, leading to the next form of evolution, to learn to acquire psychic energy, thus connecting us to the universe.'

'Ah—I see,' Roy says, clearly non-the-wiser.

'And it's written by this woman who claims to have been *channelling* all these lessons from extraterrestrials on the other side of the universe—relatives of whom claim to have been reborn on Earth as lizards. Little green men. You've heard all that nonsense. And our Jamie po-goed across the world to become one of their students.'

'I went to see Matthew,' Jamie says. 'When I got there, he'd changed.' Tears roll down his face.

'It beats me how people fall for the stuff. It's just so trite. People have been listening to them for centuries—you know, the *voices*.' She's still snarling at Jamie. 'That's what *you* used to call *art* or *poetry*. And all of sudden, some freak comes along and calls it *channelling*. That Matthew has been wading around in a pool so shallow no ideas can actually live in it.' She sighs now. 'If you'd actually spent as much time writing a book as you have pondering the meaning of life, you'd have your first novel published.'

'Oh, Mum, I was so frightened.' Jamie begins to sob.

Gloria relents, taking him into her arms. 'Come, on love. That's it, let it out.'

'They said they were going to change me... they said...'

'I know love. They were just trying to frighten you.'

'Mum, I'm sorry. I really am. I didn't mean to worry you.'

Over Jamie's shoulder, Gloria can see Freddie fooling around. He's pulled up his blazer over his head so his face is surrounded by a cowl, arms retracted inside shortened sleeves. He sticks out the forefinger of his right hand, like the alien in Spielberg's movie and mimics a croaky voice, 'Phone home.'

Gloria lets go of Jamie, leans forward and in one uncompromised motion, she hits Freddie across the head, so hard it nearly spins.

'My God!' Sandra says.

'Gloria!' Roy says. 'You need to be sectioned, you do.'

Gloria rubs her face and teases her hair. Then for the first time since it had arrived, she pulls out the little glossy catalogue for Nebular Cruises that she'd discreetly hidden in the magazine rack. 'Look at this, Roy.'

'What's this?' he says.

'That's a ship. It's called *Miracle of the Universe*, would you believe.'

Roy flicks through the booklet. 'Look at these bloody prices.'

'Yes, I know. Sometimes life is expensive, Roy. I've decided I don't want to be stuck around here anymore. I want to swim in the sea. If there's one thing our Jamie has taught me, feeling secure isn't holding onto the edge. Security is swimming out into the middle knowing you won't sink.'

The Pharmacist

Billy is in his usual spot, leaning against the wall of the pub, taking photographs and savouring a beer after a stressful week at work. Through half-closed eyes, he zooms in on an old man talking with the flower seller on the opposite side of Columbia Road flower market. A bunch of bright pink gerberas is being wrapped up, and then money is exchanging hands. Even from where he's standing, Billy can see it's more money than the cost of a bunch of flowers and the flower seller is counting it out to the old man, not the other way round. Billy lowers the camera. The old man in the cream linen suit turns and for a split second, in the fiery glare of summer, across the street, he and Billy are smiling at each other. Billy acknowledges him with a nod. But then, he appears a little self-conscious under his cream Panama. The old man looks back, shiftily, at the flower seller who's nudging him with the bunch of gerberas. He takes the flowers. Billy watches them nodding agreeably to each other and, as they are shaking hands, he sees the old man quickly pass something, a tiny packet, to the flower seller who winks as they exchange inaudible words.

Often, on Sunday lunchtimes, Billy comes here to take photographs and chat to the traders selling the last of their flowers. He's attracted by the atmosphere of the market and enjoys the eccentric postmodern revivalists, in their vintage costumes and designer accessories, who posture and parade as if the street were a catwalk. Yet on this occasion, he's gripped by this debonair gentleman. Billy disregards the transaction he thought might have taken place. It's the old man he's interested in. He must live locally. Billy's seen him at least three times before, here on the street. Unmistakable. When the old man walks, trailing rich aromatic smoke from his pipe, he holds himself taut and regal. This graceful image of a man is enough to spark Billy's interest for unconventional behaviour, and he manages a couple of good shots of the man, amid his photographs of the flowers.

From his place in the sunlight, he observes the old man doff his hat and say 'goodbye' to the flower seller, punctuated by a flourish of his hand.

Look at that, thinks Billy, the flair, the twirl. He loves that the man doesn't conform to any normal code of behaviour. Swanning swiftly through the crowds of fashionably dressed people carrying freshly cut flowers, the old gentleman disappears round the corner into Laburnum Road. Billy follows quickly to see if he can get another shot to take back to the studio. The old man fascinates him and he wonders if he may have found a new subject. The gentleman heads down the east-end street towards the Victorian maisonettes where Billy lives. It's a great surprise to him to see the old man take a key from his pocket and slip into the communal entrance of his building; Billy's building. 'Oh my God!' Billy says out loud, before reaching the front door. 'He lives upstairs.'

After that, Billy doesn't see his mystery man again for days. While he's curious about the old man living upstairs, he's hardly had time to unpack, let alone introduce himself to the neighbours. Perhaps even a week goes by before he hears anything more than the old man's footsteps, or the cackle of friends sloshing wine around upstairs. One morning, they meet in the little entrance hall to their maisonettes. They greet each other with the stiff, ceremonious air of businessmen, neither quite knowing how to react, having already met but not met.

'Albert Power,' offers the old man, replacing the pipe in his mouth, freeing up his remaining hand.

'Billy Monroe,' he returns. They shake hands, but with Billy beaming right at him, Albert's eyes fall uncomfortably to the floor. He's carrying a brown leather carry case. 'Working?' Billy asks, nodding to the case.

'Er, no,' Albert says and moves the case guardedly behind his legs. 'I don't work.' Billy wonders what might be inside and why a retired old gentleman would be carrying such a thing.

Albert steps towards the interior door of his flat, adjacent to Billy's door. 'Well, neighbours we are,' he says, inserting his key into the lock.

Billy allows his voice to deepen. 'I've knocked a couple of times since I moved in, but I keep missing you.'

'Not to worry,' Albert replies, hurriedly. 'We must keep different hours. Ships in the night and all that.' He lets himself in and turns back to Billy, now that the ice has been broken, correcting what appears as plain aloofness. A streak of sunlight through the street door catches one side of Albert's face. 'But you're here *now*. *You're* not at work *today?*' Albert asks, one eyeball gleaming like a pebble of tiger's eye.

There is a charged moment when their eyes meet, in which Billy feels a knowledge pass between them. It's the kind of cruisy look he only usually gets from young guys in bars and clubs. Billy knows he should look away, but Albert doesn't, so *he* doesn't. He feels something there—the weird sensation, perhaps, that they knew each other before. 'I'm on holiday from work,' Billy replies, and breaks his gaze.

'Ah.' Albert nods. 'You live alone?'

Billy has no reason to be anything other than transparent now, but he finds himself saying, 'Yes. I live alone.'

'No… girlfriend?'

'No.' Not a lie. Though in omitting the fact that he's actually in a relationship, he knows he's not being honest either.

'Oh?'

'What?'

'It's just that I thought I'd seen someone else coming and going.'

Billy looks up and smiles at Albert's blatant prying. 'That's Jamie. He's been helping, since I moved in,' Billy says, still being opaque. That puts an end to it, for now at least, allowing a silent moment in which Billy takes in every physical detail. Good muscles and bone structure give Albert a taut appearance. He looks younger than his attire would suggest and Billy thinks he would look more at home on the set of a Tennessee Williams play. He's curious to see an off-white shirt, collars fraying at the sides of his neck.

'Well, at last we meet,' Albert says. 'Pop up for a drink sometime.' Albert's gaze falls, less discreetly this time, over the length of Billy's body, as if stroking each downy hair on Billy's skin with his eyes. 'I'm in and out. Just knock.' Albert turns to enter his flat.

'Thanks. I will,' says Billy. He smiles and walks out into the sunlit street.

§

'I prefer Dalston to Kentish Town. And that estate agent was a right slimy fucker.'

Billy glances sideways at Jamie. It's the liveliest he's seen him for a long time. Real joy. The end of Billy's cigarette burns to the filter and he flicks it into the gutter. There are two pubs on this street. The first one they come to has a beer garden. 'Shall we stop here for a pint and talk?'

'Sure,' Jamie says.

When Billy walks over to Jamie with two pints of lager, the sales materials are already spread out on the table. Jamie looks up, takes his beer. 'Lovely' he says, and he nods as Billy slides onto the bench. 'You okay?'

He's hit a wall. The painting isn't happening. The existing ones aren't really selling. He's going through the motions while Jamie's doing so well. And it shows. He's now splashing out on boutique clothes. 'We need a fresh start. We need something new.'

'Well, looking at these… loft apartment in Shoreditch, warehouse work-live unit in Clapton… I'm not sure we can really afford any of them, especially after all those fancy holidays we've been having.'

'We can't live like this all our lives, constantly at the mercy of a greedy landlord.' Billy rubs his hands over his jeans, thighs torn and threadbare and not in an ironic way. They'd agonised over the idea of moving in together ever since Jamie had returned from New Mexico, and that had been ages ago. Despite Jamie being established in his new job at the Walter's Gallery and being rather more solvent than he'd ever been in his life, Billy actually found he enjoyed living alone. It has taken him until now to relinquish his freedom.

'I'm fed up of living out of a suitcase. It's time to set down some roots.'

He looks at Jamie studying him, working him out. 'We don't have to do this now, Billy. You know, financially, it might be better if we wait.'

Billy fiddles with his fag packet. 'I don't want to wait. Let's take a risk.'

Jamie holds one of the sheets of paper up. 'Dalston?'

'Dalston.' Billy feels his stomach drop. In his mind, there is the echo of a life now given up. He necks his beer.

'You're drinking fast?'

Billy shrugs. 'Nothing else to do. You going to book another appointment, then?'

'Leave it all to me.'

§

Another summer day, Billy is sitting on the wall outside the flats, like a lonely teenager in the school holidays. He's smoking a spliff, wistfully reading a paperback. Albert is quickly becoming one of his obsessions. He's started to note the times Albert leaves and returns to the flat, or what he wears; sometimes the cream linen suit, sometimes a shirt without a jacket, but always the Panama.

For a moment, a movement of cool air across his bare arms causes him to slip out of his fictional dream. He lets the book rest on his leg and turns to look up at Albert's open window. The gentle breeze catches the lacy curtain making it billow playfully, before Billy returns to his book. Then he's pleasantly startled by a voice behind him. 'Good day, Billy.' Albert's leaning out of his first floor window, doffing his hat. 'Isn't the light beautiful?'

'Alright, Albert.' Billy smiles over his shoulder.

'Been stood up?' Albert asks.

'You could say that. I was waiting for...' He stops himself again before saying Jamie's name, '...my friend.' Why is he holding back? He knows the old man finds him desirable. He's enjoying being a tease, waiting to see where this will lead.

Albert winks. 'If you're at a loose end, come up. I'll open a bottle of wine.'

§

At last, together in the same space, Billy drinks red wine with his new friend. It's as if they have always known each other. In this short space of time, he's learned that Albert's favourite authors are Genet and Proust, that he never eats red meat on a Sunday and that he once had dinner with Dusty Springfield.

Billy stands in the open bay window where Albert had stood

earlier. He wonders where Jamie could have got to. Maybe he'd had to work after all. This is happening more frequently since he started that blasted job at the Walter's Gallery. He's so good at his job, they just want more and more of him.

The thought lingers at the back of his throat like a bit of dry bread until he washes it down with a zealous gulp of red wine.

Cradling the glass, he leans out into the sunshine, intermittently eyeing up a neighbour washing his car. The street is ablaze with gold and green, dappled sunlight pushing through the gaps in the foliage of the sycamores lining the street. Albert stands, holding the bottle of red wine. 'Vada the bona dish on the omi-palone!' he says, extending every vowel sound, curling his words like ornate calligraphy. He's come to stand next to Billy, to stare down at the neighbour. The palm of Albert's hand gently rests on his back, warmth spreading through the fabric of his vest. Billy turns and presses his arse against the windowsill. 'Eh?'

Albert pours more wine into Billy's almost empty glass. 'I said, look at the rear end on that gorgeous queen.' Albert puts the bottle down and gulps his wine.

It takes Billy a moment to register. 'Ah, Polari. I haven't heard that for ages,' he says, but still feels a little bewildered. 'Who?'

'That guy next door.' Albert nods his head towards the man in the street. 'Don't pretend. I saw you. Couldn't take your eyes off of him.'

Billy looks over his shoulder at the man who has dropped his sponge and now has his mobile phone clamped to the side of his face. He's sneering and flaring his nostrils, looking busy. He takes lots of very quick, small steps, down the tree-lined street, shoulders pivoting forwards and backwards. After having been misled by an image of butch masculinity, this little display makes them both giggle. Billy turns back to see Albert smiling to himself, walking across the room to throw his hat on a coat stand. 'Dolly capello, old fruit,' Billy says, complimenting Albert on his hat. They both suddenly crack into laughter, surprised but united now, across the generation gap, by the ancient gentleman's slang.

For a moment there's a silence in which they stand looking at each other. 'So, what do you do?' Albert finally says.

The question makes Billy squirm. He ponders a second before

announcing, 'I'm an artist.' He knows if he's ever going to live the life he wants he must get used to defining himself so. It seems such an airy-fairy thing to say—not really a proper job.

'I knew you had to be a painter. First time I met you, in the hall, I smelt the turps. Though, I suppose when I saw you loitering in the flower market, from the way you were dressed, I thought you might have owned one of those trendy art galleries on Columbia Road.'

'You saw me?' Billy acts surprised, but of course he knows that Albert had seen him that day. He covers a smile with his hand.

'Oh come off it. You were watching me!' Albert teases. 'You even nodded at me.' His eyes glint and his cheeks flush pink perhaps with the wine. 'But didn't you say you were on *holiday*, the other day?'

Billy explains that he works part-time for an arts trust.

'Must be difficult,' Albert says. 'Working in an office as well as fitting in your creative activities.'

He's relaxed, even though the old man continues to fire question after question at him. There seems nothing guarded about Albert. From the outside, who would guess they only just met?

Billy looks around the room. It's a large space with bare floorboards and a thick rag rug in the middle. Floor-to-ceiling bookshelves run along the left-hand side of the bay window. In front of the window there's a tatty cream chaise longue, and in the corner, to the right, a writing bureau, on top of which sits an emerald green glass vase, containing eight bright pink gerberas. Billy counts each stalk and wonders if Albert has always chosen that colour.

'I'm easing myself into the painting again,' Billy says. 'But no doubt just as I build enough momentum to work towards the next show, I'll run out of money and be back to the grind.'

'Got to stay positive, Billy. You'll make it work.'

Billy continues to gaze around the room. In front of the bookshelves, there is a well-worn ox-blood leather Chesterfield and a standard lamp with a dusty cream shade. On a glass-topped coffee table sit a few books and a scattering of magazines. Some of them are pornographic, which strikes Billy as rather unusual. Is Albert too lazy to clear up, or is he making a statement?

'But you'll continue to paint?'

Billy nods. 'Right! That's enough,' he says, flopping down onto the

Chesterfield, halting further interrogation. 'You've been quizzing me ever since I arrived. What about you?'

'Me? I'm an open book. Not all that interesting, mind.' Albert bites his bottom lip as if to feign shyness. 'I am all your failed expectations in a man,' he says sadly. Billy lifts the bottle of wine and Albert pushes his glass towards him. He pours two more glasses and Albert swallows almost half of his in one gulp.

'Well, you must have a pretty pension to keep this place on. What did you do? I mean work-wise - for a living?'

'Life doesn't cost a lot now. There's no mortgage on this place. But there are no savings and no pension either, only what I get from the state and that's next to nothing. I've done some acting. Used to be a singer. All a blur now. I managed a very nice restaurant in Soho, once. But mainly, I just got by.'

'Just got by?' Billy questions. 'I can hear the jangle of old money in your voice.'

'Darling Boy!' Albert says, pointing his finger. 'You must not make assumptions about people based on the way they speak.'

'I had you down as an aristocrat. Blue blood.'

'We're not all high fliers, Billy. I'm just a survivor.'

'Well at least you have your home. How *are* you surviving?'

Albert pauses in contemplation. Billy doesn't know much about him, but he senses Albert is about to open up. 'Billy, I hardly know you. But I feel we have a connection.'

'Me too.' Billy gives him a sexy little smile, confirming a mutual trust.

'Okay, well if you can keep a secret...'

'I thought you were an open book?' Billy sits forward keenly.

'Everyone has things that they keep to themselves.' Albert slumps next to Billy on the Chesterfield and starts to talk, slurring his words a little. 'I think it's really important, at whatever cost, to be true to oneself. I hate spending my time in drag for other people's convenience.' Albert sloshes back more wine. 'I mean *drag* in terms of putting on a performance. You know, like wearing a mask, covering up the self.

'This is the way I see it. Most folks want to get married and have babies. So they have a baby, and they do everything they can to mould it, shape it, and dress it into what they think it should be. And by God, some of them want their child to be that shape so badly that they'll beat anything else out of it. You know, one is lucky if one grows up feeling comfortable being that person, being that shape. So comfortable that one forgets to think for oneself. One can get so far down that path with the job and the wife and the car, that before you know it, the whole process starts again, of making more babies to mould and shape, mould and shape... and oh...' He pauses and swallows, then continues almost without breathing. 'But for some of us, no matter how hard we try, we just don't fit a particular shape. And we start thinking for ourselves. And we come to a fork in the road. And you just know you've got to make this choice, because when you're different, if you wear those clothes and stay on that path, when you know you really should be somewhere else, then you're just doing drag. Do you see what I'm talking about Billy?'

Billy is completely absorbed. 'I think so. Yeah. But I don't really understand what this has to do with money?'

'Well, when you make that choice, when you take that fork in the road, you might have to turn around to your folks and say, 'Yes, thanks for that. But no.' With that, you're on your own. Surviving means you might end up doing things you had never expected.'

Billy waits for a moment, expecting a punch line. 'So come on then. What's your secret?'

Albert turns to Billy and looks directly at him. 'I'm in pharmaceuticals.'

Billy closes one eye, trying to draw more out of him.

'You ever go dancing?' Albert asks.

'God—all the time.'

'You know The Palais? On Kingsland Road?'

'Yeah. Been there lots of times. There's a fantastic Trance night on Fridays.'

Albert's eyes widen. 'You've never seen me there?'

'You?'

'Yes, *me*, strangely enough! Old man in a Panama. Impossible to miss.'

'No.'

'I deal drugs in there.'

Billy feels his chin drop. 'You're kidding?'

'Close your mouth, Billy. You look like you're trying to catch flies.' Albert swallows more wine.

'I don't understand.'

'It's not hard, Billy. Every Friday night I go to The Palais and I sell drugs to the clubbers.'

'What kind of drugs?'

'What kind of drugs do you think? Coke, speed, pills. A little bit of acid sometimes, but mainly E's.'

'Albert... you're an old man,' Billy says.

'Thank you for pointing that out.'

Billy rolls around, uncoiling in his place on the Chesterfield. 'Well, of course—a very *well-preserved* old man,' he giggles.

Albert smiles, his eyes sparkling, full of danger.

Billy sits quietly staring at him, pondering the old man for several minutes. Albert smiles back without complaint, until Billy asks, 'What are E's like?'

'You mean you've never done one?' Albert runs his fingers through silver hair.

'Never done anything, except a bit of grass.' Billy looks at the clock on Albert's bureau. They have been chatting for hours. An empty bottle of wine stands on the coffee table and a second, half empty, is in Albert's hand refilling Billy's glass. The sunlight is changing. It's lower now and passes through the window, causing Billy's wine glass to sparkle like a giant ruby.

'I thought you said you'd been to The Palais on a Friday night?'

'I have, but I've never done an E.'

'You? A man in his twenties, dancing around half-naked in The Palais, never done an E?'

Billy laughs. 'Well, I suppose, in the past, my attention was mainly on my work. The students who did drugs at Art College didn't get first class degrees. It would have been no good, me doing drugs. I can't even open a box of chocolates without finishing the lot.'

'Ha. I see. But most people who hang out on the club scene, especially those of your age, have tried it at least once. Part of the territory.'

Billy shrugs. 'Never been offered.'

'Never lived.' Albert chuckles and ruffles Billy's hair.

Billy is alert like a boy on his first day of school. 'Tell me what it's like,' he says, lightening the tone of his voice, playing innocent. He kicks off his trainers, falls back onto the sofa and breathes in sun-warmed leather.

'Hard to say. Like nothing you've ever felt in your life. Like being in a dream state.' Albert flutters his hands in the air, pretending to scatter fairy dust. When his hand drops, it falls casually onto Billy's shoulder. Billy allows it to rest there.

'Can't you be more specific? Dream state? Call yourself a drug dealer?'

'I'm an expert on all drugs,' Albert says. He undoes the top buttons of his shirt and removes his cravat. For a man of his age, Billy notes, his skin is in very good condition—only a slight sagginess where one might expect to see a more developed dewlap. His strong jawline reminds Billy of Marlon Brando. 'I've never ingested any substance without first knowing about all the highs and the side effects. But with E, the experience is slightly different for everyone. Generally, with ecstasy, it's all about empathy. If people around you are enjoying themselves, chances are, you'll pick up on that vibe.'

'They make you feel horny, don't they?' Billy asks, still playing dumb.

'Yes. There's that too.' Albert smiles.

A July breeze of warm air moves through the open window. Sounds float in from the street—birdsong, traffic, the wind through the trees.

'What else? People die, don't they?'

'There are risks, I suppose, but really, the few deaths that have occurred have been the result of carelessness. Overheating, or else over-hydration and all that stuff.'

'You trying to sell to me?'

'Darling Boy, I'm not a drug *pusher*. I sell to those who *use* them. If you want to try one, you are more than welcome.'

Billy is surprised by this suggestion. A man of his age, sitting around popping Es, seemed unconventional to say the least. 'Don't you worry about stuff?'

'Like what?' Albert says, clearing his throat.

'Short-term memory loss. Alzheimer's. You read things, don't you?'

'When you reach my state of decrepitude, you stop worrying. Look at me, I'm seventy. Nothing wrong with my memory. And, Darling Boy, for every brain cell that has died, a new door has opened to a magical world.'

There's a wry twinkle in Albert's eye. 'People who do drugs always say stuff like that,' Billy says, deliberately juvenile.

'I've explored corners of my mind which would've been otherwise unreachable. It has helped me to recall events from my childhood with incredible clarity.'

'What about the hard stuff? Done that?'

'I've done everything,' Albert says.

Billy rubs the insides of his legs in anticipation. 'Everything?'

'We live in a chemical world, Billy Monroe. Everyone needs some kind of medicine.' Billy forgives him the use of his surname. It makes him feel like a pupil being addressed by a teacher but he knows that Albert is playing his game.

'What for?' Billy asks.

'When I'm tired, I snort a little speed. When I'm restless, I have a bit of pot. And if I'm feeling stuck. I mean, if I feel troubled by something, I'll smoke a bit of opium to help me get through it. If I can't sleep, I slip a little something in my tea.'

'Speed? When you're tired?'

Albert shrugs. 'From time to time. Gets the vacuuming done.'

'Albert Power!' There, switching roles—he's equal now. 'You must have a liver like a piece of leather.' He sits forward, trembling.

Albert stands, moves to the writing bureau, pulls open the front and lifts out a tiny bag of white tablets, shaking out a handful before disappearing through a beaded curtain into the kitchen. A moment later, he returns with two pint glasses of water and sits down next to Billy. Albert places his hand over the table and lets the tablets fall onto the glass surface. For a moment, Billy looks at them. Then he leans and picks one up, rolls it between his thumb and forefinger and examines its tiny logo.

'Mitsubishi. Bona doobs!'

'Eh?' Billy misses the slang again.

'Don't you know your Polari, Darling Boy? Doobs. Drugs. These are good ones. Pure MDMA. Lovely trip.'

Billy's mobile phone buzzes in his pocket. He pulls it out to read the text message. It's from Jamie.

Really sorry, Billy. Had to work late. I'm not going to make it.

Billy frowns and stuffs the phone back in his jeans.

'Problem?' Albert asks.

'Not at all.' He smiles coyly, puts the pill to his mouth, lets it touch his tongue. 'It tastes bitter,' he says, pulling a face.

'Swallow it.'

The glass of water trembles in Billy's hands. Albert swallows his pill and smiles. 'See? Not dead yet.'

After washing it down with water, Billy leans back and puts his feet up on Albert's coffee table, waiting for something to happen. Albert's right. Billy is surprised, even by himself, that he has reached his mid-twenties and still hasn't tried this. It makes him feel young and naïve. They sit quietly for a minute. 'What now?' Billy asks.

'Be patient. All will be revealed.' Albert stands up abruptly. 'Music!' he says, and moves around the coffee table with the grace of a ballet dancer, slipping his hand beneath the glass and sliding open a drawer. It takes him a moment to select a disc.

Restlessly, Billy gets up and walks to the window behind the chaise longue and looks out onto the street. The shadows along the road are longer now as the sun moves even lower. But it's still very bright. 'I love these long, hot summer evenings,' he says, stretching his arms above his head. He lets his eyes follow his hands as the psychedelic folk of Goldfrapp's *Felt Mountain* begins to play. Billy breathes out. 'I love this,' he says.

'Seminal album,' Albert says.

The silver bracelet on Billy's wrist catches the sunlight. When he lets his eyes fall again, they are caught by the refracted light from a collection of coloured glass vessels on the windowsill—red, yellow, green and blue glass, tall and thin, short and wide, straight and curved. Billy marvels at the new colours created where light passes through more than one layer of glass, one in front of the other; red and yellow making amber, blue and red making amethyst.

'The warm air is lovely, isn't it?' Albert finally says, in agreement.

'So you like the sun?'

'I'm a real baby. Hate winter. Going to work in the dark and all that. Summer is my favourite time of year.' He continues to look down onto the tree-lined street, knowing Albert's eyes are lingering on him, sketching, tracing the curve of his bicep, moving across his groin. Then, to tease the old man, he deliberately turns back to face the room. Albert is taken by surprise, and spins to face the CD player, face reddening. Billy looks away to spare him embarrassment but can't help smiling. 'I can't feel anything at all.'

'Good God, child! You only swallowed it a few minutes ago. Give it chance.'

Albert's electronic sounds perforate the air beautifully. He returns to the sofa and pats the seat next to him. 'Come on, Darling Boy, it will come when it's ready.' He picks up Billy's book, which has been lying face down on the coffee table next to Billy's digital camera. 'Is that what you were reading, out there on the wall?'

'Look how splendid the light is in this room.' Billy points to the glass ornaments. 'Have you seen how the colour from that wine glass is being projected onto the wall?'

Albert turns the book over and moves it up closer to his face. 'Ah, *Catcher in the Rye*,' he says.

Billy tilts his head to face the ceiling, gazes at the room, spangled with coloured light. 'Look, Albert.'

'Yes, Darling Boy.' Albert nods, drops the book back on the coffee table and pulls his nose up.

'Why the face?'

'It's the kind of book one discovers when one is sixteen.'

'Listen to you!' Billy says.

'Well, you are an artist after all. I'd've thought you'd have read all those angst-ridden books by now. How old *are* you?' Albert asks.

Billy goes to answer and then stops himself. 'How old do I look?'

'Ha. You're asking for trouble now!'

Billy throws his head back proudly and smoothes down his eyebrows. 'I'm twenty-four.'

Albert pouts. 'I'd have guessed at thirty.'

'Cheeky sod.' Billy punches Albert playfully on the shoulder.

'Though for your manner, mind,' Albert says, 'and your confidence.

But you do have the complexion of a youth.'

Billy closes his eyes and takes a deep breath. The fresh air seems to flush through his whole body, refreshing all the way to the tips of his feet. When he opens his eyes again, he says, 'I don't think anything is going to happen.'

'Well, I suppose you might be a bit disappointed. Who knows? Just wait. It's better if you don't think about it. Listen to the music.'

Billy sits forward and thumbs through the pornography on the coffee table—groups of naked men in leather harnesses, tattoos, piercings, just his sort of thing. Then he lets his hands explore a plain-covered, glossy coffee-table book—*The Complete Guide to Recreational Psychoactives*. As he turns the pages, the silver bands on his fingers sparkle in the half-light. He reads out loud the descriptions of random substances. 'Heroin... a potent painkiller derived from morphine... produces an overwhelming sense of well-being, elation and blissful apathy... notoriously addictive, it can lead to complex physical withdrawal.' He continues to let the pages of the book fall open at random. 'Gamma-hydroxybutyrate or GHB is a sedative drug which, used in the right quantities, induces an experience of disequilibria, a euphoric state in which the user has an increased capacity for tactile sensitivity...' He looks up at Albert. 'I can't believe there's actually a book on all this stuff.'

Albert shrugs. 'A drug user's Bible.'

'You can say that again.' Billy sits back for a while, in silence. He strokes the blonde hairs on his forearms while the music tips into something more electronic. Albert sips water, stretches, postures in an exaggerated theatrical gesture and slumps back into the Chesterfield. He breathes in deeply, filling his lungs before relaxing next to Billy, who shifts uneasily in his seat.

'Getting fidgety, Darling Boy?'

'Yeah.' Billy begins to play with the zip on a cushion.

Albert flicks him playfully on the shoulder. 'See! It's beginning to work—a touch of adrenaline. That's the edginess you can feel.'

Billy rubs his sweaty palms on his jeans and looks at Albert.

'Look at your eyes!' Albert says.

'What's wrong with them?'

'Pupils are dilated, eyes are all sparkly. You look very beautiful.'

Billy watches Albert smiling warmly at him. Then he lets his eyes fall shut. Ever changing kaleidoscopic patterns spiral behind his eyelids. His palms tingle.

'Do you feel like you're glowing?' Albert asks.

'Yeah, and light as a feather.' Billy moves to the edge of his seat and lets his head fall into his hands, moving gently, synchronised with the music. 'Butterflies in my stomach. I think I can feel it, Albert. I think it's beginning to work.'

'I know, Darling Boy. I can feel it too.'

Billy tries to grasp the feeling in his head but it is indefinable. Maybe like a pillowcase of feathers exploding in his head. So soft and subtle, but intense and powerful all at once. 'Oh God. Albert, can you feel this?'

Albert doesn't answer. Moments later Billy lifts his head out of his hands and opens his eyes. He sees Albert swallowing another pill, washing it down with water.

'What are you doing?' Billy asks.

'Oh, stop frowning. It takes a bit more for me these days. People develop a tolerance.'

Billy wonders if it will rot his brain away. He notices Albert catch the look on his face. 'I don't do this *every* weekend,' Albert says, defensively.

'Not in The Palais on Fridays?' Billy imagines him stalking around in the darkness, snaking his way through a dance floor of clubbers, or rocking from side to side in a corner somewhere.

'That wouldn't be good for business. No.'

Billy feels suddenly disappointed. It's gone. The feeling has just gone away. He sits back wondering if he's imagined it and waits to see if it returns.

'I remember my first pill vividly. It's not something you ever forget.'

'Oh my God.' Billy interrupts and collapses into his own hands. He can feel the drug beginning to work again. 'Can you feel this? Tell me you can feel this.' He sighs deeply and then sits back on the sofa with his eyes shut.

Albert lifts his palms in a sign of indifference.

'This is blowing my mind.' Billy holds his arms out in front of him. Tiny beads of sweat have begun to appear on the surface of his skin, trickling along the lines of his tattoos. He touches the clammy skin at the nape of his neck.

'What can you feel?' Albert asks playfully.

'It's… indescribable. The best mood I've ever been in.' All the anxiety he's been carrying around seems to be falling away. He thinks about Jamie not turning up. Earlier, he'd been concerned, but now it's okay. It doesn't matter. All is well in his world.

'Bliss,' Albert says.

'Perfect.' Billy opens his eyes. 'Can we change the music?'

'Do whatever you like.'

Billy moves around the coffee table to view Albert's collection of CDs. His evening with Albert has been very easy. Without the history normal friendships require, he feels they both trust each other unreservedly. Billy fingers the tiny bag of pills on the table. 'Who would have thought that something so tiny could cause such an effect? Albert, I feel… how do you explain this—so many feelings all at once? There aren't words for it. I feel drunk. No, not drunk. It's not like alcohol, but I feel… Oh God, it's coming again…'

Billy, on his knees now, sinks forward and leans over the coffee table, head-in-hands as another cloud of feather-down explodes in his head and causes another torrent of pleasure to rain over his entire body.

'You alright, Billy? It's coming on a bit strong for you, isn't it?'

Billy runs his hands through his hair, feeling how wonderful it is to touch his own head, his own flesh. Then he moves and flicks through the CD collection. It's a jumble: Mozart next to Kraftwerk, David Bowie next to Sarah Vaughan. '*Six* different versions of La Wally?' Billy remarks.

'Yes. But Callas is the best.' Albert marks the air with a finger.

A few moments later, the drug has taken full grip over Billy. He can't be arsed to change the music. He sinks into the Chesterfield next to Albert, swaying and breathing deeply. He moans softly as the waves of blissful pleasure move through his body.

Albert rolls a joint. Billy is mesmerised by the intricate process, which Albert goes through, first sprinkling the tobacco and then the grass into the Rizla paper. Watching Albert deftly rolling it between thumb and index fingers, until it becomes a perfectly formed spliff, makes him feel even more bizarrely relaxed. He can feel himself going cross-eyed. Billy looks again at the clock. This time he can't see the hands anymore. But he knows it's much later. The light is beginning to fade.

He closes his eyes, gently pulls the bottom of his vest up a little to feel the soft ladder of hair above his navel. He sighs deeply. 'I feel like I'm in touch with the universe. In touch with God,' he goes on. 'Everything suddenly makes sense. Or maybe it doesn't. But everything just feels right... safe.'

He lets out a deep, refreshing breath again and shifts in his seat. 'I love you Albert,' he says without even thinking about it. For a moment, he wonders why he would say such a thing. But it feels perfectly natural. He does love Albert.

Albert gives a little laugh. 'I love you too, Darling Boy,' he says with exaggerated warmth. He ruffles Billy's hair again, lights the joint and takes a long drag. Billy, greedily, takes the joint from his fingers and starts to smoke it himself.

'Look at the state you're in. That'll knock you for six.'

'In for a penny, in for a pound.' Billy inhales long and hard and then hands it back. He closes his eyes and feels himself disappearing into an invisible cloud of delight, moaning and swaying to the music. 'I'm so hot. It's warm in here, isn't it?' He tugs at his vest and peels it away from his body. He examines the tanned skin of his abdominals glistening with dewy sweat. Albert leans towards him slightly, examining the shiny silver ring that pierces his left nipple. 'No stranger to the gym!'

'Fuck, I feel horny,' Billy moans. He closes his eyes again and begins to gently tease his nipples. He shudders at the intense pleasure achieved with each touch of his fingertips.

'This happens often, Billy. People get horny but find themselves incapable of achieving an erection. I see we don't have that problem.' When Billy opens his eyes, Albert is staring at the large bulge in his jeans.

'What?' Billy moans, and lets his eyes roll back in their sockets.

'Oh, don't mind me,' Albert says, sinks into the sofa. 'I'll just sit here.'

'Yeah,' Billy murmurs, letting his head drop back against the

Chesterfield. He strokes his chest, lets his hands wander to his groin, slipping a couple of fingers beneath the waist of his jeans. He pulsates and swells beneath the denim. He watches Albert's eager eyes eating him up. Slowly he pushes his jeans down, over his thighs. His erect penis stands up vertical as he rubs it gently in one hand. With the other, he continues to squeeze the tender, alert flesh of his nipple.

He moans. 'I don't believe I'm doing this.'

'Just let go, Darling Boy.' Albert smiles, seemingly unoffended by the unfolding spectacle.

Billy opens his eyelids again, straining to uncross his eyes. He can see two Albert's waving a spliff at him.

After taking another drag on it, he begins to rub himself harder, more rhythmically as he works towards orgasm, waves of ecstasy crashing through his mind and body—his shiny penis gleaming with pre-cum.

'My head's swimming,' Albert says.

Billy watches Albert watching him, overwhelmed, writhing before Albert's eyes. Albert has remained a gentleman throughout the entire episode. Though at this moment, he takes leave of himself. He leans over towards Billy, grasps him in one hand. For Billy, the sensation of having someone else's fingers around him takes him by surprise. He voluntarily drops his arms to his sides in submission. His hips buck, driving a warm jerky surge from his balls. Albert's hand pushes him toward orgasm, pressing the mound of flesh at the base of Billy's cock. Again, Billy bucks, pushing his hips towards Albert's head.

When Albert slides his wet lips down over Billy's penis, he gasps with pleasure. Eyes open now, Albert's head nods up and down, before Billy crashes back into the feather pillowcases in his head. He can feel every detail of the moment: Albert's bottom lip rubs along the back of the shaft, his tongue on the 'v' of flesh where the foreskin meets the head. Billy can feel Albert taking all of him in, gorging on him, while he writhes powerlessly underneath him, nearing orgasm.

Afterwards, there is a religious silence. Billy is sated. He casually strokes his cock. He looks at Albert, whose apparent fascination, perhaps even fixation with him, has turned to a look of melancholy as he seems to survey the room and his few material possessions: a collection of compact discs, a writing bureau, a few books and a leather Chesterfield.

And then a new look of admission crosses his face. There is a frank, matter-of-fact tone in his voice. 'Baggage, Darling Boy,' he begins to soliloquise, seemingly aware that Billy has slipped out of his dream state. 'I try not to carry any baggage. Frightened I might lose it, see? If one doesn't own things, one can't lose them.'

The edges of Billy's vision are disappearing as if someone has taken an eraser and rubbed them out. He lets his eyes fall closed and pretends that he's not really listening while the old man continues. 'Can't hold on, but scared of letting go. *He* was everything to me. When I was with him I knew the truth, but now I just make it up as I go along.'

With who? What truth? Billy's thoughts will not stay solid. They float in and out of his mind.

'Walks in the park, photograph albums, boxes full of trinkets, memories of a life I used to have with him. I can see the day that he came in shades of autumn. Somehow my memories all appear in sepia.' Billy tries to follow Albert's thoughts but they jump around. 'Out there, on the street, sitting on the wall, just like you were, reading a book, smoking a spliff. He used to smoke like a chimney. Took his mind in the end. He looked like James Dean. He was reading *East of Eden*. Thank God you weren't reading Steinbeck. I think I would've had a turn, Darling Boy. Of course the street was still gas-lit then, in those days. Showing my age now.'

Billy gazes at Albert, his eyes staring, unfocused. 'You loved him,' he asks—feeling, understanding Albert's loss.

Albert looks surprised. 'You were listening?' The skin around Albert's eyes is darkened and bruised where blood has flushed to the surface. His cheeks appear hollow. His eyes roll back a little as he begins to trip out. 'I lost him,' he says.

Billy struggles to focus. 'But you had your time together. That's what matters.'

Albert is moving across the room now, gently swaying. 'So precious... precious little...' he continues. 'He had golden brown hair, wavy and swept back. At the temples where the hair was shorter, he had tight little curls. I remember his full red lips, like Elizabeth Siddall in those Pre-Raphaelite paintings. He used to wear those v-neck pullovers and a rugby shirt underneath. I always thought he looked like a farm boy. I loved his soft tanned skin. Not unlike you, little more than a boy with dewy eyes and flawless skin.

'We should have made more the time. It just slipped through our fingers.' Albert gives Billy a box of tissues. 'Clean yourself up, Darling Boy.'

Billy wipes semen from his skin, dabs at where, so quickly, the warm, sticky liquid has turned cold and watery. He licks the residue from around his fingers where liquid has become dry and crystalline.

'Billy Monroe, this is one of those days you'll never ever be able to relive. But it can never be erased. One day when I'm long gone, you'll look over your shoulder, back down the road we've travelled and I'll be there waving back. You're an angel,' he says as if addressing someone other than Billy in the room. Then looks directly at him, reconnecting. 'It's been one hell of a journey, hasn't it?'

'Epic,' Billy mumbles.

'Fairy tale,' Albert says.

Billy checks himself once more, looks at his watch and stands up. 'I think I need to go downstairs,' he says. He steps closer to Albert and hugs him tightly. Albert's hands caress Billy's torso and he kisses him on the cheek; a kiss neither of them has managed to plant throughout the entire evening. He kisses the skin below Billy's ear and nuzzles the hollow in-between his neck and collarbone.

'Thank you,' Albert says. 'This has been... a pleasure.' Billy can feel him trembling.

Billy stares over Albert's shoulder at a painting. It's been there all the time, on the wall behind the sofa, a large canvas. Billy is surprised that he hadn't noticed it. The frame is gilt, quietly ornate. There is a photo-realistic quality in the image of a man. An astonishing man with a broad masculine jaw-line and just a touch of femininity in his sharp smile. His skin is dark and smooth, the colours of autumn. His face fills the frame, all but for the brim of a Panama hat resting just above his feline eyebrows. Billy studies it.

Albert steps backward to see why Billy is so dumbfounded. He turns, following Billy's eye line. 'Ah, I wondered why you were so quiet.' Albert bends over the coffee table and collects the leftover ecstasy tablets into the plastic bag and presses together the re-sealable zipper.

'It's you!' Billy says, stunned, looking at the painting.

'Yes. Hard to take in, isn't it?' Albert stuffs the bag into the pocket of Billy's jeans. 'For another time,' he says.

Billy rocks unsteadily again. 'Who painted this? It's the most beautiful thing I've ever seen.'

'*He* did. My love. He finished working on that and faded away. I lost him in life's rear-view mirror. I went back for him but he'd gone.' Albert makes perfect sense to Billy. He can hear the pang of sadness in his voice. 'Who'd have thought I would end up like this? Sad old man, dealing in pharmaceuticals.'

Billy says nothing. He thinks it's sad that there is no painting of Albert's companion. He rouses himself and looks about the room. His eyes fall on the coffee table. 'Can I borrow that book?' he asks. When their eyes meet again, Albert is smiling at him.

§

Billy goes back to his own flat carrying Albert's book—*The Complete Guide to Recreational Psychoactives* and places it on his desk. In stark contrast to the summer light that had pervaded Albert's front room earlier, Billy's back room is now dark, cavernous and magical. He often works by candlelight to hide the peeling wood-chip wallpaper and the rising damp making its way through the cracks.

He's brought home something new, something fresh, and something that will help him connect to the source, enough to get him working again. His desk lamp scarcely lights the cluttered back room that he's been using as a workroom for painting, since he gave up his studio at the arts trust. A red light flashes on the answering machine—probably a message from Jamie. Next to the machine are two recent holiday photographs of him and Jamie. Billy glances at them fondly, stroking the glass of one of the frames with a finger. In one image they are in ski-wear and in the other they're in summer vests in San Francisco. The walls are covered with pieces of paper, notes, doodles, photographs, and magazine cuttings, all to inspire his imagination. Books are strewn across the floor and paintings from his previous exhibitions lie stacked up against the walls. Tonight, however, they seem not to be needed. Even with the drug wearing off, there's a feeling of absolute concentration as he starts to work. He gathers his tools and materials, meticulously laying them out, as a surgeon does before an operation. He stretches a canvas over a frame, mixes paint and prepares the surface of the linen. When he's ready, he begins to paint. The image of a man, head and shoulders, emerges very quickly on the canvas. No preliminary sketches or background materials are gathered. There is no model. The likeness built up, as if projected directly from his own mind. Layer over layer, he builds up the paint, gradually, until the image is formed, like flesh stretching over muscle and bone.

He paints all night and then intermittently for the next few days. He paints feverishly, desperate to get some truth out onto the canvas, before it disappears from his mind. In between painting, he masturbates over pornographic videos and magazines. This, unlike reading, watching television or listening to music, does not interfere with the images and feelings that come to him. Like spirit manifesting at a séance, a life slowly seeps into the studio and onto Billy's canvas, conjured from the other side.

§

'Billy? It's Jamie. Are you there...? Hello? Where are you? I've left you so many messages... Sorry I didn't make it on Thursday. Work has gone crazy. I'll come and see you tomorrow. Anyway, please call me back. Anyone would think you're having an affair.'

§

Billy enters The Palais against a wall of sound and a backdrop of laser lights, dry ice and strobes. The soaring, woven fabric of music is perforated by a hair-raising pizzicato. Underneath breathes a floor of raging strings and an urgent drumbeat, threaded with the howl of synthesised sound.

An old recycled theatre-turned-party-venue opens out into the dress circle, from which, as he reaches the over-hanging balcony, Billy observes the mass of revellers on the dance floor below. Topless men, dancing in neon combat trousers, hang out of elaborately moulded rococo boxes on both sides of the decrepit theatre, hydrating themselves with water carried in illuminated shoulder holsters.

Billy looks down at the crowd moving together—each figure a cell of one giant animal, collectively pulsing and breathing as one.

He lifts up his camera. 'Fucking magical,' he says, aiming it into the crowd. He leans back against the edge of the balcony, craning his camera towards the upper circle, the gallery and right to the top where fingers of laser light stroke the ceiling of the gods. His E has already started to work. He recognises the signs this time: sweaty palms, tingling in the stomach, a slight rise in the heart-beat. Will Jamie join in? How will he explain? He can hardly say the old man upstairs gave them to him.

By the time Jamie arrives, Billy is swaying on the edge of the dance floor. He can feel beads of sweat on his forehead, heat in his cheeks. Jamie stares at him through the fronds of laser light passing between them.

'Hello, boyfriend,' Jamie says, and touches Billy's coiffed hair with his fingertips. 'What have you been doing today?'

Billy flexes his biceps.

'You're so unbelievably gay.'

'And you have a problem with that because…'

They both laugh. 'I spoke to Mum earlier. She sends her love.'

Billy nods. He's not in the frame of mind to talk about Gloria.

'She sends her love.'

Jamie looks great, if a little over dressed. 'Aren't you warm?' Billy asks, undoing the buttons of Jamie's shirt.

'It's cool outside,' Jamie says. 'And obviously, I'm not as worked up as you.'

Worked up? Billy bites his lip. Can Jamie tell just by looking?

They are jostled by other clubbers, a crowd of toothy grins. The music gradually gains pace, becoming steadily more intense. They dance, smiling at each other—smoke blasts at them from the side of the auditorium. Billy looks at the faces around him, noticing the dewy eyes of the crowd. Is that how he looks? Billy closes his eyes. Their bodies move with the music, like swimmers moving with the swell of an ocean. There's a drum roll and a single synthesized note comes in, chasing a racing melody beneath the drums. The note is lasting in duration, curling gradually upward in pitch until it floats high above all else, over the drums, over the strings, higher and higher. Jamie is pushed closer to Billy with the surge. They stare deep into each other. Closer. Ecstasy rushes through Billy's brain. 'Fucking amazing,' he yells. Everyone's hands are in the air, tracing the note getting higher, more and more piercing. When Billy opens his eyes, they are almost touching. He looks up, reaching with his hands, as if the note has materialized in solid form, visible to his eyes, rising with the laser light. As the sonic shape reaches its apex, high above the dance floor there is a huge explosion of bass and a flash of firework. Glitter explodes over the crowd. There is a moment's silence as they, too, are travelling through the air after that single note. As Billy's mind reaches solid ground, the beat kicks in again and everyone goes wild—

'Having a good time?' Billy shouts, struggling to make himself heard over the pounding trance music.

'Yeah, thanks.' Jamie nods, looking ever so slightly unimpressed. They are not on the same level. Billy knows he's been found out. 'Have you taken something?' Jamie asks.

Billy winces and points to his ears pretending to be unable to hear. Jamie leans into him and shouts, loud enough to deafen him. 'You look like your jaw has been wired.' He hands Billy a packet of chewing gum.

'Thanks,' he says, gaining awareness for his grinding teeth, muscles bulging in his cheeks. He takes a piece of gum and hands the packet back to Jamie. He cocks his head and nods to the club. 'I bet your mum would love it here.'

Jamie throws his eyes up. 'I don't think you'd find my mother getting off her tits in a place like this.'

He breaks off and wanders off to the bar. In a minute or so he returns with another gin and tonic. He looks a little nervous and slightly out of place. 'You okay?' Billy asks.

'I'm fine,' assures Jamie.

Billy reaches into his pocket, discreetly turning away from him for a moment. He feels around for a pill and presses one into his palm. Retrieving his hand, he holds out a downturned fist to Jamie. 'Take it.'

Jamie shakes his head. 'Not my thing,' he says. 'Where did you get them from?'

'Never mind where I got them from. Come on, take it,' Billy encourages, finding Jamie's reserve cute and slightly sexy.

'Is it safe?'

'Your mother's not watching now.'

Jamie eventually moves closer, cupping his hand beneath Billy's. Billy smiles, lets the pill drop into Jamie's hand and watches him slip the tiny white tablet between his lips. Billy pushes another pill into his own mouth. 'I wish I could feel like this forever!' he says, feeling his eyelids becoming heavy and slightly droopy.

'Forever?' Jamie asks. There is a slight look of horror in his eyes.

Billy punches him affectionately on the shoulder. 'Forever!' he says.

§

They have been dancing for some time before Billy realises Jamie is as dewy eyed and loose-limbed as himself; as if they've suddenly woken from a dream, they stare longingly into each other. Billy peels Jamie from his now damp shirt and threads it through the belt of his jeans. He rubs him affectionately on the stomach, touching the hair around Jamie's navel.

Aroused, longing to kiss him, Billy pulls him through the crowd and leads him, rather inelegantly, upstairs. On the gallery, Billy opens the door to the gents' toilet and finds a dimly lit room crowded with men. 'Where are you taking me?' complains Jamie and they bundle in.

The small room has urinals along one wall, two cubicles and a very low ceiling. This is not a *toilet*. The door closes behind them. The room becomes a little darker. Billy can just make out a group of topless men at the back. There is the sound of muffled music from the gallery and the sounds of men moving around in the dark, breathing, whispering, the shuffle of shoes on a dirty, sticky floor. The two of them lean against the wall for a moment, waiting for their eyes to adjust to the gloom.

'How long does this take to wear off?' Jamie whispers.

'Stop worrying. Just relax.'

'But I've got work tomorrow.'

Two men grope each other, playing with each other's nipples, kissing passionately: 'Action Men' types pumped with steroids with beards and army style haircuts. Billy can't stop staring. In his head he gives the guys names. The first one, *Bluto*, reminds him of the character from *Popeye*. This guy reaches for the other's hand. Let's call him *Bruno*, thinks Billy. Bluto pulls his hand and places it flat on his own flies, encouraging Bruno to rub the fabric where his cock lies beneath. Undoing the zip of Bluto's camouflage combat trousers, his mate's fingers probe inside, pop open the buttons and draw out the flesh that lies beneath. Bruno caresses him with big hands until he becomes longer, harder. Billy trembles, watching intently as Bluto loosens his combats and pushes them over his buttocks, revealing more flesh. His mound of neatly trimmed pubic hair is slightly damp, stuck to his flesh in tiny curls.

He looks over at Billy and Jamie, hungrily. Only an arm's reach away, he breathes deeply through his nostrils, biting his bottom lip. He nods, questioning—*do you want to join in?* Bruno gasps as Bluto tweaks his nipples again. An ecstatic moan comes from the back of the room as someone is penetrated. More men, on the prowl, enter, eyes searching the obscurity. Men huddle in corners, snorting bumps of white powder off the end of door keys.

Orange dots of glowing cigarette ends float around like fireflies in the dark. Condensation drips from the low ceiling. One after another, men enter the little toilet until Billy and Jamie are pressed together, flesh against flesh. Billy feels hands groping. He catches eyes, dilated, the room awash with Ecstasy. Further in, Bluto and Bruno are swallowing capfuls of something—compounds that might be found in Albert's book. He moves deeper in. Bruno is kneeling in front of Bluto, tonguing him, making him moan loudly. Billy can't wait any longer. He turns so that Jamie's face is closer to his. Parts of them touch—knees, a shoulder, Billy's finger-tips against Jamie's snake-hips. At first, they are too close for eye contact. Billy grabs Jamie and kisses him hard on the lips. He responds. They are suddenly in a clinch, hands all over each other. He holds him close. His tongue dances with Jamie's. The wetness of their spit mixes together. Jamie's mouth moves over Billy's neck, his wet tongue sliding on skin, across his throat, down his nipples. He traces circles around them, making Billy gasp. Billy's hands are undoing Jamie's jeans. A few strokes on his cock and Jamie whispers, 'Stop,' squeezing his bare shoulders, hands on his tattoos. But Billy won't stop. He races away—his mouth thrusting. 'Stop, now!'

Unreal. They are there in the dark, men standing in circles, jerking off, sucking, fucking, fingering, kissing, while the rest of London goes about its business. Billy watches as Bluto's large hands reach forward for Jamie's nipples, pinching each in between thumb and forefinger, twisting gently. Jamie gasps and falls gently back against Bluto's chest, happy to let it all happen. Billy looks at them, greedily. Bluto takes a foil wrapper out of his combats, winks at Bruno, and nods towards Jamie. The waiting is worst. Bruno takes the condom and moves behind Jamie, back to the wall. He grabs him by the waist, a hand on Jamie's groin, bends him over, pulls him firmly against him. Jamie bucks as Bruno pushes deep inside him.

§

When Billy reaches across the bedspread, Jamie is not there. A vague memory comes back to him—Jamie getting into a cab and going home to his own place. That bloody job always comes first.

Eventually, Billy rises from his slumber; he goes straight to the half-finished canvas on the easel next to the desk. The first thing on his mind is the portrait. The features are there, protruding like bone and muscle beneath flesh. He has yet to add the vital marks that will give it genuine personality.

He leans over his desk and studies his pale, ghastly face in the mirror. He touches the skin with the tips of his fingers, tentatively, as if it belongs to someone else. He feels his way around his skull, his cheekbones, his jawbone, probes his eye sockets. He breathes in again, deeply, recalling the scent of lavender filling his nostrils.

Feverishly, his eyes move across the back wall of images. He reaches, accidentally scattering a pile of cuttings, models torn from magazines. A book on 'Screen Legends' catches his eye, photography of famous actors in films. He flicks through it and begins to feel something. The air feels thicker, more conductive and there is an essence, like low voltage electricity. This is how it finds its way to him. He lifts a paintbrush from a glass jar and begins to rub it against the canvas. He remembers the loneliness of the old man. He sees Albert in his mind's eye. And then he sees this other man. The motion of his wrist provokes a link from the paintbrush to his brain and from his brain to wherever it is he sources the images from—*out there*. It's a meditation aided by the smell of linseed oil and turpentine that saturates the air. That is how the images come. No model required.

The oils on his palette are still wet from his last session. Connected, he dips his paintbrush in several colours, umbers and siennas, a bit of ultramarine, to daub and blend on the canvas. He mixes a skin tone, a touch of green here, a bit of red there. The picture gains clarity as he places a highlight on the forehead, a sparkle in the eyes, a crease between the nostril and the curl of the lip. He builds up the layers of flesh and breathes life into the emerging portrait. There it is, forming, changing and reforming before his eyes—the face of a man he's never met before.

He paints until he is satisfied with how far he's gone. He puts the paintbrush and palette down and stands back from the portrait, nodding agreeably. Then he walks to the mirror, stares at his ghostly reflection. Dark rings surround his popping eyes, pupils so dilated that there is very little of the iris left. His own changed face fascinates him, skin waxy and clammy. How do I feel? he thinks. Maybe there is the slight feeling that something is missing. A memory, something he can't think of... not quite there anymore, but he doesn't let it bother him. He shuffles into his tiny kitchen, to make tea, eats some chocolate from the fridge and then heads back to bed.

§

Billy leans against Albert's upstairs doorframe. ''Ello 'ello 'ello.'

He makes Albert jump. 'Jesus! Darling Boy.'

Billy holds Albert's door key in the air. 'You want to be more careful' he says. 'I found it in the keyhole at the bottom of the stairs.'

'Bloody hell, I must have forgotten,' Albert says, touching his forehead with the palm of one hand. 'One of these days it really is going to be the local plod standing there.'

'And you say there's nothing wrong with your memory.'

Albert is sitting on the Chesterfield, in front of a small set of weighing scales, on the coffee table. He is weighing some sort of brown mess into little plastic bags.

'A policeman's dream, this place. You could go down for five life-times!' Billy says.

'Yes. So you should be careful what you say about me to other people. Concrete slippers wouldn't suit you. I'm an unlikely drug-dealer. Small operation. That's why I get away with it.'

Billy strides into the room and throws himself down on the Chesterfield.

Albert sits looking at him. 'You're sprightly today. Thought you went out last night?'

'I did. Been in bed most of the day,' Billy rubs sleep from his eyes.

'You still feeling that nice fuzziness?' Albert enthuses, as if speaking about jelly and ice-cream.

'Yeah. Even now.'

'Hmm. Bona doobs, those ones. You look nice. Tailored short trousers suit you,' Albert says, glancing at his legs. He sits forward and organises the items on the table.

'Thanks.' Billy slips his red braces off his shoulders so they won't overstretch when he sits down. He looks at Albert's weighing scales. 'What are you doing?'

'A couple of orders. Strictly medicinal! A bit of dope for Mrs Jenkins' arthritis and mushrooms for Mr Carter's cluster headaches.' Albert points to the small plastic bags.

Cluster headaches? Billy is bemused.

'Like migraines, but worse,' Albert says. 'Very rare. And the medical industry offers no cure. But these seem to do the trick.'

'How can a mushroom cure a headache?' Billy asks, unbuttoning the top buttons of his black shirt.

'These are magic,' Albert says, holding up one of the little bags and tapping it with a fingertip.

'Yes. I know what they are.' 'Psilocybin is the active ingredient in them, which becomes Psilocyn when it's metabolised in the body. This cures the headache.'

'How?' Billy persists.

'Do you really need to know how?'

'No. I suppose not.'

'Well, let's leave it there then.' Albert scrapes up the rest of the brown mess into a plastic re-sealable bag. Looking directly at Billy again, he says, 'You shouldn't really see any of this, you know.'

Billy leans over and kisses him gently on the lips. 'I thought we were going to look at my work?'

§

The entrance to the arts trust, where Billy works part-time and used to have a studio, is hidden from view, down a narrow private side street, off Kingsland Road in Shoreditch. He had to give up the studio but some of his paintings are still stored there. Through a pair of wrought iron gates, Albert follows Billy in between the two nineteenth century factory buildings, the gallery on the left, and a rabbit warren of studios on the right, home to more than fifty artists. The street is lit from above by a zigzagged string of coloured light bulbs.

'Do you know, I've lived in this area nearly all my life and I never knew all this was here,' Albert says, quick stepping behind Billy.

Billy leads Albert up a wooden staircase on the outside of the building. At the top of the scaffold they reach a door which leads into the studio. Inside, his large-scale canvasses lean in groups against the wall of the lofty room. Some smaller ones are collected in boxes, waiting to be collected, now that a new artist has moved in.

Billy flips through some of the canvasses. He and Albert stand next to each other, looking at the work, a closeness between them— no boundary where one's personal space ends and the other's begins. Their hips are almost together, their hands discreetly touching. Another sort of substance is at work here. Billy can feel a chemistry between them.

'Well, I am stunned, Darling Boy.'

The images of faces, chin to forehead, like those infamous 'choker' shots from old film-noir movies, create a dramatic, claustrophobic effect. Each is a snap-shot from Billy's life: moments that could have been lost in the blink of an eye, now immortalised on canvas. 'I managed to attract an art dealer just as I was finishing art school. It meant that I could continue painting for some time.'

Albert looks at him, the way an older man sometimes looks at a younger man, full of lust. Billy can't quite decide whether it is nostalgia or envy in his eyes, but there is definitely lust.

'I'm intrigued, Billy. What's your motivation? Why do you paint?'

Billy pauses for a moment before answering. 'It's cathartic, I suppose.' He pulls several paintings out for Albert to view more closely: scenes of the lawlessness of school, the wasteland of childhood. He remembers how he never really fitted in. 'I paint in an attempt to understand my world.'

'So it's therapy for you?'

'No. Therapy is therapy. Painting is painting. It's not the same thing. Painting helps me to explore something. I can pick up a fragment of my life, look at it from every angle. I can explore every nuance there is within it. And then I can put it down and say, 'I know that now. I can leave it alone.' That's why some of them look so similar. That's me, revisiting, getting closer to the truth. I paint to find out who I am.'

Albert nods encouragingly. 'And have you succeeded?'

'Don't know.' Billy shrugs and stuffs his hands in his pockets again.

'Well, let's hope you don't get too close, or you'll lose your reason to paint.' Albert smiles, studying the images. 'I mean, Darling Boy, you must paint. Every minute available, you must do it.'

'I am painting.' Billy thinks of the portrait he's been working on in the back room. 'You've given me a new lease of life.'

'Really?'

'Yes. It's my best work to date, I'd say.'

Albert's transfixed by one particular canvas. 'It's obvious who this one is.' Billy smiles at the picture of the young boy around the age of five or six years, wide eyed, deep and black, surrounded by pale luminous unblemished white skin. The wells of his eyes so deep you could fall into them.

'I thought I knew everything then—who I was, where I was going.'

'And now?' Albert asks.

'Lost.'

He wishes now that Albert hadn't seen this painting. It makes him feel exposed and vulnerable. There was a whole life that Albert didn't know about—his life with Jamie. He doesn't want to talk about any of this. He enjoyed his secret time with Albert but his other life is becoming more and more difficult to hide. Thinking about who he was when he was at school fills him with shame. Billy can feel a tug in his body. Jesus, he could murder a drink.

Albert moves closer to the canvases to observe the brushwork. 'You know, Billy, I think we're actually born somebody. And then that somebody sometimes gets lost along the way. Sometimes people can spend the rest of their lives looking for that person. At the end of the day, we're all lost.' Albert nudges him on the shoulder and smiles. 'To look at you in this painting is to look at something from another universe. You've captured the essence of yourself so well. There's something very special in your eyes.'

§

At ten o'clock, Billy and Albert are entering the upstairs flat. They avoid turning on the lights. The room, while partially dusted with moonlight, remains to the larger extent in shadow. Moving across the room, Billy threads a trail of smoke through the air with a joint he's smoking. He stands in his favourite place beside the chaise longue in the open window. The warm and unmoving night air supports the smoke so that it is suspended like a grey phantasm, only very slowly dissipating. He watches Albert remove his Panama and his jacket and throw them on the Chesterfield. Then unbuttoning his shirt at the neck, Albert walks forward into the moonlight. 'Be careful with that stuff, Billy,' he says, solemnly.

'Just a bit of puff, Albert. You can't be worried about that.' Billy coughs on smoke.

Albert's face catches the moonlight. Pinpoints of light sparkle in his deep-set eyes. 'You're in the business of chronicling the past, and the nature of all drugs is to erase it from memory.'

Billy stares at him through the darkness. He offers the last bit to him, the last ember glowing orange in the dark. Albert takes the joint, draws deeply on what's left and flicks the stub into the street. Billy turns slowly away from the window and steps forward, knowing Albert will only see him cast into silhouette. They stand frozen like the smoke in the air, a dream, two men sharing the same room, something growing in the space between them.

'Give me a match,' Albert says. Billy hands him the lighter from his pocket and Albert moves gently, lighting and positioning candles around the room. 'What are you, Billy Monroe?' Albert asks. Billy waits, says nothing, detecting the room changing shape, growing brighter. 'You're my angel, from another world,' Albert finishes.

'Maybe I can give you a dream,' Billy says, huskily. He thinks for a moment about the painting downstairs and smiles. 'What are *you*, Albert Power?'

'A man,' he answers, simply and deliberately. 'Nothing more.' He stops in the middle of the room. The candlelight dances on his face.

'What am I doing with a man?' Billy says, hearing the tone of satisfaction in his own voice. 'What's happening here, Albert? What are we doing?' He moves closer to him.

'You're having an affair,' Albert says. Billy can see him smiling in the moonlight. 'With an older man!'

'Hardly an affair,' Billy says. 'I'm not married.'

'It's a secret, though. Is it not?'

'Only because *you* want it to be.'

'It will keep its magic that way. But it *is* an affair.'

'Of sorts.'

'Better to avoid too many labels. They only lend themselves to the prosaic, the mundane.' Now they are close—almost touching. 'Do you mind that, Darling Boy?'

'I don't care what you call it. All boils down to the same thing,' says Billy.

'What's that?'

'Sex.'

'Our world, Billy! Here, we can do whatever we want. No one else need ever know about it. They'd want us to be 'boyfriends', go to parties—all that palaver. You don't want that. You don't want to be seen *out* with an old man.' Albert tilts his head.

Well, that's a relief, thinks Billy. He doesn't want to think about it. 'Do you have anything to drink, Albert?'

Albert raises an eyebrow. He's silent for a moment and then he says something that takes Billy by surprise. 'Don't you think you're drinking quite a lot?'

Billy feels himself become defensive. 'Why do you say that?'

'Darling boy, far be it from me to judge but... what are you trying to escape?'

Billy thinks about the secrets on top of secrets that he's been keeping. He thinks about how duplicitous he has been to both Jamie and Albert. His lies will catch up with him. He knows this. The idea clenches inside his gut like a fist.

Disconnected from his thoughts, Billy's hands rise to Albert's shirt buttons. He undoes them one by one and pulls his shirt off. Under moonlight, Albert's skin glows like phosphorous. Billy watches Albert's hungry, luminous eyes moving down over his body. He can feel Albert's fingers trace the patterns of his tattoos.

He can't hide his surprise at the firmness of Albert's body.

'What were you imagining, Darling Boy? Rolls of fat?' Albert's hands are suddenly all over Billy, sliding across the curves of his muscles. It feels to Billy as if there are many hands on him—stroking, caressing, probing every inch of him, inside and outside—many hands, many mouths, many bodies. Now, Albert is behind him, pressing himself against him, pressing into the damp space between his firm, round arse cheeks.

They kiss, pulling clothes from each other. In moments, they are naked.

§

Then comes a speechless moment when all movement ceases. Billy feels Albert resting, still inside him. They say nothing. What is there to say? Words are meaningless and only serve to make matters awkward. Slowly and gently, he feels Albert pull away, kiss him on his neck. Albert walks into the kitchen. There's the sound of him clicking the kettle on. He returns, sending the beaded curtain skittering, and throws Billy a kitchen towel to mop up with.

Slipping away into a trance, a residue of ecstasy still working in Billy's brain, his eyes roll back into his head. Moments later, he senses Albert come back into the room and then his head being lifted into Albert's lap. 'I've made Earl Grey.'

'Got any more of those pills?'

'You don't need pills,' Albert says, stroking his hair.

'For another time.'

'A likely story. Dependency is not a road you want to go down.'

'Don't be daft.'

Albert shrugs. 'I can get you whatever you want, Darling Boy.'

Billy grins. 'Now that I am an object of your desire.'

'Drink your tea and then sleep, Darling Boy.'

§

Lying on Billy's bed, Jamie holds *The Complete Guide to Recreational Psychoactives* upright on his chest, in one hand, and twiddles a set of keys between the fingers of the other—the keys to the flat which Billy had given him.

Billy watches from the foot of the bed and at the same time, struggles to fix the television. There's a documentary about sex on Channel Four that he wants to watch. Pizza and shit TV—hangover cure. Jamie, flicking through the book, stops at random pages, reading out loud. 'Ketamine—a psychedelic, sedative drug, used recreationally to induce a state of mild disequilibrium and dissociative anaesthesia... street name—Special K... LSD—d-lysergic acid diethylamide, used in transcendental practices, psycho-nautical trips... most commonly known as Acid or Trips...' He pauses, closes the book momentarily and looks at the cover. 'Where did you get this book?' he asks. 'It's got everything in here.'

'It's been lying around for ages,' Billy says. 'I borrowed it from the guy upstairs a few months ago.'

'What? Albert? That old fella?'

'Yes. He invited me in for a cup of tea in the summer, when I was off work.' Billy continues to fiddle with the TV set, trying not to look Jamie in the eye.

'You never said you'd actually been in there?' Jamie says.

'I keep meaning to give it back to him but I haven't seen him recently.'

Jamie looks back at the book. 'Crystal meth—a powerful euphoric stimulant, with a reputation for being one of the most dangerous drugs because of its addictive and destructive qualities...' Jamie snaps the books shut. 'Funny sort of thing for an old man to have around the flat.'

Billy blows out a heavy sigh. 'Jesus, I've got a headache.'

'I'm not surprised with all that socialising with clients that you do.'

'Wooing a buyer is easier to do with a glass of wine in my hand,' Billy bites and then instantly regrets it.

'You're in a funny mood today. What are you hiding?' Jamie says. There's a seriousness to his voice.

'Bloody thing!' Billy says, punching buttons on the television, deliberately changing the subject. 'It's stuck on BBC2.' He gives the television a good thump on top and, 'Voila!', Channel Four, just in time for the sex.

Jamie finally stands up, demonstratively, with the book in his hands. Billy braces himself. 'This reminds me of when we were in that bedsit in Camden. You got the sack from that job at that Belgian fashion company,' Jamie says. 'You'd been drinking *then* as well. Do you remember?' he says with an accusing tone in his voice. 'You got pissed at one of their staff dos and embarrassed yourself.'

Billy stands, flinches almost. 'What are you trying to say?'

'You never were any good at lying,' Jamie says.

Billy knows he has to tread carefully. There's something about the way Jamie is speaking that sounds both sympathetic and yet at the same time very final.

'You carried on getting up and leaving the flat at eight in the morning every day to make me believe you were going to work, while all along you were desperately trying to find a new job. Then when you did find work, you told me you were moving to something better and that the *old* job wasn't your thing. You thought you could pull the wool over my eyes, but I can see through you, Billy Monroe. You withdrew money from the joint account three times in that month.'

Billy drops the TV remote on the bed suddenly feeling very exposed. He wasn't stupid enough to think that had all gone unnoticed. 'I'm sorry.'

'Sorry?' Jamie asks, sardonically. 'What have you got to be sorry for?'

The question hangs in the air like an accusation waiting to bite him. 'I lead you a right life, don't I? I'm not the greatest person to live with.'

'We don't live together. *Yet.*' Jamie says. 'Which reminds me—there are some forms from the solicitor back at home for you to sign.'

Billy is not used to Jamie having the upper hand. 'I've given you the run around,' he says. 'And I'm sorry.'

'All part of being in a relationship, isn't it? I don't give up so easily.' Jamie turns from Billy, perhaps a little overwhelmed, perhaps a tear in his eye. He looks back at the book. 'It says here that you can synthesise Crystal meth in your own kitchen. You ever do this stuff?'

'Jesus! Jamie! What do you take me for? That's made of drain cleaner.'

'Only asking. No need to bite my head off.'

'Will you put that thing down! We're meant to be watching this together.'

§

Travelling on the bus, from the Curzon cinema in Soho back to Shoreditch, Billy insists on sitting upstairs, right at the front. He's enjoying making Albert feel uncomfortable by resting his head on his shoulder and discreetly touching his leg.

'Don't,' Albert says, swatting him away like an insect.

Billy loves plaguing him. Stepping off the bus, he pinches his arse.

'You mustn't do that,' Albert says, as they walk along the pavement.

For all his years, Albert is unreservedly reserved. 'Mustn't what?' Billy asks.

'I don't want you to do that in public,' Albert replies, walking into the fish and chip shop.

'It's the twenty-first century! No-one cares if I touch you or not.'

'*I care*. I'm not used to that sort of thing. Please don't do it.'

Moments later they're sharing a portion of cod and chips on their way down Columbia Road. 'The nights are drawing in,' Albert remarks.

Billy laughs. 'Albert, it's October.'

'It's colder, too.'

'It's been freezing for ages,' Billy says. 'Did you miss September?'

'The months have flown by and I hadn't noticed. Anyway, what did you think of the film? I thought Marlon Brando set the screen aflame.'

Billy nods, mouth full of greasy fish. 'Vivien Leigh, porcelain doll of the silver screen. Divine.'

They are nearly at The Royal Oak when Albert looks at him sideways and says, 'We'll just go in here for a drink. That alright?'

Billy frowns at him suspiciously and discards a clump of oily paper and fish batter in a rubbish bin. 'If you want to. I thought you were keen to get back?'

'*Molly* bar,' Albert says. He shivers and points up at the tattered old rainbow flag above the doors, flapping in the breeze. 'My round,' he says, entering the public house. It's a real spit'n'sawdust kind of place with a mixed clientele. Not the world Billy's used to. Its after-hours reputation often attracts a *morning after* crowd. He recognises faces from the art set of Hoxton and Shoreditch, and there's a sprinkling of unbefitting queer punters. And you're required to be over the age of eighteen just to look at some of them. Billy stands behind Albert, while he orders two pints of lager. Albert spots someone he recognizes on the other side of the bar. He raises a hand and waves. 'Hello, Eric.'

Eric nods and comes over carrying a pint of lager. He's unshaven, in a polo shirt and tracksuit bottoms. He and Albert shake hands. He has tattoos of German Shepherd dogs on his forearms. He points to a booth, near a frosted glass window.

'We'll join you in a second,' Albert says. 'A top up, Eric?'

'Nah, I'm alright, fella!' Eric says, holding up his half-finished pint. Billy watches him walk over to the booth, taking lots of very little steps, really quickly, shoulders pivoting quickly forwards and backwards, looking really busy. Billy smiles to himself, remembering he has seen Eric before, washing his car. He waits for Albert to pay and then follows him, carrying the drinks.

'I wondered when you were gonna troll on down here,' Eric says. 'Ain't seen you in a while, Albert.'

'This is Billy,' Albert says, slipping into the booth, opposite Eric.

'Nice trade, Fungus!' Eric says, looking at Albert and then winking at Billy.

'Mind your billingsgate,' Albert says, sharply.

'Alright, fella?' Eric says, extending his hand towards Billy.

'Good, thanks.' They shake hands. 'And yourself?'

'Grand!' Eric says. Then looking back at Albert he asks, 'How's business, old fruit?'

'Picking up. Thanks for putting those film guys in touch with me.

Wanted stuff for a wrap party. No pun intended.'

Eric gets a cigarette packet out of his pocket and places it in the middle of the table. 'Usual.'

'Eight?' Albert asks.

'Yeah.'

Billy watches Albert, sitting quietly for a moment, drinking his beer, perusing the room. Everybody is minding their own business. He wonders why Albert is being so surreptitious. These people don't give a shit who or what is going down. Then, as Albert discreetly picks up the cigarette packet, he flips open the top and checks inside. He nods and puts the cigarette packet in his breast pocket. He smiles at Eric and says, 'This stuff is bona.'

'Ya never fail to please, fella!'

Albert drinks more beer before looking around the room again. He reaches into his other breast pocket to fetch out an identical cigarette packet and places it in front of Eric who picks it up quickly. He taps it gently on the table, before stuffing it into his pocket. 'Right,' Eric starts, 'I'm off to slap me onk.'

Billy acknowledges the hilarious translation for *powder my nose* and smiles.

'Have a nice time, mate.'

Albert nods. 'We must be off.' He looks at Billy and nods towards the door.

'Hang on. I haven't finished my drink yet,' Billy says and gulps down his lager.

'Cheers, fella.' Eric smiles. 'You be in next week?'

Outside, under the frayed rainbow flag, Billy shakes his head at Albert.

'Just a bit of business.' Albert strides off down the street.

'That was *it*? Christ, how much did you take?'

'Three hundred and fifty quid.'

'For a bit of sniff?'

'A man has to eat.'

'He's in the neighbourhood. Why didn't you pop round?'

'Some people like to hide in plain sight.'

'Albert, have you been carrying drugs around with you all day?'

'Yes.'

At the corner of Laburnum Road they turn and walk briskly down to the maisonettes. Billy touches Albert on the bottom.

'Billy, do behave yourself!' Albert hisses.

§

Billy stands in socks, vest and boxers, in the doorway between Albert's kitchen and front room, tangled and posturing in the coloured glass droplets of beaded curtain—a pastiche of an LA showgirl. In front of him Albert is sprawled on the chaise longue before the open window.

Drawing on a spliff, the old man looks as if he has sunk deep into an oceanic mind. 'I know *that* face,' Billy says, but Albert doesn't stir. He untangles himself from the beads and moves nearer to the window. 'Albert?'

Albert looks up. 'Oh, Billy. Miles away.' Billy touches him on the shoulder. 'What is it Darling Boy?'

'Remember when we were together on that first night?'

'Yes.'

'Just before I left, you were talking about another man. You said he painted that portrait of you.' Billy points to the painting on the wall.

'I remember.'

'He was important to you, yeah?'

'Darling Boy, he was the love of my life.'

'You were *together*?'

Albert's eyes smile. 'I met him when I was twenty. We knew each other for thirty years. He died.'

'I'm sorry.'

'Sometimes I get mixed up and I think you are *him*.'

Billy smiles. 'How did he die?'

'The secrecy drove him mad in the end. He committed suicide.'

'Albert. That's just awful.'

'Well, anyway, that's past now.' Albert lifts his arm and hands the spliff to Billy.

Billy is thinking about his palette, about Prussian blue and magenta. 'Odd question.' he says, drawing on the spliff. 'What colour were his eyes?'

§

'You've not been painting?' Albert asks.

'I've slowed down.'

'Oh, this *is* bad news.' Albert is lighting tea lights one after another and placing them on the floor around him. He takes another handful from the bag that Billy brought from downstairs, when the power went off.

'I just want to walk away from it all,' Billy says, dropping his lighter on the floor and sipping from his glass of red wine. Sitting comfortably on the floor of Albert's living room without electrical light, they are surrounded by hundreds of the little tea-lights. *Hundreds* of them! They have transformed the room into a candlelit grotto. The whole street is out.

Gradually, from the blackness, the room has grown light and the walls are alive, flickering with candlelight. 'I love what you're wearing, Darling Boy,' Albert says, eventually, now that it's bright enough to see. The blood red shirt that Billy had worn earlier to meet his art dealer is shot through and embroidered with silver, reflecting the candlelight. He traces a finger over the glinted thread. It's on the tip of his tongue to divulge that it was a gift from Jamie, but stops himself at the last second. He doesn't want Jamie creeping into his time with Albert—the job, the flat hunting. He should message him.

Aside from the canvas he's been working on downstairs, he's not been doing much in the way of painting. He's very down. Even Albert's drugs don't seem to cheer him up anymore. But with Albert it is glamorous alchemy. 'What we do together helps me recharge my batteries. And then I go back to my other life.'

Albert's eyes drop to the floor. 'It can't always be like this.'

'Why not? No one understands what we have together.'

'You should probably be with someone your own age.' Candlelight flickers across Albert's lined face, betraying sadness. 'You should be with someone with similar ambitions. Not wasting your time with an old goat like me.'

'Don't say that,' Billy says. 'It's like we've known each other for hundreds of years.'

'Well, of course that's the *only* explanation,' Albert agrees.
'Perhaps even *thousands*.'
'That's maybe why we feel we know each other so well. And we'll *always* know each other. Till the end of time.'

Billy sighs a deep, resigned sort of sigh and stares at all the tea-lights. They make him feel like he is deep underground, in a cave or a mine. 'Have you heard of Lapis Lazuli?' he asks.

'It's a colour, in paint, isn't it?'

'It's a pigment, made from crushed gemstones. The deepest, bluest, fairy tale blue you ever saw. It's a splendid colour—regal. Its sparkling quality is because of the tiny particles of pyrite within it, twinkling like microscopic stars. Created a gazillion years ago. So you could say it's been around forever. It's been used for thousands of years in many paintings. Really expensive and considered very powerful, and now it is so rare that it can only be found in these mines in Afghanistan, deep underground. Can you imagine those gemstones have been there for a real long time? Like *you* and *me*. That's how I felt when I met you. I felt like I'd found something so rare, and so indelible. This stuff doesn't fade, you see. You take a look at all those paintings of the Virgin Mary in the National Gallery. The backgrounds have paled, but her robes are still royal blue. And when the light hits it from a certain angle, it glows. Lapis Lazuli.'

'Remarkable, Darling boy!'

Billy lets his head drop back against the arm of the Chesterfield. 'I need the next show to really work. I need to sell a painting, Albert. Fuck! I need to sell lots of them.'

'You won't sell them if you don't paint them.'

§

'You look like shit, Darling boy!'

Billy looks up from his big pad of paper on the wooden floor of Albert's living room. 'I know what I look like,' he says. Even though it is getting dim the lights stay off, while he works. Today, he's making a drawing of Albert in charcoal and deep blue Indian ink. His hand moves over the paper methodically, meticulously recording the vital truths that make Albert who he is: a broad brow, hooded eyes, a slight longness of the tooth, elegant nose.

'Are you eating properly?' Albert asks.

I wish everyone would just get off my fucking case, Billy thinks. He traces Albert's jawline with a brush of indigo and smudges the charcoal around his nostrils. He exchanges the charcoal for a piece of white oil pastel and adds highlights under Albert's eyes.

'You need to get more sleep. You know what will happen. I told you...'

'Yeah, yeah,' Billy holds up a hand to halt him. 'Don't give me the third degree.'

Albert is sitting on the Chesterfield, wearing a deep green shirt with a cravat the colour of red wine. He holds a vertical posture. Arching his back regally, he says, 'How do I look?'

Billy sucks the end of his pencil for a minute. 'Hungry.'

Albert laughs. Billy moves his sketchbook aside and stands up.

'Finished?' Albert asks.

'For now.'

'We should eat,' Albert says, stretching his arms and arching his back.

'You didn't spend long on that. I thought you were trying to persevere with the work?'

Billy gets his jacket from on the back of the door. He scratches his head, fiddles with his belt buckle, rubs his eyes, avoiding further questions.

'Going?' Albert asks.

'No.' Billy reaches into the top pocket of his jacket and goes back to the coffee table. He kneels, empties out white powder onto the glass surface from a paper wrap made of a National Lottery play slip. 'Want a line?'

'No,' Albert says, folding his arms.

'Mind if *I* have one?'

'Whatever limbers you up.' Albert chews his bottom lip.

'Stop being so pious.'

Billy quickly chops a line, rolls up a twenty-pound note and snorts it. The cocaine hits the membrane at the back of his nose and crackles behind his eyes. In a moment he feels the gentle high coming on, the quickening of his heartbeat, a slight heat at the temples, a tingle in the belly. He moves to sit next to Albert.

'Where did you get that from?' Albert asks.

'From your bureau,' Billy says without looking up.

Albert loosens his shirt and removes the cravat. He places it over the arm of the Chesterfield. 'Well I can't fault you for honesty. I didn't say you could help yourself.'

'You said yourself, it goes off if you keep it too long,' Billy says, pointing at the coke with his credit card.

'Well I won't be needing it much longer.'

'What?' Billy says and continues to move the charlie around the glass surface with the credit card. He drags it into straight lines. Then, seeing the imperfections in form and length, scratches them around, obsessively adjusting, the way he might straighten a tie.

'The big clean up. *Gentrification*!' Albert says.

'What you mean is—some geezer has moved in on your patch at The Oak.'

'Selling second class gear, I might add,' Albert spits. 'It's going to be a gastropub.'

Billy knows he is just sore because someone saw an opening and took it. In the last few months, Albert's dealing has dropped off.

'I'm too old for this game,' Albert says. 'I'm getting out.'

This strikes Billy straight away. He looks directly at Albert. '*Can* you get out? Are you able to just walk away from it? Whoever it is you're selling for will lose a fortune.'

The skin around Albert's eyes tightens for a moment. 'That's *my* problem.' Then he waves a finger at Billy and then at the cocaine on the table. 'Billy, just how much of that stuff have you been doing?'

Billy feels him observing out of the corner of his eye. 'I don't think you should be judging me. You're the one who got me into this.'

'Now, hang on Billy. I didn't get you into anything.'

'You gave me my first ecstasy pill in this very room.'

'Oh, come on. You wanted to know what it felt like. I had some lying around. I didn't force your hand. And if I remember correctly, you gave quite a floorshow. A few pills, Billy. It's a bit different to you casually helping yourself to several grams of charlie.'

Billy moves the powder around, drawing it into long thin lines, tapping the edge of the credit card on the glass. He runs it across his tongue. Oh *whatever*, he thinks. 'Look, do you want a line or not.' He wipes the excess from the table and smudges it into his gums.

Albert looks up to the ceiling in a resigned sort of way and then leans over the table.

§

Wired. Riding on coke, Billy feels his desire for Albert grow stronger. There is that pull, in the tummy, like magnetism. 'Feels good? No?' Billy asks.

'Well, it's woken me up, if that's what you mean!' Albert rubs his nostril with a handkerchief. Moments later they are locked in each other's arms, struggling to remove clothes. Albert tears at Billy's shirt. They roll and fall against the leather. Breath on heated breath, they bend together, violently. Albert presses his mouth vampirously against Billy's neck. They are naked, two bodies burning. Billy loves Albert's older flesh. The more delicate parts of Albert's body are beautiful. He runs his hands over the greyness of his hair, the minor paunch of his belly, the sagginess around his thighs. Albert is by no means frail, but the differences between their bodies tantalises Billy. He notices their flesh a closer shade, now that he has much less of a tan. 'Wait! Let's have another.' Billy frantically scrapes together four more lines, powder scattering across the glass surface. He snorts two. 'Go on,' he urges.

'Not for me. Got to watch the ticker.' Billy allows himself to be pulled by Albert. He resists a little, playfully, and then he is upon Albert, muscles enveloping him, crushing him, snakelike, pushing his hardness against Albert's belly. They thrash like dragons fighting, cock rubbing against cock. Billy regains control and takes hold of them between a fist and stimulates them both as one. He sits up, astride Albert so that their balls nuzzle together. He bucks as Albert pushes a finger into his arse and rushes them towards the end. His eyes roll back beneath the lids.

'What do you want me to do?' Billy exhales, opening his eyes again.

'Cum on my face,' Albert says, looking up at him. Pinpoints of light sparkled in his eyes.

Billy isn't sure. Albert might be pushing him too far.

'Please.'

Billy feels himself suddenly more alert.

'Yes, now, quick!' Albert begs.

'Sure?'

'Yes.'

Billy shunts forward, his arse now above Albert's face. He feels the stubble from Albert's chin scratch his testicles. They work themselves to the end. Albert's wild eyes sparkle underneath him—a look of anguish on his face.

'You ready?'

'No, Billy. Not yet!'

'Now?'

'Keep going!' Albert says, frowning, resisting the pleasure. 'Ah... yes... *now*!' They let go. Abruptly, Billy explodes volcanically onto Albert's face. The *slap* sound of it stuns him, as if being shaken from a daydream. Albert appears equally stunned. 'Oh, yes... all that cum...' he growls, pleasurably. But after the first pump, there is more. It oozes from Billy like honeyed tree resin. 'Oh, Darling boy!' Albert looks up, curling his lip like a beast. Billy can't hide the fact that he's shocked. He shocked *himself*. Staring back, he knows some line has been crossed.

'What's wrong?' Albert asks. A smile dissipates with the semen running down his face.

'Nothing...' Billy tries to hide disgust, but he knows he's already made Albert feel vulnerable.

Albert sits up. 'What?'

'You look...'

'I *know* how I look.' He touches semen on his face. 'Excuse me, for a moment.'

Billy gets off, unable to speak. He knows Albert will be angry. More than that. Upset. Why this, now? Why his childish, antiseptic reaction towards sex? Albert stands up. He walks naked to the bathroom.

§

Beneath Albert's open window, Billy and Jamie sit on the wall, in woollen hats, on a silent Laburnum Road. The frosty, unmoving night is textured like layers of coloured cellophane, indigo for the trees, royal blue for the sky, and prickled with stars. Haloed in amber streetlight, they share a joint. Jamie exhales a plume of white smoke into the chill air and recurrently looks up at the window of the upstairs flat. 'Have you taken that book back yet?' he asks.

'Not yet,' Billy says. He shivers and vigorously rubs his arms under a padded jacket.

Jamie kisses Billy. They smile, gently caressing and ruffling each other's hair. 'Goodnight, sleepyhead,' Jamie whispers, as he steps from beneath the amber halo.

'Why don't you stay?' Billy asks. 'We've not seen much of each other.'

'Early start, Billy. And I've no clean clothes with me.'

'I miss you,' Billy says. It's true. Jamie is always so busy with work and perhaps Billy really hasn't made much effort recently. He can feel his life veering off course. How can he be so confused about what he really wants?

'I'll see you on Wednesday, when I come to stay. Three weeks off work. Sleep tight,' Jamie says, giving Billy a brief, but very sweet backward glance, before disappearing into the darkness.

'I'll call you,' Billy whispers, left alone outside the maisonette. He lies back on the wall finishing his joint, gazing up at moonlight through the trees. For a moment, he thinks, he sees Albert's silhouette in the window above. Billy feels himself blanch. Why has he orchestrated this whole carry-on underneath their noses? Though, he knows they will never connect the dots.

He allows the burning orange tip of the joint to dance playfully between the tips of his fingers as he points at the star-prickled sky, counting each, one by one. Then, losing interest he stubs out the joint and slips off the wall. When he turns, he looks up and this time catches Albert in the window. Billy raises a hand to wave, but Albert ducks back, as if pretending not to have seen him.

§

Three nights later Billy knocks on Albert's door. He knocks several times before there is an answer.

'It's rather late, Billy.' Albert lights up the joint he is holding in his hand and breathes out the velvety smoke, watching it slowly dissipate under the harsh, unshaded hallway bulb.

'I'm sorry. I knew you were still up. I could hear you moving around. I've brought something for you.' Billy indicates the large object under his arm.

Albert looks at him rather dubiously. 'I rather thought you'd forgotten me. I've not seen you for days. Better fish to fry. I suppose you've been spending time with that mate of yours. What's his name?'

'Jamie.'

'Oh yes, that's it. I never did get to meet him.'

'Is it okay to come in for a minute? This is pretty heavy.'

Albert pauses for a second. 'It'll have to be Lapsang souchong,' he says. 'I'm clean out of Earl Grey.' He turns and disappears into the kitchen while Billy sidesteps in with the gift he's carried up for Albert, the large canvas he's been working on. He's had it covered up, but now Jamie is actually coming to stay with him, and it's finished, he wants it out of the way. He sets it beside the portrait of Albert that hangs on the wall behind the leather Chesterfield.

Albert returns, skittishly, through the beaded curtain with a tray of cups and saucers and a teapot, hands shaking, spliff in mouth, head tilted back, eyes half closed avoiding smoke. He stoops, places the tray on the coffee table and as he stands up straight again, he speaks around the spliff. 'Ah, Darling boy. What *do* we have here?' Stepping backward to take in the whole piece, he takes a long drag on the joint and passes it to Billy. He stares at the new painting for a few moments before registering the image. Eyes the deepest, bluest, fairy tale blue you ever saw. 'Lord above!' he says, eventually, coughing out smoke at the same time. He clamps his hand over his mouth. 'How did you do this?' His voice breaks. 'How did you do this? Without a model?'

'From your description, from my imagination, from visual references. I don't know. I don't always use a model. I kind of pick up on a feeling and paint what comes to me.'

'But it's *him*,' Albert says. 'It's extraordinary.' His eyes are full of tears.

'Really?' Billy asks.

'It is uncanny. It's *him*. Alexander Kendall.'

'Alexander Kendall?' Billy asks and he sees at once a look of realisation emerge on Albert's face.

'Yes,' Albert says. 'What are you so—'

'You said, *Alexander Kendall*. You mean *the* Alexander Kendall? From those old films?' Billy is dumbfounded. He thinks of all those movies he's seen at art house cinemas. *I'm Watching You, Behind the Closet, In the Lavender...*

'I didn't tell you?' Albert asks.

'No.' Billy shakes his head in disbelief. 'It really does look like him.'

'Well, I always said you should trust in your own process.'

'He was your...?'

'We were lovers... yes,' Albert says, tears running down his face. 'What have you done, Billy? It's almost as if he's *here* in the room.'

For the first time Billy is stuck for words. 'I... I wanted to give you something,' he says, with reticence. 'You helped me find something. You helped me find my creativity. I wanted to give something back to you.'

'You certainly have, darling, Darling Boy. You've brought him home. Back where he belongs.' Albert blinks away tears.

'This flat? He left it to you?'

'Thank God! I'd have been on the streets otherwise. Caused a terrible fuss with his family. Of-course, they didn't want me to have it. It was more complicated in those days.' Albert smiles, squeezing moisture from his eyes. 'Look at me. Old queen.' He pulls out a handkerchief and wipes his face. 'So, you're painting again?'

'More than ever.' Billy looks away.

'Good!' Albert says, still transfixed by the portrait. 'Drink your tea.' Billy sidles up to him and touches him on the arm, rests his head on his shoulder. 'My God. Look at the eyes, Darling Boy. His eyes are...the colour of...'

'Lapis Lazuli.' Billy smiles, pleased that he can bring the old man a little happiness. 'Mind if I use your loo?'

'You know where it is, Darling Boy.'

Billy's just sat down on the cold black porcelain toilet seat when he hears a knock on Albert's front door—unusual and alarming at this time of night. He listens intently to Albert shuffling to the door and then the sound of the door opening. 'Oh, hello. How may I help you?'

'Er... Hi. I'm looking for Billy. I don't suppose he's here, is he?' There is a silence spiked with tension. 'Sorry, I've just arrived downstairs. He's left all the lights on and this was on the sofa. He was meaning to bring it up, so I thought...' Billy recognises Jamie's voice and he can guess what he has in his hand. *That bloody book!*

'Oh, I've been looking all over for that. I'd forgotten that Billy had it.'

'I've been calling but he's not answering his mobile. I wonder where he's got to...?'

Billy can hear Albert stuttering in the hallway. 'He... He's on the khazi. He'll be out in a minute. Come in for a drink. I'm sure I have something that will tempt you. I might even have some brandy somewhere.'

Go away, Billy thinks. Then, 'Oh, I never say no to a cup of tea.'

'A man after my own heart,' Albert says.

Billy listens as Jamie steps in and the door slams. There are muffled voices, Albert asking questions that Billy doesn't quite catch. He feels a veil of blackness falling over him and a dragging feeling in his gut as he flushes the loo, washes his hands and steps out of the toilet, into the living room. The muffled conversation suddenly becomes dangerously clear.

'Don't worry,' Albert is saying to Jamie. 'It was going to come out in the end. I'm just shocked he didn't mention it earlier.' Albert and Jamie are standing face to face with the new painting in between the two of them. When Billy steps forward, their eyes meet. Albert's face is pinched and angry. 'So that's why you've been avoiding me,' he says, glaring at Billy. 'Don't you think it would have been kind to tell me, Darling Boy?'

'I'm sorry,' Billy says, swallowing on guilt. He doesn't know what to say. He shakes his head unable to comprehend the whole perverse situation. What is Jamie doing here in Albert's flat? He can feel an outpouring of honesty coming, but is halted by Albert's next unexpected words:

'Moving into a flat in Dalston and you didn't think to tell me.'

Jamie waves at Billy, smiling, eyes beaming obliviously. 'You left this downstairs.' He's holding Albert's copy of *The Complete Guide* to *Recreational Psychoactives*. 'I thought I'd bring it up.'

'I thought you weren't coming until tomorrow,' Billy says.

'I wanted to surprise you.'

Billy cringes. He feels his phone vibrating in his pocket with received messages.

Albert points at Jamie, 'If it hadn't been for this young man, I would have known nothing about it.' He stops and looks at Jamie. 'I'm sorry, sir, I didn't catch your name.'

Billy wants to leap across the room and press his hands over Jamie's mouth. For a moment, it is as if time has slowed down and Jamie's mouth opens at the speed of treacle pouring from a tin. And then...

'Jamie,' Jamie says, beaming at Billy.

Albert pauses. He looks shocked. There is a need, just for a moment, for silence. Eventually, Albert looks directly at Billy. In a moment, a knowledge passes between them. Jamie looks at them both, a realisation forming.

'Is it possible, do you think... to be *in love* with more than one person at the same time?' Albert asks.

Billy is stunned into silence for a moment. He cautiously considers his answer. Finally, he quietly replies, 'No.'

Albert closes his eyes, his head taut with sadness. He looks as if he's been winded. 'No, I didn't think so.'

§

After all of Billy's *I-didn't-mean-to-hurt-yous*, Jamie goes back downstairs, out of the way. Billy stands next to Albert, who is resting against the window frame. Above the flats, a texture-less bruise of luminous grey-yellow spreads itself across the sky, like a patch of backlit vellum. Albert leans out of his first floor window as the first fork of lightning streaks across Laburnum Road. The cobblestones look like rivets in brown PVC, an effect of amber streetlight in spent rainwater. Billy can smell the sickly sweet stink of mildew, rising from a winter sludge, rotting on the pavement. Albert opens the window wide letting in the cool charged air. A storm is coming, he thinks, anticipating an impending thunderclap. Then it comes, not a clap, but a low hellish rumble, like the amplified sound of an impatient belly.

He watches as Albert nods to himself, loosening his tie and the buttons of his shirt and moving silently away from the window.

§

'Please stop,' Billy says, pursuing Jamie around the kitchen as he collects his things to leave. He's forcing clothes and his writing pad back into his holdall. 'Can we at least talk about it?'

'And listen to another pack of lies?' Jamie says, his voice trembling. His widow's peak and receding hairline makes him look rather more serious than he used to. His choice of clothes has taken on a streamlined, utilitarian look that fits in well with those academic types at the art gallery.

Billy feels tears coming. He feels desperate, grasping. 'One minute you're stifling me, needy, the next you're remote, closed off, wrapped up in that bloody job. If you weren't so... maybe I wouldn't feel the need to lie. Maybe I wouldn't—'

'So this is all my fault?' Jamie stops now, drops the holdall and turns on him. 'The drugs, the booze, the endless nocturnal excursions...' His face is pinched with fury. 'I *drove* you to it?'

'I didn't say that.' Billy says. 'But sometimes—'

'How could you? He's old enough to be your grandfather.'

'I just wanted to have some fun.'

Hot tears sting Billy's cheeks. He watches Jamie wrench on his jacket, pick up his bag and walk to the front door.

'Some *fun*? I hope it was worth it.'

§

The next day, Billy knows he has to visit Albert one last time. Static dust particles in the air are visibly disturbed as Billy enters the still and silent passageway up to Albert's flat. Why has he made such a mess of this? All trace of what has been before is now gone. Any semblance of an affair has now been extinguished. A little piece of him has disappeared. Maybe it hasn't been there for a while. No longer can he locate that piece of him that can make everything better, the part that could make Jamie stop crying.

As he reaches the top of the stairs, he stops. The door is ajar. In the rehearsal in his head, he'd been expecting to knock, perhaps repeatedly, and maybe have to force his way in. He knows Albert would turn him away. But he knows he must at least get in to try to make amends. But now he makes a different entrance.

Peering around the open door. Billy's breath quickens, hairs stand out on his skin. His eyes fix on the empty space between the wooden floor and the old man's feet—a ray of sunlight picks out the dust floating there. On the floor—a fallen stepladder. Billy's heart makes one violent thud, as if it has stopped. After that, there's a squeaking noise that sounds like seagulls crying. His heart beats so hard and fast his ears throb. Why can't he scream? He wobbles and loses his footing. His vision pulses dark blue at the periphery, as if the lights are dimming. He gags, and his vomit hits the floor.

Albert, hanging by his neck from a rope: face blue and swollen like a pumpkin, tongue sticking out, eyes bulging. He is wearing a white vest and underpants, yellowed and damp with urine. His hands, too, are swollen and reddened.

Billy regains himself to take in the full picture and tries to control his breathing. He wipes his mouth on his sleeve. He wants to sit but can't, not in the room with… He can't just leave. No. What? What? He averts his eyes from the body, moving further into the room. Sunlight reflects off the Chesterfield where he and Albert had sex. The large portrait of Alexander leans against the wall. Above, is the painting of Albert Power, a young man.

Out of breath, he takes his mobile phone from his pocket. He looks down at the floor, thinking about Jamie on his way to work. Who to call? The police? An ambulance? No, that would be pointless. Albert is dead.

Billy walks to the open window, rainwater on the sill, and looks out. He takes a deep breath. Everything on Laburnum Road is quiet and peaceful. No-one around. A crisp December day. He turns and stands in the bay window where Albert has arranged a bunch of freshly cut flowers in a green glass vase. Bright pink gerberas on long elegant stems, just like the ones he'd first seen Albert buying in the market. Then he sees the bureau, open, where Billy had previously pilfered a couple of wraps of cocaine. Pulling open little wooden drawers inside, he discovers pills and powders and vials of liquid lying inside. He recognises—coke, crack, heroin, K, ecstasy, LSD, GHB—the whole chemistry set. Fuck. Albert had a whole cottage industry up here. His shaking fingers move across the folding desk shelf of the bureau. There is also a little plastic bag with what look like droplets of glass inside. Crystal Meth. He fingers the contents of the bag between his thumb and index finger. He looks down at the pills. He's never seen so many drugs. He finds his hands are on them and he's stuffing his pockets with packets and bottles. And then he sees the letter. It's addressed to Billy Monroe. He picks it up and reads:

My dearest, Darling Boy,

I'm such an old fool. I don't know what I'm doing here. I don't belong anymore. I'm sad and I'm lonely. I've had this infantile idea that we could have been in love. Now I'm embarrassed by my own foolishness. Finally, after all these years, I thought I'd found someone I could be close to, someone who could make smaller the void of Alexander's death. It's ridiculous, isn't it, to think that someone like you could love someone like me?

You came into my life like a flash of lightning—a boy running in summertime. Seeing you was like seeing him come back to my life. It was unreal. In you, I felt him. But the kind of love he once had for me, I know you seem to have now found in another. I'm crushed by the idea that you cannot be mine entirely. But I'm just a creepy old man. It would be wrong to take this time from someone more able to enjoy your vitality.

I can't lift myself out of this darkness which I suspect, if I'm honest, is chemical—a result of the years I have used substances. And in any case, I'm a dead man walking. The ravens are circling. I can't remember how I got into all this—this vampirous existence. I pray you will not let this happen to you. I pray that you will live a long and happy life with the person who you choose to share your life.

I have a deep affection for you but I am terrified of looking into your eyes, to find the feeling unrequited. And were the feeling reciprocated, it would be scandalous. It only serves to remind me of that other devotion I still harbour for Alexander.

Without him, the winter days are long. Shadows surround me in this lonely flat. I can feel my soul creeping from my body, this empty husk, to find the place where he now dwells. We are shackled, you and I, in this most inappropriate and addictive relationship. Who would accept love between someone like you and someone like me? Meeting you was a joy but, nonetheless a heartache. I can't go on. I'm not the same man anymore.

You have helped me reach this place. You have helped me to realise who I am. So it is time for me to break our shackles. They say that people who write letters like this don't actually mean to do it. But I do. I have the rope that will pull me into the next world, to help me make my leap into the unknown. My only hope is that he will be there, waiting for me.

Maybe some day, we shall meet again, in another condition, my darling, Darling Boy.

All my love
Albert

Elbow Room

Jamie is shaken bolt upright from sleep as the door rattles in its frame. He cranes his neck over the arm of the sofa. Gracie wades into the warehouse flat through the weight of unopened mail that has accumulated by his front door. She rubs her nostrils. 'Is there a dead mouse in here?' She drops carrier bags on his white Verner Panton table, turns and purses her lips at him. 'Look at you, grubby, barely dressed. I can smell your underpants from over here. Have you actually washed this week?' Her eyes move to a half-eaten bar of chocolate that he's left on the glass coffee table. 'Christ, look at the state of this place.' Jamie watches her drop the keys into the pocket of her woollen coat, stride back to the door and kicks it shut.

A discarded vodka bottle trundles across the floor, launched from the end of Gracie's foot. It rolls into the pot of his dying yucca, which sits askew in waterless soil, the leaves browning at the tips.

'Babes, I *love* what you've done with the flat.'

Sitting next to him is a week-old kebab, dry and leathery like a severed ear. Alarmed, he pushes a cushion over it with his foot.

'I don't know how you'd cope if Billy had actually moved in too. It's been five months now and you're still no closer to living like a human being. Look at all this stuff! Boxes full of what?' She pulls open the lid of one of them. 'Photographs and videotapes. It's an obsession.' She smiles, drops one hip and hooks a hand onto the other in an exaggerated *vogue femme*.

He doesn't smile back. 'Did you use that key I gave you?'

'Would you prefer me to use a crowbar?'

'I gave you that key for emergencies,' he says. 'Not so you can walk in whenever you feel like it.'

Gracie waves him away. 'It's taken me over an hour to get here and I've only come from Hackney Wick. Bloody trains—do my fucking box in.' She pulls a cord to the blind, dusty as it had been when he moved in. Daylight floods the room. 'Good job I do have a key, isn't it? You could die in here and no one would know.'

She walks across the room, lifts the lid of the pedal bin with her foot and checks the refuse. 'It's empty,' she says. The empty sink too brings a surprised look to her face. 'When was the last time you ate?'

'Stop getting at me, will you, Gracie.'

'You don't look after yourself.'

'I'm fine.'

'You won't pay the mortgage on this if you keep taking sickies.'

'I had some holiday owing to me, if you must know.' Jamie heaves himself to the edge of the sofa. He feels so terribly tired. 'Look, if you've just come to—'

'Babes, I'm not having a go, but you must snap out of this... melancholia.'

'I'm not melancholic.' He could get Gracie by the throat.

'You're not right, that's for sure. I've bought you some soup.' She lifts Tupperware from the bags, places them on the kitchen work surface and exhales, impatiently. She walks over to his desk and shuffles papers around. 'I know you don't want to hear this, but I don't think he's coming back. Bloody liability. You want to have the deeds to this place put in your name immediately. Did he put any money down?'

In her hands is a photograph, crinkled and torn at the edges. She turns the photo so he can see: him standing up in Billy's old Volkswagen with the soft-top down, shortly after they first met. Staffordshire countryside. He's smiling joyfully.

'Self-harming again?'

'Please don't mess with my stuff,' Jamie says.

From her coat pocket, she pulls on a pair of reading glasses. Under Gracie's hands are piles of manuscripts he's written—novels, short stories, articles—wads of paper in plastic sleeves and ring-binders. 'Jamie baby, you need to do something with all these.' She looks over at him. 'Did you get the invite to Simon Jones's party?'

Jamie shrugs.

'It'll be a real swanky affair.' Gracie looks at the pile of mail by the door. 'Bright red sparkly envelope—difficult to miss. You should go. Everyone who was ever nominated for the Booker will be there. And their agents! Perfect place to network.'

'It must be at Billy's flat,' Jamie says, hoisting himself to his feet. 'I was going to ask him to come with me.'

She looks at him with a glassy stare. 'No plus ones, Babes. Invitation only.'

'It'll be there somewhere.'

Gracie is sifting through the manuscripts now. 'Where's the latest one you were working on? The one about your mother? You must look for it. I liked it—'

'It's fiction. It's not my mother.'

'I know that, but she's a wonderful character.' Gracie sighs. 'Maybe you can put *me* in a book one day.'

'No fucking point. They'll never be published.'

She turns on him, glasses balanced on the tip of her nose. 'Why ever not? They're good.'

'Old boy's network. You think any of them are going to let me—'

'Don't keep harping on about class barriers and glass ceilings. Preaching to the converted, Babe.' She pulls off her glasses and points at him. 'You've missed countless parties. David Cabaret had a fantastic birthday, which you didn't attend. Everyone misses you. Why won't you just talk?'

'I—I can't talk about it,' he says. 'No one would ever understand?'

'Try me. What about this Albert character?'

'He's dead,' Jamie snaps forcefully.

'Well, I knew that bit,' she replies, remaining the calm counterpart. 'How was he involved with Billy?'

Jamie turns his back on her, feeling his eyes becoming wet. 'We're going away for a while.'

Gracie draws breath. 'You and Billy?'

'Berlin.' He nods. 'A week or so out of London. I've got to make him see sense.'

'And if you can't?'

Jamie touches his forehead, turns and walks towards her. 'How is David? I must remember to give him a call.'

Gracie grabs one of his notebooks and waggles it at him. 'At least two of these manuscripts are excellent. You can't leave them gathering dust. Send them out.'

'No.'

She drops the manuscript on his desk, pulls the belt of her coat tight. 'I'd better be off.' She draws him to her—a hug, a kiss. 'Eat that soup. I made it especially. And ask *anyone*; I rarely go near the kitchen. Let's rendezvous on Thursday, Babes. I want to see one of these knocked into shape. How about the one about the cult in the desert?'

§

'Billy? Billy!' Jamie barks into the phone, clamped in between his ear and his shoulder. His voice echoes in the alleyway between *Deborah's Designer Boots* and a car lot.

'What?'

With one hand around a beer can, he uses the other to guide his trail of urine down the fence of corrugated iron, forming a puddle near his feet.

'Where are you?' Neon-lit liquid, a thin layer of petrol floating on its surface, radiates a swirling spectrum of colours. Billy's voice, down the phone, has the quality of liquid—no sharp edges. 'I'm in a bar.'

'You said you were leaving. Fifteen minutes ago.'

'Leaving?'

'Don't do this, Billy? Who are you with?'

'Just some people I met last night.'

'So just leave them and come and get your keys! I'm with David at the Joiner's Arms.'

'Keys? I don't know what you're talking about.'

'You lost your fucking keys! Have you totally forgotten the conversation we had?'

'What conversation?'

'The one about your keys.'

'No. I said I'd pick them up tomorrow.'

'What? Fuck! You're fucking deranged. You need to go to sleep.'

'I *am* going to go to sleep.'

'How?'

'When I get home.'

The playful puddle of urine, has become a window into another fairy tale world, framed by the dust and dirt floor of this one. Preoccupied, he casually zips himself up—loses balance for a second, steps in the urine and shatters the illusion.

'But you need your keys.'

'That's why I'm phoning you.'

Jamie falls against the fence. '*I'm* phoning *you!*' The fence rattles and he's stunned by the sound of guard-dogs barking.

'Don't shout at me,' Billy says.

Jamie spins round and sees the dogs snarling behind the fence of the car lot, padding around a trail of tiny pieces of glass, frosting the ground like granulated sugar under moonlight. Across the street, outside the doors of the pub, David is waving at him, looking more than a little pissed off.

'Billy, where are you?'

§

It takes Jamie seven minutes to march to Curtain Road. Jamie knows Billy must be in one of the bars so he goes in them all, one by one. Through the windows of the Elbow Rooms Jamie sees him slumped on a leather sofa, arm in arm with a guy whose unkempt face is liver-fail yellow. He strides in, past the bouncers, past a party of girls cackling and drinking cocktails around a pool table. The pulsing pizzicato of Kylie's *I Can't Get You Out of My Head* plays at a headache-inducing volume. Jamie heads straight over to Billy, scattering the crowd like skittles. Billy's eyes are shut, but Jamie can see his eyeballs rapidly moving behind the lids. He kicks Billy's leg. 'Get your coat,' Jamie says. 'We're leaving.'

'Leave it out,' the yellow guy says. 'Who the fuck are you?'

Billy's eyes roll back in his head as he strains to focus on Jamie, leaning over him. His forehead is greasy with sweat.

'I'm his boyfriend. Who the fuck are *you*?'

The guy snatches his arm from around Billy's shoulder.

Jamie kicks Billy again. 'Get your coat!'

§

'How could you lose your keys?' Jamie says, flinging open the door to Billy's flat, flicking on light switches as he goes. Billy stares into the half-light, his eyes circled by bruised skin. Behind Jamie, he walks in, unsteadily. 'Why do you get yourself in this state?'

Billy's back room is a swamp of filth—pornography strewn around, glass pipes lying in ashtrays. On his desk next to the computer is an old photograph album. It's bursting open, spine broken, pages loose, bulging with memories. Jamie grasps it, like a drowning man who's just been thrown a float—a book crammed with the contents of his life. The photographs of a holiday they had shared in Amsterdam. There's a picture of Phyllis on a night they had taken her to the bingo, screeching, no doubt at some vulgarity.

'Don't you ever learn?' Jamie says, his eyes fixed on the clump in his hands. 'If you carry on like this, you're gonna be dead.' His fingers probe in between the pages. 'Look at all this stuff. Why do you save it, if you're just going to kill yourself?'

When Jamie looks up, Billy has moved into the adjacent room. Through the doorway, he sees Billy, standing in front of the mirror—a lost man who hasn't exactly used all of his twenty-five years productively. Jamie can see his hollow reflection, the lights of his eyes turned out.

Jamie calls out to him. 'Have you seen that red sparkly envelope I left here? It was an invite to Simon Jones's party.' There's no response. 'Billy?' It's as if he doesn't remember his own name. Jamie can't reach wherever his mind may be.

'No. Why would I want to go to that?' Billy says, eventually. 'Fucking snooty bastards, looking down their noses at me.'

Jamie looks down again at the photograph album. The image in Jamie's fingers carries enormous personal weight. In it Billy is a baby, wide-eyed with luminous, unblemished skin. The camera has caught him just as his lids opened back at their widest. The deepest, blackest of pupils, look as if they contain all the knowledge of the universe— the image that inspired one of Billy's paintings.

'Well, I'm not surprised. You're always drunk. You made a right mess in David's toilet last time.'

Hard to believe that baby, such a delicate body, could host such creative brilliance. Jamie must not give up on him now. If he can get them both through this bad patch, maybe everything will be all right. Art openings and book launches. They could be the toast of London.

Billy's brushing frantically at his arms and chest, as if something is crawling over him. He shudders, in fear of the imperceptible thing. 'I'm not going and that's that,' he says.

Billy's spite makes Jamie smart. 'I wasn't asking if you wanted to go. Gracie said she'd go with me. I might meet someone who can help me get published.'

Billy sniggers. 'Still gnawing away at that bone?'

To look at Billy's derelict body, jeans hanging from his waist, it's incredible that Jamie once thought him a god. But Billy is no centrefold now.

'You used to say I could achieve anything.'

'*You* used to be fun. Who wants to read that crap you write?'

'You'd never say that if you were sober,' Jamie says. 'You're not cruel.'

'I don't know where the invite is. Perhaps it went in the bin. You're not one of *them*, anyway.'

Jamie trips and the album tumbles out of his hands. Tiredness and drunkenness get the better of him. Time expands like a bungee elastic. Seconds start to feel like minutes. Pictures from his book are dancing before him in slow motion. Photographs, postcards, love letters all pirouette in the air and come to land on the bare floorboards. The book lies ruptured amongst the other scattered items. No sign of the invitation. His eyes fall on a photograph of them both in the YMCA student residences, sending his mind springing back in time. Jamie remembers this moment as if it were yesterday. This is where it all began, when Billy still knew who he was.

§

Gracie sits before her mirror, which sits above a sink spattered with crushed eye-shadow, limescale and hair dye. Bottles of setting lotions and clothes lie strewn around the floor. Next to the bed is the sewing machine she'd used to make the costumes that hang around the bedroom. Her most recent is a lacy wedding dress affair. She pours fizzy water from a bottle into a tall glass.

'Perrier? Not very *you*, is it?'

Gracies tilts her head to one side and drinks heavily from the glass.

'Why are you looking at me like that?' Jamie says.

Gracie makes two waxy arcs of Rimmel over cushion-plump lips. Jamie loves watching her get ready to go to work at the nightclub she's hosting. She presses her lips together, spreading the colour around. 'There's still something you're keeping from me,' she says. Then she carefully paints over the edge of the lip-line.

'Oh Gracie, not this again?' Jamie clasps his hands together in front of him.

Out of the layers of powder and paint, she emerges, a living, breathing art piece. False eyelashes sit behind black cat eye spectacles detailed with rhinestones. She peers over them at Jamie.

'The way you've been living.' Gracie folds her arms across her chest, eyeing him. 'That flat—it's like a kennel.'

'It's just all that stuff with that old man and... Doesn't everyone have their ups and downs?' Jamie looks away.

A tattoo draws his eye into her abundant cleavage, oozing from a polka-dot, short sleeve cardigan. Her look, set off by a leopard print handbag goes perfectly with the night: a full moon and warm air. The gothic sounds of Shoreditch carry in through open windows. The air is spiked with cat cries, like babies being murdered, and the drunken peal of laughter from the pub around the corner.

'I'm not talking about the old man. I'm talking about Billy.'

He shakes his head. 'I can't be the life and soul of the party all the time.'

'You've stopped seeing all your friends, apart from me. It's like you've completely given up or something.'

'It's just a blip,' Jamie says. 'Stop being silly.'

Gracie has a New Romantic attitude towards getting ready, spending hours painting on her mask, curling and pinning her hair for the crowds. Jamie wonders what painful bruises lie beneath.

She stuffs the lipstick back in her make-up bag. Her eyes are wet. 'You've been having these blips for a while now. You can't fool me, Jamie Johnson. Why do you think I keep checking up on you? It's okay, Jamie. You can tell me.'

'Tell you what?'

Gracie sighs—dabs moisture from around her eyes. 'The real reason Billy hasn't moved in. Why you think you need to get him out of London?'

'We just need some space to think, to talk.' He raises his voice now. 'Please Gracie, stop hectoring me.'

'No,' Gracie snaps back.

'Why not?'

'Because I need you to tell me the truth.' She levels her eyes at him. She speaks slowly and deliberately. 'You're scared. You think you must have driven him to do it, that it's your fault. You keep going over it in your head. You convince yourself that it's normal behaviour—acceptable even, that if you could just control the situation, that everything will get better. But somehow, it never does. It's like being stuck in a bog—the more you try to help, the deeper you sink. It's an impossible situation.' A finger touches her temple. 'I've been there.'

'Been where?' Jamie holds his breath, as if he's about to dive under water.

'I'm an addict.' Gracie stares at him, sadly, for a long moment and places a leaflet on the table in front of him. 'I always thought I'd be able to control it—just one glass at a barbecue, just one cheeky line in a nightclub—and I'd be able to leave it alone. But as soon as the wine touched my lips—all bets were off. I might go home early to bed. Unlikely. I might embarrass myself at a party, insult a friend, sleep with a stranger, lose my job. I did so much coke once, I attacked my best friend. She called the police. I woke up the next day in a cell. Believe me. I'm not making it up. It's dark. You hurt anyone who comes near you. You start to make a mess of their lives too. You drag *them* down. And *you* know how that *feels*, don't you Jamie? Because it's happened to you, hasn't it? Billy's an addict.'

Jamie nods. There is a long pause.

'Did you find that manuscript?'

'Yes.'

'Good. Did you find the invitation?'

'No.'

'You need to be at that party.'

She's powdering in-between her boobs now, smoothing down the creases in her dress, pushing her black meshed feet into leopard print sling-backs. 'And Babes, I think you should get as far away from that man as possible. He's an imploding star—a black hole from which nothing can escape. Not even light. You get too close to that and you'll be turned into... what's the word? Anti-matter!'

§

Jamie watches Billy sipping iced orange juice. Daylight floods the deserted Berlin bar where they are checking their emails. 'Been invited to two job interviews,' Billy says, looking up from his laptop.

'Maybe you could think about moving in then?' Jamie suggests.

'It's going to work out, isn't it?' Billy says, smiling. His skin looks less spotty and he's begun to gain weight again. The tension has dissipated and Jamie is enjoying their day trips and early nights. The fog that shrouded their future has started to clear.

At the end of their holiday, they meet an English couple in that very same Kreuzberg bar. After offering to buy a round of drinks, Billy returns from the bar with shots of tequila for them all. 'What happened to the orange juices?' Jamie asks.

'Oh come on, Jamie. We're having fun.'

Just before the fourth round of drinks, Philip, the portlier one of the two, leans over and whispers in Jamie's ear, 'My God, I thought I could drink fast, but your other half can really sink 'em!' and before he knows it, they've been carried away to find Berlin's elusive underground scene. The club is away from the main drag, down a dark and narrow alleyway, behind some buildings, down a flight of stairs in the basement of what could have been a disused abattoir. It's closed-in and claustrophobic and Jamie finds it unnerving. He's only two drinks from sober, unlike Billy who is intent on turning his liver into foie gras.

'This is your last blow out, Billy Monroe. Remember what we said? We're getting our life back on track.'

Jamie tries to dance but soon grows bored of the club. True, it's nearest to nightlife they've been since their arrival. But he can't stand by watching Billy pour that poison into his body. The English couple gawp at them, as Billy dangles his glass of vodka defiantly in front of Jamie's face. 'Please don't drink any more,' Jamie says.

'Why shouldn't I? You're not my fucking keeper.'

'You've had enough. If you drink any more, I'm going back to the hotel.'

'Go on then,' Billy says, barely able to stand up.

Outside on the rain-drenched street Jamie chokes on angry tears. He looks behind, half expecting Billy to come dashing after him with apologies.

§

Awake at the crack of dawn, Jamie senses the absence of Billy's body, not for the first time. His hand slides across the cold sheets. He sits up, picks up his mobile, calls Billy.

From the thirty-sixth floor of the Hotel Alexanderplatz, the panorama is dizzying. Directly ahead of him, the wide carriageway of the Prenzlauer Allee stretches away into the dust-grey distance. The Berlin horizon is scattered with cranes; mechanical animals reworking a dismantled city.

He stands, walks about the room, searching for a stronger signal. Over to the window, he presses himself against the glass, attempting to reach a space out there where the signal might be stronger. The call connects, just long enough for the phone to ring three times. Then he gets cut off again.

The view unsteadies him but he can't resist looking down. People crawl about silently on the pavements below. Jamie pulls a single hair between trembling thumb and forefinger, follicle still attached, and runs the hair between his lips before placing it precisely on the surface of the bedside cabinet.

Alongside, there are one, two, three more, which he must have placed there last night when he arrived back at the hotel. He dials again. This time the call connects immediately and he listens to it ringing.

In the bedroom mirror, his reflection is cut off at the neck—a decapitated milk white face, tight lips. A fingernail investigates creases beneath tired eyes, while Billy tells him he's on his way back. They exchange a few brief words. 'Why didn't you come back last night? I'm worried about you.' Then the signal drops out again.

Jamie tries to call back. 'Billy, look I'm sorry about what I said,' he appeals to his voicemail. 'I didn't mean those things. Just come back.' He hated that begging tone in his voice, the one he's started adopting to get Billy's attention—to manipulate him, even. 'Please just call to let me know you're safe.' He shouldn't have left Billy in that club, on his own, in a strange city. What a stupid thing to do! And if they hadn't argued, if only they hadn't argued, they might be enjoying their holiday together, planning what to do with their day. Instead, he lies on the bed alone, tears behind his eyes, blaming himself.

Jamie prepares himself for the worst. Knowing Billy, anything could happen. He is prone to vanishing for long periods of time without explanation. Fretful and hemmed in, Jamie tries to distract himself with a stroll to Brandenburg gate. He knows he should eat, but he has no appetite. At least he can be sure of a signal outside. He catches a glimpse of himself in the polished shop windows, biting his nails, scratching the itchy part of his wrist.

At half-past ten, Billy calls. 'I'm okay—I've met some people— We're just having fun.'

'Fun!' Jamie cries. He feels the eyes of sightseers on his face and hides puffy eyes with a hand.

Then there is that *don't-give-me-a-hard-time-I'm-not-as-drunk-as-you-think* voice of his. Jamie listens to Billy moaning down the phone to him, while others cackle with laughter in the background. Are they laughing at him?

'Stop making a fuss,' Billy mumbles, his voice distant and distracted.

'Are you speaking to me, or someone else?' Jamie asks.

'Who else is on the phone?' Billy replies.

'Where are you?'

'I'm in a cab.' Each word is sluggish.

'Going where?' There's a prolonged silence. 'Going where?'

'Some warehouse. A party.'

'In Berlin?' Jamie persists, at the same time aware of his finger twisting a single hair around itself.

'No. Somewhere else.'

'Oh my God. You can't leave this city.' Jamie's voice reaches out to him, suddenly demanding, 'You have to come back this instant,' as if

Billy were a child. Jamie hates the role: mother to a rebellious child. It's not beyond the realms of possibility for Billy to board a plane and fly out of Germany. But Billy's passport is at the hotel. Jamie can hear the drone of the taxicab's wheels on tarmac and the sound of the phone rubbing rhythmically against the collar of Billy's shirt. 'Billy!' No answer. Billy may have actually dozed off. 'Billy!' Jamie snaps, trying to wake him.

'What? Eh?' his voice comes back.

'You fell asleep.' A thousand thoughts rush through Jamie's mind at once. He's being kidnapped. Someone has spiked his drink. He's so vulnerable. 'What have you taken? Someone has given you drugs.' It's difficult for Jamie to believe he could be this incoherent on alcohol alone.

'Who?' he slurs. 'Who could give me drugs in a foreign country?'

Jamie's not stupid. He's familiar with Billy's behaviour now. Billy would hang around cubicles of bars and clubs with those who kneel and pray before lines of cocaine on a toilet seat. Billy can sniff the stuff out anywhere.

'Don't be fucking stupid. I've just... had... a drink.' Billy stumbles over his words, struggling to put one in front of the other. 'I've been drinking water for the last hour.'

'Swear on my life that you haven't done drugs.'

'I'll be back soon,' Billy says, but his voice trails away.

'Please, Billy. I love you. Come back to the hotel.' Jamie's voice slips like bone china from a high shelf. 'I need you to be here. Now. This is our holiday, and I'm here on my own,' he shrieks.

Then the line goes dead.

When Jamie calls him back, he answers straight away. There's the sound of Billy's sluggish footsteps on concrete. This time he issues the obligatory ultimatum. 'Come back, right now, or I'll leave you.'

'You're trying to control me again,' Billy says, indignantly.

And then the threats... Billy, get in a cab or I'll burn your passport... Billy, get in a cab or I'll phone your mother... Billy, get in a cab or I'll scream... Billy, get in a cab or I'll call the police... Billy, get in a cab or I'll kill myself. Jamie takes a deep breath, lowers his trembling voice and says, 'Billy, if you love me, get in a cab.'

Silence. And then, 'Alright, I'll come now.'

'Stay on the line until you're in the cab,' Jamie implores.

'You don't trust me?'

'Please just get in the cab.'

Jamie begins to sob. He waits until he hears Billy say 'Hotel Alexanderplatz' to the driver. Then the line goes dead. Jamie runs from where he is at Brandenberg Gate to the hotel—a half hour walk in under ten minutes, past the imperious buildings of Mitte and the graffiti decorating every spare piece of the city's concrete.

The run gives him enough time to go over everything that has happened. Stay calm, he thinks. Don't make things worse.

From the hotel window he looks at those people meandering like insects, wondering if one of them is Billy. If he presses his face right up against the glass and peers down, he can just about see them entering and exiting the hotel doors below. From this angle he can see a man getting out of a cab, brown hair, and Billy's blue jacket. That must be him. Jamie thought for a moment about his jackets in the wardrobe. Billy had been wearing his blue jacket, hadn't he? Jamie tried to convince himself. He waits just long enough for the figure to reach the hotel foyer... long enough for him to enter the elevator... maybe there is a queue. He counts the floors in his head, all the way to thirty-six, the journey of a few minutes. But Billy doesn't appear.

§

Lying on the bed, Jamie is flicking through photographs on his mobile—photographs that Billy had sent to him. The clock reads 3.30. One particular image catches his eye: a photo of Billy in dark blue jeans, scuffed white trainers and a white vest with red seams, his trademark look. He has a good tan, skin colour offset by deep green Victorian calligraphy tattooed into each of his gym-pumped arms, a florid lacework of curlicues and serif fonts inked from shoulder to elbow. The tips peep out from behind the neck and sleeves of his shirts, but the rest is there underneath, written across his chest, curling around a nipple.

Happy times. Jamie took that picture with Billy's little camera. That camera went everywhere with them—Sunday afternoon picnics, drinks at Brick Lane art galleries, the roof of a squat party in Dalston where it captured Jamie lit by the flame of Billy's clipper. Though it could not record Billy's whispers, telling Jamie he loved him. Jamie continued flicking. Three photos of a wonderful holiday in San Francisco, a bar in the Castro, an image of them cycling on Golden Gate Bridge. Jamie remembers they had played with the idea of moving, starting a new life, in Sausalito on the other side of the bay. Billy wanted this as much as he did. Billy wanted to be saved.

§

At six o'clock Jamie calls again. 'Where are you?' Jamie grips the phone in wasted fingers, silver rings hanging loose above the knuckle.

'I'm in a bar,' Billy says, as if mystified by the question.

'What are you doing in a bar?'

'I needed the toilet.'

'You said you were in a cab.' He begins to cry again, feeling himself being drawn into Billy's vortex of madness.

'What cab? I don't know what you're talking about.'

'Billy, don't joke with me. You were in a cab, coming back to the hotel.'

'I never said I was coming back.' Billy burps into the phone.

'You're drinking again! I thought you needed the toilet?'

'I just picked one up while I was here. There you go again, trying to control me.'

'I'm not trying to cont…' Then Jamie feels his words splinter into quick discordant snatches. 'The plane leaves first thing in the morning. I can't take anymore. Why are you doing this to me?'

'I'm not doing anything to you.'

'Oh god-oh-god-oh-god-oh- What am I going to do?

Billy hangs up.

Jamie hurls the phone across the room.

He doesn't come back. At eight o'clock Jamie really starts to worry about what to do if Billy doesn't return at all. It's a possibility.

At nine o'clock in the evening, Jamie picks the phone from the floor and leaves the building to search for a reliable signal. Outside on Alexanderplatz, the phone rings in his hand. Billy's smiling photograph appears on the cracked screen. Sudden relief washes

over Jamie. Billy will have sobered up. He will say... this is what
we'll do... we'll forget this ever happened... we'll put it all behind us.
Everything will be all right.

Jamie answers the phone. It's Billy's phone number, but not Billy's
voice.

'Who is this?' says an unfamiliar voice.

'I'm Jamie. Who is *this*?' Jamie asks.

''Ello, my name is Petronella. I am the waitress of the bar your
boyfriend was drinking in last night. I am so sorry...' The voice is
foreign, but not German. It's artificially soft.

'Oh my God, is he alright?'

'I am calling on Billy's phone, because I saw that you had called so
many times.' The woman raises the tone of her voice at the end of her
sentences, turning everything she says into a question. 'He said such
lovely things about you last night.'

'Were *you* at the party?' Jamie's voice is rushed and impatient.

'He is with me,' she says, failing to reassure.

'Can I speak to him please? We're supposed to be catching a plane
in just a few hours.'

'I am afraid not. He's in my guest room, in... how shall I say this?
Unrousable sleep.'

'Oh no! What do you mean? Is he alive?'

'Oh dearest... what I mean to say is, he is in a very deep sleep.'

'Can I come and get him?'

'Of course. He has just been having a lot of fun, you know? Come
over to the apartment and have dinner with me. He can sleep it off
and...'

'I need to get your address.' Jamie looks up at the Hotel
Alexanderplatz, dwarfing him. He thinks of his pen and notepad
lying on the dresser, up there in the sky and the damned phone signal.
He looks around for a newsagent, a stationary shop. Nothing. 'If I
hang up and find a pen and paper, will you answer the phone when
I call back?'

'Of-course. Try not to worry.'

'Thank you so much, Petronella.' Remember that name he thought.
Petronella.

It takes him five minutes of waiting for the elevator before he eventually reaches the hotel room and his pen and paper. He looks at the little digital display on his phone, showing no signal. He holds the phone at arms length and whirls around the room, like a dervish, chasing the signal. He gets as close as he can to the window and dials Billy's number. Finally, face pressed against that panoramic window, he manages to call out. Paper and pen clutched in hand, he listens to the brrr brrr sound of relief. Petronella doesn't pick up. No one picks up. He calls again and again and feels the fabric of the universe bending, pulling him towards a black hole.

From the thirty-sixth floor of the Hotel Alexanderplatz, the panorama is dizzying. The glass of the window is so clean, it seems he could fall right through it. The skyline darkens gradually and streetlights begin to illuminate. He checks the bathroom twice to see if Billy is there, playing a trick on him. Maybe he has made the whole thing up. Jamie flies about the room, shrieking, 'How can this be happening?' He has no idea which district of Berlin Billy is in, or if he is even in Berlin. Was Petronella telling the truth? Terror flashes through Jamie's head. Has Billy been kidnapped? Are his vital organs being, at this very moment, sold on the black market? He pictures Billy lying on the floor of a guest room, disemboweled, in a pool of blood.

He gets undressed. He showers. He dries. He dresses. He gets undressed. He showers. He empties his suitcase. He scrambles through clothes, as if Billy might be hiding away at the bottom of the case with the roll-on deodorant, a nail file and tweezers. He finds the leaflet that Gracie gave to him. '*Are you an alcoholic?*'

He reads the list of twenty questions. 'If you can answer 'yes' to three or more of these questions then you are an alcoholic.' Jamie looks at three of the questions and raises an eyebrow.

Is drinking making your home-life unhappy?

Do you ever have a complete loss of memory because of your drinking?

Do you lie to others about your drinking?

He wants to add, *Has your drinking ever ruined a perfectly good holiday in a European country?*

Jamie thinks of their home life in London, how he's found vodka bottles hidden inside the cushion covers of Billy's settee. He thinks of the times Billy invited complete strangers back home completely smashed out of their heads. He thinks of the times when he woke to find Billy sleepwalking, standing naked at the foot of the bed, trying to take a piss, unaware that he hadn't reached the toilet. Pissed while skiing, Jamie had to get him airlifted off the mountain.

It's late. Billy has now been gone for over twenty-four hours. Jamie stares into the mirror. There's a centimetre gap in his eyelashes where he has methodically pulled them out. It's the pulling that gives him some sense of control: the pulling of hair, the pulling of an eyelash, the tearing of a fingernail from its root, the picking of a scab, the marking of flesh. He used to have gorgeous brown hair. Now there is a bald patch the size of an onion where his crown used to be.

He considers the police. Will they speak English? Think of the humiliation. *I'm on holiday. I'm catching a plane at six in the morning. I've lost my boyfriend. How careless!*

He can't just get on the plane without him. He has his luggage and his passport. He falls into a frail, futile sobbing. Billy can't be saved.

Jamie rummages through Billy's suitcase—clothes, books, razor, toothbrush. At the bottom of the case is a pile of bits of paper—scraps with random notes written on them. He sifts through, searching for Billy's passport until his hands fall on a shiny red envelope. There's no more logic to this than finding Billy's house keys in the microwave, or him hiding empty beer bottles at the back of his wardrobe. It's just there, randomly—an envelope, red and sparkly.

§

'So, you phoned your mother,' Gracie says.

'What else could I do?' Jamie asks, sobbing uncontrollably. He thinks of the pieces of himself he left discarded in the hotel bathroom sink—fingernails smudged in blood and hair clogging up the plughole. 'I did what she told me to do. I left his passport at the reception desk with his suitcase and I caught a cab to the airport.'

Gracie smiles. 'I want to meet your mother. She's got her head screwed on.'

Jamie falls helplessly into her arms. 'I abandoned him. I left him and our life.'

Gracie surrounds him, arms squeezing. 'I know, baby. Sometimes, you have to cut off your own legs, if you're to climb out of the swamp.'

Fairy Tale Metropolis

'Let me speak frankly: separate but equal is a fraud. It is the language that tried to push Rosa Parks to the back of the bus. It is the motif that determined that black and white people could not possibly drink from the same water fountain, eat at the same table or use the same toilets.'

> *Commons debate that preceded the vote on the*
> *marriage (same-sex couples) bill, 2013*
> DAVID LAMMY 1972—

Sotto Voce

On the other side of the glass, Gloria can see falling snowflakes, fine as caster sugar and soft enough to stick, lit by the orange glow of Oxford Street. Determined spiked-heeled shoppers carry bags of gifts along frostbitten pavements under this year's Christmas lights—a bit tackier than usual. A woman, perhaps a movie star or a mafia wife, in dark glasses, cuff hat and mink coat, hails a black cab. A bus spills its cargo onto the pavement. The tide of festive retail ebbs and flows, a scene not unlike something in a seasonal children's movie. She spots other women like herself, a little lost—out-of-towners in wax jackets, sporting practical template hairdos. Though she'd never have hair like that, drab and sexless. A couple of them are standing, gormlessly looking at an A-Z, amid the fast lane of pedestrians.

She's glad she and Sandra sought shelter in this bar, away from the chaos. Gin and tonic before lunch time. Daring. She cradles her mobile phone, allowing her thumb to rest on the dial button before pressing it. Gloria refocuses, able now to see her reflection in the glass—an anonymous woman, independent even.

This must be how Jamie feel—no curtain twitchers, no nosey neighbours knowing all your business. You can be whoever you want to be here. Though she worries about him, all alone in this place—workaholic, no partner, never mentions dates. God only knows what he does for kicks these days.

'Jamie?' She presses the phone against her ear to hear more clearly over the jukebox, which is playing one of Jamie's favourites. She's seen him bopping around his kitchen to *Comfortably Numb* by the Scissor Sisters, many times, with or without a drink inside him.

'Mum?' Jamie's voice, at the other end, is surprised. 'Where are you—'

'I'm calling on this new mobile thingy. Just getting used to it. I'm in London.'

'In London? You didn't say you were coming?'

'I *did* tell you I was coming. You just don't listen. I'm with all my ladies. Coach trip.'

Gloria whispers into the phone. 'Sandra's birthday treat. Freddie's up to his old tricks. Don't say anything, but she caught him snogging that woman from the pharmacy counter in Boots again. She's been a bit down.' Gloria turns and looks at her sister mock-flirting with Vince, a grey-haired fella who they'd befriended at the bar. Sandra had been asking him if he'd ever seen *Phantom of the Opera* but now she's asking him if he knows anyone who can get Freddie kneecapped.

'Are you going to come and meet us?' Gloria asks, letting her voice return to normal volume. The bar is quiet, save for someone playing the fruit machine and what look like a couple of regulars gossiping at the other end of the room.

'Erm...'

Gloria listens into his silence for a few seconds before running out of patience. 'You can't sit moping in that flat forever.'

'I'm not moping. Where are you?'

'A little olde-worlde pub at Marble Arch. The coach dropped us off first thing and we started our Christmas shopping, but it's frantic, so we thought we'd get out of the crowds for a bit. They're ever so friendly in here, and this lovely man in leathers has just bought us both a drink. He's been telling us all about some club he goes to in Vauxhall. It's an education, I can tell you.'

'Jesus. What's the name of the pub you're in?' Jamie says.

'Daddies,' she says.

'*Daddies!*'

They've got a lovely grand piano. She looks up at the cheap holographic foil Christmas decorations. Not what she'd have in her own home, but whatever turns you on. 'You know I had the feeling we were in the wrong place when I saw the clientele—proper flouncy Liberace types—hissing and calling each other Violet and Blanche. We're like a pair of sore thumbs. Sandra wanted to walk right back out but you know... I said, 'Sandra, it's your birthday. Fuck it. Let's have a drink.' And they made us both feel ever so welcome.'

'Mum, that's where all the old men and rent boys hang out. They call it The Elephant's Graveyard.'

'I don't see the problem,' she says. 'You're always telling me to take a risk.'

'It's a gay bar.'

It's a bit more traditional than she'd expected. No Muscle Marys. 'I thought you'd be pleased.'

'Mum, I don't go out to gay bars.' Jamie's voice sounds weary at the end of the line.

She thinks of all the knitting he did as a child. 'Why not? You *are* gay aren't you?'

'I go to the local boozer with my mates.'

'Perhaps you're not really gay then. Gay men listen to Kylie and lift heavy objects at the gym, don't they?'

'Well thank you, Mother, for that painting of gender-identity in the twenty-first century.' She can hear him sighing impatiently at the other end of the phone. 'I'll come and meet you. But there's no way I'm coming to Daddies.'

§

As they walk down Old Compton Street under an umbrella, Sandra barks at Freddie on Gloria's mobile. Useless bugger can't look after himself, not even for one night. Gloria listens in. 'No Freddie. I don't care. After what you've done—why should I give a shit whether you eat or not?' Sandra turns and throws her eyes up at Gloria. 'There's eggs, there's bacon, there's ham. You could make yourself a sandwich. There's fresh bread in the pantry. There's cheese. If you go in the freezer compartment there's oven chips, waffles, there's beef burgers. There's even a piece of steak if you could be bothered to defrost it. There's potatoes in the—What? No. I don't know when I'm coming back. What...? Well, you should have thought about that before you started playing silly buggers.'

Sandra hands back the phone to Gloria and squeals. Jamie is in front of them, arms wide. Sandra runs at him. 'Bab! I ain't seen ya for ages.' Jamie flings his arms around his auntie and hugs her. Then he releases her and turns to Gloria.

'Hello Mum.' He squeezes her tight. 'You deign to visit me then.'

She wriggles free. 'When was the last time you ventured north of the M25?'

'I've been busy.'

'You're in grave danger of turning into a hermit. Even your dad isn't as boring as you, and that's saying something. Have you missed me?' she asks, turning to meet his eyes now. She'd forgotten how tall he is now. Thirty-four, but still her little boy.

'Course I've missed you.' He smiles.

'He's dressing like his dad now too.' Sandra tugs at his smart jacket, running her fingers over the black lapel. 'Look at how grown up he is,' she says. His thinning hair is cropped, beard groomed into neatly shaped stubble. He's handsome, tanned but perhaps still not altogether *together*.

Gloria looks up and down the street. 'So this is your stomping ground then?'

'Used to be. I'm more East London these days.'

She stretches her fingers round his skinny waist. 'Eating like a sparrow. I don't think living on your own suits you. Too much time on your hands.'

'You do look a bit peaky, our Jamie,' Sandra says. 'Not still pining for Billy, are you?'

'Of course, I'm not *pining*,' he snaps. 'It's been five years.'

'Has it been that long? Blimey. No one else on the scene?' Sandra asks.

Jamie pulls free of both of them. He's a difficult little bugger at times. 'Leave me alone, will you,' he groans. 'I'm perfectly fine.'

Sandra purses her lips. 'Needs a new boyfriend, if you ask me,' she says.

'I'll pass on that, thank you. Last time I went on a date, it was with a holidaying Columbian.'

'Sounds yummy,' Sandra giggles.

'He gave me six weeks of diarrhoea and a trip to the Hospital of Tropical Diseases.'

'Racist!' As Sandra steps away to look in one of the nearby windows, Gloria's eyes follow her toward the flashing neon frontage of a sex shop, *Vids, Mags, Poppers, GHB*.

'Don't say anything,' Gloria says, returning to her son. 'I'm taking her to the opera tonight. Neither of us have been before.'

'Better switch that off!' He points to her mobile. 'Don't want to put the diva off.'

She pushes the new contraption into her handbag. 'Have you got your spare key with you?'

'Why?' Jamie asks.

'We're sleeping at yours tonight, that's why.'

Jamie's mouth falls open.

'You don't expect us to book ourselves into the Ritz, do you?'

'Could have given me more notice. I'm writing.'

'Oh, he's *writing*. He's in the *zone*.' Gloria grabs Jamie by the arm, steering him away from oncoming traffic. 'I'm *your mother!* You wouldn't say that if it was one of your fancy London friends who'd just stopped by to *touch base*.'

Jamie pulls a bunch of keys from his pocket and slides one off the key ring.

'Come on, let's go and have a drink in there.' Gloria points to the first bar she sets eyes on.

'The Admiral Duncan? People know me in there.'

'That's nice. You can introduce us.' She stops en route outside a shop called *Clone Zone*. The window is a London skyline of black rubber dildos, backlit by pink neon. She points to one huge twelve incher and laughs. 'That one's like your dad's.'

'Mum! How much have you had to drink?'

Gloria turns from the window and glares at him. 'I'll say one thing for Billy. He knew how to have a good time and he never looked down his nose at me.' She extends her fingernail and jabs him in the stomach.

'Ouch. That hurt!' he winces.

Sandra comes running across the street. 'Gloria! What's pole dancing?'

'Honestly, Sandra, anyone would think you were born yesterday.' She tugs Jamie towards the bar and looks over at Sandra. 'Come on.'

Jamie resists. 'Mum, you know that's the pub that got bombed, don't you?'

'Yes, funnily enough, I do.' Patronising little shit. She does actually watch the news. 'Come on. I want to go and have a look at the memorial,' she says, striding into the bar, busier and gaudier than the last one. She slaps her purse on the counter. 'Right what's everyone having?'

'Surprise me,' Sandra says, disappearing to the loo.

Jamie slides reluctantly onto a barstool, looking round him, probably in case anyone notices he has his mother with him. A welcoming smile from the greying barman with watery blue eyes defies a life of adversity that Gloria can only begin imagine. He hooks his wrists over the beer pumps. 'What can I get you, sweetheart?' And before she knows it, there are drinks and packets of crisps in front of her, they're on first name terms and she's got a full history of the place.

Sandra returns from the toilet. 'You won't believe it, Glo. There's no ladies'. It's all unisex.'

'It's London, not Welston,' Gloria says. She points at the memorial chandelier above them—'Look at that sculpture, Sandra. Do you know, those metal ribbons are for the people who got injured in the bombing? It's unfathomable why anyone would do such a thing.' She looks at Jamie, sitting on a bar stool, sulkily flicking through a magazine. 'You know our Jamie, I don't know why you don't come to these places more often.'

Winston, the barman looks at Jamie. 'Is this your sister?'

Gloria laughs. 'That kind of talk'll get you places. I'm his mother, you soft sod.'

'Sweetheart, he's no stranger to a bar stool. He's always in here, checking out the trade.'

'And I thought he didn't do gays bars anymore.'

Jamie blushes.

'You're so lucky having all this on your doorstep,' Gloria says. 'Just think, all we've got back in Welston is *The Pink Flamingo*.'

'How do you know about *The Pink Flamingo*?'

'Me and Sandra went to a hen do there.'

'Right, Sarah-Jessica, those spaces exist for our safety. They're not there so you and your hetero friends can commandeer our dance-floors.' Jamie glances at Sandra disapprovingly, who has one of the men from the bar, up and out of his seat, bopping to *I saw Mommy Kissing Santa Claus*.

'Aren't you lucky,' Winston asks of Jamie, 'to have a mother that would come in a place like this with you? She's making a real effort.' She's glad someone appreciates her. Look at him, her son, hanging round like a bad smell. She thought this might be fun. She had been saving him the spare ticket to the opera in her handbag, so he could join them. They were on offer in one of her magazines. But she's not having this. She'd rather it go to one of the other girls who were on the coach. Maybe Janice or Angie would like it. She doesn't need Jamie to have a smashing time. He's a proper wet weekend. She moves over to him and pulls the magazine away. 'Give me your wallet.'

'What?'

'When you were little, everyone used to think you were a lovely little boy.' She wrestles with him until he hands over his wallet. 'Now look at you! Complete pain in the arse.' She pulls out a handful of notes. 'Is that all you've got?'

'There's about eighty-quid there,' he says, indignantly.

'That'll have to do.'

'What?'

'It's probably best you leave me and Sandra to it,' Gloria says. 'We can look after ourselves.'

'But I've only just arrived.'

'Well, I can tell you're preoccupied!' She bashes him with the rolled-up magazine. 'We'll see you after the opera. And make me a hot water bottle, would you? Sandra's got cold feet.'

§

'No Jamie, I'm not dead in a ditch,' Gloria says, running her fingers across the ceramic Belfast sink. 'What on Earth makes you think that? We just decided to stay out a bit longer. You're not the only one who can have fun you know.'

They had sinks like that when she was at school, stained with powder paint and glue grime, but here it's reinvented as a stylish interior embellishment.

'You said you'd be back before midnight,' Jamie says, the signal dropping in and out.

'Well, I know we said that, but well...' she presses the phone against her ear. 'We don't come to London very often and we thought we'd make the best of it. I can't win with you, can I?'

Gloria surveys the room—soap in a wall mounted dispenser, marble walls. She traces the edges of the tiles on the floor with her toes—she can feel sheer luxury, even through her tights. Under-floor heating. She's always wanted a 'wet room'.

'I just wanted to know you're okay,' Jamie says.

'Of course we're okay. As I said, we said goodbye to the other girls from the coach and then me and Sandra went to the Opera House. You should have seen her face. I wish I'd got a picture.'

'You're not there now though?' Jamie's voice is impatient at the end of the phone.

'No, love,' she lowers her voice, even though she feels like raising it. 'We left a few hours ago. We all decided to hang around Covent Garden for a bit.'

'All?'

'The thing is, we met this lovely couple of girls and we decided to stay on and have a drink.'

'What were their names?' Jamie asks.

'Beryl and Maureen.'

'Where did you meet?'

'Beryl bumped into me at the bar of the Opera House. Spilt my drink. That's how we got chatting.' Gloria smiles to herself. They'd clicked. Just like that. They'd asked them if they wanted to join them for a drink and a bite to eat. 'It's such a lovely night—the snow, the twinkling lights and these girls were such a good laugh... one thing just led to another.'

'What do you mean 'one thing led to another'?'

'That's what I mean. *One thing led to another*. Listen, I know we promised to be back but it's only one o'clock in the morning, I'm not a child, Jamie. I can look after myself.'

'My mother the socialite. How are you going to get back?'

'We'll get the night bus.'

'The night bus? Lord above!' Jamie says. 'Don't sit upstairs. Don't make eye contact. In fact, forget that. Just get a cab.'

'A cab? You think I'm made of money?' Gloria whispers.

'You stole eighty quid from me. Why are you talking so quietly?'

'I'm in the toilet, in Maureen's flat if you must know,' she cups her phone with her hand. 'They've got this lovely flat in Covent Garden. Just around the corner from the Opera House. You wouldn't believe

it. They've got a beautiful Bichon Frisé. You'd be in your element.'
Down the corridor, she can hear the other girls laughing in the kitchen. Sandra is recounting some story about the time they fell foul of street peddlers in Luxor.

'How much have you had to drink?'

'What the bleedin' hell has my drinking got to do with you?'

'Tell me.'

'Three? Four? I don't know. There's a bottle on the table.'

'So you've been out for something to eat?'

'Yes, Italian.'

'With those two women?'

'Yes. With *those two women*!'

'And now you're back at their place?'

'Well… yes,' she says.

'What do you think Dad will say?'

'What do you mean '*What do you think Dad will say*?' I don't give a tinker's cuss what your dad thinks. I expect he'll have had his feet up in front of Panorama or some such rubbish he's recorded from the telly. I'm out having a nice time with my sister. That's all. I don't know why I didn't start coming to London more often years ago.'

'Doesn't it bother you that they might be lesbians?'

'Of course it doesn't bloody bother me, you soft sod.'

'You didn't say that twenty years ago.'

'You know, considering you're my son, you can be a right jumped up little shit! I didn't want to say anything because I knew Sandra might freak. You know how… pedestrian she can be. She's only just learnt what pole-dancing is. I knew something was amiss when Beryl was feeding me scallops off her fork.'

'Mum!'

'I was flattered, you know. I just thought it would be better to keep quiet and go with the flow.'

'You've been picked up by a couple of rich dykes!'

'Don't use that word!'

'What?'

'It makes them seem… well something that they are not. They are nice sophisticated ladies.'

'No idea what they see in you then?'

'You know what your problem is? You're too uptight.'

Finally, he laughs. 'You're probably right.'

She looks down at her feet and thinks of the thick white snow outside. 'Right, listen. We'll be home soon. My glass slippers turned back into plimsolls over an hour ago.'

She Doth Protest too Much

'Remember that Boy George wig you made for our Freddie to wear at that fancy dress party? Those were the days.'

Jamie remembers it vividly—in his grandmother's council house where he'd eaten cheese and piccalilli on pieces of cracker-bread or Shippam's fish paste on sandwiches of bleached bread. How different he is now. It almost feels like a betrayal, now that they are talking about it. He'd no sooner eat Shippam's fish paste than eat dinner at the Ritz. Though every time he passes the condiments aisle in the supermarket he's tempted to pick up a jar just for old times' sake.

'You've always been good at making things.' Gloria's voice calls from Jamie's bathroom, echoing with bright resonant optimism, over the sound of music issuing from his iPod. On his knees, Jamie folds a large sheet of stiff red card into an origami papal mitre—a design he'd found on the internet. The floor of his flat is covered with placards and banners that he's made to take on the demo. 'You can't keep holding onto the past, Mum,' Jamie says. 'I know it makes you feel secure, but it's actually keeping you stuck.'

When Gloria steps from the bathroom, sashaying to Plan B's *She Said*, her Brigitte Bardot hair is perfectly sprayed and pinned into position. She sighs and hooks a dangly earring into one undecorated ear. 'You used twenty-four balls of my best black double-knit on that bloody wig.'

'I'm sorry you lost your job at the wool-shop, Mum. I know how much you loved it.'

'That went years ago, Jamie. It's a betting office now.'

'I know, but you loved it there.'

'Sign of the times, love.' She's applying orange lipstick and gabbing at the same time. 'Everything is closing down.'

'You'll find something else, Mum.'

'Jobs in Welston—rare as rocking-horse shit,' Gloria says.

Jamie smiles at her attire. 'Mum, what in God's name are you wearing?' There are not many people who can carry off an orange lipstick like his mother. However, he raises an eyebrow at her dungarees, the colour of Bird's Instant Custard.

'I picked these up in Oxfam. I thought they were rather, you know—*Greenham Common.*'

'There's the spirit. Stand up and be counted, Mum,' Jamie says. 'Fight back!' He fixes together a placard.

Gloria sighs. 'Don't you think it would be easier to accept the way things are?'

'Have you asked yourself why they are that way?' he asks, handing her the placard and starting on another one.

'We haven't had it all that bad,' she says.

'Mum, when you were younger, you were poor. Trapped in a cycle of poverty, not by accident, but by design. *Their* design.'

Gloria gasps. 'We were *not* poor!'

Jamie knows that picture in his mother's head—an idea of her life she can't stand being spoiled, no more than she can stand a mark on a freshly washed and ironed white shirt.

'I suppose you've forgotten the black depression your own father was pitched into during Thatcher's reign?'

Her face relaxes now. 'It was a rough time, yes. And your grandad was one of the casualties.'

'But you can't see how government after government have failed ordinary people?'

'We were taught to just get on with things.'

'You were taught to know your place.' Jamie wishes he wasn't so annoyed by her.

Gloria waves his lecture away. 'Look, we don't have a bad life. I can still afford to get my nails done. Your dad pays for us to go on a nice holiday every year.'

'Oh well, everything must be right in the world if Gloria Johnson can still get her nails done.'

'It's important to look one's best.'

'Existence is resistance, Mum. We can't afford to be apathetic.' He

watches her slipping her feet into a pair of kitten-heeled sling-backs—
hardly appropriate for a day of walking—but he feels a smile come
back to his face.

'Oh stop harping on, will you. I'm coming on your demonstration,
aren't I?' she says. Jamie is folding a second origami mitre. 'What's
this protest in aid of, anyway? Come on, I want to know what I'm
getting myself into.'

He stares at her, frustrated. 'You don't listen. I've already told you
twice. We're condemning the Pope. Get your coat on.'

'The Pope? What have you got against him?' Gloria inspects her
fingernails.

'Er... his stance against homosexuality, women's rights, abortion,
his irresponsible condemnation of condoms to prevent the spread of
HIV.'

Gloria places her hands on her hips. 'I suppose you could say the
same of a lot of other people.'

'Yes, but his visit to the UK is being paid for by *your* taxes.'

Gloria's eyes widen. 'Oh well, when you put it that way... But why
have you made so many placards?'

'Everyone is coming. David, Gracie...' Jamie pushes his hand inside
the form of the paper hat, stretches it out and pulls it onto his head.
'How do I look?' When he looks up again, Gloria has pulled on a
black donkey jacket. 'Mum, where in god's name did you get that?'

'I borrowed it from your dad. Best look the part.'

'Mum! It's not the Battle of Orgreave. This is a peaceful march—'

'You're not seriously expecting me to wear one of those pope hats?'

§

Helicopters circle overhead. Gleaming sunlight. Police officers cordon
the edges of the demonstration to keep the pavements clear. Piccadilly is a sea of demonstrators wearing the papal mitres and condoms
blown up into giant balloons. Jamie, David, Gracie and Gloria stand
behind a group of lesbians carrying a sign saying *Pope Hid Sex Abuse.*
Pope to Resign. David is head to foot in a comical white cassock and
mitre—a satirical gesture that neither Jamie nor his mother are quite
sure they understand. 'Everyone's here, Mum. Richard Dawkins,

Peter Tatchell. Ian McKellen.'

'Oh, Gandalf is such a nice man. Think we'll get on television?' Gloria asks.

He flaps his hands at one of the many cameras. 'Make sure you wave at Dad.'

'It's a good turn out,' Gloria says. 'Though this bloody hat is messing up my hair.'

Jamie hands out placards to his friends.

'So lovely to meet you, Gloria,' Gracie says. 'I've heard so much about you.'

Gloria purses her lips. 'What's he been saying about me? Bloody little bugger.'

'You're a living legend,' Gracie says, smiling warmly at her. She squeezes Jamie on the arm. 'Baby doll, don't look now... but that's Simon Jones standing three feet away.'

Jamie turns to look. It's true—there he is—tanned, dressed like a Soho dandy. His hair is a little bit different and he's wearing a dickie bow, but it's him all right. Jamie would recognize those looks, anywhere. He's wearing a patterned shirt underneath what looks like a boy's school blazer.

He and Simon had met for a drink at the George and Dragon in Shoreditch—a date manufactured by Gracie. Simon had turned up, dressed in what he'd described as his favourite white shirt, neatly embroidered, starched and pressed to within an inch of its life. Jamie had returned from the bar with drinks for them both. He tripped and spilt red wine all over it. That got things off to a great start. In truth, both of them were a little morose—Simon licking his wounds after a failed film project, Jamie, even after many years of being single, still only tentatively playing with the idea of dating.

The next day, Jamie sent Simon a nice message. *I had a really nice evening with you. But I don't think I'm ready for this. Do you think we could be friends?* To which Simon had responded, *Yours is the seventh message of this nature I've received this year. I have enough friends, thank you very much.*

This had been just one chapter in a collection of experiences Jamie had resolved to compile into a book titled 'How to Drive a Man Away'.

'Oh God!' Jamie pushes his sunglasses tight against his eyebrows and swaps his placard to the other hand to shield himself.

'What?' Gloria says, nudging in between Jamie and Gracie. 'What's wrong?'

Jamie winces, speaks quietly through clenched teeth. 'That guy next to me.'

'Oh I know,' Gloria says, licking her lips. 'Gorgeous, isn't he?'

Jamie feels himself flush with embarrassment. 'I know him.'

Gloria grabs another eyeful. 'And is he single?'

'How do I look?' Jamie says, smoothing down wrinkles in his shirt.

'Stop making a fuss,' Gracie giggles. 'You're drawing attention.'

The procession starts slowly walking forwards, towards Piccadilly Circus. Jamie looks at his mother. 'His name is Simon. He's an artist who's been on the scene for years. We went on a date, after I finished with Billy.'

'What's wrong with him?' Gloria asks.

'It was *me*. I wasn't ready. I gave him that whole *let's just be friends* malarkey.'

Gloria looks over Jamie's shoulder. 'And?'

'He didn't want to be *just* friends.'

'He doesn't have anyone with him,' Gracie says. 'I'll have to say hello.'

'No!' Jamie snaps.

'He's edible,' Gloria bites her teeth together, miming animal sexual hunger. 'I might even have a crack at him myself.'

'Mum!'

David pulls Jamie's placard away from him. 'Bring me a knife and fork!'

'I couldn't possibly.' Jamie slows his walk, letting Simon get ahead of them.

'Grow old and lonely then. See if I care,' David says, swishing his cassock.

Gracie links arms with Jamie. 'Don't let us bully you, babe,' she softly says. 'How's the writing? Finished anything?'

Jamie relaxes and quickens his pace. 'I finished plenty of stuff.'

'Did you use the contacts I gave you?'

'It didn't really lead anywhere, I'm afraid.'

'Nothing at all?'

'A few short stories.'

'I'm surprised.'

'I'll try again soon.'

Gracie nudges him. 'Life doesn't come to you.'

'I know,' Jamie agrees. 'But if I find the right person, I want to make sure I'm ready for them.'

'Simon is very ambitious,' Gracie says. 'Probably one of the most creative people I know. And he's a connector. An enabler.'

They are just rounding the corner and heading towards Trafalgar Square. A surge in the crowd behind them causes Jamie to lose his footing. Gloria leans, deliberately, onto him. Suddenly, Jamie finds himself pressed against Simon's shoulder. 'Oh, sorry,' he hears himself saying, and this time, takes the opportunity to look him in the face. He can't pretend any longer. 'Hi,' Jamie says, lowering his sunglasses. 'Remember me?'

Simon curls his lip. 'Oh, it's you.' He coolly looks away.

Jamie's going to have to work hard to thaw the ice between them. 'How are you?'

'I'm fine, thanks.' Simon looks away.

They've reached Trafalgar Square and are edging towards parliament. 'Are you here on your own?' Jamie asks.

Simon looks around him as if to verify that he is actually here alone. 'No law against it, is there?'

There—a chink in the armour. Jamie senses that, behind all that bravado, Simon is actually feeling a little lonely. 'What are you doing later?' he asks.

'I'm going to the rally to listen to the speeches. I want to hear Peter Tatchell.'

'You're a fan?' 'He's a good man. His head is screwed on.' Simon says. Jamie hesitates. 'A few of us are going for a drink after this. Would you like to come?

'Well...' Simon's starting to defrost now. 'I suppose I could have one drink with you.'

§

The Retro Bar is busier than usual for a Saturday afternoon, punters, especially the smokers, spill out into the alleyway just off The Strand. Gracie and David dance to Culture Club. Jamie watches his mother from the bar; she is chatting to Simon at a table they had managed to bagsy. He picks up their drinks and as he approaches them, he hears his mother say: 'He never used to be this much trouble when he was a little boy.' Jamie does an exaggerated eye roll at Simon.

'Come on!' Gracie calls from across the room.

'I don't dance,' Simon says, which sounds rather ill-mannered.

'Oh, this is one my favourite songs,' Gloria says, looking at Jamie.

'Go on, Mum. Knock yourself out.'

She launches herself at Gracie and David.

Jamie looks at Simon and beams a warm smile in an attempt to melt the remaining ice.

'What did you think of Richard Dawkins then?' Jamie asks.

'Bit of a dork.' Simon raises one eyebrow. 'Have you read *The Selfish Gene*?'

'No,' Jamie says. From across the room, Gracie winks at him.

'Fascinating examination of the human condition. But I'm not sure he's got it right.'

David waltzes over. 'Alright, ladies.'

Simon smiles. 'I'm just nipping out for a cigarette.'

David curls his lip. 'Snooty old so and so.'

'You've changed your tune. I thought you liked him?' Jamie says, a little taken aback by David's cattiness.

'Madam Simon, makes out she's bulletproof. Where are her friends? Can't smell her own breath, that one,' David says, before swooping away to dance again.

Culture Club comes to an end and Bob Marley takes over. Jamie can't help mouthing the words. *Get up, stand up.* Simon returns and their conversation resumes. They count the various protest marches they have both coincidentally been on, yet not bumped into each other.

Despite Simon's insistence on not staying, he's somehow now on his third drink. His eyes linger comfortably upon Jamie. A warm, excited feeling rises up in Jamie, just the way it had when he'd first met Billy and he knows in his heart this feels right. Simon can try his hardest to fool him but, once or twice, the little fingers of their hands touch on the bench. Jamie consciously leaves his fingers there. So does Simon.

Jamie wishes he hadn't fucked it up last time round. Would it be foolish now to make a second attempt?

'Oh, there'll be more protesting,' Simon says. 'More marches, more striking. There always is with a Tory government.'

Gloria comes back to the table, bopping in front of them, singing, 'Get up, stand up, stand up for your rights.'

The two boys exchange glances. 'I'm just nipping to the toilet,' Jamie says.

Downstairs—he watches his urine trickle along the porcelain, picking up blue dye as it passes a tablet of disinfectant on the way. It collects in the drain cover, inches away from his toes, a retro yellow-green-blue wash smelling noxious.

No matter how far he progresses in life, men's toilets always smell like this.

Jamie steps backwards away from the trough and moves to wash his hands in a grimy ceramic basin. He stares at himself in the mirror, runs a hand over his bald head, checking for spots his Turkish barber has missed with the razor. His skin is smooth, even in colour, a few spots. He's older but still handsome. He frowns at the wrinkles beneath his eyes. He's looking a little worse for wear these days. He thinks of Simon. They're the same. Jamie is slimmer, faster—like a whippet. Simon is calmer, more robust, but they complemented each other. He's interested in the world—Jamie's world. Jamie's eyes are as bright and vital as his. In the mirror he can see guys, walking in and out of the toilet. Some of them are in their forties, others much younger. Their eyes are similar, bright pearls set in optimistic faces, like a great joy has been bestowed upon them. Jamie feels fluffy, a little light-headed, happy.

He walks out of the toilet and over to the table where Gloria is showing Simon a photograph of him when he was a baby. 'Mum!'

Jamie glares at her.

'Alright, alright, I know when I'm not wanted.' She pushes the photograph back into her purse, gets up and walks off towards David and Gracie.

'Cute little thing, weren't you?' Simon says.

Jamie's eyes fall to the floor.

'Even cuter now,' Simon says. 'Quite a handful, isn't she, your mum?'

'You noticed?' Jamie asks.

'Does she come to London a lot?'

'She comes with her friends,' Jamie says. 'You know those long lines of women following each other down Oxford Street, doing their Christmas shopping? Arriving together on coaches from out of town?'

'Yes.'

'My mum's the one at the front with a clipboard.'

Simon laughs. 'Yes, I can imagine that.'

Jamie takes a deep breath and holds it in, like a pearl diver about to swim underwater. 'I know I made a mess of it last time. But do you think we might start again?'

'I'm not sure you deserve another chance after you gave me the brush off last time.'

Jamie's eyes fall again. He breathes out, feeling suddenly beaten. But Simon nudges him and smiles. 'I've got tickets to an exhibition later. A private view. Would you like to come?'

Jamie lights up again. 'Sure. What's the show?' He can see his mother whispering in the corner with Gracie.

'Humanity and mortality. It's at the Wellcome Collection.'

Gloria is suddenly in front of them again, eyes beaming, her hands flapping enthusiastically in the air. 'Gracie says there's a fantastic karaoke night at this bar round the corner. Why don't we all go there?'

Jamie doesn't know what to do. He doesn't want to exclude his mother but he wouldn't be seen dead at a karaoke bar.

'Oh... But Simon just asked me if I wanted to go and see an exhibition with him.'

It takes his mother a moment to read the situation. She eyes Jamie and Simon carefully. She seems to be concentrating on how close they are—the way their legs are touching. Then she smiles and Jamie feels himself relax. 'Oh, you know me and art, darling.'

Simon shakes his head. 'It's not art, Gloria. It's science.'

'Oh, you know me and *science*, darling. Sworn enemies.'

'Mum, I didn't mean to—'

Gloria is closer now, close enough to silence him with the tip of a finger against his lips. 'Darling, go and have fun.' She laughs at herself. 'Look at me. Hardly dressed for an exhibition.' She's right, her attire—part bombshell, part land-girl, in those lurid yellow dungarees.

Simon laughs. 'I think I might give my body to science when I'm dead. The university up the road offer a service.'

'Maybe I'll do that,' Jamie says, pleased at Simon's attempt to move conversation on a little. 'I'd like to think I'd be useful after my death.'

'There are no fees,' Simon says. 'They just come and collect the body.'

Jamie looks back at Gloria. 'Well, in that case, I might give my mother's body to science too.'

'At least it won't come out of the inheritance,' Gloria says, dancing now to Gloria Gaynor's *I Am What I Am*.

'My problem, really, is what to do with her while she's still alive,' Jamie laughs. 'Do you think I could give her body to science while she's still with us?'

'Cheeky little bugger,' Gloria says, pinching his cheek.

They laugh. 'Will you be alright, Mum?'

'Yes, darling. I've got your spare key. I probably need an early night.'

Congregated, moments later in the alleyway outside the pub, they are all ready to depart. Jamie looks at his mother and David dancing drunkenly with each other—one strap of Gloria's dungarees undone and David tripping over in that silly Pope costume.

'I'm doing Elvis,' David says. 'Gloria, you can do Whitney.'

'I'm not doing Whitney. I've told you, I'm doing Peggy Lee. Gracie?'

'Dusty Springfield,' Gracie says, drawing hard on a cigarette. 'Who else?'

'Are you sure, Mum?' Jamie says, as Gloria pulls on her donkey jacket.

'Darling, it's fine. I know sometimes I get in your way. Perhaps I try a bit too hard because I want you to know how much I love you. But I know I don't have to now. But you can like art and science and I can like karaoke. And that's okay.' And there is the look she'd given him when he was a child, like he could do no wrong.

Gracie and David have already walked off. 'You'd better catch them up.'

Simon and Jamie are almost alone, save for a few smokers. The soft touch of Simon's hands on his skin makes Jamie tremble. Everything feels suddenly more real. He feels he can tell Simon anything. Under an autumnal blue tissue paper sky streaming between the buildings, the two of them are, lost in a daydream.

Simon places his hands at the side of Jamie's neck and kisses him, softly, and then with a fieriness that makes Jamie grip him by his blazer—holding on, as if the foundations of the world might move away. His waiting mouth parts for Simon's eager tongue, arousing from Jamie a rush of sexual joy. Jamie kisses him back. And then, they are walking off, hand in hand, into their life together.

He's Done Ever so Well for Himself

Out of the darkness of the black cab, they step onto the sharp salty gravel of The Mall. Jamie points to the doors of London's Institute of Contemporary Arts under a haze of moonlight. 'Simon's special night!' Gloria speaks. 'I can't wait.' A cold sweat prickles Jamie's skin beneath his costume. His shallow breathing, anxiety for himself or for Simon already inside; he's not sure which. He pays the fare and then follows Gloria, Roy, David and Gracie into the building. David goes first. He's in the most elaborate costume—dressed as Tretchikoff's Blue Lady—blue face, red lips, kimono—and is carrying around with him an old wooden picture frame.

The long corridor towards the bar and auditorium is lit from overhead fluorescence and occasional scribbles of neon on white walls. This contrasts with the riot of punks, goths and new-romantics they weave through to the boom of Frankie Goes to Hollywood's *Relax*. It's almost as if this giant cuboid light-box were intended for this special event—the fiftieth birthday party of the late performance artist, Leigh Bowery.

'You mean Simon's organized all of this?' Gloria asks. Jamie had asked her to doll up and as usual, she has not disappointed. When he'd shown her vintage photographs of all the eighties club kids dressed up to go out on the town, she'd been positive of the look she was going to go for and today had spent all afternoon in the hairdressers.

'It's just what he does, Mum,' Jamie says.

Gloria's hair, styled into a skyscraper of a beehive, is paired with a taffeta dress worthy of Mari Wilson. She's arm in arm with David.

They pose for pictures as they go—David carefully positioning himself inside his picture frame. 'Gloria, you'll be in all the mags. ID, The Face, Attitude.'

Even Roy has made an effort. He's in a blazer over a black polo neck sweater, aiming for an older Simon Le Bon but somehow looking like Del Boy.

Gloria says. 'You wouldn't think it is two-thousand and eleven, would you? It's like the eighties all over again.'

'I think that's the point,' Jamie says.

'Well, where is he?' she says. 'I want to say hello.'

'You'll be lucky,' Gracie spouts from behind them. 'Simon Jones, say *hello*? Think again.'

Jamie tucks the braids of his wig behind his ears. He surveys the space, feeling himself on the edge of an abyss between the possible and the impossible. This whole scene defies the laws of physics. Imaginary beings, mythological creatures glimpsed for just a second then lost again to the shadows. Jamie wonders if he will get to see Simon at all before the show.

They reach the end of the corridor where it opens up into the bar area. Roy clears his throat and asks, 'Can I get anyone a drink?' Just then, a high-heeled Simon Jones glides through a set of double doors, followed by his entourage. He's wearing an androgynous suit, fashioned entirely of animal print. The black quiff of his hair rides high, like an alicorn upon his head. His face is stark with white powder, eyes lined with kohl. He's talking as he walks, giving instructions, gesturing.

'There he is!' Gloria cries.

As Simon approaches them, an unearthly delight, for a split second he looks at Jamie and winks. Then, almost as if he was never there in the first place, he's gone again. Jamie looks at Gracie, crestfallen.

'What did I say, darling?' she says. 'Total control. Total concentration. He's working.'

'But I've gone to all this trouble to dress as Boy George for him.'

'Oh, don't make out you did it all for him. You couldn't wait to put on that Kabuki make-up.'

'I'm supposed to be his *boyfriend*. He didn't even say hello.'

She squeezes his arm. 'Darling, he winked at you! All the

years I've known him, when he's working, he's never even looked my way.'

'Where did he go?' Gloria asks, who has turned for a moment to speak to Roy about drinks.

'He'll be making the rounds, I expect, just before the show starts,' Gracie says.

Jamie wants to pursue him, to get another glimpse of something so unusual, perhaps even fabled, but Roy drags them all to the bar. 'Your mother's never fully relaxed unless everyone has a drink in their hands.'

'Dad! You don't have to. Let me get them.' Jamie pulls his wallet out of his carrot legged trousers.

They wait patiently until, armed with gin and tonics, Roy permits them to venture further into the party. They pass through the doors to the darkened auditorium, a crowded dance floor before an enormous stage where the show will take place. It's a voluptuous scene, rabid with *faces*, *figures*, *celebutantes*—all bringing out of retirement looks that had been popular during Leigh Bowery's reign over club culture at his infamous nightclub *Taboo*.

'It's filling up,' Roy says.

Overcoming his own cowardice, Jamie pushes through the hordes to penetrate the main room. His parents and David and Gracie are behind him. If they want to hang back, let them, but he wants to get a good vantage point for when Simon comes on stage. He'll be right bang smack in the middle when the celebration begins and he doesn't intend to miss a thing, even though he is already three-quarters down his gin and tonic and could do with a refill.

Jamie is surrounded by mythology. Holly Johnson from Frankie Goes to Hollywood is standing just a few feet away, arching his back, stretching his arms out as if he were a winged horse. There are a whole host of avant-garde personalities, dancers, buffoons, lip-synchers he recognizes from the world of cabaret—all wearing concoctions of Westwood, thriftshop, Judy Blame and designer mimicry. Jamie's glad he made the effort now.

He looks behind him at his parents lingering at the back with Gracie. Roy looks a little uncomfortable. Gloria has linked arms with him, as if he needs protecting from all these freaks. The next time Jamie looks back, Roy is talking to an anguished punk whose PVC dress has come undone at the back. Roy holds up his palms in a calming gesture. Resourceful to the end, he fixes the broken zip with a hairpin from Gloria's beehive.

Gracie gives a little wave to Jamie, and an enthusiastic nod, while mouthing, *it's starting. It's starting.*

As the lights dim and Jamie turns back towards the stage, he arches his back and stretches his arms out like a winged horse. He knows he's just Jamie from Welston. But aren't we all *multifaceted?*

'Ladies and Gentlemen, welcome to the ICA for Sunshine Night Time.' The lights come up on the emcee for the evening. He's walking rather gingerly in his heels—a man who Jamie thinks he knows. The figure on stage, not quite real, is alchemic. This is the man he'll catch a cab home with tonight, the man he will wake up next to in the morning, with the residue of make-up underneath his eyes. But the figure on stage is not really that man. 'A celebration of what would've been, give or take a few days, Leigh Bowery's fiftieth birthday. Leigh was a man who made a huge contribution to the arts.' The man on stage is untouchable, intangible. 'My name's Simon. I'll be your Master of Ceremonies for the evening.'

The crowd clap. Jamie watches Simon's hands move through the air, fluttering as if talking, gesturing to the audience, captivating, casting a spell over them, until they fall silent. His body is so lithe it could almost be liquid.

'And I'll be introducing some of Leigh's collaborators and contemporaries, as well as some new contemporaries whose work may have been inspired by Leigh.' He is untamed. He trots across the stage. His zebra jacket falls open exposing a pierced nipple, the tattoos Jamie knows so well, the chest he has fallen asleep upon so many nights now. It is Simon. It is… But those eyes, black and gleaming, that's not Simon. Those eyes, black and full of magic, magic that must be many thousands of years old, the magic of a shape-shifter, the magic of a shaman. The audience are cheering and whistling. The atmosphere has an almost tangible quality, charged like the air just before a thunderstorm.

And then, like a genie in a pantomime, Simon disappears. This creature is gone and the first act enters the stage. Gracie touches

Jamie on the elbow and exchanges his empty glass for a full one. 'He's amazing, isn't he?' she says. Jamie can't speak. He can feel his Boy George make-up melting.

They watch the show without exchanging a word. Hours after the last act, they find themselves back in the bar. Jamie's mum and dad look just the same as they always have. Even with her huge beehive, Gloria is still Gloria, his mum, his father's wife, wearing a little more make-up than usual. His father, still awkward looking. If Jamie knows who they are, how can he be feeling the way he does, still trying to work out who he is, now that he's no longer the person he was?

David is touching up his blue face in a compact. Gracie is teasing his wig out.

'Never forget who you are, baby,' Gloria says.

Jamie blushes, as if he's just dropped his trousers in public. How could she know what he's thinking? 'What makes you say that?'

'I can see you changing,' she says, touching him on the cheek.

'Mum, I'm thirty-eight. I think, if I was going to change, I'd have done it by now.'

Gloria looks at Roy. 'He's done ever so well for himself, ain't he, Roy?'

'We're proud of you son,' Roy says.

'Oh, bring me a bucket,' David says. He grabs Gracie. 'Come on you. Buy a lady a drink.' They stagger off to the bar.

Jamie feels bewildered.

'Your book will be published soon,' Gloria says. 'A new beginning for you. We always knew you could do it.'

His mother is right. He is changing. The universe is arranging itself around him. A door is beginning to open.

Over Gloria's shoulder he gets another glimpse of something rare. Boy George is stood, in full Leigh Bowery drag, brightly coloured shiny paint dripping down his forehead. He's looking right at Jamie. It takes him a few seconds to remember that he himself is dressed as Boy George.

Then Simon is beside him. His make-up more or less removed; just a smudge of eyeliner remains. Gloria is smiling. 'Well? Are you going to go and speak to him?'

Simon follows their sightline to Boy George. 'I'll introduce you if you like.'

Jamie arches his back again. He feels a power surge through him. 'This is a meeting for which I need no introduction.'

Narwhal

It's quiet, bar the ticking of the clock on the mantelpiece. Tea from an actual teapot. Jamie pours for himself, Simon, Gloria and his grandparents and hands around mugs from a tray on the floor. He sips his own, blowing at the steam, careful not to burn his lip. He's full of nerves for tomorrow. His mind is in two places. He's forever living a double life. It feels strange to be in this room again. He catches his reflection in the mirror where Phyllis used to do her hair, when she was young enough to care about such things. For a moment, he sees a different version of himself—the Welston one. He feels nostalgic for a life he might have had... the one where he's settled down, married... because they can get married now... in a two-bed semi... the one where a different set of dreams came true.

Phyllis's voice draws him from his fantasy. 'Ain't it quiet?'

'Don't get used to it,' Alf pipes up. 'All hell will break loose once the that lot arrive.'

Phyllis moves to Simon, who is standing awkwardly on ceremony. She touches him on the elbow. Her fingers move to the gold buttons on his red waistcoat and then she teases the ends of his curly moustache. 'Don't worry, old fruit. I'll protect you.' Simon's reaction looks like a mixture of gratitude and cold fear.

No sooner has she returned to her armchair than there is the sound of a car pulling up, doors slamming and laughter. Phyllis tucks a strand of long silver hair behind her ear. She gets up out of her seat, not as agile as she used to be, walks to the window and lifts the net. 'It's them.' The net drops from her fingers and she points at Alf in his armchair. One leg is propped up on his wheelchair in place of a footstool. 'You! Don't move!' she says, as if his arthritic knees could possibly carry him anywhere fast.

Alf huffs and puffs and pulls his dressing gown around him. 'Here we go,' he says. 'We're going to have a houseful again!'

'Oh give it a rest, father!' Gloria snaps, behind him. 'You're nothing but a bloody party pooper.'

Phyllis moves around the room collecting up her things—library books, knitting, a book of word-searches and clears them out of the way. 'Put the kettle on, Glo.' She turns and looks at Alf. 'And move that pork pie! You know he eats whatever he sees. It's like having an unfed dog about the place.'

Jamie picks up the pork pie and gives it to Gloria who takes it into the back room. Then he is startled by the thump of a knuckle against the window and a face pressed against the glass.

'Oh, look at ya!' Phyllis moans at Sandra's face through the curtain. Phyllis adjusts her pinny, goes into the hallway and there's a cheer as Sandra appears.

Freddie is still hidden behind the door. 'Is he here?'

'Of course he's here,' Phyllis says. 'He's been waiting for you.'

Freddie sticks his head in sideways. Jamie notices his hair is salt and pepper grey. Freddie pokes his tongue out and says, 'Where's the red carpet then?' The rest of him appears, in a Marks and Spencer's plaid shirt, pushed in by Phyllis.

'Get in there—pest!' she says and gives him a good whack around the ears.

Freddie looks past Jamie at Alf, who's halfway into his tea. 'Alright, Pops?'

'Oooh, that's a lovely cuppa that is,' Alf says.

'What you drinking tea for? We've bought bubbly.' Sandra waves a huge bottle and in the air.

Alf mumbles. 'I'll have a drop of red wine. That sparkling muck plays havoc with my waterworks.'

Jamie gestures to Simon. 'Everyone, this is Simon. Simon, this Auntie Sandra and Uncle Freddie.'

'*Varmint*,' Phyllis corrects.

'Lovely to meet you, Simon,' Sandra says. Everyone shakes hands, crossing arms and bumping into each other in slapstick pandemonium.

'Welcome to the family,' Freddie says.

'Welcome to the madhouse.' Jamie sits back into his seat, next to Phyllis, smiling at the whole commotion.

'Alright, our Jamie?' Sandra leans and gives him a big kiss. 'Congratulations, bab. Didn't I always say you could do anything if you put your mind to it?'

'Wouldn't have done it without Simon's help.'

Gloria comes back from the kitchen. 'Hello all.'

Sandra hands Gloria the bottle of champagne. 'Get that open, Glo.' She looks at Jamie and says, 'Veuve Clicquot. Your mum says it's your favourite. We went all the way to ASDA for that.'

Gloria disappears into the kitchen again.

'So, when do I get my signed paperback then?' Freddie asks, boisterously. He perches himself on the arm of the settee, folds his arms and sits looking at Jamie. Sandra stands by the gas fire, warming the backs of her legs.

'I've got you all a copy,' Jamie says. He fetches one of the books out of the bag beside him and hands it to Freddie.

Freddie runs his hands across the cover. 'Amazing, Jamie. You know we're all dead proud of you.'

Across the room, Alf throws his eyes up.

Gloria comes dashing back in from the other room. 'Mother! Have you not got any champagne flutes?'

'Oh, I never thought of that,' Sandra laughs. 'Freddie, why didn't you remind me?'

Phyllis adopts her Queen-of-England voice. 'No, we do not have flutes, I'm afraid. We do not drink champers.' She slips back into broad Welston. 'We only drink PG Tips.'

'Lord above!' Gloria says.

'We'll have to have it out of a mug, and lump it,' Phyllis says.

Gloria draws breath and throws her hand on her hip. 'Mother! We're *not* drinking bubbles out of a mug!'

Freddie laughs at her. 'Oh lighten up, Glo. He can do it for old time's sake. I don't suppose our Jamie will be drinking anything out of a mug again. It'll be bone china all the way, from now on, Royal Doulton, now that he's going to be on *The Southbank Show*.'

Gloria disappears once more and comes back with another tray of mugs and a look of disgust painted across her face.

'I'm not Steven Spielberg, Freddie,' Jamie says. 'It's just a—' and then he jumps in his seat as Gloria releases the champagne cork. They all cheer like children at a fireworks show.

'He won't want to know us,' Freddie says, leaning over and

prodding him on the shoulder. 'Now that he's famous.'

Alf shakes his head. 'He's just playing at it. He hasn't published a real book. Not like those you see in the book shops.'

Sandra puffs up with sudden anger and shrieks at Alf. 'What's the matter with you, Dad?' She grabs the book from Freddie and thrusts it in front of Alf's face.

'I told him years ago,' Alf says. 'Wild goose chase. Too many people at it. Too much competition. People like us—'

'Sandra, I've told him it's true but he won't believe me.' Gloria starts handing round mugs of champagne, tutting as she goes. She's poured a little extra for Simon on account of him being stiff as a board. 'Here, get that down you.'

'Thank you,' Simon says, shifting his weight from leg to leg.

'You'd better knock that back and loosen up, y'miserable bugger,' Phyllis says. 'You're making my nerves bad.' Simon looks bewildered. Phyllis narrows her eyes. 'Perhaps his foreskin is a bit tight today.'

'Nan!' Jamie snaps. 'Jesus!'

Alf doesn't even look at the paperback that's been handed to him by Sandra. 'Old boys club,' Alf continues. 'They'd never let someone like him in. Working class lad.'

'It wasn't easy, Grandad,' Jamie says.

Gloria says. 'Dad, we are *not* working class.'

Alf looks up at her. 'Says you, drinking champagne out of a mug. Our Gloria, always thought she was a cut above the rest.'

Gloria glares at him.

'We *are* working class, Mum,' Jamie says.

'Jamie, how can someone like you be working class? You're educated. Written a book.'

'I'm talking about my roots—'

Gloria towers over the old man now. 'Yesterday we all went down to London to see him read at a fancy literary event. Everyone was there. Ray, Angie, Paul and Debbie...'

Jamie feels himself light up. 'How is Debbie? I didn't got chance to talk to her.'

Gloria smiles. 'We had quite a nice chat. She teaches History now at Kings College.'

'Always was a bright girl,' Phyllis says.

'Mother wanted to come, didn't you mother. But she wouldn't leave you here, in your bloody wheelchair. I've no idea why, you nasty old goat. How would you get on, cooking your own flaming dinner?'

'He did his reading ever so well,' Sandra says. 'You'd have thought he'd been doing it all his life.'

'Nobody told me,' Alf says.

'We did tell you,' Gloria says. 'You just weren't bloody listening.'

Phyllis stands in front of the fire now, warming her legs. 'Alf, cut it out now. I've heard enough. If you don't stop, I'll have Freddie wheel you to the top of Welston High Street and let the brakes off. Can't you just be happy for the lad?'

Freddie and Simon are giggling at Alf's antiquated CD collection.

Alf opens the book and leafs through it. He pushes his glasses up his nose, tilts his head to peer through the lower lens of his bifocals. They all watch him as he runs his fingers over the dedication. *To my family. Thank you for believing in me.* Alf swallows and looks at Jamie, his eyes a little wet with something that might be pride.

Then there is another thump of a knuckle at the window and they all turn to look; even Alf this time. 'That'll be Roy,' Phyllis says. 'The dependable one.' She goes to open the front door. 'You've come at the right time. Gloria's just popped the fizz.' Her voice can be heard in the passageway. 'Have you fixed it?' She comes back into the room with Roy behind her.

'Running like a dream,' Roy says.

Phyllis points at Alf. '*You* ought to be grateful.'

'What needed to be fixed?' Alf asks.

'Roy's car was on the blink, but he's mended it so he can drive you to Birmingham tomorrow.' Phyllis puts her hands on her hips. 'Our Jamie, nip upstairs and fetch me the photograph album. I want to show Simon.'

'What do I want to go to Birmingham for?' Alf moans.

'Jamie is reading from his book at the Midlands Arts Centre. So we'll get to see what we missed in London.'

'Alright everyone?' Roy says, standing in the doorway. 'Is this a private party or can anyone join in?'

§

Nan's bedroom hasn't changed one bit. It's still the orange of a gold-fish you get at the funfair—walls, bedspread and even the carpet. Jamie likes it here. It feels cosy and full of pretty things that she's collected, like photographs, postcards and letters that Jamie has sent her over the years. Jamie sits on the edge of the bed. His head is still throbbing from last night's celebrations.

Downstairs music has started up abruptly and the whole family seem to be cheering. 'Well done, Simon!' The volume shoots up and booming music vibrates the floorboards under his feet. Jamie can hear Tony Orlando singing *Knock Three Times* at full pelt. Perhaps Simon has somehow got Grandad's old music system working.

Jamie stares at his reflection in the mirror, surrounded by lights. They remind him of the mirror in the green room at the Purcell Room. Just thinking about it makes his heartbeat quicken. It's all so fresh in his mind.

The green room at Southbank's Purcell Room has monitor screens, which allow a view of the stage and the audience to the performers waiting to be called. Jamie stares at the screen from the sofa where he is sat, checking to see if they're all back in their seats. Around him there's a buzz from all the authors who have already done their spot before the interval. Everyone is drinking champagne. A man with a clipboard and a headset approaches him, carrying a large bunch of flowers.

'I think these are for you, Mister Johnson,' the man says with a wide smile.

Jamie takes the flowers—white roses. He reads the little card in trembling fingers.

> *Well done, Soft Lad.*
> *Wouldn't have missed it for the world.*
> *I'll see you, afterwards.*
> *Love, Billy x*

Jamie smiles warmly. 'Thank you,' he says to the man. 'Is it my time?'

'A few minutes. Interval is nearly over.'

Jamie stands, places the flowers on the sofa behind him with the notes for his acceptance speech, which he's practised and practised. He knows his story by heart. Though he's still bloody nervous.

'Through here.' The man leads him out of the green room and into a little corridor situated behind the black stage curtains, like an airlock separating him from outer space. There are more monitors and bits of electrical equipment on shelves to one side. Another man is twiddling knobs, adjusting sound, pressing headphones to his ears. 'When the music stops, you're on. I'll give you a little push and you go straight through that curtain there, like we did at the sound check. Okay?'

'Okay?' Jamie says. 'How long?'

'Two minutes'

'Two minutes,' Jamie repeats. His heart flutters. He looks around him wondering where Jamie has gone: Jamie from Welston, Jamie the supermarket checkout operator, Jamie the art educator.

His phone buzzes. A text message. He slips it out of his pocket to glance at the screen. It's from Simon. He knows exactly how Jamie is feeling right now—weeks of coaching in front of the mirror.

'Better turn that off,' the sound guy says.

'Yes,' Jamie agrees, before reading the text message.

There's always a quiet space at the centre of a storm
Step into that, and perform.

Jamie switches off the phone and tucks it into the breast pocket of his electric-blue Tom Ford suit. Someone closes the door to the green room behind them, shutting out the light. The sound guy starts counting down. 'And ten. And nine.' No turning back now. 'And seven...' He can't be who he was before.

On stage, Jamie can hear the voice of the emcee of the evening making an announcement. 'And next up, ladies and gentlemen, we have Jamie Johnson, reading from his debut.'

'And two... And one...' The man with the clipboard gives Jamie a little push through the curtains. He holds his breath as if he's about to dive into deep, cold water. The dense, black fabric brushes his cheeks and then he's on stage. He swims out into the velvet blackness facing the auditorium. He closes his eyes for a moment against the shimmering stage lights. Through the light, all there is out there is blackness. He cannot see the audience. Wherever his family are, wherever Simon and Billy are, he cannot see them now.

But he is with them. He can feel himself smiling, muscles stretching tightly across his face. In the middle of the black marine is the outline of a lectern and microphone, spot-lit from above. He moves towards it. 'Good evening, Ladies and Gentlemen...'

Jamie Johnson, a mystery of the ocean, rare but real, is on the other side.

§

'Jamie? Jamie!' Gloria's voice calls from the bottom of the stairs.

He realises where he is again—Nan's bedroom, holding a photo album, open at the picture of them all—Gloria, Roy, Freddie, Phyllis, Alf and himself, eating potato fritters and chips out of newspaper on the cemetery wall. 'Yes Mum?' he calls out.

Gloria is laughing at the bottom of the stairs. Jamie can hear them all laughing—the warm convivial sound of home. 'Come quick! I think your dad and Simon have had too much champagne. You'll never guess what they're doing now.'

Acknowledgements

To the wonderful people of the West Midlands and of East London, who inspired the many characters in this book.

To my beautiful parents, Joy and Dave, for putting up with all the moaning. To my beautiful boyfriend, Nathan, for putting up with all the moaning. To all of my beautiful friends who have listened to my endless moaning for many many years, especially Michael Jones, Joe Mateo, David Cabaret, David Cabreza, Elizabeth Pisani, João Florencio, Gustav Grass, James Maker, Paul Buchanan, Lisa Goldman, Kit de Waal, Sophie Morgan, Joshua Davies, Bartholomew Bennet, Annie Murray, Gaylene Gould, Jake Jones, Kat Dixon, all at Leather Lane Writers, Jonathan Kemp, Matthew Westwood, Tessa Garland, Marcel Baettig, Michael Barry, Michael Bradley, Karen Livingstone, Anthony Psaila, Jacqueline Haigh, Anna Sutton, Emma Bourgeois, Toby Rye, Paolo Biagetti, Katie Vermont, Eddie Doherty, Chris Atherton, Amy Redmond and Stephen Morris.

For their generous help and support in the creation of this book, I am deeply grateful to: Daren Kay, Christopher Hamilton-Emery, James Greig and my Goldsmiths workshop group.

Thanks to Uli Lenart and Jimmy MacSweeney at the very splendid Gay's the Word Bookshop, Matt Cain, Patricia Routlege, Annette Badland, Neil McKenna, Paul Burston, Paul McVeigh.

Very special thanks to Andrew M Pisanu, who wrote, composed and recorded the heart-breaking track, *Proceed Undeterred*, to accompany the release of this book.

Very special thanks to all the wonderful people who generously gave up their time to courageously bring to life the characters of this book in photographic form.

Inkandescent is a new publishing venture. Their fourth publication *The Pale Ones* by Bartholomew Bennett, a horror novella, is due for release in 2018.

Cast

in order of appearance

Freddie — Nathan Evans

Alf and the Blue Lady — Paul Buchanan & David Cabaret

Angie — Rose Thorne

Billy — Alexis Gregory

Gloria — Sarah-Louise Young

Phyllis — Thom Shaw

Matthew — Antonio Blanco

Albert — Jonathan Kemp

Gracie — Polly Wiseman

Sandra — Rhyannon Styles

Simon — Billy Boland

Roy — Marcel Baettig

Jamie — Daren Kay

Also from Inkandescent

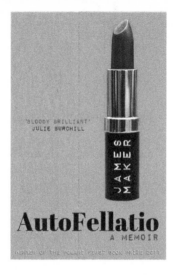

AutoFellatio
by James Maker

Apart from herpes and Lulu—everything is eventually swept away

According to Wikipedia, only a few men can actually perform the act of auto-fellatio. We never discover whether James Maker – from rock bands Raymonde and RPLA – is one of them. But certainly, as a story-teller and raconteur, he is one in a million.

From Bermondsey enfant terrible to Valencian grande dame – a journey that variously stops off at Morrissey Confidant, Glam Rock Star, Dominatrix, Actor and Restoration Man – his long and winding tale is a compendium of memorable bons mots woven into a patchwork quilt of heart-warming anecdotes that make you feel like you've hit the wedding-reception jackpot by being unexpectedly seated next the groom's witty homosexual uncle.

More about the music industry than about coming out, this remix is a refreshing reminder that much of what we now think of as post-punk British rock and pop, owes much to the generation of musicians like James.

The only criticism here is that – as in life – fellatio ultimately cums to an end.

'a glam-rock Naked Civil Servant in court shoes. But funnier. And tougher'
MARK SIMPSON

Also from Inkandescent

THREADS
by Nathan Evans & Justin David

If Alice landed in London not Wonderland this book might be the result. Threads is the first collection from Nathan Evans, each poem complemented by a bespoke photograph from Justin David and, like Tenniel's illustrations for Carroll, picture and word weft and warp to create an alchemic (rabbit) whole.

On one page, the image of an alien costume, hanging surreally beside a school uniform on a washing line, accompanies a poem about fleeing suburbia. On another, a poem about seeking asylum accompanies the image of another displaced alien on an urban train. Spun from heartfelt emotion and embroidered with humour, Threads will leave you aching with longing and laughter.

'In this bright and beautiful collaboration, poetry and photography join hands, creating sharp new ways to picture our lives and loves.'
NEIL BARTLETT

andescent

Sign up to our mailing list to stay informed about future releases:
www.inkandescent.co.uk

Follow us on Facebook:

@InkandescentPublishing

and on Twitter:

@InkandescentUK